THRONE
OF
ISIS

OTHER BOOKS BY JUDITH TARR

Lord of the Two Lands

The Hound and the Falcon
Alamut
The Dagger and the Cross

The Hall of the Mountain King
The Lady of Han-Gilen
A Fall of Princes
Arrows of the Sun

Ars Magica
A Wind in Cairo

His Majesty's Elephant

THRONE
OF
ISIS

JUDITH
TARR

A TOM DOHERTY ASSOCIATES BOOK   NEW YORK

THRONE OF ISIS

Copyright © 1994 by Judith Tarr

English translation of Horace, *Odes* I.xxxvii, copyright © 1994 by Judith Tarr

This book is printed on acid-free paper.

A Forge Book
Published by Tom Doherty Associates, Inc.
175 Fifth Avenue
New York, N.Y. 10010

First edition: April 1994

Library of Congress Cataloging-in-Publication Data

Tarr, Judith.
        Throne of Isis / Judith Tarr.
                p.   cm.
        "A Tom Doherty Associates book."
        ISBN 0-312-85363-7
        1. Cleopatra, Queen of Egypt, d. 30 B.C.—Fiction.
    2. Egypt—History—332–30 B.C.—Fiction.   3. Queens—
    Egypt—Fiction.
    I. Title.
    PS3570.A655T47   1994
    813'.54—dc20   94-4057
                                                           CIP

Printed in the United States of America

0 9 8 7 6 5 4 3 2 1

To Bruce and Tracy

for all the help, advice, and moral support,
particularly the input on matters military

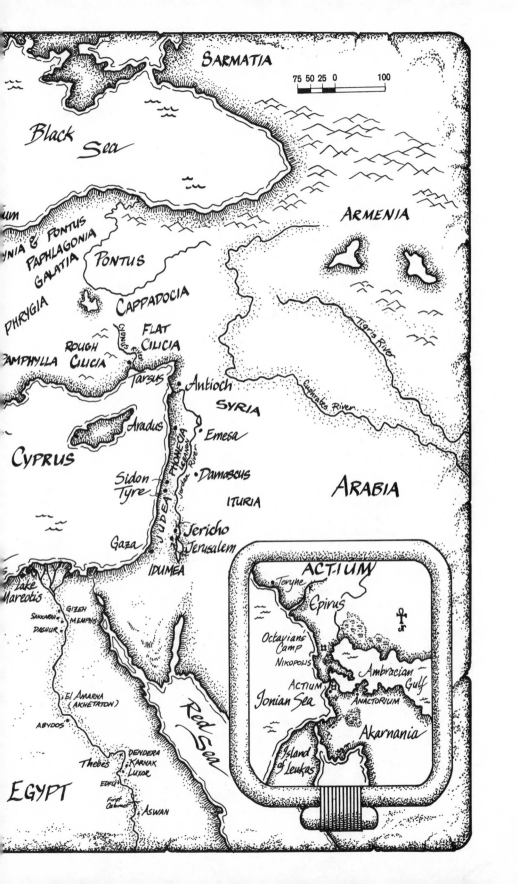

Now's the time to drink,
now's the time to strike the earth with freedom's foot,
now's the time to deck the couch of the gods
with the banquets of the dancing priests,
my friends.

Before this it was a forbidden thing
to draw the Caecuban wine
from our grandfathers' cellars,
while the mad queen was preparing
ruin and destruction
for the Capitol and the empire

With her flock of freaks and perverts,
frenzied enough to dream of victory,
and drunk on sweet good fortune.

But the escape of scarce one ship from the flames
moderated her rage,
and Caesar brought her mind,
mad drunk with wine of Mareotis,
under the power of true fear—

Driving her with ships in close pursuit
as she flew from Italy,
as the hawk pursues the tender dove
or the swift hunter the hare
in Haemonia's wintry fields—
that he would lead in chains

That prodigy of fate.
She, seeking a more noble death,
did not in womanly wise fear the sword,
nor seek hidden shores with her swift fleet.

And she, bold woman, looked even on her fallen palace
with serene face, and bravely took in her hands
the savage serpents,
to drink deep their black poison.

Fiercely she resolved to die,
loathing to be borne in cruel Liburnian galleys,
loathing to be led, cast down from her throne,
in a Roman's haughty triumph—
no humble woman, she.

> —Horace, *Odes* I.xxxvii
> (trans. by Judith Tarr)

Nunc est bibendum, nunc pede libero
pulsanda tellus, nunc Saliaribus
ornare pulvinar deorum
tempus erat dapibus, sodales.

Antehac nefas depromere Caecubum
cellis avitis, dum Capitolio
regina dementis ruinas
funus et imperio parabat

Contaminato cum grege turpium
morbo virorum, quidlibet impotens
sperare fortunaque dulci
ebria. Sed minuit furorem

Vix una sospes navis ab ignibus,
mentemque lymphatam Mareotico
redegit in veros timores
Caesar, ab Italia volantem

Remis adurgens, accipiter velut
mollis columbas aut leporem citus
venator in campis nivalis
Haemoniae, daret ut catenis

Fatale monstrum. Quae generosius
perire quaerens nec muliebriter
expavit ensem nec latentis
classe cita reparavit oras.

Ausa et iacentem visere regiam
voltu sereno, fortis et asperas
tractare serpentes, ut atrum
corpore combiberet venenum,

Deliberata morte ferocior,
saevis Liburnis scilicet invidens
privata deduci superbo
non humilis mulier triumpho.

—Horace, *Odes* I.xxxvii

ACT ONE

ALEXANDRIA AND TARSUS 41–40 B.C.

ONE

Once, the chamber had been all gold. Now it was gold and crystal, and in the center of it, dead image of a living name, the king.

The embalmers of Egypt had done what they could to a man dead of fever in the Babylonian summer. They had not wrapped him, or he had been unwrapped long ago, even before the splendor of his golden sarcophagus was sold off by a successor king with debts to pay. His armor glittered in the light of the lamps. His face was now in shadow, now in light. The life that had animated it and, the tales said, made it beautiful, was gone. Flesh had sunk in on strong bones: strong brow, strong arched nose, strong chin. The hair was bright still, near as bright as the gold, cut and combed to fall like a lion's mane.

Dione traced the carved letters of the name. ALEXANDROS—Alexander. The rest of it, the titles, the prayers, the grandiosities of kings, mattered little, as little as the death that in its way had made him immortal.

She looked from the dead face to one as alive as any could be. The dead man was the prettier, but for character there were few to match this woman who had turned from the bier to pace the wide gleaming chamber. Even, Dione suspected, the great Alexander.

"Gods, I miss that man," said Cleopatra.

She did not mean Alexander, who in any case was three centuries dead. Dione raised a brow. "Still?" she asked.

The queen stopped before she struck a pillar, and spun to face Dione. She could mince and sway like a court lady when she chose, but her native gait was a light free stride that was nothing at all like a man's. "Still," she said, "I could wish him devoured by dogs and not burned on a pyre in Rome, for haunting me with such persistence."

Dione's hand flew up in a gesture of warding. "Avert the omen!"

"Dear good little priestess," said the queen, not kindly. She tilted her head toward the man entombed in crystal. "Now if *he* haunted me, I'd be delighted. I can face the ghost of a god dead three hundred years. A man dead a mere three . . . ."

"A god," Dione said, "if you believe the stories that come out of Rome."

Cleopatra curled her lip. Her nose seemed longer than ever, her chin the more pronounced with the vividness of her scorn. "Gaius Julius Caesar was a great man, a brilliant general, and a perfect scoundrel. If any god owned him, it would be his Mercury, who so loves thieves."

She was entitled to say so. She was herself Isis on Earth, mother and goddess. Even Caesar had granted her that—Caesar, who granted nothing that was not to his own advantage.

Dione wondered now and then if Caesar had loved his Egyptian queen, or merely found her amusing. When he was alive she had never been able to tell. That the queen loved her witty, cynical, thoroughly unscrupulous Roman, Dione had never doubted.

"I was going to seduce him coldly," said Cleopatra, "bewitch him as I very well knew how to do, wind him round my finger, win Egypt for myself and Rome for him and rule a world. And what became of him? Rome! He had to go back, he had to take what it offered him, he had to court his death as eagerly as he ever courted me."

Dione was silent. Cleopatra moved toward the bier and looked down at the body within. "He envied you," she said to the dead king. "He wanted what you had: all your fame, and your death, too. Do you know how many wounds it took to kill him? Twenty-three. They counted. Romans count everything. Then they seize it. Or if it objects, their legionaries trample it under their feet."

"Including Egypt?" Dione asked softly.

"Oh, no," said the queen with quiet that was remarkable if one knew her temper. "Egypt will conquer Rome. Yes, even with Caesar dead. He would have been Osiris to my Isis. Now he is Osiris indeed, lord of the legions below. Even Roma Dea has no power against that."

Dione sighed a little. She had not meant it to be heard, but Cleopatra's ears were quick. "What, my friend? Do I bore you?"

"No," said Dione truthfully enough.

"But we came for a purpose, and I've been wasting the time in nonsense. I maunder too much. You should stop me sooner."

"It does no harm," Dione said. "It exorcises him, after a fashion."

"You, too?" Cleopatra asked.

Dione shrugged. No, she thought but did not say. He did not haunt her. Not so much. She had admired Caesar, enjoyed his wit, taken pleasure in his company, but she had found him cold as all Romans were, caring for nothing but their own and their families' gain. He could have been so much to Egypt, but he had chosen Rome, and Rome had killed him.

Cleopatra laid both hands on the sarcophagus. They were long hands, beautiful as her face was not, ringless in this place of the dead, with fingers both slender and strong. Dione felt the air stir, here where the doors were shut, the windows barred. The banks of votive offerings seemed to tremble, flowers both fresh and withered, amulets of stone and bone and metal, wine, bread, images of the god-king that bore varying degrees of resemblance to the man in the tomb. Petals quivered as if something had brushed against them. One of the images toppled sidewise upon a silver salver. The metal rang softly, like a bell heard far away.

Dione started at the sound; then rebuked herself for an idiot. There was power here. How could there not be? Here was Alexander, dead. Here was Cleopatra, living. Here was Dione herself, priestess of Isis in the Two Lands, voice of the goddess from her childhood, gifted with magic beyond the lot of simple mortal women. It spread its cloak about her before she even willed it, shielded her from the white heat that was Cleopatra.

The queen lit the incense in its golden censer, sent the sweet smoke on its course toward heaven. She poured the libation from golden cup into golden bowl. She spoke names of gods and powers, one by one and in order as reverence decreed. Dione murmured the words with her, but otherwise did nothing, said nothing. This was not her rite or her invocation; it was not for her to step forward in it, except as friend and fellow priestess.

Cleopatra bowed to the power of the gods that was in this place, and returned to the sarcophagus. Again she laid her hands on it. "Give me a sign," she said. Her voice was much as it always was, low and sweet, like silk over the steel of her will. "Show me what I am to do. My Osiris is dead. My Horus, my Caesarion, is a child still, and has no father. My kingdom, my Two Lands, will be devoured by Roman vultures, unless there is more strength in all of us than we have needed before."

The tomb was still, a stillness as unnatural as the wind had been before. Dione stood silent, not even breathing, eyes fixed on Cleopatra. This was no formal ritual, no invocation of the gods in the temples of the Two Lands; therefore the queen wore no sacred vestments, only the simple gown of a lady of the Hellenes. She looked like any woman in Alexandria, taller than some, maybe, and plainer than many, though a familiar eye might call her handsome. And yet there was no mistaking what she was.

The gods above all knew their daughter, and spoke to her when the mood was on them. Now, it seemed, it was not. She waited long, motionless, wordless, an image of pure will. But no answer came.

At last she moved. Her head bent; she drew a slow breath. "Silence too can be an answer," she said.

"Or the answer will take longer than you were willing to wait," said Dione, which was as close to *I told you so* as she wanted to come.

Cleopatra shot her a glance. "You were always more patient than I, and more willing to wait on the gods' pleasure."

"I'm not a queen," said Dione, "only a voice."

The queen arched a brow. "You're somewhat more than that, I think." She sighed, shook her head. "I should have known better than to hope they'd answer me, even here. They've been silent since Caesar died. Maybe his death killed them, too."

"That's nonsense," Dione said. It was also very like Cleopatra. "They talk to you every day, in everything the world is."

"But they won't answer questions."

"Maybe they do answer," said Dione, "and you aren't listening."

Cleopatra's anger was quick, but it passed quickly; she laughed in spite of herself. "And that, I'm sure, is the voice of Mother Isis, bidding me be patient and stop vexing heaven with my silliness."

Dione did not answer that, which made Cleopatra laugh again. "Come, my tactful friend. Since the gods would have me be patient, then patient I must be. Even a queen can hardly compel heaven, when heaven is in no mood for compulsion."

That was wise, Dione granted her: a wisdom of necessity, to be sure, but better that than no wisdom at all.

TWO

Dione parted from the queen at the door of the Sema, the tomb of Alexander. Cleopatra's litter, walled in guards, went up swiftly to the palace. Dione's much less pretentious chair, with its four burly bearers and her mute but keen-witted maid, made its way through the morning crowds. Unlike the queen she had no one to open a path for her, although she could by rights have had a brass-voiced majordomo to bellow, "Way! Make way for the Voice of Isis!"

Secure in the solitude of her chair, with a jar of almond oil and citron to lighten the curtained stuffiness, Dione allowed herself a smile. Cleopatra thought her much too modest for her station. And so she was; but she was comfortable in it.

She followed the progress of her bearers by ear and by feel. The ever-present hum of the greatest city in the world had its pauses and its variations: softer near the Sema, underlaid by the harbor with the song and scent of the sea, rising to a crescendo as they passed round the fringes of the greatest of the markets. If she listened she could catch the rhythms of a dozen languages at once, from the lovely liquidity of Greek to the sonority of Latin to the rapid gutturals of traders' Persian. Someone was singing in Egyptian, a high pure voice that could only have been trained in a temple, but what it was singing was sublimely secular and thoroughly Greek, about a boy with buttocks like a peach.

Past the market square it grew quieter by degrees, until the chair took the sharp turn and turned again into the street and then the gate of Dione's house. There it stopped and lowered gently. Dione heard the gusty sigh of relief from the right front man. Marsyas was the strongest of the four, but he was also the laziest. As she emerged blinking into the bright sunlight of the courtyard, his head was down like the others', but he had a grin for her. The corner of her mouth quirked in response. She thanked each one by name, and Marsyas last. The bearers, dismissed, went to their rest and their dinner.

"He fancies you," said a voice in the shadow of the colonnade. "Do you fancy him, Mother?"

"Timoleon!" Dione was less shocked than she sounded, but there was no need for him to know that. "That's not proper at all."

"Well, do you?" asked the younger of her sons as he came into the light. As always at sight of him, she suppressed a sigh. He was much too pretty for a mother's comfort, with his big eyes and his glossy black curls. Sometimes she thought it might be wise to hand him over to a temple, where he would be safe from either his own vanity or the importunings of men who loved beautiful boys, but he had no calling to that life, and she could not bring herself to force it upon him.

"You are reprehensible," she said to him, but without heat. "Of course I don't fancy Marsyas."

"Lady Deianira fancies her chamberlain," said Timoleon. "Androgeos says that when her husband finds out, he's going to do something terrible to both of them." He paused. "He won't tell me what. What do they do to ladies who fancy their slaves?"

"Terrible things," said Dione. "Is Androgeos here, then?"

"He's in the fountain court," Timoleon said. "But, Mother, *what—*"

"When you're older," she said with serenity as unruffled as she could make it, "you'll know. Come, out with you. You should have been at your lessons these hours past."

"We finished early," said Timoleon. "Perinthos got us a bowlful of tadpoles so we can watch them grow into frogs. And then he had us read all about frogs. There's a play with frogs in it, did you know? They even sing: *Brekekekex koax! koax!*"

He ran ahead of her, grubby tunic, grubby bare feet, and sweet young voice croaking the chorus of Aristophanes' play. Dione laughed as she followed him.

Androgeos was in the fountain court as his brother had said, tidy as Timoleon never was, quiet and composed, reading a book while he waited for his mother. Unlike Timoleon, whose face and coloring were Dione's, Androgeos favored his father. He was tall for twelve, and narrow, with a thin face that never seemed to smile, and straight brown hair cut severely short, and cool grey eyes that measured everything and found it wanting.

Dione shook herself sharply. It was not fair to the child to think of him as she thought of his father. He was certainly a prim creature, but she should be glad of that; unlike his scapegrace brother, he behaved well always, and always observed the proprieties. He rose as she approached, took her hands and kissed her as a dutiful son should, and waited politely for her to speak.

"I see you've been gossiping with Timoleon," she said. "And how

did you find out about Deianira? Have you of all people been chatter-
ing with the slaves?"

"Of course not, Mother," said Androgeos. "He overheard the slaves
talking, and he asked me to explain. *I* heard Father speak of it."

"And I suppose your father is going to broach the matter to
Deianira's husband."

"Of course," said Androgeos. "He can hardly do otherwise."

Dione might have disagreed, but there was no profit in arguing
justice and mercy with a child. She sat on the fountain's rim and put
on a smile. "So, then. And how is your father?"

"He's well," said Androgeos, no more or less stiff than he ever was.

"And your father's wife?" she inquired.

"Lady Laodice is well," Androgeos said. "She delivered herself of a
son yesterday evening."

"Did she? How fortunate for her."

For all his air of worldly wisdom, Androgeos was too young, Dione
hoped, to understand the complexity of her response. She had parted
with Apollonius long ago, when Timoleon was still a young child. It
had seemed inevitable then, for all the disapproval it bred. She had
been surprised not that he married again, but that he waited so long
to find the proper, youthful heiress. Laodice was young, lovely, and
patently fertile, and dowered with the revenues of a substantial province. She was well chosen for a man with ambitions, a court function-
ary of middling rank who wished to rise higher.

He had thought to gain that with Dione. Her family was of the
noblest, though she was the last of it. Her father died of a fever before
she was born, her mother died bearing her, leaving her all that they
had: lands, estates, wealth enough to content any fortune-hunter. Isis'
temple had raised her, been all the mother and father that she ever
knew, till she left it to be heir and steward of her house, and to wait
on the queen her kinswoman. But she disliked ostentation, she preferred to live simply, and she had no gift for the social niceties that
could advance a man through the offices of his wife.

She should have been a better wife, maybe. But that art was not
given her. Apollonius needed a woman who was not inclined to
forget everything in the needs of the goddess, who knew how to
entertain the intolerable silliness of courtiers both male and female,
who had patience to spare for her husband's more incalculable
whims.

And yet, she thought, she had given him two sons. He had kept the elder son, and left the other to her. And now he had a son whom he need not share with her.

Androgeos did not seem to mind that he had a rival for his father's affections—and possibly, later, his father's estate. Probably it had not occurred to him that he need fear any such thing.

"Did you come to tell me about your new brother?" Dione asked him. "What is his name?"

"Father wants to call him Ptolemy," Androgeos said. "Laodice is insisting that he be Demostratos, after her father. Laodice will win. Her father is going to gift the boy with his own incomes and properties. He'll be a prince."

There was no envy in Androgeos. That much he had from his mother: a lack of ambition that his father no doubt found deplorable. Dione smoothed his hair. He tolerated it, which was a rare concession. "Will you stay for dinner?" she asked him.

"Oh, I can't. They're celebrating the birth; I have to be there, to keep them from talking. They all think I should be wanting to strangle the baby in his cradle."

"Which of course is absurd," Dione said.

"I could wish that the first one had been a girl," Androgeos admitted, which also was rare. He was troubled after all, but not, Dione thought, by the kind of jealousy that led to fratricide. "Did Father still have time for me when Timoleon was born? I can't remember."

Father had not had time for either of his children, but Dione was not about to say it. "He had as much time for you as he ever did," she said: and that much was true. "He always has preferred young men to children and babies. He'll pamper his wife, admire his new son, and come back to you in relief. *You* can carry on an intelligent conversation."

Timoleon would have whooped with mirth. Androgeos shrugged slightly, as humorless as his father could ever have been. "I hope so. He's acting as if he's sired the heir of Alexander."

"But you," said Dione, "are more honestly that. Apollonius' family is merely Greek, and Laodice's descends from a Macedonian soldier, not even a lord or a commander. Ours comes from Lagos himself through King Ptolemy's brother."

That put a little sheen on him, though it was no new thing. But being Androgeos he had to take the vividness out of it. "Nikolaos Lagides never had a son of his body, legitimate or otherwise."

"True, and the Lady Meriamon was barren," Dione said, "but they adopted a whole tribe of sons. *And* daughters, and one of them both

Macedonian and Persian, who married an Egyptian, and their daughter married a Greek, and they had daughters, and on it went, all the way down to us. You can be proud of what you are. I know Alexander would have been."

"How can you know the great Alexander?" Androgeos demanded.

"The goddess tells me," said Dione, which silenced him. Even he was in awe of that other thing which Dione was; foolish, but useful for stopping a child's impertinence. She took his hand, which he saw fit to allow, and said, "Now then. Tell me how you've been."

Androgeos was a much too proper young man, but when coaxed he always told more than likely he meant to. Dione was simply glad that he would still talk to her, and that he visited regularly if not often. He was her firstborn, after all, and however like he might be to his father, he was part of her, too.

THREE

The queen in state was quite a different person from the woman who had gone all but solitary to the Sema. Dione, summoned with formal words by a chamberlain in full court dress somewhat rumpled from passage through the city, kept to the position she preferred: near the throne but not beside it, among the robed priestesses of Isis.

Cleopatra now was visibly Isis on Earth. It had not been the way of her predecessors to keep overmuch of Egyptian custom in clothing and conduct, Macedonian Greeks that they were and never forgetful of it, but she could, when she chose, be truly queen of Egypt. Today she so chose.

Whatever the failings of her face in the canons of beauty, her form was beautiful, and it showed to advantage in tight wrappings of linen so thin as to be nearly transparent. She wore the jewels that went with it, great pectoral of gold and ivory and lapis and carnelian, belt of gold, bracelets and anklets of gold and lapis. She carried the crook and the flail of the Great House of Egypt, and wore the two crowns, the Red and the White, and the golden vulture and the golden uraeus serpent of the Two conjoined Lands. Her face was painted like an image in a tomb, her eyes drawn long with kohl and malachite. She knew, none better, that she looked best so, her arched nose and strong chin well able to balance the weight of the crowns, and her eyes large and dark and long enough that the paint did not diminish them.

Beauty, no, thought Dione, but splendor like none other in the world. This hall of marble pillars was Greek but its colors were all Egypt: red and gold and white and blue and green. The court that filled it wore Greek chiton, Egyptian kalasiris, Persian coat and trousers, Judean robes, even Roman toga. Scribe in kilt sat next to scholar in Greek mantle, recording the proceedings in Egyptian and in Greek.

The queen, who spoke both, kept careful watch over the translators. It was one of the wonders that made her Cleopatra: that she had learned to speak and to read every language that she must need in her courts of judgment, and many that would serve her in the arts of diplomacy.

There were, at the moment, a number of matters for her to consider. An embassy from Herod of Judea, with sweet words and friendship, to which she replied with equal sweetness. A matter of finance from a monarch of the Thebaid, grain taxes due and excuses made for a portion that had not come in with the rest—the nomarch would make it up, the queen decreed, from his own resources. A question of legality concerning the marriage of a woman from Alexandria and a man from Memphis, with the income of an estate at issue, and the custody of a round half-dozen children. That, Cleopatra settled by granting the estate and the children to the mother, and bidding the husband begone: a summary judgment but, as she herself observed, perfectly just in the circumstances.

As the man from Memphis departed scowling, a stranger was led forward. The chamberlain announced him in Greek, which was the language most often spoken here, but the man who faced the queen, proudly upright in armor with helmet under arm, was anything but a Hellene.

Romans were always blunt, even when they were trying to be floridly Greek, as this man was not. His style of oratory was of the simple style called, these days, Caesarian—it was no more than pared-down Attic—and his accent was cultured as Roman accents went. Dione did not recall his face offhand from her time in Rome, nor did she remember a man named Quintus Dellius. There had been so many names and faces when she lived in Rome with the queen, so many of them so much alike.

He came, it seemed, from someone whom Dione did remember:

Marcus Antonius, who had been Caesar's friend. That one was ruling Rome now, or rather sharing it with Caesar's nephew Octavian, as Dellius was pointing out with delicacy that bordered on the insulting.

"Ah," said the queen to that in her most colorless tone and her most Attic Greek. "The heir."

Dellius glanced swiftly at the child who sat at the queen's feet. Ptolemy Caesar—Caesarion—like his mother was dressed as an Egyptian. He knew how to be still in the linen kilt, and how to be patient, which was something that his father had had to learn through hard lessoning.

There could be little doubt as to who his father was. He was much fairer than his mother, fair brown hair, fair white skin, cool grey eyes in a handsome and completely un-Greek face. He met Dellius' stare without expression, as a prince should, but Dione could tell that he wanted to burst out laughing. He would keep it for later, and proba-bly for Dione. No one else, he told her often enough, could under-stand that sometimes even princes needed to laugh. Caesar had told her that too once, after a particularly excruciating meeting of the Senate.

Caesar's son leaned lightly against his mother's knee. His mother seemed oblivious to him.

"The heir," she said, "Gaius Octavius, who styles himself Gaius Julius Caesar. How little imagination you Romans have when it comes to names."

Dellius smiled not too uneasily. "We make do, your majesty."

"There was only one Caesar," said Cleopatra. "I hope that he is remembered in Rome. I would not wish that sickly clerk to be the only memory your people have of his name."

"They're not likely to forget, majesty," Dellius said.

"Names matter," said Cleopatra. "Names are power. What does Antony want of me?"

Dellius was an agile man: he was not thrown altogether off balance by the suddenness of the shift. It took him a bare half-dozen heart-beats to reply, "Majesty, he asks that you visit him."

"Does he?" asked Cleopatra as if such a thing were of little interest. "And where?"

"He waits now in Tarsus, majesty," Dellius answered her.

"He could," said the queen, "visit me here in Alexandria."

"So he would," Dellius said, "but affairs of state keep him in or about the fringes of Greece."

"Affairs of state keep me here," said Cleopatra. "I am queen of Egypt. What, this month, is he?"

Dellius was unperturbed, or seemed to be. Wise of Antony, Dione thought, to send a man with iron nerves. "This month, majesty, he is one of the triumvirs, the three equals who serve the Roman state."

"And can they be equals? Must not one be their master?"

"Rome is their master," said Dellius, "majesty."

"And why does he wish me to visit him? Has he not sufficient companionship among the Greeks?"

A less canny man might have taken the bait. Dellius forbore to treat the queen as if she were an idiot child. "Majesty, he wishes to discuss an alliance."

"Alliance?" the queen inquired. "Not conquest? Or claiming of a putative possession?"

"Egypt, in the mind of Marcus Antonius, is a sovereign and power-ful state. One with which he wishes—wisely—to ally himself."

"Indeed," said Cleopatra.

"Then, majesty," said Dellius with careful delicacy, "will you accept his invitation?"

"I may," said the queen.

That was as much as he could reasonably expect, and he seemed to know it. He accepted dismissal without apparent reluctance. The queen went on to other matters. Dione, having seen all that she had need to see, slipped away.

"Well?"

Dione turned from the window. Here in the queen's study, high up in a tower of the palace, she could look out over the whole of the city and the harbor to the Pharos on its island, blinding white in the light of late afternoon. The room, though well lit and airy, seemed dark in comparison, the queen a shadow and a glitter, coming to stand beside her.

Cleopatra had taken off her crowns and her finery but kept the linen gown and the least of the necklaces and bracelets. She wore a rich scent, both sharp and sweet. "Myrrh," Dione said, "and roses. And oil of cloves?"

"And a little ambergris." Cleopatra brushed Dione's cheek with a fingertip. "Not a fleck of rouge or white lead, and you bloom like a lotus flower. I should be bitterly jealous."

"I washed it off," Dione said. "Your baths are as large as my whole house."

"Your whole house could settle itself here in much greater comfort than it enjoys in the city."

"Ah," said Dione, "but it's *my* house."

Cleopatra sighed, but she was long inured to Dione's intransigence. "How long do you think this will remain my palace, if I come running to the Roman's call?"

"As long as you live," Dione answered. She was not trying to speak for the goddess, or for anyone but herself. But as she said it, she knew that it was true.

So too did Cleopatra: she eased a little, just enough to see, just enough to mark how great her tension had been. "Still," she said, "Rome is a bad guest, and a treacherous ally."

"As Caesar was?"

"Caesar died."

"Nor have you ever forgiven him for it."

"He doesn't deserve to be forgiven." Cleopatra leaned on the window's edge. "Wise men live to finish out what they began. Fools die."

"Fools, and those whom the gods have touched."

"There's a difference?"

"You're a cynic today," Dione observed.

"And tomorrow I'll be a Peripatetic," said Cleopatra.

Dione laughed, but she was not so easily distracted. "You're going?"

"I think I may," the queen said. Her hand ran along the window-ledge, as if of itself; her eyes were fixed on the blaze of the Pharos. "Egypt needs Rome. We may deny it; we may resist it. But Rome is a Power, and no nation can afford to ignore it."

"It hasn't even a king," said Dione. "Republic, it calls itself—free land for free men, and any man with enough money and enough power can call himself a master of it. Caesar came as close to kingship as any Roman ever has. And you know what happened to him."

"They stabbed him to death in their own senate house." Cleopatra's voice was utterly quiet. "They abhor kings, and any man who seems to them to be claiming the title of king. Let him call himself dictator, general, high priest, First Man—that, they'll swallow. But never king. And yet," she said, "a king they need, at the very least—and an emperor soon, if they go on as they've begun. That's what all their wars have been for, you know. Marius and Sulla, Caesar and Pompey, Brutus and Cassius the so-loyal sons of the Republic against Caesar's toadies Antony and Octavian: it was all for the power behind the word. All and simply to rule the world."

Dione shivered. "The word is power," she said. "To deny it—to call it by another name—that's living a falsehood."

"How Persian of you," said Cleopatra dryly, "to so abhor the Lie. A Roman will tell you that all's well if only you alter the name."

"But it's not," said Dione.

Cleopatra sighed. "It's clear you'll never be a queen, or much of a courtier, either. Whatever a Roman calls himself, the fact remains that he is a Roman. And Rome is too strong to ignore."

"But what is Rome now?" Dione demanded. "A pack of squabbling boys, no more."

"Certainly," said Cleopatra, "but those boys have armies at their backs, and a power greater than armies: the fear of what they could do if they ever settled their quarrels and left one man to rule them all. That will happen, Dione. It's written in the stars. Rome's wars are nearly over. And when they end, then, by whatever name he calls himself, the victor will be emperor of a wider realm than Alexander ever knew." Her eyes were glittering. She was seeing as a goddess might, more clearly than any mortal could.

"Rome will rule," she said. "That is as certain as that the sun will rise in the morning. But who will rule Rome—there, my friend, we have room to choose. We can shape the world, we of Egypt. We can name the man who calls himself its master."

There was a silence. It rang faintly. There was a name in it, if Dione listened. "Antony?" she inquired, more to fill the pause than because she needed to say it.

"Maybe," said Cleopatra. "Do you remember him?"

"He was and is no Caesar," Dione said.

"No one is Caesar. Least of all that puppy who has stolen his name." Cleopatra's temper was slipping its leash. Dione watched her call it back to heel. "Him too I remember. Antony is a braggart, a wastrel, a runner after women—but at the very least he carries himself like a man. Octavian is a prim little miss with a perpetual sniffle."

"I think you underrate him," Dione said.

"Oh, no. I rate him very well. He has all of his uncle's intelligence, but none of his wit."

"But Antony has none of Caesar's intelligence, and little of his wit."

"Antony can command an army. He also," said Cleopatra, "has an eye for a woman."

Dione studied her profile limned in light from the city. There was nothing soft about it, or about the mind behind it. This woman, while hardly more than a child, had disposed of a pair of inconvenient brothers and a sister, exiled another sister, and seduced the wiliest of the Romans. Maybe she had not bent him precisely to her will, but she had won much from him that he might not have granted to a man or to a woman with less force of character. Beauty was fleeting. Character endured. And Cleopatra could teach a courtesan the finer points of the trade.

Nor was she so very old, at that, or so very decrepit. Twenty-eight years—old for a woman as men thought of it, but young for a man, or for a queen. She had barely begun to come into her prime. What Antony would think of her, Antony who was forty if he was a day . . .

"Antony has a wife," said Dione.

"So he does," said Cleopatra.

"And such a wife," Dione said: "mind and will enough for both of them, and ambition to match it. She'll make him all that Caesar was, they say, and rule at Caesar's side, as Caesar's wives never did."

"I was Caesar's wife," said Cleopatra.

"Not in Rome," Dione said.

"He ruled at my side in Alexandria. In Rome," said Cleopatra, "Romans came to me to beg for favors, to beseech my intercession with Caesar, to bow at my feet as queen and goddess. What is a wife to that?"

"I think," Dione said, "that I may pity Antony. He'll be no match for you."

"You think so?" asked Cleopatra. "I wonder." Her mind seemed to drift; she shook her head abruptly as if calling herself back to the moment. "I'll go. I'll see what he wants of me, and act accordingly. But as to how I'll do it . . ." She smiled slowly. "He thinks he can call me to him like a tame cat. But cats are never precisely tame. He'll learn that, will my lord Marcus Antonius."

FOUR

"A proper mother does not lay her children open to the blandishments of evil. A proper mother does not run off to sea with a fleetful of rakes, libertines, and grubbers after power. A proper mother remains at home in modest seclusion, performing her duties as the gods have ordained, attending to the rounds of—

"Madam, have you heard a word I say?"

Dione sighed. Apollonius was a blathering ass, but he was not, alas, a stupid one. "I hear you," she said tiredly. "It's the same speech you always trot out when the queen or the goddess needs me."

Her late husband, now the devoted consort of the beautiful, wealthy, and fertile Laodice, looked perilously close to disarranging his carefully coiffed curls. But since he never actually did, and since she had much to do if she was to sail in the morning, she spared him no pity.

"Dione," he said with a transparent effort at conciliation, "the queen of course rules all, and the goddess is the goddess, but surely one of them would acknowledge that you have responsibilities to your children?"

"They acknowledge precisely that; and they agree that Timoleon should accompany me. I can hardly leave him here in the company of slaves and servants."

"And has he no father?"

"He has a father," said Dione with chilly calm, "who, when queen and goddess called me to Rome before the death of Caesar, informed me that I would choose: I would go, and be no longer his wife; or stay, and be a proper modest mother, and there make an end of it."

Apollonius opened his mouth, but she was not ready to let him speak again. "I went," she said, "because my goddess called me. I left the one of your sons whom you deemed worthy of you, and took the one whom you had long since branded incorrigible even by the rod. And when I came back, I was no longer your wife. I am not your wife now. I permitted you to invade my house, disrupt my servants, and hector me, but you have no right or power to compel me to your will."

"When I had such right and power, you ignored it," said Apollonius. He sounded suddenly as tired as she.

"I belong to the goddess," said Dione.

"You belong to yourself," Apollonius said. He rose from the chair into which he had invited himself—her own chair, no less, relegating her to the one reserved for guests.

She could remember dimly why she had married him. His family lacked the distinction that hers had, but he had been presentable, and the terms that his father offered had been generous. Her guardians in the temple had offered no objection, if no great encouragement, either. She had thought them merely disappointed that she had not chosen the temple over her duty to her house. Marriage had been a part of that, marriage and childbearing, and a child to inherit when she was gone.

She could not say that she regretted her choice, although it had been clear within a month of the wedding that Apollonius was not overfond of women who put both a goddess and a queen ahead of his sovereign will. But there had been no difficult choices in the beginning, and they had got on well enough. He was intelligent if not witty; he treated her well, denied her little, even suffered her absences in temple or palace.

It had never gone sour, exactly. When the children came, he was as happy as she had ever seen him, proud of his elder son, tolerant at first of the younger's escapades. But then the queen was invited to Rome. She had a baby at the breast, her first, and though she might never admit it, she needed Dione. So, in her way, did the goddess. And Apollonius did not.

He needed a wife, to be sure. But that wife did not have to be Dione. So she chose, and gave up her elder child but kept the other, and gained this house that was hers, where she was free to do as she would.

Yes, he would believe that she belonged only to herself. He had never understood the half of her that was not simply a woman of Alexandria. He thought her cold and hard and given to claiming the gods' will when it was no more than her own whim. He did not believe in magic, or even, much, in gods.

He stood over her, trying to loom as men always did, thinking that size was all that mattered. "Will you at least leave Timoleon with us? His education—his studies—"

"He can share the prince's tutor," said Dione. That stopped him, as she had known it would. "Apollonius," she said, "we are going. You won't stop us. Will you leave now, please? I have preparations to make."

She had insulted his dignity, perhaps beyond recall. She did not care. He spluttered for a while, but in the end he went away.

After he left, Dione sat alone in the room in which she received guests, and lowered her aching head into her hands. Oh, she was free, yes, so free that she went wherever queen or goddess bade her, dragging her son behind.

Her son was singularly unperturbed to be so maltreated. "We're going on a *ship?* With *sailors?* Can I work the sails, do you think? Will they let me take an oar?"

"I should hope not," said Dione.

He was not listening. He was already running to boast to all his friends that he—yes, he—was going to be a sailor.

Dione sighed, but she smiled, too. She saw both of them packed, gave the servants their orders to follow while she was gone, all but Hebe who went wherever her mistress traveled, and bundled them all to the harbor in the dark of earliest morning, the day the queen set sail for Tarsus.

The boat of the sun rode high, casting its rays on the water. The boats of Egypt rode a swift wind, sails of purple and gold stretched taut on the limber masts, oars shipped and sailors praising the gods who saw fit to ease their labors. The queen's ship sailed in the center of its guard of lesser vessels. Here away from the land, a month's leisurely sail from Alexandria, its splendor was veiled. Its decks were covered over with matting of reeds from the Nile, its crew in plain kilts or in nothing at all. Its passengers idled where there was room, or leaned over the rails to watch the foaming of the wake, or else to give tribute to the gods of the sea.

Dione, who was never seasick, spared a moment's pity for the exquisite young courtier who was trying to vomit his vitals into the water. Since he had long since cast up anything he could have eaten for the past handful of days, he had nothing more to offer the sea-gods, and they were as displeased as one might expect.

"There now," said a friend of his with the callousness of the hale for the wretchedly sick, "that'll pay you for going ashore at Cyprus. Only way to cure the seasickness is to stay at sea. Stay aboard for a month or two this time, and you'll actually want to live again."

The sufferer might have murdered him, but lacked the strength. His tormentor went off laughing. Dione stayed to hold the boy's head, a favor he did not appreciate. She did not trouble to tell him that she was working a small magic on him. Not much, not enough to defy the sea-gods, but it got him off the rail and into the cabin he shared with the rest of the eunuchs. It would put him to sleep eventually, and when he woke, if the gods were kind, they would be at anchor in Tarsus.

"We'll raise the mouth of Cydnus in the morning," said Timoleon, dropping, it seemed, from the sky. He was as naked as a newt and brown all over, and clean only by virtue of his having fallen recently from the masthead into the sea. There were new calluses on his hands, and blisters half-healed on his feet. He was gloriously happy. "And then it's up Cydnus and anchor at Tarsus, and show the bloody Romans what Egypt thinks of them."

"You won't be showing them your nut-brown backside," Dione said. "It will be decently covered and facing away from them, and you will be remembering that you are a gentleman and not a sailor's pup."

He looked mutinous, but he had had the lecture on mutiny; Dione had heard it. She had not known that the queen's oarsmen could be so eloquent. "Yes, mother," he said, which was also a consequence of his sojourn with the sailors. They were in awe of her; unlike Apollonius, they knew the goddess, and believed wholeheartedly in magic.

She was only glad that someone had found a way to civilize her son. Maybe, she thought, she should leave him with the sailors. He would leap at the chance. But whatever his father might think, she had some small sense of responsibility to her rank and station. Timoleon might grow up to command ships, but he would never be simply an oarsman in one.

"Is Cleopatra seasick?" he asked her, having taken a bare moment to be sulky.

"The queen is never seasick," she said. "She's in the cabin, keeping Caesarion company."

"Caesarion is as sick as a dog," said Timoleon. "He's a Roman, even if he's only half. Romans want to rule the world, but they don't understand the sea at all. It's a curse, Gyges says." Gyges was one of his friends, the enormous Nubian with the copper ring in his ear. Dione had half dreaded to find a ring like it in Timoleon's own ear, but so far he had forgone that tribute. "Gyges says Romans hate the sea, and the sea hates them right back. That's why they want us to give them ships. They know we aren't sea-cursed."

"And how do you know that it's ships they want?" Dione inquired.

"Oh, everybody knows that," said Timoleon.

Everybody probably did. It was Dione's firm conviction that the people knew what their princes wanted before the princes were even aware that they wanted anything. The people lacked magic in themselves, but in their aggregate they had more real power than a temple full of priests and seers.

She drew a long breath of air that smelled of salt and sun and the sea. The rail was warm under her hands, its gilding protected beneath a wrapping of mats, the woven reeds both prickly and smooth. They remembered the Nile, the great slow river that was the lifeblood of Egypt and the wellspring of its magic. While she traveled the sea on this ship out of Egypt, she was a part of it still. It was not as it had been in Rome, that cold alien place, even with queen and goddess to be her strength. Here was still Egypt. Here she was strong, with the sun in her eyes and the wind in her hair. She drew up magic out of the deck beneath her feet—cedar from the Lebanon, but matted with reeds and full of Egypt—and gave it wings, and sent it up like a prayer into the sun.

When she remembered earth again, Timoleon's eyes were round. "I never saw you do that before. Will you do it again?"

"No," said Dione. She snared him before he could escape, and sent him cabinward. "Now, in with you. Sailor's pup or no, you'll have your hour of Greek, and no mutiny." Since that was just what he had been contemplating, it silenced him conclusively. But then he liked the tutor whom he was sharing with Caesarion, who, though a eunuch, had, the sailors whispered, borne arms in Caesar's wars. That was enough to keep Timoleon in hand, even if Rhodon would not confirm or deny the rumor. In fact it was true, but Rhodon was modest, and a scholar. He was not proud to have found fighting so congenial.

Timoleon went to his hour of Euripides. Dione stayed in the sun while it lasted, and when it went down, went reluctantly to wait on the queen.

Cleopatra was not in one of her better moods. Queen or no, she would fret over her son's indisposition, and no matter that she knew exactly what it was. Her pacing and snarling aggravated his sickness; no one but Dione was bold enough to say so.

Dione was not one to be flayed by looks or even words. She got the queen out of the boy's cabin and into her own, where her maids could tend her. Cleopatra was no more grateful than one might expect. "All our wealth, all our knowledge, all our power, and we can't even comfort a seasick child."

"That's to keep us humble," Dione said. She lent a hand with the queen's hair, taking it out of its knots and plaits and combing it, soothing her as one soothes and strokes a cat. She hissed as a cat will, and showed claws, but Dione took no notice. "You'll meet Antony tomorrow," she said.

"If the wind and the gods allow," said Cleopatra.

"They will," Dione said. "They sail with us. Don't you feel them?"

"I feel nothing but that my son is half a Roman, and that half, at sea, is too much."

And yet, Dione thought, she was calming slowly, waking to what Dione had known since they left Alexandria. They were in the gods' hands. The air was full of it. The lamps swayed, casting shadows that seemed possessed of shape, birds and beasts, winged, furred, taloned, and one that, man-bodied, jackal-headed, bared white teeth in a smile. Dione bent her head in respect to that oldest of the guardians of her house, guardian indeed of all who walked the paths of magic and of the dead. While he was with her she had no fear; and he had been close to her, in and out of her shadow, since she set foot upon this ship.

The queen's breath hissed like the snake of shadow that seemed for a moment to crown her. "Ah, so *he* has come. No wonder you laugh at my nonsense."

Dione did not deny it. Cleopatra bowed to him more deeply than Dione had. "My lord," she said. Maybe he bowed in return. Maybe his eyes, sulfur-colored and perfectly alien, granted her both indulgence and respect. She was human and mortal, but she was Isis. He who was both shadow and Anubis, knew her fully for what she was.

FIVE

Marcus Antonius, triumvir, master of the eastern world, was reviewing his troops.

"Samian," he said, strolling down the ranks. "Coan. Cretan. Cyprian. Falernian—ah, Falernian! But these," he said with the deep pleasure of a man who has come home at last, "are the real, the only, the true Caecuban."

The winejars stood in their ranks, marching away into the gloom of the cellar. The general had been conducting a proper inspection, tasting as he went, but when he came to the Caecuban he filled his cup full and drank deep.

He was not drunk. Antony seldom was: his capacity was legendary. But he was in what his intimates called a Caecuban mood, warmly expansive, urging the crowd of them to find cups and fill them, too, and carry the jar out into the sun. The door to the wine-cellar of this villa in Tarsus was placed conveniently close to the dining hall, but also and pleasantly to the garden that looked on the river.

They took time to sort themselves out. Lucius Servilius the Augur, who liked a cup of good Caecuban, but not in the early afternoon, wandered to the wall and up the flight of steps that went to the top. Some previous tenant of the villa had set a marble bench there, where one could sit in comfort and watch the ships come and go in the harbor.

"Is she here yet?"

He looked down. Antony stood at the foot of the steps, winecup full as it always seemed to be. The rest were gathered round the jar, oblivious. Lucius was reasonably certain that Antony had made sure of it before he spoke.

Lucius answered the question easily enough, with a glance at the river to be sure. "No. Not yet. Not, I think, until tomorrow."

"That's an augury?"

Lucius forbore to lose his temper. Antony did not vex him with his office as too many others did; or not often. "That's common sense," he said. "And an ear for rumor. The natives can tell to the hour when the fleet will come to harbor."

"So they can." Antony climbed the steps more lightly than his bulk might have suggested. He was a big man, not much run to fat, yet, nor much softened by the wine he drank so much of. As he came to the top, he did not sit as Lucius did, but leaned on the rail that edged the wall. "She's taking her royal time," he said.

He sounded less impatient than bemused. Lucius observed, "It's fitting, I suppose. She is the queen of Egypt."

"You don't remember her, do you? You were out of Rome when she was in it."

Lucius nodded. "Gaul," he said. "Then Spain, on Caesar's errands. And only after that, and after she was gone, Rome." He rather regretted that he had not been able to see Egypt's conquest of Rome—or so they called it where authority was lax enough to permit such levity. "I gather she was—is—unusual."

Antony laughed, a rumble in his throat. "Unique, more like. She's as plain as a post, you know. Beak of a nose. Chin that goes halfway to meet it. But let her move or open her mouth, or bring those big brown eyes to bear, and she could be a black Fury for all you care what her face is. She's better than beautiful. She's interesting."

That, from such a connoisseur of beauty as Antony, was praise indeed. Lucius raised his brows at it. "Then you expect an interesting interview."

"It will be that," said Antony. He looked down, seemed to realize that there was wine in his cup, drained it in a gulp that would have sent Lucius reeling, and set the cup carefully beside his foot. Rather surprisingly, he did not go to fill it again, though he glanced over his shoulder at the winejar and its court of admirers. "It would be like her not to see me at all."

"Her ships are on the sea," Lucius said. "Surely she wouldn't come all this way for nothing."

"*She* would," said Antony. "Just to put me in my place."

"Rome is your place," said Lucius.

"Exactly." Lucius did not have anything, on short notice, to say to that. Nor did Antony add to it.

It was hardly silent, with the triumvir's general staff long gone in Caecuban, but there was a certain peace in sitting apart from them, in the sun, with the wind in his hair. Antony was not an unrestful companion. He was the kind of man who could be still. Like a lion, Lucius thought, sleeping the day away, till he roused to the swift violence of the kill.

They had not known one another long. Lucius was half a decade the younger, had been away when Caesar died, had come back late and for his family's sake, to bury a father and then a mother. When the mourning was done, he was bid remember his family and his fortunes, both much depleted. Antony had been mounting an expedition into the east, to make it his own and to raise war against the Parthians. It had seemed a less dreadful thing to go away again than to stay where he had estates to maintain in a style that his resources would not much longer permit, sisters who required dowries in order to marry respectably, clients and slaves who had to be fed and clothed and looked after with endless solicitude.

So he had gone, attached as legate to the triumvir's train. And somehow, on the long voyage and the longer muster of forces in Greece and in Asia, Lucius had found himself inclined to talk to his commander. It was not anything he sought. He was a poor hand at currying favor, did his duty with competence and kept himself to himself, but Antony was the sort of man a man could talk to. Even such a man as Lucius Servilius the Augur.

Antony went down after a while to see to matters of state and the queen's welcome. Lucius stayed where he was. Antony came back in time and in panoply, to stand watch again, this time with an edge of eagerness, perhaps even apprehension.

"Look," he said suddenly. "Out there."

At first Lucius did not know what Antony was seeing. There were always ships on the river, beating up from the sea, sailing down to it from the harbor of Tarsus.

These came in order like a fleet. The sun blazed on them, catching them just as it came down from the zenith.

No, he thought. It was not only the sun. There was gold on deck and rail and prow, and their sails—dark at first to his dazzled eyes— were the purple of Tyre, and of kings. One ship was larger than the rest, riding ahead of them, its three great banks of oars swinging to the beat of a drum that he felt in his bones though he heard no sound, yet, with his ears. The oars were bladed with silver. The decks were sheathed in gold.

The wind, shifting, brought music with it, the wailing of flutes, the deep sweet voice of the aulos and the shrill twitter of the pipe, and under them the pulsebeat of the drums.

Antony's voice was almost as deep as the drums, with laughter in it, and more than a hint of admiration. "Never the expected. No, never. Not with Cleopatra."

People were running along the river's banks, a vast throng of them, lured by the gold and the music and the sweetness that rode on the wind: perfumes both subtle and strong, rich with the strangeness of Egypt. The crowd's voices were like the cries of birds, too feeble to drown the music that came from the ship. Some flung themselves into the river and swam among the fleet, taking no heed for the slow relentless beating of the oars. The water curled over them, caressing them with white foam-fingers. Almost Lucius could see the curve of white breasts, sea-blue hair, sea-green eyes of water-nymphs skimming with the great ship, making it light, bearing it over the sea.

"There," said Antony, soft with wonder. "There she is."

Lucius had been waiting, taking in all the rest, tasting something that, if not magic, then was as close as made no matter. Now he let himself look at the ship's high deck, where the gold was blinding in its brightness. But not too bright to conceal the couch that stood there, or the one who reclined on it. There was no face to see from so far away, only a form that unquestionably was a woman's, robed and crowned, surrounded by children wielding fans of gold: boys, beautiful and quite naked except for the conceit of gilded wings. Women and maidens stood beyond and about them, robed in foam-green and foam-white, with their hair streaming upon their shoulders: mortal images of the half-seen, half-imagined spirits of water and of air.

"She comes as Venus from the sea," said Antony, "in her court of loves and graces, with an honor guard of sea-nymphs. How like her that is. How . . . eloquent."

"You're besotted with her," Lucius said. He did not know what had got into him; he was never so blunt or so impolitic. What approached on the river was a spectacle of vulgar ostentation, a message so blatant it invited nothing but contempt. Its magic was mere human credulity, its immortal escort a figment of dazzled eyes and fuddled brain. And yet it moved him. It made him forget the requirements of tact.

Antony grinned at him, unangered and completely unrepentant. "Why, so I am, aren't I? Aren't you? Isn't she splendid?"

"She is—" Lucius began to say, but stopped. "So. The rumors are true. She does have magic to use against us."

"Of course she has," said Antony, not even mildly appalled. "She's the queen of Egypt. She's Isis on earth. She breathes enchantment."

"Not on me," said Lucius. "Not if I can help it."

"What, you're afraid of her?"

Penetrating question, dangerous perhaps to answer. But Antony did not wait for Lucius to speak. He was halfway down the steps, bellowing for his aides. One of whom, Lucius was; but Lucius was powerless to move from his seat on the wall.

Magic, he thought. *She breathes magic.*

Of course he had known that. Egypt was the fount of the art; an art which he had studied, and respected but never greatly feared. But this was something more than the dry words and drier potions of the old magicians. This was power, honed like a blade, aimed straight at Rome's heart.

And Rome, here, was Antony. Antony the lover of wine and

women. Antony the more than half besotted, even before she came with her gold and her music and her perfumes and her spells.

"Father Jupiter," said Lucius Servilius the Augur. "Gods of heaven and earth and the world below; powers of all names and none: defend him now. Keep his wits about him. Let him remember. Egypt she may be, but he, of all men in the world—he is Rome."

SIX

Cleopatra was a mistress of illusion. It was her great gift to show herself as she was, goddess on earth, in a form that mere mortals could understand. Thus the gold and the perfumes, the costumed Cupids, the music that turned it all to magic. Of real magic there was little, no more than was in the queen by her nature. She did not waste power when its semblance would serve.

Dione, clad in white and wearing an aspect of one of the Graces, stood just behind the throne. Half of her was caught up in this play of the queen's. Half kept a wary eye on her son. Timoleon had yearned to be a Cupid, had objected strenuously when his mother refused to let him stand naked on a ship's prow for the world to stare at. He had been mollified when she permitted him to mingle with the sailors; his tunic was still on him, for a wonder, as he clung to the rigging a heart-stopping distance above the deck.

The oars lifted like wings. A light wind caught the sails and bore the ship forward. As smoothly as the great vessel sailed, it seemed almost that the ship stood still and the land moved toward it, laden with its cargo of shouting, singing people.

There were Romans among them. The scarlet cloak of the legionary was a thing no eye could mistake, vivid as blood among the many colors of an eastern city. They were forming ranks along the quay; the hoarse shouts of centurions carried over the water, even through Cleopatra's music. So would Rome always conquer, with rough efficiency.

Cleopatra meant to be stronger. Dione let her eyes return to the splendor that was Egypt. There for a while she rested, until she could look outward again, and see what waited on the quays of Tarsus.

*   *   *

The fleet bent toward the shore, riding wind and oar. The music continued beneath the shouting of captains and the pounding of feet, bringing the ships to their moorings. Egypt floated in the harbor of Tarsus, more exotic than ever, and somehow less gaudy than it had seemed from a distance.

Lucius Servilius the Augur stood somewhat nearer the quay than the market square, on the edge of a portico raised above the level of the street, so that he could see over the heads of the crowd that rimmed the harbor. Out of the corner of his eye he could see Antony on the dais set up on one side of the market square, where he heard cases and administered justice in this part of the world—and where now he expected to receive the queen of Egypt. Antony, like his staff and his troops, was in full panoply, and no sign in him of the haste that had brought him here. He sat in the curule chair that was all the throne any Roman needed, posed as if for a sculptor, seeming oblivious to the weight or the discomfort of his armor.

Lucius had stopped on his way down from the wall to put on the toga. Armor might have been more comfortable. The sun was warm, and the toga was wool, and heavy. One learned to ignore the weight and the itch, and to walk with ponderous dignity lest the folds be disarranged and the lot of it fall in an ignominious tangle. Soldiers could stride out even in parade armor. Togaed notables must keep to a more sedate pace.

Even so, he came in time to take a place where he could see, and his toga held back any who might have contested his right to stand there. Not that any did. Every eye in Tarsus was bent, it seemed, on the ship in the harbor.

It rocked gently in a swell. The music went on as it had for an hour and more now, since the fleet came to port. The people on board stood like images in a temple, as if they never grew tired or restless or footsore. No boats went down, nor did the queen move to greet the men who waited to conduct her to the triumvir's seat.

For a long while, as the sun beat down, Antony neither moved nor spoke. Not when the crowd about him drifted one by one toward the ships and the river and the bright lure of the Egyptian fleet. Not even when his own men, some furtively, some more boldly, joined the exodus to the harbor. At last he sat all alone, awaiting a tribute that did not come.

The woman on the ship seemed as solitary as he, though all eyes were on her, and her attendants stood all about her. She sat immobile in their midst, her long, heavily painted eyes fixed on a prospect far above anything of earth.

Lucius wondered briefly if she was not a woman at all but a carved image or an illusion—if the ship was full of dreams and mockeries. Then something stirred in the rigging—a sailor, young from the look of him, and agile as a monkey, standing on a narrow bridge of rope as if it had been a stone floor. One of the Graces bent a stern eye on him. They had the same delicate oval face with eyes as wide and dark as a doe's, and the same rich curling hair, so black it shone blue. The child's form was boy-lean, the woman's richly rounded, but they stood in the same way, light and supple, swaying as the ship rocked. Brother, then, and sister? Or son and mother?

The boy caught the woman's eye, fine dark brows drawing together. The woman frowned very slightly. The boy's chin firmed. But the woman was a match for the child. He stilled, eloquent of resistance but clearly unwilling to test his mother's will—for mother it must be, no sister had quite that weight of authority.

Lucius discovered that he was amused. The glittering abstract that was Egypt was suddenly a human thing: a son plotting mischief, a mother catching him before he began. There was no fear in the child's manner, no tyranny in the mother's. He was almost disposed, for a moment, to feel kindly toward a queen who had such servants.

Whatever charity the queen might keep for those about her, she had none for Rome. She made no effort to disembark from her ship, but floated at anchor as if she expected Rome to come to her. Rome, unmoving, was treated to the music's sinking into silence, and to the drawing of curtains about the queen and her court. The play was done, the gesture said. The audience might applaud, and then it should go home.

Lucius glanced at Antony. He seemed calm, undismayed.

Then at last, when it seemed that Egypt would remain aloof even in the harbor of Tarsus, a boat lowered from the ship's side. It was a small boat, but gilded about the prow and along the gunwales, with oarsmen in shining white kilts. A personage sat among them. He wore what must have been Egyptian formal dress, or else the robe of a priest, white linen so fine as to be nearly transparent, with a heavy golden pectoral, and hair—no, a wig—in elaborate plaits. The face under the weight of the wig was wizened and brown, with eyes painted in that fashion which even Egyptian men affected.

But, thought Lucius Servilius, Cleopatra was a Hellene; she was no more Egyptian than Antony was, no matter where she was born. They said that she spoke the language of her kingdom—if she did, then she was the first of her line to do it. All the rest had spoken the Greek of their heritage, or even the Macedonian patois of their first ancestor, who had claimed to be half-brother to the great Alexander. Lucius doubted that old Ptolemy had been any such thing. It was a convenient rumor, that was all, and a useful pretext to seize power in a land that Alexander had not conquered, but which had welcomed him as a savior from the yoke of Persia.

Credulous Egypt had accepted the falsehood as truth, and named Ptolemy pharaoh and savior. His descendant seemed determined to remind Rome that she was Egyptian as well as Greek—for Greece after all was conquered, but Egypt still fancied itself free.

Her messenger disembarked with dignity nearly as stiff as that enjoined on a Roman by the toga, and, leaning on a gilded staff, faced Antony's officers. Lucius could not hear through the crowd's roar what he said to them, or they to him. They spoke at some length. Then the Egyptian turned away from Antony's messengers and began the ascent from the quay. Legionaries with spears opened a way for him. He walked slowly but ably enough through the throng into the emptiness of the square. Antony waited, silent, solitary in his splendor.

Somehow, as happens on occasion even in mighty crowds, there came a silence, a stillness in which no voice spoke. In it Lucius heard the tap of the staff on the stone that paved the square. The staff was carved, its head the head of a serpent, the hooded cobra of Egypt. The eyes were set with jewels, rubies like drops of blood, glittering almost as if the thing were alive.

And so it might be, if tales were true. Rod into serpent was an old trick of the Egyptian priests. Would this one fling down his staff at Antony's feet and bid the living snake sink fangs in the Roman's heel?

It seemed that he would not. The staff remained a staff, gilt over wood. The priest approached the triumvir. Some paces from the foot of the dais he halted. He did not bow, although he inclined his head in lofty respect. When he spoke, he spoke in Greek, in a clear, high, ancient voice.

Stripped of flourishes, his speech was simple enough. The queen of Egypt bade the ruler of the Romans to dine with her on her ship at sunset.

The ruler of the Romans revealed emotion at last: he frowned. "We had wished her to dine with us," he said, "before sunset."

The queen of Egypt, said her emissary at length, regretted that she was unable to accept; but she would be most pleased to entertain the ruler of the Romans, as it were, on her own ground.

Now that, thought Lucius, was an argument well calculated to sway a soldier. Certainly it swayed Antony. He was angry: his words were bitten off short. But he said, "Let it be, for this one night, as the queen wishes."

"A soldier goes straight in," he said to Lucius as the sun was sinking. He had taken off his armor to rest and to attend to things that needed doing, but now he was putting it all back on again. "If I were a proper senator—no offense to you when you come to it, Lucius Servilius— I'd be playing every game in the field. And I'd lose to Cleopatra. She's been a master since before her breasts were budded."

Lucius was not offended. He happened to agree with Antony concerning the duplicity of senators as a breed. Still he said, "You shouldn't have given in so quickly. She'll think she can wrap you around her finger."

"And let her think it," said Antony, with a hint of an edge. "I'm not immune to her, I grant you that, but I think I can hold my own, on my own ground."

"You're going to hers tonight," said Lucius.

"But I'm going as a soldier." Antony grinned a white wolf-grin, raising his arms so that his servant could fasten the golden cuirass. It was his best, his parade armor, embossed with the triumph of Dionysus. The long skein of satyrs and dancing maenads wound all about it through a thicket of vines and grape-clusters. In the center stood the god, crowned with vineleaves. It seemed a strange thing to adorn the armor of a warrior, but the god's face, if one looked closely, was terrible: a still, cold, beautiful mask, with eyes that were quite blank and quite mad.

Lucius was not a soldier, but he had seen enough of war. He knew its face. He bowed to the god, offering up the thrill of cold fear that was the god's due.

"Come," said Antony. "There's a battle waiting."

"He sees everything as a soldier must see it," said Cleopatra as her maids prepared her for the banquet. "To him this will be a battle, and I the enemy, to be taken by storm if he can, or by stealth if he must."

Dione was ready long since. Her face felt stiff in its armor of paint, under the plaited richness of the Egyptian wig. Her gown was of the ancient style of the Two Lands, so transparent that it concealed nothing; she had learned not to blush in it. Its great virtue was that it was cool, even with the weight of the jewels that made splendid its simplicity.

The queen was as nervous as a bride on her wedding night. She held herself still, kept her face immobile under the brushes of her most skilled handmaid, moved only at the direction of the lesser servants who dressed her, arranged her hair, put on the jewels she had chosen. But her tongue ran on as if it had a will of its own.

"He has no subtlety," she said. "Everything he does, he does direct, with no more pretense than would deceive a child. And yet," she said, "such simplicity can be dangerous. I must not underestimate him. Don't let me slip into that, Dione."

"Can I stop you if you're set on it?" Dione inquired.

The queen rounded on her, scattering servants. Dione smiled serenely.

"You," said Cleopatra, "are impertinent."

"Certainly," Dione said.

Cleopatra's outrage faded as quickly as it had risen. "Ah, you," she said. "Now I remember why I keep you."

She might have said more, but a page slipped into the dressing-room, bobbed his head in respect, said, "Lady, they've come."

So they had. Dione, listening, heard the ring of armor, the thud of feet, the rumble of Roman voices.

Cleopatra had drawn up like a cat at gaze. Dione watched her soften every tensed muscle, turn back to her maids, submit herself to their ministrations. Most of them knew how to read her expression; they moved in leisurely fashion. But one, the child who attended the queen's sandals, tried to quicken her pace.

Dione touched her gently on the shoulder. "No, little one. Slowly. Queens never make haste. They make bold foreign warriors wait."

And wait. And wait. The queen, once arrayed past any expectation of improvement, settled herself on the couch that stood against the wall of the room, and called for her book. "Read," she commanded Dione.

Dione thought Hesiod unbelievably dull. But read she did, while in the banqueting hall, no doubt, the Romans learned the virtue of patience.

So this was Egypt, thought Lucius Servilius the Augur. It reeked of perfume. Everything that was not painted was gilded, and everything that was not gilded was inlaid with colored stones. One would not know, sitting in this hall of many couches, that it floated in the harbor of Tarsus. Its walls, to be sure, were not marble or painted plaster but wooden pillars and gauzy draperies stirring gently as a breeze blew through them. The sky beyond was light still though it was well past sunset; stars had come out one by one.

Within was a splendor of light. Great circles and squares, arcs and clusters of lamps were let down from the ceiling, or stood among the pillars or on the tables or behind and about each couch. All that hall was as bright as noon, but the light somehow was softer, less merciless. It even softened, somewhat, the gaudiness of the appointments.

Servants in Egyptian kilts offered wine, of which the guests partook liberally, and small delicacies on, of course, golden platters, and excuses for their queen's failure to appear. Lucius was mildly surprised that Antony had not lost his temper even yet. He was close to it: the high color was higher than usual, and he was downing wine at a rate prodigious even for him. But he reclined apparently at ease on the couch to which he had been escorted, in the place of honor beside the empty one. Lucius, well down the ranks, caught snatches of his exchanges with those nearest him. His humor was growing cruder as the hour—hours—advanced.

Not all the guests were Roman. There were dignitaries from Tarsus, nervous and sweating in their best robes, and courtiers in the garb of Hellenes or Egyptians. Most of the conversation was in Greek.

Lucius, granted the unusual privilege of a couch to himself, rather enjoyed his solitude. It gave him leisure to appreciate the full ostentation of the appointments. He was rapt in contemplation of a carved and gilded depiction of either a nymph astride a goose or Leda post coitum with the swan, when a shadow fell across him.

It was brief, slipping past, taking the place that had been left vacant, but it altered his focus to the face of the one who cast it. "Why," he said without thinking, "it's the most interesting of the Graces. Did you lock your son in a sea-chest, to keep him from joining you?"

The queen's attendant regarded him with remarkably little surprise, and no censure that he could detect. "Very nearly," she replied. "Do you know me?"

"Why," he said, stammering a little, "why, no. That is—I saw you on the ship. You were a Grace. The sailor in the rigging—it was your son, I couldn't be mistaken. He looks a fair scamp, that one."

The Egyptian lady laughed. Her laughter was full and rich and completely without affectation. "Oh, he is! He was ready to go over the side, or to dance on top of the mast, or something equally inadvisable." She raised her brows. They were painted in the Egyptian fashion, but he could see that they were fine under the paint; her eyes were nearly as long as the paint made them seem, bright and dark at once, and lively with curiosity. "Are you a priest?" she asked.

"Why," he said, stammering again—oh, damn his tongue, it never knew how to behave in front of a beautiful woman—"yes, yes I am. But how can you . . . ?"

"I, too," she said, nodding as if he had confirmed something that she needed to know. "My name is Dione of the house of the Lagidai. Though not," she added with a glint, "the royal branch. I am priestess of Isis in the Two Lands."

"Lucius," he answered her, for once without tripping over his tongue, "Servilius the Augur."

"Ah," she said. "A seer. What do you see in that really quite dreadful dado on the beam yonder?"

His eyes followed hers. For no reason that he could explain, he blushed. "It is awful, isn't it?" he heard himself say.

"Ghastly," said Dione. Women in Rome were outspoken, sometimes to the point of pain, but Lucius had never met one quite like this. "I'm glad someone in Rome has taste. The queen's shipbuilders insisted that Romans require at least a hundredweight of gilt per roofbeam in order to be even mildly impressed."

"No doubt they were taking a cut of the proceeds," Lucius said. "I am impressed, I admit. I've never seen anything quite so . . ." His voice died.

"Appalling," Dione said for him. She was sitting on the couch, he noticed belatedly, like a child on a stool: alertly upright, hands folded in her lap. Her gown was Egyptian. It left nothing to the imagination.

His cheeks were aflame. His eyes dropped, fixing on the first thing they came to, which happened to be a wine-stain on his otherwise pristine toga. Since his winecup lay untouched on the low table beside him, he could not imagine where the stain had come from. It vexed him quite out of proportion to its magnitude.

When he could look up again, he found admirable distraction. The queen had, at last, seen fit to make her entrance.

SEVEN

Women past first youth and never greatly gifted with beauty were said to prefer the dimmer lights, a lone lamp or the moon. Cleopatra, it seemed, preferred the full blaze of light, whether it came of the sun or of a myriad lamps. She came as queen and goddess, arrayed in gold. Courtiers surrounded her, attendants waited on her. None of them mattered. Many were taller than she, and many more beautiful. It made no difference. Only she was Cleopatra.

Lucius Servilius willed himself to resist her spell. It was not magic, not in the sense of potions and incantations. It was the sublime surety that she was royal, and that the world existed to serve her. She was a queen of a race of kings. She was born to receive homage.

So she might think, mused Lucius Servilius the Augur. Antony rose at her coming, out of a courtesy native to him; the rest followed suit, the easterners rising only to bow to the gaudy carpets, the Romans standing at attention as soldiers should. She acknowledged them graciously, Antony no more than the rest, though he held the place of honor.

Her couch was set beside Antony's. She reclined there with grace that was quite remarkable considering how heavy and unwieldy her robes must have been. Once she was settled, with her attendants dispersed about the hall, the feast began.

It was of a piece with the rest: twelve tables spread in succession, perhaps in honor of Rome's Twelve Tables of the law, perhaps in mockery of it. Lucius, who had had to order the preparation of a state dinner or two himself, could admire both the resources and the resourcefulness of a woman who, after a voyage of some days' duration and with but the fraction of a day to discover the capacities of the market in Tarsus, produced so splendid a range and variety of courses. Most of them, inevitably, were fish, but there were roasts of lamb, duck, goose, and something succulent in a spiced sauce that was, the servant said, gazelle. There were figs from Persia, dried and honeyed or spiced with cloves and cinnamon; apples of Damascus baked in little caskets; dates from Jericho, dried grapes from the queen's own vineyards, juice of pomegranates from her garden in Alexandria.

There seemed no end to it, either in abundance or in variety. The queen was apologetic: "If I were in my own house," she said in her voice that was as beautiful as her face was not, both low and sweet, "I would prepare a proper feast."

"This is proper enough," Antony said. "I doubt that I could do as well in my house in Rome."

"Your wife, they say, is an enterprising woman," the queen said. Was there a barb in it? "She keeps the state required of your station, yes? But that, in Rome, implies a certain Roman austerity."

"But this is the East," Antony said, "my lady of Egypt."

Cleopatra smiled.

The queen, Dione was pleased but not surprised to see, had lost her nervousness somewhere between her dressing chamber and the hall. The effect of her entrance was all that she could have wished. The Romans were struck to silence. Even the young augur seemed to have lost a fraction of his scorn for anything that was not Roman.

Dione watched him out of the corner of her eye. Roman faces tended toward a certain cragginess, noses like the prows of ships, cheeks deep-furrowed with the weight of self-importance. Lucius Servilius the Augur had self-importance in plenty, but his face was more cleanly carved than most, his nose less monumentally arched. In fact he was quite handsome; pretty, for a fact, if his mouth had had a shade less character. It was long and a little crooked, and looked as if it did not smile enough. With his fine olive skin that looked as soft as a girl's, and his black curls and his big brown eyes, he looked like a boy. But there were fine lines at the corners of those eyes, and a look in them that spoke of more years than his face admitted.

She rather liked him. He found her shocking, she could tell, but unlike most Romans he did not presume to lecture her on the proper conduct of women in public. Nor did he reckon quality by the quantity of gold that went into it. Quite rarely for a Roman, he had taste.

He ate in silence that maybe he meant to seem aloof. To Dione it was merely shy. She might have coaxed him out of it, but she was watching the two who led the feast.

Antony's armor was gilded, flashing in the light of the lamps. Cleopatra's robes, like golden armor, dazzled the eye that rested on them. Dione trained her eye to see through the veil of splendor.

They had spoken little beyond their exchange of greetings and slightly barbed civilities. And yet, Dione thought, something had roused that had nothing to do with words.

Maybe it had been there when they knew each other before, in Rome while Caesar was alive. But then there had been Caesar, for whom words were both armor and weapon; with him Cleopatra had been always on her mettle, her wit honed to its finest edge. Antony was not, had never been, a witty man.

He had gained in flesh and in substance since that last terrible night in Rome, when Caesar was dead and Cleopatra knew no wisdom but flight. He had aided her, as calm in grief as she was, but under the calm a white rage. The rage was gone now, the stocky solidity softened a little about the edges, the heavy shoulders braced beneath the weight of empire.

Cleopatra's own rage had never truly died. Dione had half expected it to burst out in mockery of this Roman; but something, prudence perhaps, restrained it. As the feast went on in its blaze of light, Dione watched that rage transmute into something quite unlooked for. It was not peace. Cleopatra had never been a peaceful creature, nor could she ever be. But here, somehow, she found calm.

He understood, or seemed to. When the wine had gone round, and round again, as all the lights seemed to swim in a sea of Caecuban and Samian and pale gold Chian, eye met eye across the golden couches. Later, maybe, the words would come, the long winding skeins of alliance and counteralliance, prices paid and prices to be paid, all the impedimenta of kings. Now there were only the two of them.

"Aphrodite comes to Dionysus for the joy of Asia."

The voice was Dione's, soft beneath the roar of conversation. It seemed no part of her, as always when the goddess spoke. No more came than that, though she laid herself open to it.

The young augur was staring at her. He must have seen the goddess: his eyes were white around the edges. She found a smile for him. "You shouldn't mind me," she said. "It's only divinity."

"You are," he said slowly, but without the stammer that seemed to vex him. "You *are* a priestess."

"You doubted me?" Dione asked.

His blush was charming, like a boy's, darkening the fine olive cheeks to crimson.

"There now," she said, meaning to soothe him if she could, "no one ever believes it till he sees it. I'm the goddess' voice in the Two Lands—and, for that matter of that, outside of them, too."

"But," he said, "such things need order—ritual—sacrifice—"

"I am the rite and the sacrifice," said Dione. "She's never needed more than that. And why should she? She's a goddess. She can do whatever she pleases."

Poor punctilious Roman, he could not understand a goddess with a mind of her own. All his gods were safely bound in cords of ceremony, their priesthood reduced to political office, their power shrunk to a shadow and a name. No wonder Egypt appalled him. Egypt's gods were alive, and lively with it. Their names meant something outside the walls of temples.

If Lucius Servilius the Augur could not comprehend divinity, Marcus Antonius the Triumvir had no need to. On this night, in this company, he was divinity himself. Glittering in gold, expansive with wine, he rose. The wine caught him; he stumbled, but he laughed, and steadied himself, holding out a hand. The queen smiled up at him, took the hand he offered, let him draw her to her feet. He swayed again, or she softened, bending toward him. Briefly; not even an embrace, so swift as it was, but it said all that words did not.

Dione might have protested, but there was nothing to her but eyes; her voice was mute. No one else seemed to see. They were all well gone in wine, or absorbed in watching the dancers whom the queen had brought from Nubia.

So soon? Dione meant to say. *So absolute?*

If they had heard, they would not have cared. Maybe Cleopatra knew what she was doing, and did it open-eyed. Maybe Antony, too. Dione could not know.

But then, having not quite embraced, they parted. Cleopatra slipped through the curtains that swayed behind her couch. Antony walked out of the hall. Dione, sharp-eared with startlement, heard him call for his boatmen.

She found that she was staring at Lucius Servilius. He for once was staring back, neither lowering his eyes nor blushing. The corner of his mouth curved very slightly up. "Not tonight," he said.

"Not yet," said Dione.

EIGHT

Dione, accompanied by an armored guard, a maid with a basket, and the children—her own Timoleon, and Caesarion escaped from his tutor's guardianship—walked up from the harbor of Tarsus. Behind her the boatmen backed away from the quay, returning to the queen's ship. They would return when the sun came to noon.

It was still early morning. The queen was abed though not asleep, attending to matters that could be attended to in comfort. Most of her courtiers slept the sleep of the dead or of revelers who had drunk till dawn. Dione suspected that the Romans were in similar case.

The market was lively. So were the children. Timoleon objected in principle to the company of, as he put it, a toddling infant. The infant, who was all of three years younger than Timoleon, smiled much too sweetly at him. As much of a hellion as Timoleon could be, Caesarion was the child of Caesar and Cleopatra. He had their wits and their arrogance, and their capacity for trouble.

Dione did not fancy herself a match for them, but she had one thing that even Caesarion did not: the gift of command. Both of them had tested it before and discovered that once she had laid the Word on them, it held them until she pleased to release them. The threat of it was good for almost an hour's obedience. That got them off the ship and onto the land, and even into the market.

There, before they could erupt into rebellion, Dione turned them loose in the custody of the guard. "But mind," she said to Timoleon, "that you stay with Caesarion and watch out for him. Any mischief either of you gets into, I'll hold you to account."

"That's not fair," said Timoleon.

"Of course it's not," said his mother.

He opened his mouth, then shut it again. Some children would have argued with the inarguable. Timoleon was wise for his years: he settled for what he could get. It was hardly freedom, but it was better than a long dull morning of dangling at his mother's heel.

Trailing the smaller boy and the lithe young soldier, he darted off toward a vendor of sweets. The guard held the purse, another insult to Timoleon's pride, but Dione was not a merciful creature. She saw them off with a mingling of relief and mild alarm. "The gods know what they'll get into," she said to her maid.

Hebe was mute, but her ears were as sharp as a cat's, and her mind was keen. She grinned whitely in her dark Nubian face. She was not so much older than Timoleon that she had forgotten the joy of mischief well committed.

Nor, for that matter of that, had Dione. She answered the maid's grin with a wry smile, and began her own circuit of the market. There was little enough that she honestly needed, but after a month on shipboard, even with as many pauses as they had made to come to harbor and to show the queen's majesty to a dazzled populace, it was a pleasure to stand on solid earth again. She chaffered over a bit of wool that the seller claimed was Tyrian purple but Dione knew was berry-dyed and sure to fade in the first washing; picked through a tray of silver brooches and armlets; bought a grapeleaf filled with spiced meat and barley, and ate it still scalding hot, sitting on the plinth of a statue dedicated to foamborn Aphrodite. She felt quite as young as Timoleon, and rather more free to do as she pleased.

That was enough of a rarity that she took time to savor it. Hebe was amenable; she could move quickly when she saw the need, but she loved to drowse in the sun, blinking like a great glossy cat.

Their resting place was just at the edge of the market square, near the platform on which Antony had sat so very much alone—was it only yesterday? Dione had to admire his coolness in the face of such humiliation.

He was not there this morning, or perhaps only not there yet. The dais was empty even of the triumvir's seat, his curule chair that went where he went. He had not brought it onto Cleopatra's ship. Perhaps he meant something by that. Egypt was a sovereign nation still, whatever Rome might think.

She ate half of her grapeleaf, fed the rest to a little sun-and-shadow cat that came to investigate. It was a shy and skittish thing, all bones and eyes and enormous, preposterous feet. Mother Bastet had blessed or cursed it: its paws were strange, with an extraordinary count of toes. When it dropped a bit of meat, it reached as a child would, and picked it up in its paw that was like a hand with a thumb, and ate it.

Hebe hissed. Her hands flashed in a sign against evil; she swooped toward the cat as if to drive it away.

Dione stopped her with a hand. "No. This is Mother Bastet's child. See, she understands us"—for the cat had paused in its devouring of the grapeleaf to answer Hebe's hiss with a hiss of its own. But then it turned its head to blink shyly at Dione, and inquired in a voice so soft it was barely to be heard, *"Mao?"*

"Mao," said Dione. The cat butted its hard round head against her arm and purred.

When Dione got up to go on, the cat followed. Dione was careful not to acknowledge her new companion. If the cat chose to remain with her, then she was blessed of Bastet; but she was too wise to force matters. Cats belonged to no one but themselves and their goddess. Sometimes, however, they chose humans for their servants.

A little distance from Aphrodite's statue was a fishmonger's stall. Dione bought a handful of small silver fish, not for the cat, not exactly, but the cats who owned her house in Alexandria were fond of just such a dainty. Farther down, she found a woman willing to sell a cup of goat's milk fresh from the udder. Some of it she drank herself, some she gave to Hebe. There was enough left for a small cat who had eaten a pair of the fish and showed an inclination to drink as well.

While Dione sat on a step by the goat-woman's stall with cat and cup in her lap, she realized that she had an audience. Of course she knew that Romans only wore the toga for state occasions; it was much too unwieldy to be comfortable in. Even so, she was mildly surprised to see Lucius Servilius the Augur in a tunic and sandals like any man in Tarsus, insofar as any man in Tarsus wore fine new linen and fine soft leather and a cloak that was not berry-dyed purple, but was the lesser Tyrian, the lucent amethyst that Dione rather preferred to the deep-dyed vermilion of kings. He seemed amused to see her there, and not surprised. "Good morning," she said to him.

"Good morning," he replied civilly, with only a hint of a blush. "Do you adopt cats whenever you visit a market?"

"I should hope not," said Dione. "This cat adopted me."

"They have a way of doing that," said Lucius Servilius.

When the little cat purred, she purred from head to tail. She looked up from her breakfast to study the Roman, and pronounced her verdict: *"Mrrrrttt."*

"She says you need a mother," Dione translated, "but she isn't adopting multitudes today."

"Particularly Roman multitudes?"

"Cats don't care for tribes or nations. A human is a human, poor thing, wherever it comes from."

Lucius Servilius laughed. In daylight, in public, he seemed more at ease than he had been at Cleopatra's feast. He did not offer to pet the cat, which Dione thought remarkably perceptive of him.

"Probably you have dogs," said Dione, considering him.

"Dogs are charming," he said, "but frightfully servile."

"Don't Romans prefer servility to independence?"

He caught her meaning: his eyes sparked. But he did not seem angry. Interested, rather. Diverted. "Romans may," he answered. "This Roman does not."

The cat's purr rose to thunder. She was done with her breakfast; she sat on Dione's knee to wash her face. Lucius Servilius, after a moment, sat beside Dione. He did not seem to have the Roman propensity for standing on his dignity wherever he was. He sat boy-like, clasping his knee and watching people pass in the street. He was quite beautiful, Dione thought, and quite evidently unaware of it.

The cat finished her toilet and curled in Dione's lap. Hebe, squatting against the wall a little distance down the street, regarded the cat balefully. The cat paid no attention to the maid's mistrust. Dione decided to follow suit.

"Is your son in the city today?" asked Lucius Servilius rather abruptly.

Dione's heart forgot, briefly, to beat. "Why? What was he doing?"

"Nothing," said Lucius Servilius. "He had a younger boy with him, and was leading him a merry chase. Did he own a bright green tunic before you turned him loose?"

"Goddess, no," said Dione. Then she drew a breath of relief. "If that's all he's done, I'm content."

"It was quite a shocking shade of green," the Roman said. "Bilious, at the very least. I hope he didn't pay a fortune for it."

"He wouldn't have. Diomedes has the purse."

"Diomedes is the guard," Lucius Servilius deduced, "and the boys are your sons."

"One of them," said Dione. "The elder. The younger is the queen's."

He started, not obviously, but enough for her to see.

"Yes," she said as if he had spoken. "That was Ptolemy Caesar: Caesarion."

"And the queen—his mother—you—let him run wild in the streets of Tarsus, as if he had been any commoner's child?"

"You did not," Dione pointed out, "object when you thought he might be my child. And I am not a commoner."

He caught the edge in that; it brought him up short. "The queen has—had—sisters—but—"

"No, I'm not Cleopatra's sister," said Dione. "My family began with the brother of the first Ptolemy who ruled in Egypt. We never wanted to be kings, or queens either. But neither are we the sweepings of the street."

Lucius Servilius looked half mortified, half angry. "I never said you were. But Caesar's son running loose in Tarsus—if Antony hears, he'll be outraged."

"Antony is not Caesarion's father," said Dione coldly, "nor his guardian."

"Perhaps he should be."

"Why?" Dione asked. "Because an Egyptian queen is no fit parent for a Roman's get—even one born out of lawful Roman wedlock?"

"That is Caesar's son," said Lucius Servilius.

"And Cleopatra's," said Dione.

They glared at one another. Dione did not know which of them realized first how truly absurd they were, sitting on a doorstep in the market of Tarsus, glowering over the head of a small peculiar cat. Dione laughed first, but Lucius Servilius grinned before he laughed.

When the gust of mirth passed, Dione leaned back against the doorframe. The cat butted her chin. She sighed a little. "I can see that Rome and Egypt have much to do by way of compromise."

"Why should Rome compromise?" demanded Lucius Servilius. But before her temper could rise again, he shook his head. "I'm too stubborn by half. Ridiculous, too, debating matters of high import with my feet in a gutter."

"That should stop you?" Dione asked. "It never stops anybody in Rome that I ever knew. Even the gladiators have political opinions."

"Politics are important," said Lucius Servilius. "The most important thing in the world."

"I don't think so," Dione said.

"A woman wouldn't."

"You sound like my husband," she observed.

He looked startled. She did not see why he should. Respectable women did not bear children outside of marriage. Unless of course they were queens.

"In fact," she said, "you remind me of why he divorced me. He can be unbearably self-righteous."

There. He was startled all over again. She had rather hoped he would be.

While he stared at her, struggling to fit her into his conception of the universe, she stood. The cat did not wish to ride in her arms: it poured itself out of her grasp and sat beside her foot, smoothing its ruffled fur with its tongue. "I had better find my offspring," Dione said, "and Cleopatra's, before they decide that a green tunic is only the beginning and dye themselves green all over."

He rose more slowly than she had. He was of middling height for a Roman, tall beside her smallness, but not too tall for comfort. "May I escort you?" he asked.

She thought of refusing. The goddess knew, she had done everything she could, knowing or unknowing, to antagonize him. Maybe this was his revenge.

She did not find him hard to look at. If he had other things in mind, he would learn that she had more defenses than met the eye. Even, maybe, the eye of a seer.

For the moment he seemed moved simply by courtesy, and perhaps a touch of curiosity. He would want to see Caesar's son, of course. They all did.

Trailed by the maid and the Roman and the cat, Dione went back into the bustle of the market. It was not unduly difficult to find the children, although it took some little time. She simply went where a child would be most inclined to go.

Sweetseller, vendor of clothing both lurid and shoddy, juggler in a whirling crown of knives, fur-clad savage leading a dancing bear, seller of meat pasties, blind singer with a dog crouched at his feet. Dione paused to listen to him. The dog was asleep with its head on its paws, but its ears were alert to anything that might threaten its master. The little cat hissed; the dog ignored it. Dione retrieved the cat before it could begin hostilities in earnest.

A body hurtled into her. She staggered; strong hands caught her before she fell. She took no notice of them or of the Roman who belonged to them. Caesarion had caromed off her and come to a stop, breathing hard. "Dione! Dione, come quick!"

She caught him before he could bolt. "What? Who is it?"

"Timoleon," he said.

She was running before he finished the word.

It did not look like a threat to life or limb. A lesser square lay beyond the great one, with a fountain in it, dry and choked with refuse. Past the fountain was a circle of people, mostly men, laughing and shouting. Inside the circle was a man with a stick, and a very small donkey under a very large burden, and Timoleon.

His tunic, Dione noticed, was even more ghastly than Lucius Servilius had led her to expect. It was also much too large for him. He had tied it up with a bit of cord unearthed from who knew where, but the hem trailed grubbily out behind him. He was taking no notice of it at all. "You let that donkey go," he said in his clearest and most imperious voice, "or I'll have my mother turn you into a snake."

"You just do that," said the donkey's driver, to the raucous approval of his audience, "and I'll turn right around and bite you in the foot. Now you get out of my way, little cock, and let me get about my business."

"I will not," said Timoleon. "That donkey's load is too heavy and its back hurts."

"Who says?" the man sneered. "The donkey?" Others echoed him. Still others cheered Timoleon. They were laying wagers on how soon the man would tire of the play and give the impertinent child a taste of his stick. He was close to it, if not there already. "The donkey says this, the donkey says that. The donkey's owner says he's carrying this load of oil-jars to market, and that's that."

"You can carry them yourself," Timoleon said. "Or drag them, since you're going to be a snake. Do you like mice? Or would you rather eat crawly things?"

"I'd rather take a piece out of your hide," snarled the man, slashing his stick through the air.

Dione caught it before it struck. She had no memory of movement from outside the circle to within it. She was simply there, with a stinging hand and a startled drover, and the stick between.

Her expression must have been alarming. The drover backed away from her. The rest of the circle had gone mute. Timoleon looked as if he could not decide whether to be dismayed or furious. Dione fixed him with a terrible stare. "What did I tell you?" she said very quietly.

"I—" he said. "I couldn't—"

"Back to the ship," she said. "Now."

"But it's not noon yet," he protested. "There won't be anybody to take us across."

"There will be," said Dione. Her glance encompassed the guard, who slunk in Timoleon's shadow. At the moment she did not particularly care if Diomedes vanished from the face of the earth.

Timoleon got a grip on the donkey's neck, and clung grimly. "I'm taking him, too," he declared.

"You can't take him on the ship," Dione said. "Come with me."

"No," said Timoleon, as stubborn with his mother as he had been with the drover.

"You may come," said Dione, measuring each word, "on your own two feet. Or you may come on four, or on none. But you will come. Do you understand me?"

"You won't do it," Timoleon said with a lift of his chin.

Dione raised her hand. The people nearby, she noticed distantly, had scrambled out of the way. Some of them were shrieking.

Idiots.

"Well?" she demanded of her son. "Since you were so free with my powers, trumpeting them to every ear in Tarsus—what is it that you want to be? Snake? Goose? Dog?"

Timoleon's chin rose higher. "You can't turn me into a puppy. That's just for sticks and snakes."

"Yes?" Dione said. Her magic was there, in the depths of her, where the goddess was; it was never absent. Nor did it know mercy, or the scruples that bound human will. She could transform this child of her body, not without cost, but not with great difficulty, either.

She let Timoleon see that. Timoleon was young, but he was not entirely a fool. All at once he wilted, transparently considering tears, but determining that his mother was in no mood to be swayed by such expedients. "But, mama," he said in a small voice, "if we leave the donkey here, he'll be beaten worse than ever."

Dione could not deny it. The drover had the look of a man who beat his animals and his children the harder, the more the world thwarted him. He was terrified still, and silent with it, but that would not last much longer.

She gestured sharply to Hebe. "My purse." Her maid produced it from the basket, face eloquent of disapproval. Dione flung it at the man. "This for your miserable beast and all he carries."

She got out of there before he could recover his wits enough to haggle. And what she would do with a mangy, fly-bitten, underfed donkey—

"I can take it, I suppose," said Lucius Servilius. "I'm sure there's some use that we could put it to, somewhere in the triumvir's following."

"You have to be good to it," said Timoleon, "and feed it, and not make it carry too many things at once. It's carrying too many now."

"So it is," said Lucius Servilius, who was singularly undismayed by so outrageous a child. He stopped in the middle of the street and began to unload the donkey's cargo. "I'll send men back for this," he said.

"Do you honestly believe it will still be here when they come?" Dione asked. "No, leave it. It's only rancid olive oil and bad crockery."

Even at that, beggars were circling, ready to seize the largesse. Lucius Servilius shrugged and stripped the beast of its burden, even to the saddle, which looked as if it had seen half a dozen generations of hard use. The donkey's back was raw with sores, and scars under that. Timoleon, seeing it, cried out in rage. "Oh, *mama!* Make it better, mama, please."

"Not in the middle of the street," said Dione.

"The triumvir's stable," Lucius Servilius said, "would know how to look after such wounds as these."

"Mama will make it better now," Timoleon said in a tone that booked no opposition.

Dione slapped him lightly, to get his attention, and said, "Lucius Servilius and the triumvir's people will make it better as soon as you let them get to it."

"I want to see," said Timoleon.

Dione's head had begun to ache. There was this stranger, this Roman, who seemed to find nothing surprising. There was Diomedes the guard, looking as if he expected to be flogged at any moment, and well he deserved it, too. And there was Caesarion, clinging to Hebe's hand and keeping quiet, and Timoleon expecting his mother to work miracles simply because he asked her to.

Dione was weak: she surrendered to Timoleon's whim. "Very well," she sighed. "We'll go to the triumvir's stable. But only as long as it takes to make sure this beast is settled. Then we have to go back to the ship."

"Yes, mama," said Timoleon, all sweet reasonableness now that he had had his way. "May I lead the donkey, please?"

"Yes," said Dione wearily, "you may walk beside him. And no more bold rescues. Promise. Or we go straight back to the ship."

Timoleon jibbed at that, but he had won enough to be magnanimous. "I promise," he said.

NINE

"And how long do Timoleon's promises last?" asked Lucius Servilius.

The donkey was established in the triumvir's stable, its back salved, its manger filled with good barley, its stall bedded with straw; it rested as well as any horse in Tarsus. Timoleon would have no less.

Now they were all returning to the harbor, where the boat should be waiting to take them back to the queen's ship. Lucius Servilius seemed determined to see the end of the adventure; Dione could not see why else he would accompany them. "Timoleon's promises," she answered him, "last just as long as he remembers them, which is anywhere from an hour to a week. I give this one a day at most."

"I see you know him well," said Lucius Servilius. The corner of his mouth had turned up again in his crooked smile.

Dione smiled back. "Oh, we knew early on that he was trouble incarnate."

"And other things, too?" he asked with a return to his Roman gravity.

"Such as a call to the goddess' service?" Dione inquired. "No; that only happens to daughters in our branch of the family."

"Not sons?"

"No," she said. "We belong to the goddess, you see. She prefers daughters."

"I see," said Lucius Servilius, as if in fact he did not. "And yet she gave you sons."

"Oh, yes," said Dione. "They drive me quite as wild, too, as if they had been goddess-brats, but in different ways. Timoleon has decided that he wants to be a sailor, chiefly I think because he doesn't need to wear clothes to do it; and you've seen what he does when he's loose in the market. Androgeos is his father all over again—such a stick, but endearing when it's young. He stayed in Alexandria. His father keeps him, since he's the eldest son."

"You have another?" asked Lucius Servilius.

"My husband does. His new wife is much more to his liking than I ever was. I have opinions. Laodice lacks that failing."

"I suppose it is a failing," Lucius Servilius mused as they came down the steps to the quay. The boat was indeed waiting, and Timoleon, who had run ahead, was with it, hopping with impatience. "You took your time," he said before Dione could speak. "Caesarion is being a baby again. He keeps whining for his mother."

"I do not!" said that prince from where he sat on a piling. *"You* are jealous because your mother wants to talk to someone else besides you."

"I am not," snapped Timoleon.

"That," said Dione, "will be enough of that. Get in the boat, Timoleon, and stop your nonsense."

Timoleon did not even pretend to obey her. "Do you know what they'll call you in the city? The little goddess."

"That is arrant nonsense," said Dione.

He grinned at her. "You are, you know. Which goddess are you? You can't be Mother Isis. That's Cleopatra."

"Offhand," said Lucius Servilius, "I would say Aphrodite."

Timoleon shot him a dark glance. "I'd rather she was Artemis. Artemis hates men. She turns them into deer and hunts them."

"Oh, she can't be that," Lucius Servilius said. "She's a mother, after all."

"You're supposed to say I'm a bloodthirsty little sprat," Timoleon said. "Why don't you?"

"Because I don't like to be predictable," said Lucius Servilius.

Timoleon stared. Lucius Servilius gazed back, half-smiling. Abruptly, astonishingly, Timoleon grinned. "Why, you're almost worth it! I know you, too. I saw you with Antony. Aren't you a soldier? Why didn't you wear your armor?"

"Because it's beastly uncomfortable," Lucius Servilius answered him, as calm as ever. Dione could not help but admire his aplomb. Surely it was tested to the utmost, but he gave no sign of it.

"So's the toga," said Timoleon.

"True," Lucius Servilius conceded, "but the toga comes off a lot more easily."

"Do you have any armor?"

"Two sets," said Lucius Servilius. "One for parades and one for use."

Timoleon, Dione could see, was settling in for a long interrogation.

She pushed him toward the boat. "In, sir. You'll have time later to wear this gentleman out with questions."

"Oh," said Timoleon, "but he can't be a gentleman, can he? He's a Roman. Romans are all commoners."

"Except when they're patricians," said Lucius Servilius. He did not look at all insulted. Dione would almost have thought that he was laughing behind his solemn face.

"Are you a patrician?" Timoleon asked.

"I'm a priest," said Lucius Servilius, "and I'll be dragged into the senate, I suppose, when I go back to Rome—my father was a senator. I'm head of the family now he's gone, I was foolish enough to hold office when I was younger: I was a quaestor, which is a kind of paymaster, except it's very respectable. There's no getting out of that purple-striped toga, short of staying forever away from the senate house. That's as close to a patrician, these days, as most people get."

"Oh," said Timoleon, just before his mother was moved to gag him and throw him into the boat. He got in with the grace of a sailor born, and swung Caesarion over the gunwale squawking, "I can get in *myself!* Let me *go!*"

Hebe sat already in the bow with her knees drawn up, keeping out of the way of feet and oars. The oarsmen were in their places. Dione was left on the quay, wondering exactly how to apologize to Lucius Servilius for her son's various transgressions.

"Never mind," he said as if he could read her thoughts in her face. He smiled. "You have a very interesting child."

"You have a gift for understatement," Dione said. She bent her head to him. "Thank you, sir. I'm a little saner for that you were with us."

"I hope so," said Lucius Servilius. He offered his hand. She thought about it for a moment, then took it, and let him help her into the boat. The cat followed, bristling and starting at shadows, but determined to be a sea-cat if it must. When Dione had settled herself, the cat came to her lap, sitting upright in it, staring hard at the land as they were rowed away from it.

The Roman stood watching, nor did he move until Dione had returned to the queen's ship. Then he raised a hand and left the quay, turning back toward the triumvir's villa.

The feast that night was of Antony's making. He could not begin to equal Cleopatra's splendors, therefore he did not try. No more did he try to make a Greek banquet out of it. He served Roman dishes in the Roman style, men reclining, women seated at tables, although for the queen he had set a couch on which she might recline like a man. She did not refuse it. She was, after all, no common woman but a queen.

Lucius Servilius had seen how they met after their day apart: cool courtesy, fair words, and a heat beneath that burned him from half the hall's distance. Tonight Cleopatra was Greek rather than Egyptian, her attendants dressed as Hellenes of the court of Alexandria. Dione was not among them. He managed to ask, and to get an answer from a man reclining near him. The queen's friend—so the man called her—was occupied in some rite of her priesthood. "She's the voice of Isis," he said, "after all. Sometimes the goddess rides her hard."

Lucius found himself annoyed with the Egyptians' goddess. She could have let her servant have an evening's respite.

He reined himself in before he said what he was thinking. His companion took his silence for polite disbelief, and said with a touch of heat, "You Romans don't believe in gods, do you?"

"Of course we do," Lucius said mildly. "I've heard the goddess speak through her priestess. It's rather disconcerting."

"Rather," said the other, softening slightly, but not enough to carry on a conversation.

Lucius was left to himself, as he preferred to be. He found himself missing his companion of the night before, the light on her face, the sharpness of her wit and the sheer unexpectedness of so much that she said. He wondered if the little cat had taken well to life on shipboard, and if Timoleon had forgotten his promise yet.

Even as distracted as he was, he could not mistake what went on at the head of the hall. There was as little conversation between the queen and the triumvir as there had been the night before, and as little need of it. It was as if they looked at one another and knew all that there was to say.

As before, they left early and unobtrusively, and separately. But tonight there was something in the way they moved, some signal passed, that Lucius did not think he had mistaken. If the queen returned to her ship tonight, she would not return alone. And if she remained, it would not be as a guest in her own chamber.

Some might think it sudden. He, having heard Antony speak of her, knew that it was years in the doing. And yet the woman had no beauty of face, and little enough youth; she must have been thirty, or nearly. She was not what one might imagine Antony falling blind in love with. Unless one had seen her, and heard her speak; felt the force of her presence. She had more than beauty, more even than allure. She had Egypt.

Egypt gave itself to Rome. Rome took, and taking, was conquered. Lucius saw it as clearly as if he stood in the bedchamber, watching the oldest of dances.

Was this, maybe, the rite that the queen's friend was making? Did the goddess wield her voice to seduce the triumvir?

No, he thought with supernatural clarity. Cleopatra needed no rites or magic. She was sufficient in herself.

He roused with a shiver. The hall was warm with wine and revelry, but he was cold. He muttered an excuse to no one in particular, and stumbled out into the cooler air of the garden.

The stars were bright tonight, no haze of cloud to soften them. The air was warm and cool at once, sweet with the scent of green things. Lucius made his way to the wall and climbed the steps, and paused by the bench at the top. The city was silent, buried deep in shadow, save here and there where a lamp was lit above a door, or a group of late revelers made their way home by torchlight.

Out in the harbor the water was full of stars. Lanterns hung from the prows of the queen's ships, and a whole jeweled necklace of them on her flagship. Lucius saw no one on the decks. No doubt those who were not at Antony's banquet were asleep.

All but Dione. He knew that as he sometimes did, with a surety that owed nothing to rational thought. It was the same gift that made it so simple for him to perform the sacrifices that were part of his priesthood, to read the entrails or the omens and render their meaning in words that others could understand. They were not always the omens that he had been asked to provide. That was a difficulty. One day, maybe, it would be his ruin.

Not tonight. Tonight was his own. Dimly he was aware that his body had seated itself on the cold marble bench. His sight, fixed on the ship of lights, blurred and dazzled.

When it cleared, he seemed to stand face to face with the priestess from Egypt. She was clad in white of a stark and ancient fashion, her hair concealed beneath a heavy wig and a tall headdress like plumes of lapis and gold. The room in which she stood might have been small, a ship's cabin, yet it seemed as wide as the world. Its walls were alive with painted creatures, the writing of the old priests who worked magic before Rome was born. She sang in a pure voice. He could not understand the words.

Even without understanding, he knew that she sang a hymn to her goddess. She was not working magic here. This was worship, and tribute. She had companions: the cat that had followed her from Tarsus, and what at first Lucius took for a man in a mask, a Nubian perhaps, with a jackal's head on his wide dark shoulders. But if it was a mask, it was remarkably lifelike, with lips that curled as a living jackal's will, to bare white fangs in a grin. Its eyes were the color of sulfur burning.

Lucius shivered, though he had no flesh here to feel either cold or fear. Gods in Rome, true gods, did not wear living faces. They were shadows full of power, ancient, numinous. Of the Greeks' squabbling flock of divinities he took little notice.

But this was real. This was alive in the world, standing guard on a slender priestess and a small peculiar cat.

The priestess offered gifts of wine and honey and white barley, and a mouse with the marks of sharp cat-teeth in its neck. Her hymn rose to a crescendo and faded. She sank down before the sea-chest that served as an altar, and lay there, until Lucius was sure that she had fallen asleep.

But then she raised herself, looking straight into his eyes. "Good evening, *ba*-spirit," she said. "What brings you here tonight?"

Lucius started, nearly falling back into his body. But something held him within those painted walls, and made him answer. "My eyes brought me here. Your pardon if I trespass."

"No," she said. "I only wondered. I didn't know a Roman could fly on the wings of his spirit to visit other people's altars. I give you welcome."

"I'm . . . not spying," he said.

"I didn't think you were." She took off her headdress and her wig and unbound her hair. It rippled down her back and over her shoul-ders. She rolled her head on her neck, sighing. "Ah, that's better. I don't know which is heavier, the wig or the crown."

There was something utterly charming about a concern so trivial in a place so full of strangeness. Lucius was not even there, not in his body, and yet she addressed him as if he had been standing in front of her. Maybe in Egypt such meetings were common.

"In Rome," he said, "if I appeared to you so, you would be convinced that I was dead and bearing omens."

"But of course you're not dead," said Dione. "The *ba* can leave the living body when it wells. Now if I saw your *ka* too, your twin-of-the-soul, I would be running to be sure that you hadn't fallen dead where you sat. A person can't release too many pieces of himself at once; that's perilous."

"I don't understand you at all," said Lucius.

"People often don't," she said, serene. "You are alive. Believe that. And very talented, too. That's a very complete *ba* you're showing me. Your spirit is a falcon, I see. I rather hoped so."

"Why?" he asked. Not that he expected to understand that answer, either. But he seemed unable to withdraw, and questions were better than the gibberings of fear.

"Why," she said, "if you'd been a vulture, I'd know I'd misread you. Not that Romans aren't mostly vultures, feeding on the carrion of nations. You just seemed to me cleaner, somehow."

"Thank you," he said dryly.

She stroked the cat, who had come to curl in her lap as she sat cross-legged by the altar. It was an odd cat, truly, brindled black and gold, with a mark like a flame on its forehead. Lucius had no doubt at all that it belonged to a goddess.

It seemed content to conduct itself like any common lapcat, purring as Dione rubbed its chin. Its eyes blinked lazily at Lucius. Dione's own eyes, dark though they were and not green-in-gold, had the same feline tilt, the same deceptively mild expression.

"They make the Great Marriage tonight," Dione said suddenly.

Her expression had not changed. Her tone was as soft as ever. And yet Lucius knew that she was not speaking entirely for herself; that the goddess was there, speaking through her priestess.

Nor did he need to ask who "they" were. Only two in Tarsus would make a Great Marriage, a marriage of gods and not of simple mortals.

"There has been no rite," he said, knowing as he said it what she would think of him, and how she would answer.

As she had when he spoke before of rites and proprieties, she said, "They are the rite. They need no more than themselves. She is Isis and Aphrodite and Venus of the Romans. He is Osiris and Dionysus and Bacchus, Father Liber of the wine and the holy madness. Do you hear the earth singing? It knows, Roman. It knows that the gods walk upon it."

Lucius heard only the silence, and the lapping of water on the ship's hull, and the murmur of voices in the city. Human voices only. No gods anywhere but here.

"Ah," said the goddess through her priestess. "You see; you do not hear. Look, then. See."

He was not given to choose. The goddess commanded; his eyes obeyed. He saw the god in the goddess' arms, and the light that wrapped them about.

TEN

The light was lamplight, pale gold in a room neither Greek nor Roman but something of both. Its walls were painted with nymphs in a strange sea-garden, dancing skeins of them about Aphrodite as she was born from the foam. The floor was a pattern of tiles: vineleaves weaving endlessly, and clusters of grapes. Under the couch with its carved lion-feet lay Dionysus with his rod of ivy. There was armor on a stand near Aphrodite's wall, its martial glitter strange beside her foam-pale loveliness, and a soldier's chest, much battered and scarred, and half flung over it, half trailing on the floor, a cloak the color of blood.

The two on the couch had come to a haven of sorts after the storm that had scattered garments from one end of the room to the other. The queen's pallium was tangled with the triumvir's tunic; his toga lay in a knot that would win shrieks from his bodyservant in the morning.

He said as much, lying in her arms, tracing lazy circles round her breast. It was full and firm despite her having borne a child, the nipple large and sweetly dark, rising to his touch. But she was calm, evidently unmoved, smiling down into his lifted face. "Let the man wail," she said. "He lives for the trouble you cause him."

Antony laughed in his throat. "Doesn't he? And don't you, too? Even when you were Caesar's woman, and not for a moment did you let anyone forget it, you could knock me down with a look."

"I was never Caesar's woman," she said with cool precision. "I was his lady and his queen. And he was my consort—no matter what Rome said to that. I chose him; he was mine long before he knew it."

"So was I," said Antony, but not as if he minded it. "But when I called for you, you came. Why didn't you try to make me come to you?"

"Because I never do the same thing twice," she said. "Caesar came to me. I chose to come to Antony. But when I was here, you dined at my table first; for a night, you were in Egypt."

"And now you're in Rome." His hand traveled lazily down her belly to rest on the mound that, Greek-fashion, she plucked and oiled smooth. "You do have a beautiful body."

"Unlike my face?"

She did not sound bitter. He traced her cheek with a finger. "You're beautiful to me," he said.

"Flatterer," said Cleopatra.

"They say you live for flattery," he said.

She laughed with a touch of surprise. "Why, Antony! That was witty. Should you ruin your reputation so?"

"Even a blunt-tongued soldier can turn a phrase now and then."

She kissed his crown where the curling hair had grown thin. "So he can. He's not half the fool he seems, nor ever has been. You were a brilliant subaltern, my dear. But can you rule?"

He stiffened at that, drawing himself up level with her, face to face across an expanse of crimson silk. Crimson was not his color—it clashed with the ruddiness of his face. But it was hers, dark as she was, with her long dark eyes. She smiled lazily, as a cat will.

"Haven't I been ruling, then?" he said, half growling it.

"Certainly," she said. "With Octavian. Caesar's heir."

"That eats at you, doesn't it? You wanted the inheritance for your son."

"Caesar's son," she said.

"Oh, of course, Caesar's son. But yours, too. Rome sticks at that. It wants no foreign by-blows calling themselves lords on the seven hills."

"So its leaders informed me," she said. "Repeatedly."

There was a pause, with blades in it. There was nothing absurd about it, though they were naked on the couch, flushed as much from lovemaking as from anger.

"Now look," said Antony at length. "I can't give you Rome. Not yet. There's still Octavian. But I've got the east. The whole of it. I hold the power where it matters."

"Only Rome matters to a Roman," said Cleopatra.

He shook that off. "Never mind it now. Rome will be mine when

I'm ready to take it. I'll have the east first, all that's been ours since we made an empire here. Parthia, too."

"Ah," said Cleopatra. "Now we come to it."

He nodded. "Parthia's defied us from the beginning, just as it defied Alexander. He conquered it. I'll conquer it, too, and make the conquest stick. That was one thing he never did. He died before he'd sewn it all up tight."

"But before he took Parthia, Persia as it was then, Egypt gave itself to him. They lay under the Persian yoke; he freed them from it. Do you imagine that we need freeing from anything but our own freedom?"

"I think I need Egypt," he said, "and Egypt needs me. I can keep you from being devoured by Rome. You can help me conquer Parthia."

"How so?" she demanded, as if she did not know.

"Ships," he said. "Sailors. Rome has never been much of a sea power. Even when we're winning battles afloat, we're lubbers to the bone. Egypt, though—Egypt lives between the water and the desert. With your ships, I could take the whole coast of Asia, and hold it till the moon came down."

"Should I want you to do that?"

"If you held it with me—if Egypt remained a sovereign state in alliance with Rome."

"Are you threatening me?"

He looked into her narrowed eyes and shivered. But he was god to her goddess, and he ruled in Rome, whoever might share that honor in the city itself. Here, he was Rome; there was no other. He said, "Is it a threat to tell the truth? How long can you hold Egypt if Rome wields all its power against you?"

"Longer than you might possibly imagine," she said, but her answer lacked force.

"Remember how you rose to the power you hold," he said. "You outlasted two brothers; two sisters, too, all of them determined to rule in Egypt. Caesar helped you then. Where would you be without him, or without Rome?"

"He made it easier," she conceded, "but I would have won. The gods were with me."

"Maybe," said Antony. "Maybe they were with Caesar."

"I am alive," she said, "and queen of Egypt. He is dead."

"Dead and a god," said Antony. "So, then. You want to bargain. What will it cost me to win your alliance—and your ships?"

"I have a sister," she said promptly. "Arsinoe." She all but spat the name. "She wrested the queenship from me once when I was weaker than I like to admit. She escaped and ran for Ephesus. Kill her for me."

"Kill . . . ?" Antony shook his head as if to clear it. "Pollux! You're bloody-minded."

"I am queen," she said, implacable, "and that little bitch thought herself capable of contesting it. I'd kill her myself if I could get my hands on her. Give me her heart in a casket, or you get no ships from Egypt."

"I'll think about it," he said, crisp enough, all things considered. "I don't suppose that's all you want?"

"Of course not," said Cleopatra. "There's the high priest of Artemis at Ephesus, who sheltered Arsinoe when she ran crying to him. He'll die, too. And the governor of Cyprus—he betrayed me for Arsinoe. He's in Tyre now, or thereabouts, repenting his sins. And in Aradus, perhaps worst of all, is a blathering idiot who calls himself my brother-king. Ptolemy of course is dead, drowned in the Nile like a proper pretender to the throne; but fools and liars will believe a boy who calls himself the king come back again. Rid me of them all."

"And?" said Antony, now past surprise, past even horror, perhaps; or simply biding his time.

"I'll need lands," she said. "Give me Cyprus, for the shipyards. Give me the Lebanon, for the wood to build the ships."

"And?" he said again.

She smiled and combed her fingers through the hair of his chest. "That will do for a while."

"You don't come cheap," he observed.

Her smile widened. "If I did, would you want me?"

"Probably not," he said. "I'll think about it."

"Think about it quickly." She raised herself over him, letting her hair veil them both. It was beautiful, dark with red lights, fragrant with musk and frankincense. He breathed in the scent of it, and gasped as she mounted him.

"Blackmail," he managed to say.

She laughed. "Anything that I can do—anything at all—to win advantage for Egypt, I will do. Did you ever think I would not?"

"No," he said with the last breath he had for coherent speech.

"Good," said Cleopatra.

ELEVEN

Lucius Servilius the Augur plummeted out of dream into vision, and thence into his own body, cold and stiff, lying on the wall of the triumvir's villa. There were no words for what he felt. If Antony ever discovered that he was watched in his lovemaking with the queen of Egypt—such lovemaking, half politics and half war—he would rage. Or, thought Lucius, he would laugh till he wept. Antony had the ability, unheard of in a Roman, to laugh at himself.

Lucius lacked any such gift. He got himself somehow into the villa, to the room in which he slept, and dropped down onto the couch there. His body ached as if with bruises. His head felt as if it were made of glass, and was about to shatter.

The worst of it, perhaps, was that he had performed no rite. He had willed and it was so: vision of the ship, dream of the royal lovers. It was all highly improper.

Dione would laugh at him. He did not want to think of Dione.

He tried to will sleep as he had willed the vision, but sleep was no docile servant. He lay awake until cockcrow, while thought pursued thought in a fruitless round.

Dione, for her part, slept the sleep of one who has labored long and wrought well. Of Cleopatra's methods she might not wholly approve, but if they succeeded, then well indeed for Egypt. She slept wrapped in the goddess' arms, with the cat in the hollow of her body, and woke warm and rested and wondering for a moment why she was so richly content.

The queen and the triumvir made no secret of their alliance both in love and in politics. The world saw that Aphrodite indeed was come to Dionysus, and the sun their brother smiled on their union. The Great Marriage was made. The queen's prices were paid: blood sacrifice on the altar of Ephesian Artemis, in the temple of Melqart at Tyre, in the precinct of Cyprian Aphrodite. And so it came full circle, and Aphrodite ruled as queen of Cyprus, and built ships there of cedar from the Lebanon.

Dionysus—Antony—gained ships for his wars in the East. Yet once he had the promise of them, and the queen in his bed, he seemed to forget that he had wars to wage.

But the queen did not. A month nearly to the day after she sailed into Tarsus, she dined with him as they had made a custom of doing, one evening on her ship, one in his villa, turn and turn about. Tonight they dined on shipboard, with the curtains drawn back to admit what breeze there was, and slaves with fans to raise such wind as they might. The usual revelry was muted, drowsy with heat. They drank wine cooled with snow, or cold clear water from the sources of the Cydnus, brought in earthen jars and kept cold by sinking them in the harbor.

Antony pressed his cup to his sweat-streaming cheek. "Ah," he said. "Cool." One of the slaves brought the jar of snow wrapped in its blanket of straw, and dipped a spoonful into the cup. He filched another, rubbing it on his cheeks and down his neck and breast. "They say there's snow still on the mountains in Syria. I'd give anything to fly there like a god, and roll in it till my balls went numb."

"Would you?" Cleopatra raised a brow. "Then why don't you?"

"I don't have wings," he pointed out.

"You have ships," she said.

"What ship is fast enough to take me there tonight?"

"Why, none," she said. "But one could be in port tomorrow, and fast horses waiting to carry you into the mountains."

"Are you trying to get rid of me?"

He was laughing, but she was not. "No," she said, "but you lie idle, and the world goes its way without you. So too does Egypt without me. I'm sailing tomorrow."

"Sailing?" he asked, puzzled. "Where? Syria?"

"Egypt," she said. "I'll expect you when winter comes. Then when no one wages war, we'll wage love in Alexandria, and take our pleasure till the spring."

All the wine that was in him fuddled his wits, but he had enough left to say, "That's high-handed of you. Who gives you leave to go away from me?"

"I do," she answered. "I have duties in Egypt. You have duties in this eastern province of yours. Perform them, then come to me. I can't say I'll wait; I have more to do than that. I'll look for you when the Nile's flood has ended."

"Octobris," said Lucius Servilius, reckoning aloud. "Or thereabouts."

Antony shot him a glare. Cleopatra smiled. "Octobris," she said. "And what do you call this month that wears us all out with its heat? Sextilis? But no, how could I forget? It's Julius now, for the great Caesar."

"That's time enough to win me another queen," muttered Antony.

Cleopatra's smile turned deadly sweet. "Do that," she said, "and see how many ships you get from my yards in Cyprus."

He buried his temper in another cup of wine. She sipped her goblet of melted snow, which was, Lucius thought, no colder than her heart.

"Queens have to be cold," said Dione. She had not been at the feast, but Lucius knew where she usually was: up on the foredeck with her Nubian maid to fan away the heat and the flies, and her odd little cat hunting moths in the light of a lantern. Tonight she was alone but for the maid, which was a rarity. He seldom saw her without at least one of the children, either hers or Cleopatra's. Sometimes he wondered if she used them as a shield, though against what, he could not have told. Vexation, maybe, beyond what they themselves could cause.

She did not seem unhappy to see him, nor did she bridle when he called her queen an ice-hearted woman. "No queen can afford a soft heart," she said. "Not if she wants to go on being queen."

"I suppose not." Lucius lay on the deck in the wash of air from the fan, and sighed. "She's really leaving tomorrow?"

"Really," said Dione.

"Even if it costs her Antony?"

"It won't." The cat, having captured and devoured a moth nigh as big as a sparrow, came to curl purring in her lap. She smoothed the particolored fur, idly, gazing out over the water. "We brought Egypt with us, and that was well, but I feel it growing thin under our feet."

His fist thumped the deck. "It feels solid enough to me."

"Don't talk like a Roman," she said with rare impatience. "You know what I mean."

He did not point out that he was a Roman, and therefore entitled to be obtuse. "Your power is waning," he said.

"Not waning," said Dione. "Not exactly. But we need to go back. Egypt lives by the inundations of the Nile, flood and ebb and flood again. So too do we."

"That could be a weapon," said Lucius, "for your enemies. Take you out of Egypt, trap you till your strength is gone, then overwhelm you."

"Then I hope you're not my enemy," she said.

"Not now," said Lucius.

Her eyes slanted toward him, and then away. She would be thinking what he was thinking, that Rome was Egypt's ally now, but who knew how long that would last?

She drew a breath, not quite a sigh. "We do as we must," she said.

"Is there something you're not telling me?" he asked her.

"No," she said in all apparent honesty. "Will you come to Egypt with Antony?"

"Unless Rome calls me back," he said. He was surprised to discover how reluctantly he said it. He wanted to see Egypt. He wanted to see Dione; he was sorry that she must go.

He could not say it. They had spoken together often; it seemed to happen that one was where the other wanted to be, or they were given the same couch at dinner, or one ran an errand and met the other on the way. There never seemed to be any design in it. He was not even sure that they could be called friends. It was easy to talk to her, an ease that for Lucius was a rarity.

When she was gone, he would be alone again, solitary in his moods and his shyness. There would be no one to vex him with visions unsanctified by ritual, or to coax him into laughter, or to descend on him with her scapegrace son and her mute glowering maid and one small cat.

"Hebe will be glad to be rid of me," he observed, "and sorry to see me again."

The Nubian's smile was white in the lamplight. Dione's frown quelled the smile but not the gleam of the narrow black eyes. "Hebe is convinced that you mean to corrupt me."

"Why, what can I do? Make a Roman of you?"

"Goddess forbid," said Dione.

Lucius laughed. He did not mean to, but she looked so solemn, so nearly angry, and her maid was all but gloating. "You see? You're safe from me."

"Are you dangerous?"

"You always ask the hard questions," said Lucius.

"Oh, you are," she said. "You're perilous. So am I. So is anyone alive; and the dead can be worse."

He shivered. He was aware, too suddenly, of the dark beyond the lamp's light, and the whisper of breeze in the rigging, that might have been the breath of ghosts. *"Absit omen,"* he said.

"I speak no omens," said Dione. "Only truth."

"Truth is terrible enough," said Lucius Servilius.

ACT
TWO

ALEXANDRIA
AND ANTIOCH
40– 37 B.C.

TWELVE

Dione dreamed of silver and gold. Silver lit with the moon, gold aflame in the sun; then silver was the moon and gold the sun, folded in the queen's arms. The queen was herself, and yet also she was Isis, goddess mother of the Two Lands, and the shadow behind her was Osiris, now wound in his grave-wrappings, now bound about with vineleaves and clusters of grapes. The grapes were Tyrian purple, royal purple.

Dione woke all at once, clutching the sides of her bed. Only slowly did she realize that it was not rocking, nor was she lying in her cabin on the queen's ship. She was home, in Alexandria. The warm weight against her side was the cat that had taken possession of her in Tarsus. She could, if she listened, hear the murmurs of the city in its sleep, the near-inaudible sigh of Timoleon's breath in his room near Dione's, the soft snuffle that was Hebe on her pallet by the door.

The dream hovered still, gleaming almost visibly in the gloom. Silver and gold. The moon and the sun. Goddess and god in the heart of the Two Lands.

Dione sat up. The cat, roused, began to purr. She shivered slightly. It was cold in the room, with a scent of old stone: a memory of tombs. Swiftly she banished the omen, promise, whatever it was. She rose, putting on a robe, sandals. The cold was not all of the heart. Winter was coming, touching the air with its chill.

It was the dark before dawn, the cold time, when the dead were most in their element, and dreams turned strange. Dione lit a lamp against the darkness and carried it with her through the house. She was not searching for anything, nor had she any purpose but to assure herself that all was well. The cooks were up, yawning and rousing the banked fire for the morning's bread. The rest of the servants were asleep still. Timoleon was sprawled across his bed, all bare brown cold-pebbled skin and blue-black curls. Dione spread the blanket over him and smoothed his hair. He smiled in his sleep.

Dione, watching him sleep, knew a flash of memory, the wingbeat of her dream; and a small stab that was, of all things, jealousy. It had been three months since they left Antony in Tarsus. No, nearly four.

The Nile was receding from the flood, leaving the rich black earth that was its gift and its magic. Soon, perhaps even today, Antony would come, and as was his right, he would be the first besides the queen to know that she would bear him a child. Or children.

And yet Dione had seen Cleopatra nearly every day; had waited on her, worshipped the goddess with her, eaten and drunk and even bathed with her. Though not that last, now Dione thought about it, in a month or more. The queen would, just about then, have begun to show her pregnancy to eyes that were sharp enough to see.

Ah well, thought Dione. If Cleopatra had not seen fit to tell the one whom she called her friend, the goddess had repaired the omission. And Antony was coming at last, or so he had promised. He had wrought what order he could in Syria, and as far as Dione knew, done nothing to further his invasion of Parthia. That, if he were wise, he would keep for the spring. Winter was the fallow time, the resting time. Spring was the time for war.

While Dione's mind ran on, Timoleon's body curled as if of itself, and his thumb crept into his mouth. He did not stir when Dione kissed his cheek.

It was too close to morning to be worth going back to bed; and in any case Dione was wide awake. She dressed without Hebe's help, combing her hair and plaiting it and coiling it out of the way. Hebe would be reproachful, and would do it all over again, but by then it would be full morning. Dione said the prayers of the waking day, offered thanks to the goddess for the dream of splendor in the dark. The goddess' warmth wrapped her round.

A little after sunrise, accompanied by the cat and by her glowering maid—and duly bathed and dressed as Hebe required—she went out into the city. She had somewhat to do in the temple, and somewhat else in the market. By midmorning she was near to the harbor, and had heard the rumor that was running through the city: ships out to sea, ships such as the Romans favored, and the sails of the largest were the purple of kings. Or, as people said, of Roman triumvirs with ambitions—however much they denied it—to be kings.

The afternoon was to be Cleopatra's. The queen had found a new scholar whose wits she was minded to try, and for that, she insisted, she needed Dione. Dione was not particularly quick at that kind of disputation, but Cleopatra, who was, required an intelligent audience. An audience that, as she observed, did not applaud her merely because she was queen.

Dione had not expected that Cleopatra would alter her intentions simply for the rumor of Antony's coming. Nor did she. The court was atwitter. Would he come today? Would he come with his army as Caesar had, and infuriate the rabble? Would he march into the palace and announce that he was its master? The queen took no notice. The scholar, a pale young man with a wispy beard and the round moist eyes of a hound, proved to be quite as intelligent as Cleopatra had hoped, and fearless as Judeans tended to be.

"We have only one god," the scholar said when Cleopatra remarked on his courage, "and our god is powerful in his jealousy of any god but himself. The whims of kings rather pale beside that."

Cleopatra smiled. She was utterly at ease, and in fine looks, too, though she affected no great splendor today: Greek simplicity, and no ornament but the gold in her ears and on her arms, and the ribbon of the diadem woven through her plaited hair. "Indeed, sir," she said to the scholar, "I think you may have bested me. What reward will you take?"

"Why, none," he said. "I did it for pleasure. It's rare to find a woman, and a foreigner yet, who understands the greater disputations of the Law."

"Ah, but I'm a queen," said Cleopatra. "I drank in the law with my mother's milk."

"So did kings," the scholar said, "but too many of them colicked on it."

The queen laughed, rich and full. "Oh, sir! You are a rarity. Go with my chamberlain now; ask of him whatever you wish. We'll speak again—perhaps you'll dine with me tonight?"

"Oh, I can't," said that astonishing person. "It's our holy day, after sunset, you know. And tomorrow. Maybe the day after?"

"Certainly," said Cleopatra, much amused.

In that splendid mood she received the news that she had been waiting for; that Dione had been expecting since before dawn. Antony had come to Alexandria. Would the queen receive him?

The queen would. Her face was calm, her voice unmoved. But Dione saw how the light leaped in her eyes before she veiled them. She had not doubted Antony, but time, fate, the power of Rome— those she had both doubted and feared.

He came without state, as a simple citizen of Rome. Instead of his armor he wore the toga with its senatorial stripe, and nothing about him to distinguish him from any other Roman of rank. No soldiers accompanied him, no weapons defended him. He knew, none better, how Caesar had erred when he first came to Alexandria: arriving with armed escort, bearing the insignia of a consul, proclaiming to the wary city that he came as ruler and conqueror. The city had resisted him with armed force.

Antony, wiser, entered as guest and friend of the queen. If the friends who walked with him happened to be good fighting men as well as respectable Roman citizens, then that was nothing that need concern the city. Alexandria welcomed a man who granted it its pride.

Dione saw him coming from a high window of the palace. He did not draw with him the mighty throngs that had followed Cleopatra's fleet along the shore to Tarsus, but the city's crowds were thicker where he was. He moved in a circle of clear space, in a company of friends, all in the stainless white of the newly cleaned toga. The people of the city clustered thick ahead and beside and behind.

He came on at walking pace, neither too swift nor too slow, as if he were a sightseer in this greatest of cities. Once or twice he paused. He must know or suspect that the queen awaited him in her hall of audience; maybe he was trying to show her that he too knew how to make a petitioner wait. Or maybe, being Antony, he honestly was struck by the sights of the city.

It was a splendid day for them: cool, clear, with a brisk wind blowing, the same wind that had carried his ships so smoothly into the harbor. The Pharos on its island was a white fire in the sun, no need of the beacons that guided sailors by night and in fog. The sea was pure deep blue touched with foam; the city was white and green and red and gold.

Dione leaned on the windowframe with the little goddess-cat in her arms. She was not sure she wanted to admit that when she looked at the cluster of Romans in their togas, she looked first, not for the big florid man who led them, but for one smaller and slighter and darker. He would be somewhere in the back, wrapped in solitude that was not loneliness but simply a preference for his own company.

If of course he was there at all. Rome could have called him back. Dowries for his sisters, he had said. Estates. Clients. Duties and obligations that could keep him from Egypt. He could have left Antony of his own accord, or decided to remain with the ships, escaping the tedium of these games of kings.

Just so had she done, in her way. She should be in the hall among the priestesses. She had escaped on the pretext of a call of nature, and simply not gone back. There was time yet, if she wished, to see how Antony met Cleopatra after their months apart. It could be a cold meeting if Cleopatra was minded to make it so, or if Antony wanted to punish her for leaving him in Tarsus.

Up here in the window, with the sun warm on her face, it did not matter. What mattered was whether Lucius Servilius the Augur had come to Alexandria with the triumvir.

How strange, thought Dione, that she had not understood until now. She had not even been missing him overmuch. There had been so many things to do, family to attend to, a queen to wait on, a goddess to serve. Odd moments had come back to her, usually when she was alone or trying to sleep, bits of memory, a word or a glance or a crooked smile. None of them had struck her with this blinding clarity.

She would be very disappointed if Lucius Servilius had not come to Alexandria with Antony.

Lucius Servilius the Augur would not admit that he was disappointed. Not with the city, oh, no; it was quite as magnificent as reputation made it, and the palace was splendid beyond words and almost beyond taste. Certainly not with the queen, who received Antony in somewhat less than her most formal estate. Her court was larger and richer but, for this occasion, rather less pompous than the other courts in which Antony had presented himself. She was in Greek dress, almost without pretension, and her throne was a simple gilded chair.

She remained sitting in it as Antony approached the foot of the dais. There he stopped and gave her as much obeisance as any Roman might: an inclination of the head, a cool, "Your majesty."

Her expression was as cool as his, her eyes as fiercely intent under the lowered lids. "My lord triumvir," she said. "I welcome you to Egypt."

"Thank you, majesty," said Antony. "I come to you as a private citizen, a friend who happens to be a Roman. I hope you'll accept me as such."

"Wherever Antony is, there is Rome," said Cleopatra. "But if Antony, being wise in the ways of this city, wishes to be merely Antony, then Egypt is pleased to oblige him."

"Egypt?" Antony raised a brow. "What of Cleopatra?"

"Cleopatra," she said, "is Egypt."

"Then I'm delighted to come to Egypt," said Antony, with a glint that Lucius at least could not mistake.

Nor, it seemed, could Cleopatra. She stiffened a little, but then she smiled. Away from her throne, maybe, she would have laughed. She rose and descended from the dais and offered him her hand with that air of hers which was both imperious and utterly winning. He took it like the gift it was, and kissed it. "Ah, lady," he said, "it's good to see you again."

"And you," she said with a glimmer of the self that lay under the queen. Then she was the queen again, commanding him as if she had every right in the world: "Escort me to my chambers."

He bowed with exaggerated deference. "As her majesty desires."

It was shocking, everyone agreed, Alexandrian courtiers as well as Romans. That the queen had taken a Roman lover was public knowledge, but she did not need to be quite so blatant about it. Dragging him to her bed straight from her throne—how utterly unseemly.

Lucius Servilius took little notice. There were priestesses near the empty throne, small dark women in white. One or two were very pretty. None was Dione.

He had not been missing her company. No, certainly not. But she should have been here. She belonged in this place, near the queen whom she served so loyally.

Perhaps she was ill. Perhaps—

Nonsense, he told himself. And utter nonsense to find this whole great city dull and flat and thoroughly disappointing, because she was not there to tell him what an idiot he was being.

The others were renewing acquaintance with those of the queen's court who had gone to Tarsus, or discovering what diversions were to be had in the palace and out of it. A chamberlain approached Lucius. "Sir, if you please, the queen bids you be comfortable. If you wish food, drink, a place to rest—"

"No," said Lucius. Then, ashamed of his rudeness: "No. No, thank you."

"There's nothing you'd have?" the enuch asked. He was young, polished but somehow ingenuous, and not yet gone to plumpness as his kind tended to do. Lucius thought that he might be a Mede, with his olive darkness and his black curls. He was quite handsome. He looked, in fact, like Dione's son Timoleon.

The thought bred words before Lucius gathered wits to stop

it. "Have you seen the priestess, the queen's friend? The Lady Dione?"

The eunuch betrayed no flicker of surprise. For all Lucius knew, he had expected precisely that question. "Why, sir, as it happens, I have. Will you please to follow me?"

Almost Lucius refused. He had no business to transact with her, no call of duty. She might be occupied. She might not even remember that he existed.

The eunuch had turned already and begun to make his way through the knots and clusters of courtiers. A moment more and Lucius would lose him. Lucius hastened in his wake.

They had gone inside the palace. Dione knew she should go down to the hall, but she was comfortable here, high up over the city, with the cat for company. The room behind her was bare but for a couch, somewhat worn, and a table, and a chest that contained nothing but dust and a faint odor of cedarwood. The wind played in it, driving a bit of dead leaf across the floor, with the cat in pursuit.

Dione's mind emptied as she lingered there. She had not been able to tell whether any of the Romans was Lucius Servilius. After a while it ceased to matter. She must go soon, if not to the queen then to her son, who was expecting her to share his dinner. Canny Timoleon had made her swear to it.

"That child is going to make a truly formidable man when he comes to it," Dione said to the cat. The cat, having driven the leaf to lair under the couch, turned to fix its eyes on the door.

Dione had left it ajar. No one came up here, not even the servants to clean; this part of the palace, though convenient for watching people arrive from the city, was little frequented. Some of the slaves insisted that it was haunted.

Dione had never met a ghost here, nor sensed one. The footsteps that approached were solidly alive, two sets of them, one a little heavier than the other. She hoped that they would stop before they reached her, sighed when they came on, mustered a smile for the young chamberlain who peered round the door. He smiled back a little shyly and said to the one behind him, "Here, sir." And with a glance at Dione: "Lady." He ducked his head in respect and vanished.

Lucius Servilius was darker than she remembered, burnished with wind and sun, but even that could not hide the flush that stained his cheekbones. Perhaps it was merely exertion: this room was high up, at the end of a maze of corridors and staircases.

He glanced over his shoulder. Dione heard the retreating sound of the eunuch's steps. "Drat the man," said Lucius Servilius.

Dione laughed. It was nothing like a proper greeting, but he was too purely comical, flushed and rumpled and annoyed, with his toga slipping down over his shoulder. He shrugged it irritably into place and scowled at her. "Did I come all this way to have you ridicule me?"

"I don't know," said Dione. "Did you?"

He blinked. After a moment he said, "Jupiter. I forgot what you were like."

"I'm sorry," Dione said.

"Don't be," he said. Snapped, for a fact.

"Such a peremptory Roman." Dione's gesture encompassed the room. "Will you sit? Rest? I regret I've no wine to offer you, nor anything else but wind and light and a disastrously dusty couch."

"And a cat with too many feet," said Lucius Servilius, "and a tongue like no one else's. I missed you, I think. Other people are dull beside you."

He sat gingerly on the couch. The cat directed herself toward his lap. Dione stayed where she was, standing by the window with the sun shining warm on her back. "Alexandria wasn't dull," she said. "Not with Cleopatra, and Timoleon. But I'm glad you came."

"Are you?" He rubbed the cat's chin just as she liked it, neither too briskly nor too slowly. "I thought I'd see you with the queen."

"I meant to be there," said Dione. "But it's so much quieter up here."

"It is," he agreed.

There was a silence. It was pleasant, rather; not uncomfortable as it would have been with anyone else, particularly if she had not seen him since the summer. She had forgotten just how beautiful he was. He seemed as careless of it as ever: made no effort to pluck the strong black brows that grew together on his forehead, let his hair fall in rough curls rather than in carefully ordered ringlets, wore a scrupulously clean but slightly threadbare tunic under his toga. His sandals at least were new, and of the best quality as all his belongings were.

After a while she said, "I have to go soon. I swore a solemn oath to Timoleon that I would come home for dinner."

"Certainly you mustn't break your word," he said.

"No," said Dione. And paused. Then said, "You can dine with us. Unless, of course, you're engaged elsewhere. If the triumvir . . . the queen . . ."

She trailed off. She had never asked him to dinner before. In Tarsus there had been no occasion: they were always part of the queen's party and the triumvir's. Neither of them had had a house to invite the other to, nor thought to find one.

He was so long in replying that she was sure he would refuse. Then he said, "Will Timoleon mind?"

"I doubt it," said Dione.

He thought about it. "Then I'll come. If he objects, I don't think I'll mind finding a frog in my cup. Or is it snakes now?"

"Neither," Dione answered with the dawning of something very like delight, and rather like terror. "The last time he tried anything, he replaced the servants' beer with something I really don't like to mention."

His brows went up. "Cat piss?"

A gust of laughter escaped her. "You *do* know Timoleon."

"I know Egyptian beer," said Lucius Servilius with a wry face.

"Tonight we'll have a decent Chian. Or," said Dione, "reasonably drinkable water. I doubt my offspring will have had time to prepare a surprise for you. Though there was the time he served one of my guests with pure Alexandrian water—from under a dock in the harbor."

"Was it green?"

"And irresistibly alive." Dione shuddered with the memory. "Oh, I *am* glad you're here. No one else understands about that child."

"He's perfectly understandable. Just . . . very interesting."

"Incorrigible." Dione gathered herself together. "Shall we see what he's prepared for us tonight?"

THIRTEEN

Timoleon had nothing in store for his mother's guest but a long look and a cool, "Oh, good. I hoped you'd come tonight. Did you bring me anything from Syria?"

In fact he had, which Dione thought was considerate of him. He brought a dagger in a sheath for Timoleon, and for Dione a jar of Caecuban wine. "Which I hope stays Caecuban," he said with a glance at Timoleon. "Water of Alexandria is all very well, but the red wine of Caecubum deserves to remain in its natural state."

Taking all in all it was a very successful evening. At the end of it, when Timoleon had gone to bed clutching his knife in its sheath, Dione filled the best silver cups with the strong wine and said, "I suppose you'll have a room in the palace."

"I suppose," said Lucius Servilius. He looked comfortable on the couch reserved for honored guests, in the fine crimson robe that had been Apollonius'. It had never fit Apollonius properly; and it had made his pale skin look sallow. Lucius Servilius was dark enough and just tall enough to carry it off.

"You could," she said, "guest with us. We have room, goddess knows." His glance was swift and too easily readable. "No, I don't care what people will think. Unless *you* think it."

"No," he said, flushing. "No, I don't. But you have a reputation— honor—your son—"

"I offer you guesting and friendship," she said, framing each word with care. "No more than that, if no less. I know what a warren the palace is. Nobody but the queen can get any thinking done there, and as for time to oneself, there's no such thing. That's why I have this house. When Apollonius divorced me, the queen asked me to move into the palace. I refused. I need a place that's mine."

"And you're asking me to invade it?"

"You're not an invasion," said Dione. "You're quiet. You have manners. Timoleon likes you. I can offer you a whole suite to yourself. It's next to the library, and not far from the garden. It's only a short walk to the Museum."

He was tempted, she could see it. But he said, "People will talk."

"Do you care?"

"Yes."

She sighed. "I knew you'd say that. Very well then. Live in the palace. Share a room with one of Antony's soldiers—or were they going to put you in with the chamberlains? I'm sure you'll make do. You always have, haven't you?"

"I've always had a room to myself," he said stiffly.

"Maybe you will, then." She shrugged as if it were a matter of supreme indifference. So it should have been. A woman living alone, neither widowed nor wed, had no business inviting a man to live in her house, no matter how innocent the invitation might be.

And why, she thought, rebellious, should that matter? "You'll be miserable," she said. "Admit it. What if I tell you there's a passage between the men's part of the house and the women's, and a door of its own, with a lock? It's like another house, almost. I'll charge you rent—a woman can do that, even a woman without a man to do her thinking for her. One jar of Caecuban for each month that you stay."

"That's high," said Lucius Servilius.

"Well then. This jar of Caecuban as security, and lessons in Latin for Timoleon."

"That's too low." But he was smiling, not too willingly from the look of him, but as if he could not help it. "The wine was a gift. I'll teach Timoleon, and pay you in a copy of Caesar's *Gallic Wars.*"

"Oh, please," said Dione. "Don't punish me. Latin lessons, and Terentius' *Mother-in-Law* in a fair hand."

"Done," he said. Then: "Why the *Mother-in-Law?*"

"I like it," she said.

He laughed, but then he frowned. "I'm not sure . . ."

"This is a fair contract," she said. "I'm your landlady; you're my tenant. Even a Roman matron would be hard put to quarrel with that."

"A Roman matron will dispute points of order with King Minos at the judgment seat." Lucius Servilius shook his head. "So, I think, would you. You do know how to break a man's will. Threatening me with the queen's chamberlains—that was low."

"It worked," Dione said. "It's true, too. They'll be crowded up there, at least till Antony's men find accommodations of their own. They're bound to come asking me, once they know I've got the room. None of them's as good company as you are. And Timoleon enjoys you. He didn't even fill your winecup with vinegar."

"Which I suppose he'd do if I refused you." He sat back with the air of a man who has lost a battle he did not honestly want to win, and drank a draft of his wine. "Well then. May a tenant trouble his landlady for another of those interesting cakes?"

She passed the plate. "They're made with almonds," she said, "and honey. The spices are the cook's secret."

"May it prosper him," said Lucius Servilius, biting into his cake, "and you, since you've made yourself a woman of business."

Dione raised her cup to him and drank. "To prosperity," she said.

People talked, of course. They always did. But it did not matter to Dione, or to Timoleon. Lucius Servilius was by no means an obtrusive guest. He came and went through his own door, did whatever his triumvir needed of him, spent most of his unoccupied hours in the Museum, the great library and academy of Alexandria, or exploring the city and its environs. He taught Timoleon his elegant Latin, and Timoleon taught Lucius his rapid, colloquial Egyptian.

It was quite the most pleasant winter Dione could remember. The storms that came were fierce enough, and cold, but there was warmth in the house, the sound of voices intoning Latin verbs or Egyptian doggerel. Most evenings, when they were not wanted in palace or temple, she dined with Lucius Servilius, or sat with him by the brazier, talking of whatever came to mind.

Lucius Servilius was a happy man. He was not accustomed to thinking of himself in that way, but it came on him slowly, that winter in Alexandria, when he should have been yearning for his dear distant Rome. This foreign city came quickly to seem all familiar, with its polyglot populace and its crowds even in the side ways. The day he returned a drover's curse with one even more improbable, and got a round of applause for it, he went back to his landlady's house in a state of considerable but happy confusion. He felt—why, he felt almost like an Alexandrian.

Although it was not time for his Latin lesson, Timoleon was sitting in Lucius' study, in Lucius' chair by the brazier. He jumped guiltily as Lucius came in, though Lucius could see nothing to be guilty about: the boy had not got into anything, had not even scribbled on the wax tablet that lay open on the table. He looked as if he had been sitting with his feet tucked up, doing nothing at all.

Lucius raised a brow. "Well? Is there a frog in the inkpot?"

"No!" Timoleon's denial was prompt, but Lucius detected no falsehood in it. "I've given that up. I'm going to be a gentleman."

"You weren't born one already?"

Timoleon scowled. "You know what I mean. I've stopped being incorrigible. I'm going to be a model of the young philosopher."

"I wish you good fortune," said Lucius gravely.

Timoleon shot him a look, but he was master of his expression. The boy's eyes stayed wary. "You're laughing at me," he said.

"I'm reflecting that I decided to be a gentleman once, too. I was just about as old as you."

"And did it work?"

"I don't know," said Lucius. "Do you think it did?"

"I think," said Timoleon, "that you think I'm being silly. I'm only a child. I can't know what I'm doing."

"You're what, ten years old? That's well past the age of reason, and well advanced toward young manhood."

"Oh, I am *years* from being a man. I'll die of impatience before I even get there."

"No, you won't," said Lucius. But he shivered. It was cold beyond the brazier's reach, and the shadows crowded in. He moved closer to the warmth.

Timoleon's eyes were lethally sharp—as one might expect considering his mother. "What was that? Did you see an omen?"

"No," Lucius said, a bit too quickly perhaps. "Of course not."

"Mother says your gods talk to you. They send you messages, but you have to perform rituals to keep from being afraid of them, and to open your ears so you can hear. You close them too tight, she says. You're a priest, but you don't want to be what a priest is."

Lucius kept a firm grip on his temper. This was only a child, albeit excessively precocious. "A priest is an official of the Roman state. He performs the rites, and if he is an augur, takes the morning omens in his proper turn, and sees to it that all is performed in due and proper order from beginning to end, without error or interruption. There is nothing mystical about it at all."

"That's not what Mother says," said the priestess' child. "She says you're a real priest, not just a person who's paid to wear the robes and say the words. When you take the omens, the omens are real. It gets you in trouble, doesn't it? Do you keep quiet when the omens are bad and somebody powerful wants them to be good?"

"We are all," said Lucius, "real priests. And we all take the omens as we were taught."

"You don't make them up," said Timoleon. "I know the others do. I watched this morning. You weren't there. The old man who looks like a goose was digging around in the entrails, and he pretended there wasn't any liver. But I saw it. He just pushed it out of sight. He wanted people to think that this was going to be a bad day, because somebody slipped him a purse to say so. I think it had something to do with somebody racing his horse against somebody else's."

Lucius shook his head and sighed. "Did you spy on the augurs before or after you decided to become a gentleman?"

"Before, of course," said Timoleon with the air of a man enlightening a dull-witted child. "Why do people need to make up omens? The gods aren't hard to read, if you've got the eyes. Mother does. She says you do. The gods don't lie to you, and you don't lie to anybody else."

"The gods don't lie, no," Lucius said. "Men can, because they are men. It's the way they're made."

"But not you."

"Oh, I'm as imperfect as anyone else," said Lucius. "And no more or less a priest than Publius Annaeus Anser, either."

"Old Goosebeak doesn't see a thing. He was so busy hiding the liver, he didn't even realize that he'd forgotten to count the warts on the intestine. I did. There was a lucky number. And sure enough, Mamertinus' horse won its race. Dellius was in a right snit."

"How many—" Lucius began, but he caught himself. Jupiter! the brat had him going like a bear on a chain. "Is there a purpose to this encounter? Or are you simply regaling me with your latest round of misdeeds?"

"Oh, now I've made you angry," said Timoleon without a glimmer of remorse. "I wanted to know if you'd take the omens for me. I can't get you a sheep, but cook has a brace of fat geese. Will they do?"

"What in Hecate's name do you want omens for? Your mother is a seer."

"She only sees what the goddess lets her see. And that's never anything interesting."

"No," said Lucius dryly. "Merely dull matters of war and politics, and the lives and deaths of kings."

"They are dull, aren't they? She doesn't see the things that I'd like to see. Like who will win tomorrow's chariot races. And will Thais the Younger scratch the Nubian Beauty's eyes out when she finds out who's been playing with her pet Roman on the side?"

"You have a low mind," Lucius said.

"At least I'm not boring." Timoleon bounced in the chair, which now that Lucius thought of it was the only comfortable chair in the room, and he still standing, still in his cloak and his shoes. The boy did not even notice. "Well? Will one goose do, or do I have to use both? Will you show me how? Then I won't have to bother you again."

Lucius fixed him with a hard, cold eye. "You've been experimenting."

Timoleon's cheeks flushed faintly. He looked, had he known it, suddenly and poignantly like his mother. "No. No, my word on it. I've been watching the augurs, that's all. Seeing how they do it. But you could explain, you see. Do I need to say the same words all the time, or can I make them up as I go along?"

"Do you think that I would tell you? These are secrets. Mysteries. If your gods had called you, you would know—isn't that how it's done in Egypt? You wouldn't need to ask me to take the omens for you. You'd have them already."

"But you said," said Timoleon, "it doesn't take—you don't need—"

"You aren't a Roman," Lucius said.

"And I'm glad!" Timoleon leaped up. "You're just as bad as Mother."

"I think I'd call it wise," said Lucius. "It's never sensible to make light of the gods' gifts. They make you pay in the end—and they set the price high."

"Old Goosebeak didn't look as if he was having any trouble."

"How do you know he isn't? He's on his fifth wife. He's yet to see a son live past infancy. He's adopted sons twice. They both died. When he's gone, so is his line. And he goes on falsifying the omens, telling lies in place of the gods' truth."

Timoleon was rebellious still, but Lucius had cowed him somewhat.

"Swear me an oath," said Lucius. "Swear that you won't try to force the gods to tell you their secrets. If they want to—let them. But no compulsion. And no slitting some innocent beast's throat simply because you want a look at its liver."

"But *you*—" Timoleon began. He seemed to think better of it. Maybe Lucius' stern expression quelled him; or maybe Lucius' words had finally sunk in. "If I swear, what do I get for it?"

Alexandrian to the core, that one, Lucius thought. "The gods won't make you pay for your presumption. And I won't whale your hide if I hear that you've been trying to become an augur on your own."

One of those arguments at least was potent enough to overcome Timoleon. "I swear," he said, not willingly but clearly enough. "Will you tell my fortune, then? At least a little bit of it?"

"Easily," said Lucius, startling him. "You'll leave this room, you'll have your supper, you'll go to bed. You'll dream—of vanishing livers, no doubt, and men who lie when the gods tell the truth. And that's as far in the future as any man needs to see."

"Is he dreadfully dull?" Cleopatra asked Dione. It was the first bright day after a full week of rain and wind. Antony was out hunting in the marshes round Lake Mareotis. Cleopatra would dearly have loved to go with him, but her pregnancy was vexing her; she was too rotund already to ride, and too queasy to follow the hunt in a boat. She lay as much at ease as she could, in the airiest of her winter chambers, with the sun shining through the opened shutters, and braziers to soften the chill.

Although her body was swollen and slow, her mind was as quick as ever, her wit as merciless. "He's such a shy thing," she said, "hardly a word to say for himself. But lovely to look at—I grant you that. He's really quite beautiful."

"He has plenty to say," Dione said, knowing better than to seem indignant, but determined to defend the innocent. "He just doesn't say it to everyone who happens by."

"Really?" Cleopatra raised a brow. "What does he say when he says anything? Long disquisitions on the minutiae of Roman law? The full conjugation of the Greek preterite present?"

"He's teaching Timoleon Latin," said Dione, still as serene as she knew how to be. "His gods talk to him, you know. He won't admit it. He gets angry if I mention it. But he sees true. Just the other day he said, out of nowhere in particular, that you were going to have twins, a boy and a girl, and you should name them for kings."

Cleopatra's hand rested on the swell of her belly, as if to protect it. "I'm not seeing anything. It's as if I've gone blind."

Dione nodded slowly. "That happens when one bears a child for the gods—when all that's in you is focused on that and that alone. Or so," she said, "I'm told. It must be terrifying."

"No," said Cleopatra as if she meant it. She shifted on her couch, striking irritably at the maid who sought to restore the scattered cushions. "So your Roman has eyes to see where all the rest of us are blind. I should have him read the omens. My priests and astrologers are as sightless as I am—as if they can't see for the light."

"I can see," said Dione, "and hear. The goddess is in me still, though she's quiet more often than she speaks. This is the waiting time. We've only to be patient, and be glad. It won't be long before the waiting is over."

"It's been too long already," Cleopatra said darkly. She levered herself to her feet, glaring at anyone who offered to help. Once she was up, she was agile enough; she still had her long panther's stride, stalking round the room from sun to shade to sun again.

Pregnancy suited her, Dione thought. It softened the harsh angles of her face; her skin seemed richer, smoother, like honey and cream. She worried that Antony would find her altered body repugnant, but as far as Dione could see, he was enchanted with her. He handled her as if she were made of glass, which made her snap at him; then he laughed, more delighted than not, and called her his queen of cats.

"What else does your Roman see?"

The question was abrupt, and very like Cleopatra. Dione answered, "He sees nothing but that, that I know of. He spends most of his time denying that he can see at all. Magic is for foreigners, he says, and women. Men are priests because the state requires them to be. They don't talk to gods, or serve as messengers for them, no matter what they might pretend."

"Little he knows," said Cleopatra. "Antony is no better. This morning he told me he wanted the priests of Amon to make an omen for him. He needs a sign or two, or maybe three, to keep his soldiers happy, for when he takes them into Parthia."

Dione sucked in a breath. "He dared *that?* What did he say when they told him what they thought of him?"

"He didn't—they didn't. I sent him hunting before he could say a word to them. With the gods' help he'll have forgotten all about it when he comes back."

"I wouldn't wager on it," Dione said.

Cleopatra smiled an edged smile. "I would. I'll see to it myself."

The hunting party came back well before the women had expected, laden with spoils: ducks, geese, even a young river-horse that had blundered into the beaters' circle and been cut down by Antony's own spear. He was flushed with the elation of the kill, but there was something odd under it, a whiteness about the nostrils, a tension round the eyes. He bowed to the queen, then kissed her none too decorously in front of everyone. She returned the kiss with a signal lack of shyness, seeming not to notice the constraint with which he moved.

Dione would not speak of it if Cleopatra did not see it. The rest of the hunters had the same vaguely frenetic air, the same quick shooting of glances. She regretted that Lucius Servilius was not with them. He had gone to the Museum, observing mildly that while he saw the virtue in hunting for one's supper, he preferred to hunt for treasures among the philosophers. If he had been there, she could have pried the truth out of him.

As it was, she held her peace. It was not her place to interrogate the queen's consort, nor could she speak unless the queen spoke first. Cleopatra was occupied with exclaiming over the river-horse, ordering the hunters' dinner, dealing with an hour's worth of dull but necessary business while Antony bathed and rested. Dione might have left her then; it was nearing evening, and there was Timoleon to think of, and Lucius Servilius who would be returning from the Museum and looking for her to share his dinner. But she stayed, she did not know why, only that she should do it.

As Cleopatra frowned over a roll of accounts, questioning this line and that and listening keenly to her minister's explanations, Antony came in and sat in the chair beside her couch. He was always larger than the rooms he stood in, especially in this palace with its fussy opulence and its predilection for gilt and silk. This evening he was notably restless, fretting with a pen that the scribe had dropped, peering for a while over the queen's shoulder, getting up when it was clear that she would not immediately devote herself to him, and prowling from wall to painted wall, from frieze of lions to fresco of river-horses in a forest of papyrus. He was never angry when she was too busy to give him more than a smile and a nod; unlike Caesar, who had expected her full and focused attention whenever he was present, he understood that she was queen as well as lover, and must tend to the ruling of her kingdom.

Dione watched him unsmiling. He wandered over to where she sat, and peered down at the book in her lap. "What are you reading?" he asked.

"Terentius," she answered.

"Ah," said Antony. "I like Plautus better myself. Have you seen him performed on the stage?"

"Certainly," said Dione: "when I was in Rome."

"Ah," he said again. "I forgot you were there with the queen."

"Yes," said Dione.

The silence stretched. He did not move away, but he did not speak. She refused to be uncomfortable; she went back to reading her book.

After a while the queen finished what she was doing and dismissed the scribe and the minister of finance. She sat for a while, rubbing her eyes as if they ached; then she smiled at Antony. "All done," she said. "There's duck for dinner, and goose, and a fat ox. Shall we have the Chian or the Samian to start?"

"Both," he said. He was still standing near Dione, looming over her. She gave up trying to read with him blocking her light.

Cleopatra seemed at last to realize that something was amiss. She lifted her brows. "Is something wrong?"

"No," said Antony. "No, not at all."

"You're a terrible liar," she said. "What is it? Did one of your bully-boys break another vase?"

"No," he said. "There's nothing wrong. Really."

"Of course there isn't," said Cleopatra. "You're twitching like a horse in a swarm of flies. It isn't your wife, is it? Has she announced that she's coming to drag you back to Rome?"

"Gods forbid!" said Antony with all the force of truth. And yet Dione's skin shivered.

Finally, as if he could hold it in no longer, he came out with it. "I do have to go. But not to Rome."

Cleopatra held herself still. Dione saw the effort it cost her: her lips were tight. "Parthia?"

He nodded. The tension ran out of him in a wash of relief. "It's bad. The Parthians got tired of waiting for me to attack them. They've marched on Syria. That's enough to get me moving, but they've got Romans with them—renegades, Caesar's enemies from back before he came to Egypt. They're moving on two fronts that we know of."

" 'We'?" asked Cleopatra.

"I left people in Syria, obviously. One of them found me as I was coming back from the lake. He was going to look for me in the palace; then you'd have heard it as soon as I did."

"But I didn't," she said. "I knew there were forces moving in Syria—I suspected that Parthia would tire of waiting. But not so soon."

She was angry, deeply and coldly furious, not at him but at herself and her nets of spies. Dione wondered if Antony knew it. There was no telling. Sometimes he seemed all block-brained soldier; then he showed a flash of wit, a keen intelligence that hid behind the heavy fighter's face.

He seemed oblivious to Cleopatra's mood, even relieved that she had not given vent to her temper. "I thought we had a while longer, myself. But there's no use in moaning over might-have-beens. I'll have to get my men together and sail to Syria as fast as I can go. I've got good men there, mind you, but they'll want their commander."

"Watch them," said Dione, "that they don't go over to the enemy."

Both of them turned to stare at her. She felt her cheeks flush, but she went on as the goddess urged her. "The Romans who fight with the Parthians—they can be persuasive. And you've been in Egypt, bedding down with foreigners yourself. They'll be thinking to follow your example."

Antony growled in his throat. "They wouldn't dare."

She bit her tongue. It was Cleopatra who said, "I wouldn't deny the possibility, either. Yes, you have to go. I'll count every hour you're gone; I'll pray you win your war and come back as soon as can be."

"That won't be soon," said Dione, goddess-ruled again, and fighting it, because this, Cleopatra would not want to hear. "Look to Rome, too. There's rebellion everywhere, war, friend turning on friend and Roman on Roman—do you know what your wife is doing, Marcus Antonius?"

"My wife is here," he said roughly, "ruling Egypt."

"Your Roman wife has hopes of ruling Rome."

"Absit omen!" said Antony.

"You had better go," Cleopatra said, cold and steady. "You have much to do if you hope to sail within the week."

"It can wait till morning," he said.

She shook her head. "No. Go now. I'll look for you at dinner."

He hovered still, reluctant, but she ignored him. She said to Dione, "I think you had better go, too. Isn't your son expecting you?"

Dione stiffened as if at a slap. She had never been dismissed so, no matter how bluntly she spoke to Cleopatra.

But the queen was giving her nothing now, not patience, not understanding, not forbearance for a woman who was a goddess' instrument. Bad enough that Antony must abandon his queen for Parthia. Dione, or the goddess, did not have to foretell that more than a brief war waited; that Rome itself would beset him with rebellion— rebellion led by his own, Roman wife. Cleopatra never forgot Fulvia, nor thought of her truly as a rival, but neither did she like to be reminded of the woman's existence.

Dione bowed, scrupulously correct, and went as she was bidden.

She saved grief for later. Maybe she would not need it. Cleopatra's temper could be as quick as it was fierce; and she had had an unpleasant shock. Dione herself might have done no better.

FOURTEEN

Everyone said the queen was taking the news with remarkable aplomb.

"But she isn't," said Dione. "They don't understand that when she screams and throws things, she's much safer than when she goes all quiet and calm. She was dead calm about Arsinoe."

Lucius Servilius was supposed to be packing his belongings, of which he had managed to accumulate a surprising quantity. He had a slave to do it, of course, and Dione had offered her servants, but some things needed his personal attention. Or would, if he could bring himself to do them. He picked up a sandal that he only vaguely remembered owning, and put it down again. "Do you think she'll try anything to keep Antony with her?" he asked.

"No," said Dione. "She won't stoop to it."

"And yet they're saying in Rome that she snared the triumvir with spells to bind him to her bed, and keeps him lolling in luxury while the world crumbles around him."

"They always say that," Dione said. "They said it of Caesar, who never even knew what lolling meant. Keeping up with him would have exhausted a god. Antony's not what Caesar was, but neither is he the bloated bladder that rumor makes him. Nor would the queen want him to be. She'd despise him if he stayed."

"She'll hate him if he fails to come back," said Lucius.

"That's with time and the gods," she said. She found the other sandal and handed it to Lucius' slave, who packed it with silent efficiency.

Lucius knew how great a vexation he was to his servant. Sometimes he was contrite. This morning he was too sorely tried by circumstance. He did not want to go to Syria. Neither should he stay, though if he asked, Antony no doubt would give him leave.

This was the eastern luxury that sent virtuous Romans into frothing fits. It was not so much the excess of wealth as the comfort, the urbanity of people who had been civilized when Rome was a cluster of huts in a marsh. There were more books in the Museum than Lucius could ever read, more beauties to revel in than a man could encompass in the span allotted him.

One of those beauties folded a rumpled shirt and smoothed it with her deft small hands. He was learning to read her. She was never as serene as she seemed, a serenity that she cultivated, for it served her well in contending with a fractious child and a difficult, dangerous, deadly clever queen. And, if he would admit it, a lodger who demanded as much of her as any of the rest.

"You'll be glad to see me go," he said. "You'll have this part of your house back again, and your evenings. And Timoleon will stop dredging up horrible jokes to tell in Egyptian."

"I won't miss the jokes," she conceded. "The one with the Roman and the dockside whore . . . oh, dear. Am I too terrible a mother for not tanning his hide for that?"

"You did very well with your few well-chosen words," said Lucius gravely.

She bit her lip. Laughter escaped in spite of her efforts. It was infectious. Lucius did not even try to fight it.

They laughed themselves to tears; and every time one managed to stop, the other went off again in new gusts and gales of it. It was quite without reason. It was utterly irresistible.

They were still laughing when the storm blew into the house.

It was only Apollonius. He swept ahead of Senmut the house-steward, the image of righteous wrath, so impossibly ridiculous that Dione collapsed, prostrate with mirth.

It took a very long time to recover her coherence. By then Lucius had gone all cold and Roman, and Apollonius was rigid with fury. Dione could not make herself be properly concerned. She wiped away the tears of laughter and composed herself as much as she could, but still smiling. "Apollonius. What a pleasure. Senmut, tell cook to send wine—some of Lucius Servilius' Caecuban, I think, we have a little left—and whatever there is to eat."

As stiffly affronted as he was, her quondam husband was easy enough to move out of Lucius Servilius' bedchamber and into a room more suitable for receiving guests. Lucius Servilius came with them. He would not have done it, but Dione got a grip on him and dragged him bodily out. His slave at least was grateful to be able to finish packing in peace.

She had hoped that Lucius Servilius' presence and the distraction of food and drink would stop the tirade that Apollonius had plainly prepared. She could even guess its subject. He had not appeared in her house since the Romans came to Alexandria, nor communicated with her, nor had Androgeos paid one of his infrequent but regular visits.

"Apollonius," she said once they were seated, "do you know Lucius Servilius the Augur? Lucius Servilius, this is Apollonius, who was my husband."

Lucius Servilius inclined his head in that way he had, so like a prince's, but thoroughly Roman. Apollonius merely glowered. Neither of them was about to express pleasure in the meeting, even to be polite.

Dione suppressed a sigh. She said as brightly as she could, "Lucius Servilius has been my lodger this winter. He's taught Timoleon a lovely elegant Latin." And Timoleon had taught Lucius Servilius dreadful indelicate Egyptian. Her eye caught Lucius Servilius'; she clenched her teeth on a new eruption of laughter.

"Your son is an excellent pupil," said Lucius Servilius a little hastily. "You are to be commended in your offspring."

"He owes little enough to me," said Apollonius. "I gave him completely to his mother when we settled the matter of our marriage. She wanted it so; I saw fit to oblige her."

Lucius Servilius went cold. It was not immediately obvious, but Dione knew him well enough to recognize the way his eyes went flat and his long mouth straightened into a line. He looked older then, almost as old as he was. "Indeed," he said. "How kind of you to surrender the incorrigible and keep the dutiful son."

Apollonius drew himself up. "Are you insulting me, sir?"

"That depends on what brings you here to disturb the lady Dione."

"You would know that better than I," said Apollonius with a curl of the lip.

"What, she needs your permission to entertain a guest in her own house?"

"More than a guest, if what I hear is true."

"Why, what do you hear?"

Dione tried to get a word in. "Please—"

Neither of them paid her the least attention. Apollonius had all the encouragement he needed to go into full spate. "I hear that a Roman lives in the house of a daughter of the Lagidai. That that Roman has lured her with blandishments, corrupted her with gifts, and seduced her with a prettiness that indeed I see is quite out of the ordinary. I hear too that her name is dragged in the mud of the harbor, as if she were a courtesan, or less than that, a common whore."

"Surely," said Lucius Servilius with sweet reason, "you exaggerate."

"Was it exaggeration that I found her in your bedchamber, beside your bed, all but swooning in your arms?"

"How little you must think of her," Lucius Servilius said, "if you can believe that she would do anything less than scrupulously honorable."

"She is a woman, weak and impressionable. She has beauty; I know well how it can lure a man into indiscretion. She values her name too little, her honor less—out of modesty, I fondly hope, and not out of wantonness. She is easy prey for a foreigner who can delude her, seduce her, and abandon her when the novelty palls."

"As you did?"

Apollonius went white.

Dione intervened before there could be murder committed. Lucius Servilius had a lazy look, one that she had not seen in him before, but knew from crocodiles in the lake. He was getting ready to devour his prey.

"I do wish," she said in the most prosaic tone she could manage, "that men could be a little less like stallions in a herd. Apollonius, I'm not your wife any longer. What I choose to do is no responsibility of yours."

"What a Roman chooses to do to a noblewoman of Egypt is the responsibility of every man in the Two Lands," declared Apollonius.

"You are pompous," said Dione. "This Roman is as harmless as a man can be. *He* has never given me such insult as you have since you burst in uninvited and called me a common prostitute. It's as well I'm a woman. If I were a man, I might kill you."

He, of course, did not believe her, though Lucius Servilius seemed ready to wrest a dagger from her hand if she should produce one. "Don't be ridiculous," said Apollonius. "Did you even think before you let this man into your house?"

"Certainly," she said. "He's a man of honor and discretion, and he paid for his lodging by teaching my son Latin."

"And keeping you warm of nights?"

Years of contending with Cleopatra's tempers served Dione well. She kept her hands in her lap, though they were fists, and said with icy calm, "I do not need your permission to do as I see fit."

Apollonius opened his mouth. Lucius Servilius spoke before him. "There has been nothing between us but strict propriety and a thoroughly unexceptionable friendship. Do you understand that word, friendship? Or is such a concept beyond you?"

Dione heard Apollonius grind his teeth. "There is nothing proper about a man who lives with a woman who is neither his wife nor his kin."

"Clearly," said Lucius Servilius, "you don't understand 'landlady,' either. Are all Egyptian Hellenes so clouded of wit? Or is it only you?"

Dione was more than fond of Lucius Servilius, but at the moment she hated him cordially—almost as much as she hated Apollonius. "Oh, please," she said with the last rags of her patience. "Will you stop strutting like cocks in front of a hen? I thought better of you at least, Lucius Servilius. Can't you ignore him till he goes away?"

"He insults you with every word he utters," said Lucius Servilius, stiff with outrage.

"Whatever makes a man," said Dione to any god or spirit that could hear, "surely it must be a poison, to strip even a sensible person of his wits." She faced them both. "Will you please go away? Separately. And no fighting. I won't have your blood on my conscience."

"I am not done yet," said Apollonius. "Send this foreigner away, and let us talk."

"No," said Dione. "You would talk at me, and I would lose what temper I have left. I want you to go. And don't come back until you can speak to me sensibly, without this vileness that's no more than jealousy."

"And leave you here with him?" Apollonius demanded with a jab of his chin at Lucius Servilius.

"He leaves for Syria in the morning," said Dione. "And he spends the night alone, as he has since he came here. Unless you wish to count the cat that warms his feet when I'm delayed in palace or temple?"

Her irony escaped him, as she had known it would; but Lucius Servilius let out a bark of laughter. It won him a murderous glare from Apollonius.

Dione raised her voice slightly. "Senmut!" Her house-steward appeared with promptness that indicated an ear pressed to the door.

"Senmut, please see my lord Apollonius to the door. And send Gaius to attend Lucius Servilius."

This too she had learned from Cleopatra: to dispose of troublesome guests before they could find voice to object. The queen could put them out of her mind once they were gone, to be recalled only when she had leisure or patience to spare for them. Dione did not have that gift.

Her head was aching abominably. A sip of wine only made it worse. She propped her elbows on the arms of her chair and lowered her head into her hands, gingerly, lest it topple from her neck.

The cat appeared from wherever it had gone to escape the storm, and curled about her foot. It was small comfort, but large enough to go on with. It kept her from bursting into tears.

FIFTEEN

Next to tears, the best refuge of a woman in the face of men's intractability was in the simple round of living from day to day. For Dione that meant tending her son, grown rebellious with the departure of his sometime tutor, and serving in the temple, and attending Cleopatra. For Cleopatra it meant being queen, and being mother to her own son, and waiting to give birth.

Dione felt like a field left fallow. She looked at Cleopatra, vastly pregnant, and despised herself for the envy that stabbed her. Oh, to have damned all restraint and taken even one night, and to have something more to show for it than Timoleon's rude tongue. It did not matter then that Lucius Servilius had never indicated that he would have been willing, or even interested. He had said a cold goodbye, with bloodless thanks for her hospitality; she had responded as coldly, out of a heart gone chill and small.

Maybe Cleopatra was as serene as she was because she had decided that Antony was coming back within the year. She was coolly distant with Dione, but that faded little by little to a semblance of their old amity. She did not seem to notice that Dione kept that distance for herself.

"Oh, what an idiot I am!" she cried when she was alone but for the cat. The cat was not listening: it was asleep. It usually was of late. It had grown sleek since it adopted Dione in Tarsus; now it was fat, and given to lolling in the sun. That it would be thinner soon, even gaunt, with nursing kittens, Dione did not want to consider.

"I am such a fool," she said to the sun and the quiet of her portico, with its columns like papyrus sheaves, and its Greek fountain. The nymph looked unusually vacuous. The dolphin grinned with maniac cheer. "I was never this silly about anything. I don't even *like* lying with a man."

If there had been anyone there, he would have pointed out that she had never lain with any man but Apollonius, for whom bedding his wife was a duty like any other, and pleasing her was not a thing that he need trouble himself with. He had asked once if he was hurting her. Since he had not been, not more than usual, she had said no, and that had been that. He should have asked if he was giving her pleasure. Then she could have told him the truth.

And would he have cared? For that matter, would Lucius Servilius?

"What do I know of him?" she asked the air. "He's polite, he's witty, he's shy in company but relaxed enough when he's with someone he knows. He comes of a good family, most of whom I'd know if I met them, from what he's told me. He doesn't believe in magic, not really, even though he has a gift for it. Oh, I know all the things that a friend can know—he's even called me that, as if he means it. But a friend isn't a lover. He could be a monster in the inner room."

Nonsense, said her better self. Lucius Servilius with a woman would be as sweetly shy as he had been when he first met her, or else as warm and witty and wise as the man who had sat so late, so many evenings, with the wine forgotten and the hours running unheeded toward morning.

"But he never, never once, even suggested that he would want more than he had," Dione said. "He hasn't a wife, he told me that, and I know he wasn't lying. He had a mistress in Gaul, but she left him for a man who could marry her and make her a respectable woman. He never brought anyone home, or visited the brothels that I ever knew. If he wanted me, he only had to ask."

Oh, and did he? And how would she have answered him? Would she have even wanted him, if he had been the one to speak?

"Idiot," she said fiercely. "Idiot, idiot, idiot." And whether she meant him, or herself, or both, she could not tell.

* * *

Cleopatra grew huge with pregnancy, so huge that walking was discomfort, and sitting her throne was a thing that she preferred to avoid if she could. She even, for once, put off what could be put off, and handed some of the rest to her ministers. What was left she saw to from a couch in a chamber of cool airs and dim shade, or floating in the great pool of her bath. There she was as comfortable as she could be with all of her body subordinate to the mountain of her belly. As her time grew closer she spent long hours in the water, coming out to be oiled and stroked and cooled with fans, then going back again.

"No wonder Taweret looks as she does," she said to Dione. "What better incarnation for a goddess of childbearing than a river-horse?"

Dione smiled sleepily. It was as hot as Egypt could be at the gate of its summer. She had let Cleopatra bully her into the bath, and drifted there, for once almost content. If she turned her head she could see the queen in her wonted place, seated on a ledge, breast-deep in water. Her maids were swimming at the farther end of the pool, giggling and splashing. At this end was relative quiet, with only Cleopatra there, and Dione.

"I don't recall," the queen said, "that you were ever as gross as this, even at your time. I could hate you, I suppose. You're always beautiful, no matter what you do to yourself."

Dione roused at that. "I never had twins, or I'd have grown enormous, too."

"The doctors say it's only one. The astrologers agree. It's a son, they assure me, with the thews of Heracles."

"Nonsense," said Dione. "There are two, son and daughter, prince and queen who will be."

"What, he won't be a king?"

"I didn't say that," Dione said. Her lazy mood was gone. She swam toward the side of the pool and lifted herself out, sitting with feet in the water and body in the air, not far from Cleopatra. "She's your only daughter. Of course she'll be a queen. Whereas you have a son already."

"That's true," said Cleopatra. She leaned her head back against the sea-green tiles and sighed. The sigh caught. Her voice when it came was as calm as ever, but her words brought Dione to her feet. "I rather think it may be starting. The water muted it, but now . . ." Her smile was a lioness', white and feral. "And not before time, either. Tell the goddess to bring the girlchild first—if girlchild there is. I want her to be queen beyond a doubt."

One did not tell the goddess anything, but neither did one tell the queen so. Dione clapped her hands. "Charmion! Helena! Come quickly!"

The queen went about childbearing as she did everything, with fierce concentration. She had her doctors, her astrologers, her priests and priestesses, her maidservants to fetch whatever she needed. In that throng Dione was lost, nor had she any place there. She belonged elsewhere.

The place of the queen's magic was the kind of secret that was kept best by its openness. To those who wandered in, it seemed to be a chapel, a shrine of Isis set comfortably near to the queen's chambers. It was adorned in the Egyptian style, the walls painted thick with the old words, the old prayers, and yes, the old magics marching in their ranks from wall to wall and from ceiling to stone-paved floor. The altar was simple, black stone on red, for Black Land and for Red Land that together were Egypt. The image of the goddess was very old, brought up from Thebes by the first Ptolemy. She sat in a stone chair, crowned with the sun, and in her arms sat her child Horus, nursing at the breast. In this image he was a human child, human-headed, and yet he perched also on the throne's back, embracing his mother with falcon-wings.

This to Dione was Isis as she loved her best, mother and goddess, protector and protected. It was most fitting that Dione seek her now, when the queen was brought to bed of the sun and the moon. Nor was Dione astonished to discover a new figure in the grouping, one that stirred and yawned and sprang somewhat ungracefully from the goddess' lap to the floor, and wove about Dione's ankles. Bastet's cat, heavy with kittens, should well be here for this long day and longer night.

Something in her weaving spoke of urgency, of hours wasted, of help that might have come too late. It pressed her toward the altar, and held her there until she laid her hand upon it.

Once she touched the hallowed stone, she knew what she should have known from the first. This rite should have begun before the queen's waters broke. That was an hour past. And the sun was sinking, and the night was coming, full of beasts that hungered after infant souls.

Superstition, part of her thought. Children were born every night, came safe into the world, souls and bodies intact. But not such children as these. Dione had dreamed that Cleopatra bore the sun and the moon: that she and Antony between her had conceived magic, twofold for the Two Lands. And such magic at birthing was fragile, as fragile as air, or a child's first breath.

There were priests whose power was at least the equal of Dione's, priestesses who could sing the stars out of the sky and raise mountains out of the level land. Some of them were with the queen now. Dione hesitated, half-moved to go back to them, to call them to the working. But the cat tangled itself in her feet and held her back.

Night was coming, night without stars, like the beast that devours the moon. Dione shivered so hard that she nearly fell. She had nothing here that she should have, no powders, no books of enchantments. She had only herself and the cat, and the goddess silent within her. And a shadow that stood by the wall, jackal-headed, sulfur-eyed.

Briefly she remembered what god that was, Anubis who conducted the dead to the netherworld. But he was guardian here, defender against the dark things that lived behind the moon. He held up his hands and bowed his sharp-eared head and smiled his fanged smile. She had no strength to smile back, but his presence warmed her. With him here, she felt stronger, if not precisely strong enough for what she must do.

She drew a long breath. In the royal chamber, in a corner of her awareness, the queen fought the battle that every woman fought if she would bear a child. Dione, who had fought it twice, knew in her womb the power and the pain.

She must build the world about the two who strove to be born. She thought briefly, wryly, of the ways in which the gods were said to have done it: spending seed upon the void, rending a brother-god in pieces, conceiving clay of nothingness and shaping the earth as a potter shapes his pot.

"Yes," she breathed. "Yes." She spread hands above the altar. "Earth," she said, the simple word, the name, the power that was in the name.

She felt it in her body, bones that were bones of the earth, feet that stood on stone that stood on earth under the vault of the sky. It was dark; it smelled of growing things, and of dying things, and of the dead. All that was alive was part of it. It was the Black Land that was the gift of the Nile, the rich soil that fed this part of the world. It was the Red Land, the desert as bleak as the Black Land was rich, embracing the living earth with its sand-dry arms. The altar was made of it, set firm upon it. It was the solidity on which all else must rest.

She stood anchored in it, hands pressed to it, massive and heavy.

It dragged her down. She fought its weight. She must be part of it, yes, all flesh is, but so also must she be free of it, be spirit, be magic.

"Air," she said.

With the word she floated suddenly light, but bound to earth by the force of earth's magic. A wind blew through that windowless room, plucked at her hair, at her gown, made the lamps' flames leap and gutter. It strove to tug her free of the earth, to make her all a part of it. Yet that too she must not permit. All that air was not, earth was. Earth was solid, firm, unchanging. Air shifted always, was never still. And yet without earth, air was nothing, a dance of atoms in the void. Without air, earth was empty, with nothing alive upon it. They danced their ancient dance. They wrought the beginning of a world: earth underfoot, air overhead.

But that was only half of all that was. "Water," said Dione, gasping it, balanced between air and earth, while each did battle to possess her.

Water was silver, water was cool, water poured out across the black earth, danced with spray at the touch of the air. Water was the moon, changeful yet constant. It ran in the blood of living creatures. It filled the womb of a woman, salt like the sea, and her child swam in it like a strange fish. Water was most familiar of all to the child who looked to be born; it was the child's first element, its first memory, darkness and comfort and the sigh of the sea.

Water was woman, and moon, and bright magic in the night. Selene, Artemis, Luna of the Romans—all those, and the oceans too, and rivers, little streams in a garden and the mighty flood of the Nile. Water was life, brought the Black Land into the Red Land, made it rich and made it whole.

Dione floated between air and earth, mutable as water, with its soft strength that could conquer stone. It was tempting to linger so, in ease and in peace. But even yet the world was not wholly made. Earth to stand on, air to breathe, water to breed life—but life itself was the last of the elements.

"Fire," she said—cried out, a cry half of pain and half of triumph.

Fire of the sun, fire of gold in the forge, fire hot and pure and clean, cleaving the darkness of the air, hissing as it touched water, leaping wild on the earth. Fire was life. At its touch, earth became flesh, water transmuted to blood, and air to breath in the lungs.

And yet, even yet, the working was not complete. All that was of the world, Dione had named and therefore made. But there was the fifth element, the most elusive of them all, the one that she could not tame with a word, and yet must be, or all the rest was empty wind. That essence was the goddess' to give. She could not be compelled. She could only be asked, and that softly, while magic grew weak and spirit slow, and the shadows circled.

All that Dione had wrought hung like a sphere of glass. The queen lay within it, laboring, while her priests prayed and her astrologers cast their horoscopes and her doctors muttered learnedly of nothing. Let the goddess lift one finger and the globe would shatter, and the night come in, and death, of mother, of children, one or two or all of them.

"Into your hands," said Dione, barely more than a whisper, "mother and goddess, I give all that I have made. Without you I am nothing; the world is void, and vain. Only speak; bow your head; incline your heart to this working. Did you not intend it from the beginning? Have we not done all as you would wish?"

The silence was immense. Shadows closed in with hungry eyes. Dione clung to the altar, stripped of strength. She had given it all into the goddess' keeping.

In the heart of the stillness came a sound. It was tiny, like the throat that made it; weak, as a kitten is when it comes into the world. Dione raised her head that seemed as heavy as stone. Horus was gone from the goddess' lap. In his place lay the cat, and a thing that glistened wetly, groping blind for its mother. Even as Dione stared, the cat's belly convulsed; a second kitten slid into its nest.

Beyond the shrine, Dione heard a sound that, faint with distance, seemed as thin as the kittens' mewling. It reverberated in her skull. It was a paean, a song of victory: the birth-cry of a queen, and swift upon it, a prince.

The goddess had spoken. The night was vanquished. The moon and the sun had risen in the Two Lands.

SIXTEEN

Alexander Helios and Cleopatra Selene were, from the moment of birth, inseparable. That was to be expected of twins, but there seemed to be more to it than that. Dione had built a world for their souls to enter safely into, and kept out the night and its creatures until there was no danger of its overcoming them. The most obvious result of that was their utter fearlessness of the dark; but sometimes she wondered if she had stopped too soon, and left room for only one soul to enter the two bodies.

They seemed sturdy enough, and they certainly were not alike in character. Helios was the boisterous one, quick-tempered and head-strong. Selene was quieter but also more skilled in getting her way. Where her brother would batter against an obstacle until he reduced it to rubble or himself to tears, she puzzled out ways to evade it or to persuade it to shift of itself. Together they could be perilous: no nursemaid was proof against them, and the queen's guards were their devoted slaves.

They were, Dione thought, like two halves of the same creature. Selene was like her mother, dark-haired and dark-eyed, even at birth. Helios was born with but the barest hint of pale down on his head; as he grew, he grew fair, and his eyes never lost their newborn blueness. He was lighter even than Caesarion had been, who was still a fair brown child, grey-eyed as the Julii could be. Sometimes Dione wondered if the name shaped the child. The great Alexander had been a fair-haired man, and gold was the color of the sun.

Whatever alchemy had wrought the two of them, they made a handsome pair, even as newborn infants. Cleopatra saw to it that a messenger went to their father with word of their birth. She was not fool enough to think that it would bring him hastening back, but as the summer passed and the Nile flooded again, she looked for him. Foolishly, thought Dione; stupidly, for a fact.

Antony was having an ill time of it. Octavian was out of his way for a while, contending with the son of that Pompey who had been Caesar's old ally and enemy. Pompey the Great had died in Egypt, though not at Cleopatra's instigation, and his head had been Egypt's gift to Caesar when he came to Alexandria. Now Pompey the younger, who was called Sextus Pompey, ruled as a pirate king in the waters of Greece. Octavian brought to that sea-war the talents of his friend Agrippa, who had a gift most mightily rare in a Roman: he was a sea-commander, and a good one—even brilliant. He was also loyal, if not to Rome, then to Octavian.

With his chief rival occupied in clearing the seas of Sextus Pompey's pirate fleets, Antony was free to wage his war in Parthia. But that disintegrated almost as soon as it began. Antony found his troops in Syria turned against him as Dione had foreseen. Even as he dealt with them, his Roman wife rose in rebellion in Italy. He had to turn back from the eastern war, in what state of mind Dione could well imagine, only to find that Fulvia's uprising had failed and she had fled. He met her in Greece, in rage that lost nothing with the telling, then left her to follow as best she could, descending on Italy with as many of his armies as he could gather. She died before he came there, of mortification perhaps, or spite.

"Now he'll settle Italy," said Cleopatra when she heard of that, "and come back to me."

Cleopatra did not want to hear what truth Dione could speak; therefore Dione said nothing. And when word came that Antony had made peace with Octavian, still Dione kept silence, and still Cleopatra waited for her lover to come home. "Your father will come," she said to his children, now grown out of infancy, and crawling, and being a terror to the servants. "He'll bring you the treasures of kings, and give you each a senator to be your servant."

Dione did not believe that Cleopatra had become quite so fondly foolish as she seemed. Some of it surely was desperation. And some was willful blindness. When Caesar was alive she had said more than once that she feared no human rival, either woman or man; but Roma Dea was another matter. No woman, however great her powers of mind or body or magic, could stand against a goddess.

If Caesar, who yielded to no man and to few gods, was soul's slave to the goddess Rome, then what was to be expected but that Marcus Antonius too should give way before the power of his city? It seemed logical enough to Dione. But she had borne him no children. She had no reason to want him back—if anything, she was glad that he was gone, with his wine and his boisterousness and his propensity for distracting Cleopatra from matters of consequence.

* * *

Dione had seen her son Androgeos once since she came back from Tarsus, and that at a distance, passing on one side of a street while he strode past on the other. Of Timoleon she seemed to see little more. He had friends, some of whom had known him since he was small: boys and youths of respectable family who congregated in the gymnasium near Dione's house, shared lessons with a teacher of rhetoric, learned riding and hunting and even some use of weapons from a master of whom Dione had heard nothing but good. All of that seemed sufficient to occupy even a mind as restless as Timoleon's. He was never home; he was always out with this boy or that, or at lessons, or in the gymnasium learning, as he put it, to be a man.

Dione could not escape the implication. Since she had failed to provide him with adequate education in the art of being a male, he must find it for himself—and never mind whose purse paid for the rhetorician, the riding master, the horse and its caparisons and a groom to go with it, and all the rest of the necessities of his station.

At least, Dione thought as she contemplated a long evening alone with the cat and a new copy of Heraclitus, she knew that her son was being brought up properly as a young man of Alexandria. It did not make the evening less empty or the book less flat. She would even have welcomed the edge that always seemed to be on Timoleon's tongue of late.

The little cat kneaded and flattened itself a bed in her lap. Fortunate beast. It had weaned its kittens some time since. As was only fitting, the red-gold he-cat had gone to Alexander Helios and the black-and-silver she-cat to Cleopatra Selene. As young as the children were, they seemed to know that they were gifted with cats; more than once Dione had found all four in a heap, with the cats purring and the babies smiling as they slept.

The kittens' mother had returned to its queenly solitude and its protection of Dione. Dione stroked the sun-and-shadow fur and sighed. "If only it were that easy with children," she said.

Perhaps tomorrow she would visit the temple. The priestesses of Isis would welcome their sister and their pupil; they would be glad to have her back again, however briefly.

Dione sighed once more. The room was very quiet. The lamps barely flickered, the air was so still.

Faintly she heard voices. The servants were closing up for the night, early though it was. The kitchen fire would be banked, a supper laid aside for Timoleon if he should come back wanting it, though he had sought and obtained permission to take dinner with one of his friends. He would not be back unduly late, Dione expected. He was still a child, after all, manly though he tried to be.

The voices grew louder. She frowned slightly. Her servants had what some considered unseemly freedom to speak as they pleased in her house, but she did not encourage shouting or quarreling.

Just as she was about to rise and investigate the now very distinct clamor, the door opened with no more warning than a sudden cessation of the voices. Senmut stumbled in backwards, expostulating. A much taller and much burlier figure thrust him aside and dropped to one knee in front of Dione.

"Marsyas," she said. "What in the world—"

"Lady," he said, "if you please, and if this idiot will stop blathering, will you come with me?"

This was quite out of the ordinary, and thoroughly out of bounds. A lady's litter-bearer did not burst in on her while she sat alone. Senmut was saying so, at great length and with much embroidery, till a hand clapped over his mouth. The hand was as dark as mother Night; Hebe glared him into silence. Something in the way she looked at Marsyas told Dione much that she did not, at the moment, see any need to know.

"Lady, please," Marsyas said. "I'd never crash in on you like this if I hadn't reason."

True enough, Dione conceded. He never had before. "What is it?" she asked him. "Has someone been trying to rob the hayloft?"

He flushed under the deep bronze of his skin. "We weren't in the hayloft, lady. We were in the city, taking a bit of the air. You did give us leave, lady. Don't you remember?"

She did, at that, but she did not remember their asking to go together. The maid had begged a bit of silver with signs that said she wanted something pretty to wear, and the litter-bearer had asked for an evening's liberty to visit a friend who was a servant in another house. Hebe was indeed wearing a new gown of a particularly brilliant shade of saffron bordered with blue, which must have cost most of the silver piece.

"What is it, then?" Dione asked them both.

They glanced at one another over Senmut's head. Neither, suddenly, wore any expression at all. "It's your son," Marsyas said at last, dragging out the words one by one. "Timoleon."

Dione was moving before she had time to think. "What? Is he ill? Hurt? Dying? Dead?"

"Nothing that bad," said Marsyas quickly. "But, lady, I think you should come."

He would not say any more, and Hebe was tugging at Dione's arm. Dione snatched a shawl that was near to hand and wrapped it hastily about her, regardless of Senmut's renewed sputtering, and ran after her maid and her manservant.

It was not yet dark. The sky was full of light, with stars faint in it; the western horizon was the color of blood. Marsyas had a torch, which he lit from the one set at the gate to welcome Timoleon home. Visions of him broken, bleeding, dying, haunted Dione, for all Marsyas' assurances that she need fear no such thing. What could be worse than that, that her litter-bearer should drag her from her house in the gathering night and lead her into the city? She did not give more than a moment's thought to the fact that this could be a trap. Enemies, if she had any, would have found a better way to snare her than through two of her more loyal servants.

They moved rapidly though the streets were still crowded. Dione, preoccupied with keeping up with Marsyas and being pushed along by Hebe, realized only slowly that they were going toward the harbor and not toward either the gymnasium or the house in which Timoleon was supposed to be dining. The ways were darker here, dingier, redolent of fish and stale piss.

Dione had time in plenty to wonder what her servants were leading her to. They refused to tell her, only dragged her onward. Had Timoleon signed on a ship as a sailor, then? He had said nothing of such a thing since Antony left Alexandria; but children, as she knew too well, could go quiet, dangerously so, if their wants and their mother's failed to coincide.

She had heard of dockside taverns. She had even known to expect the reek and the crowded, sweating bodies, and the air that seemed thick enough to drink. Much of the stink here was not beer but sour wine. That, she knew, not knowing how, marked a Greek tavern rather than an Egyptian.

She froze just inside the door, all her senses appalled. The light of smoky lamps was wan in the pervading gloom. Figures in it seemed to writhe, howling, like spirits in the jaws of the Eater of Souls. They were talking, laughing, swilling, singing. Even, on a table near the back, copulating, a tangle of hairy limbs and smooth: sleek young body and wiry older one. The smooth one was a boy—not, thank all the gods, Timoleon. His face was no older in years but far more ancient in weariness, waiting with blank patience for the other to be done.

Marsyas and Hebe both pulled Dione forward, nearly toppling her. The litter-bearer's strong arms caught her and lifted her. She was only glad that she need not set foot on that floor; she did not want to know what stained it, or how long it had been since anyone swept or scoured any part of it.

Suddenly she was in fetid darkness. It was quieter here: a stairway going up, no light—Marsyas had rid himself of the torch somewhere, probably in the street—and a reek less of wine and mansweat than of cats. It felt almost clean after the midden below. Marsyas set her gently down; she did not need to be told to climb the stair, groping from step to step, with Marsyas a breathing bulk behind and Hebe just ahead, within hand's reach.

Hebe halted. A latch rattled. She slid it aside, and opened a door slowly. Light stabbed Dione's eyes.

It was dim enough, but after the dark it was blinding. The room it illuminated was as large as the one below, but rather different. The scent here was of a better wine, with a suggestion of honey, and an almost cloying perfume of flowers. There were fewer people, or seemed to be, and they made less noise. Dione could hear music, aulos and drum, and the plucked notes of a lyre.

As her sight cleared, she saw that it seemed to be a banqueting hall with an array of couches and low tables. Its walls were painted with images that made her blush and look away. Scenes like those on the walls were enacted on many of the couches, man and woman sometimes, more often man and boy.

Her heart was clenched tight. No use to deny what kind of place this was. It served a more elegant clientele than the cesspit beneath it, but in its way it was worse.

She did not want to search the faces, but she had no power to forbear. One of the boys was familiar; she had seen him with Timoleon. Likewise the one on the couch next to his. They were well gone in wine, giggling as their partners fondled them.

There was a dancer, too; Dione had taken no notice of him in her near-panicked search through the couches. But none of the boys on the couches was her son. The dancer was utterly shameless, abandoned in wine or worse, brown supple body oiled to a sheen, black curls crowned with a garland, whirling from light to shadow and back to light again. One of the revelers grabbed at him. He eeled away laughing, falling into the lap of a man endowed like a bull.

His laughter caught in a gasp; the man stopped the rest of it with a kiss.

Dione did not even remember coming into the room. Someone caught the trailing end of her shawl and whirled her free of it. Someone else lunged and caught her gown; it tore, baring a breast. She barely paused to flatten him. Neatly, with no effort that she could afterward recall, she plucked her son from the bull-man's embrace.

Timoleon was blind drunk, but not too blind to know his mother. He looked briefly shocked; then the giggling overwhelmed him again. "Pretty mama. Pretty, pretty, pretty mama."

She looked about. The bull-man had fallen back to his first companion, a woman with a great quantity of brass-bright hair on her head and curly black bush between her legs. No one else was paying any attention to her, except to leer and make suggestions as to what she should do with her lovely young prize.

She snatched a cloak from the nearest couch. The three on the couch were too busy to object. She flung it about Timoleon, who slumped against her still giggling, nuzzling her breast till she slapped him to make him stop.

When had he grown, that she had not noticed? He was half a head taller than she, leggy as a yearling colt, and utterly helpless. As she braced herself to knock him down and drag him, Marsyas appeared at too long last and slung the boy over his shoulder.

Timoleon's giggling stopped somewhere in the street. So did Marsyas, abruptly, all but throwing him down. He retched into the gutter while the others waited, the servants making no effort to help him, and Dione unable to try. She was angry, maybe. Or maybe only numb.

When he stopped vomiting up his night's worth of wine, and probably every meal since breakfast as well, Marsyas heaved him up again, quiet this time, and carried him onward.

It was a green-pale, shivering, thoroughly cowed child who faced his mother in the sanctuary of her own house. She had had him bathed; he was dressed decently in a linen tunic, his hair combed, the garland taken away and burned. She sat in the chair she favored, in the room where she liked to read in the evenings, and regarded him with a still, cold stare.

"Well?" she said at last, when he showed no sign of wanting to begin.

If he had tried tears, she would have done something unforgivable:

beaten him, railed at him, sent him to his father. His eyes were swimming, to be sure, but he kept the flood in check. "I'm sorry, mama."

"Sorry doesn't do it," she said, as cold as ever. "How often have you gone there?"

"Only the once, mama. Truly."

She considered that. He looked as if he spoke honestly. "Who took you there?"

"It was a dare," he said. He bit his lip. It was bleeding from being chewed on, no doubt to keep him from bursting into tears. "Andronikos goes there sometimes. He has a friend—a man, he calls him uncle but he's not really, he comes to the gymnasium and admires the boys—he told Andronikos he should bring a friend or two the next time. Meleager was going. He wanted to see what it was like. I said I knew, it couldn't be any different from Lord Antony's parties. So they both dared me to come and see."

"You lied to me," said Dione. "You told me that you were dining at Meleager's house."

"I didn't either!" he cried, stung. "I asked if I could go to dinner with Meleager. You said I could. You didn't ask *where.*"

Dione's head was throbbing. She lowered it carefully into her hand. "Oh, goddess," she said. "Is this my payment for being so vexed with the queen?"

"I wasn't going to do anything," Timoleon said. "Really, mama. They gave me wine. I had to drink it. I couldn't be impolite, could I? They kept giving me more. I was hot, so I took my clothes off. Nobody else was wearing any, either. They kept wanting me to do things, so I thought, if I got up and danced, they'd leave me alone. Am I beautiful, mama? Or were they just trying to get me to kiss them?"

Dione looked at him. He blanced under her stare, and fell silent. "Don't play the child with me," she said. "You knew very well what you were doing. I can believe you danced to get their hands off you—I'd have done the same thing. But you liked it, didn't you? You wanted them to look, if not to touch."

He jerked as if she had struck him. "Mama!"

But this was no time for mercy, however her heart yearned to gather him in, stroke him, comfort him as if he had been no older than Helios or Selene. "You're not a child now, Timoleon. You're a boy, almost a young man. Were you curious to see what it is that Andronikos does with his uncle who is not an uncle?"

"I know what he does," said Timoleon. "He told me."

"And still you went?"

He lowered his head, and his voice with it. "I wanted to see."

She nodded slowly. "And did you?"

"Yes, mama." It was hardly more than a whisper.

"I don't think," she said, "that I'm going to whip you. That would be too easy a punishment. I might insist that you go back there and watch everything and consider whether you want to live as those people live. Wasn't that why you went to begin with?"

That was real panic that made his eyes roll white. "No! I don't want to go back there!"

"All the more reason to make you," she said.

He flung himself into her lap. "No, mama! No!"

"There," she said. "Stop it. What's so terrible about it? It's only a den of rutting beasts."

"That's why," he said, coherently enough in the circumstances. "Please, mama. I'll be good. I won't do it again. Goddess' honor."

"Yes, but what else will you do?"

He raised stricken eyes to her face. She sighed. She did not know whether she wanted to weep or laugh. "Oh, child. I was so afraid for you, and then so furious—I could have killed you. How Marsyas even knew where you were—"

"He saw me in the square of the ships," said Timoleon, half in tears himself. "I saw him. I yelled at him, and he went away. I never thought he'd go straight to you."

Dione stroked his damp curls. "Yes," she said, thinking aloud. "Yes, that's what I'll do. You need someone strong enough to keep you in hand, and fast enough to keep up with you. Marsyas will do very well."

He blinked. A tear escaped a corner of his eye and ran down his cheek, but his mind plainly was not on it. "Marsyas? You're giving me Marsyas?"

"I'm giving you to him," she said, "with my permission to take a strap to you if you seem to need it."

"But I like Marsyas," said Timoleon. And caught himself. He would not be wanting to name someone he liked less, or not at all. Such, thought Dione, as Senmut, or dour Darayavaush who tended the stable and the garden.

None of them was as strong as Marsyas, or as quick-witted. Dione took Timoleon's face in her hands. He did not pull free as he had taken to doing of late, even when she set a kiss between his eyes. "Go to bed, child. I can wait till morning to flay your hide."

He did not smile, no more than she. "I am sorry, mama," he said.

"I'm sure you are," said Dione. She even believed him.

SEVENTEEN

Cleopatra had a man in Antony's camp, an Egyptian astrologer and diviner who had no gift for magic but much for observation, and a mind that forgot nothing it saw or heard. It was through him that she had heard of the troubles in Syria, Fulvia's revolt and eventual death, and Antony's descent on Italy. In between, by swift courier, he sent lesser news, gossip, even messages from Antony.

Cleopatra hoarded those like the rarities they were. She had had a letter from him after he left, a dance of formal phrases such as one head of state sends to another in gratitude for hospitality. Through her servant she had messages that meant something. Dione heard some of them. Antony was well, one said, but missing his lady's warmth of nights. Or he had had a fever but was recovered, she was not to worry, he was as tough as old leather. Or there had been an encounter with some prince or other, the man had been a perfect fool, his lady should have been there to beat some sense into his head.

There was once even a message for Dione. It was not from Lucius Servilius, not that the messenger knew, but it bade her know that her son's donkey was still in Tarsus and living the life of a king, and some of the citizenry had decided that it was a god, or a god's mount at least, and brought it offerings of fresh grass and flowers. Dione had to pause to remember that one of Timoleon's many adventures. She laughed when she remembered, laughter grown too infrequent of late; her sides hurt afterwards, but she felt better than she had in long days.

Not more than a half-month after that, Dione was attending the queen at one of her philosophical gatherings. It was natural philosophy this time, with learned disquisitions on the mating habits of birds, the climatic variations of the Antipodes, and, just as the courier was ushered in, the sources and origins of the Nile. Since no two philosophers agreed on that particular question, it was quite as boisterous as one of Antony's dinner-parties, and perhaps a shade less decorous.

Cleopatra had been enjoying the fray, taking part in it with the enthusiasm of a philosopher born. She took note of the messenger's arrival: a flicker of the eyes, an infinitesimal pause in the spate of her discourse. Only couriers from Antony's camp would come in this way, unannounced, unprevented by her guards or her chamberlains. She always went on with whatever she had been doing, but heard the messages as soon as she could.

Dione, less engrossed than she, noticed that the man looked pale. He must be ill, she thought. She did not allow herself to admit the possibility of bad news. If Antony had died or was gravely sick, Cleopatra would know. There was that much binding between them, that much awareness of one another's bodies, even at an ocean's remove.

It seemed an unconscionable while before Cleopatra wound to a close and eased her learned guests into the hands of the chamberlain who was to see them fed and pampered as they pleased. They left with alacrity. Scholars, Dione had observed often before, were remarkably fond of their victuals. One or two, more absorbed or more ascetic than the usual run of their kind, seemed inclined to linger, but the queen smiled them out.

The messenger had had time to compose himself, but he was still white around the eyes. Cleopatra, who was as subtle as a serpent, could be devastatingly direct when she wanted to be. She fixed the man with a clear, hard stare. "What is it? Has he lost a war? Sunk a fleet? Given up his triumvirate and retired to a philosopher's villa?"

The man swallowed visibly. "No, majesty. Nothing like that at all. If anything, he's won a war and gained an empire."

"So? Is that ill enough news to set you quaking when I look at you?"

This was a brave man when all was considered. He had come here, after all, with whatever news he was carrying, knowing perfectly well that the queen could be murderous when she was crossed. He said, "It's good news if you ask Rome, majesty. He's met Octavian at Brundisium; they've made their peace and divided their empire again, and Antony's got the lion's share. He's as close to being king of Rome as he can be while Caesar's nephew is alive to get in the way."

Cleopatra's eyes glittered. "And?"

"Well," said the messenger, faltering as he came to the point. "He didn't get his treaty for nothing. He had to give something to Octavian."

Cleopatra waited. She might have seemed to be at ease, but her hands on the arms of her chair were stiff, the knuckles white.

"Or rather," the messenger said, stumbling on, "Octavian gave something to Antony. They've sealed the peace with a living token. Octavian's sister—Octavia—she's the pledge and the promise. Antony's married, majesty. He's taken Octavia to wife, and all's amity between the masters of Rome."

Cleopatra did not say anything. Her expression did not change. Her breath did not quicken; her hands did not even twitch.

The messenger, who knew her, but not well, relaxed perceptibly. "It was a bit complicated," he said. "She was a new widow, with three children—no doubt that she's able to give a man heirs—and she couldn't marry, not legally, for months yet. But the Senate gave her a dispensation, and they married just as soon as it came. She's a pretty thing. Sweet. Doesn't crimp her hair or paint her cheeks, carries herself as modest as a maid, never says anything but 'Yes, my lord' and 'No, my lord' and 'Whatever my lord desires.' "

Cleopatra had moved before Dione knew she was going to. Her face was still set, still expressionless, like a white mask, artfully painted under its elaborately crimped coiffure. She laid the man flat in midbabble, a blow that would not have shamed Antony himself, who claimed the strength of Heracles.

Even half knocked out of his wits, the messenger did not seem to understand what danger he was in. Or maybe he did, and it held him frozen, helpless, with the queen stooping over him. Dione did not doubt for a moment that Cleopatra would kill him.

As small as she was, Dione was strong enough, just, to thrust the man away from the queen. "Go," she commanded him. "Now!"

He took so long that she was ready to give him up, or to offer herself as the sacrifice. Then, just as Cleopatra recovered from the shock of Dione's insolence, he shrieked like a dying rabbit and bolted.

Dione was left to face the storm alone. There were servants, or had been, but they had taken one look at the queen's face and fled. Dione was aware, dimly, of white faces and goggling eyes in doorways, behind pillars, even in one of the windows.

None was of the least use. Cleopatra in a blood-red rage was mercifully rare. The last time, she had sworn to have her sister Arsinoe's head on a salver. She had not got it then, since Arsinoe had prudently fled to Ephesus. She had settled for destroying a roomful of priceless crockery, some of it as old as the Pyramids at Giza—and waiting until she could find someone to capture and kill her sister.

Dione had been witness to that, too, but had been able to get out of the way before Cleopatra noticed her presence. Now she had no such escape.

Just so must a dove feel when the hawk stoops—just so, the mouse as the cobra strikes. It was long yards to any haven, door or window or portico. The queen's chair would not shield her for more than a moment.

Cleopatra's fixed, terrible stare softened infinitesimally. "There, there, dear friend. You look horrified. Am I that close to a madwoman?"

"You know better than I," said Dione, a little faintly, but clear enough. "If you're going to throw things, would you be so kind as to throw pillows or pearls, or something equally unlikely to shatter?"

Cleopatra laughed. It was almost a natural sound. "I'll consider it. You had better go. I don't know if I can keep myself from throwing the pillows at your head."

Dione wavered. But there was nothing she could do—nothing but be a target. She told herself that Cleopatra needed to be alone, to run through her rage in solitude. Then she could be reasonable. Then she would be fit to stand among humans again.

The cobra-glitter was back in the queen's eyes. Dione ducked her head and fled.

She did not flee far. Pure common sense would have sent her home to sanctuary, but she could not be that reasonable. Some delusion that the queen might need her, combined with a thoroughly inexcusable curiosity, kept her in the palace.

The sound of shattering crockery never came. Nor did the thump of hurled cushions. It was deadly silent in the queen's chambers. No one was bold enough to inquire as to what Cleopatra was doing, though the maids babbled of knives and poisons and the queen lying dead on the floor. Dione went cold at that, but not as cold as if it had been a true seeing. Her own death was the last thing Cleopatra wanted now. Antony, however, or his new Roman wife . . .

That thought fed in the back of Dione's mind, while the front of it grew progressively more irritated. She did not know which was worse, the chatter of servants or the natter of courtiers. The servants at least kept their minds on the queen. The courtiers, as light-minded as ever, wandered off almost at once into old gossip, new scandals, and the latest fashion in eyepaint.

Idiots, every one of them. She was sorely tempted to afflict them with a demon or a plague of boils, simply to teach them sense.

That she thought such a thing at all was proof of her dismay. Magic was never anything that she took lightly. It belonged to the gods; it was a gift, and precious, and not to be squandered on trifles.

The hours stretched long. The sun sank. There was a storm brewing, Dione thought, and not only in the queen's chambers. The air had that feeling, uneasy, touched with sparks. It tasted of thunder.

If she was to go home before it broke, she should leave soon. But she lingered. As she hung about one of the hallways, avoiding a cluster of ladies who disagreed shrilly on the proper way to wield a crimping iron, a supple body appeared from nowhere to press against her leg. She looked down into the green-gold eyes of Bastet's cat. Both of the cat's kittens were with her, the sun-gold male already half again as large as his mother, the silvery female smaller but slender and long-legged like a temple cat. The three of them together wove intricate patterns about Dione's ankles.

There was meaning in those patterns. At first Dione refused to heed it, reading it as hunger, for food or for attention, or as cat-inscrutability. But the cats were tenacious. The male sang a song that wavered from soprano to tenor and back, comical if it had not been so urgent. He raised himself nearly to her waist, stretching, flexing claws. His eyes were bright gold, like coins. His sister's were clear green; their mother's were both together, fixing Dione with their wise inhuman stare.

She had power to resist them. Cats were not creatures of force. They seduced; they persuaded. They also persisted, and three of them together were enough to knock Dione over if she tried to go any way but one. That, she was unsurprised to note, was toward the queen's chambers.

"Very well," she said to them. "If she kills me, I'll haunt you till you die, and then I'll hound you through the Netherworld."

They were not alarmed by human threats, however dire. The male led; the females pressed close behind, lest she try to escape.

It was a strange cat-stalk through the queen's chambers, sometimes in the long light of sunset, sometimes in the dimness of lamps. Usually there were people everywhere, servants, courtiers, scholars, petitioners let in out of the queen's magnanimity. Now there was no one. They had all retreated from the thunder-reek of the queen's wrath, or hidden till it should pass.

They were wise. Dione followed her sharp-clawed guides to a part of the queen's wing that was not often used. It was old as things went in Alexandria—a mere work of yesterday for the rest of Egypt. It breathed dust and dimness and a scent of age and forgetfulness, although it was kept scrupulously clean, aired and dusted with care lest the queen should wish to go there. What it was, Dione thought, was disuse. No one lived here; no one remembered it unless, as now, there was reason.

Dione had been down this passage before, but not in long years. The old king had been alive then, and his daughter a headstrong child with a restless, searching intelligence. It was Cleopatra who had led her friend, telling her tales of the second Ptolemy, who had been a mage as all the Ptolemies were, but his magics had been deeper than some and stranger than most. The books reckoned him a great king. "And so he was," Cleopatra had said, "but he never stopped asking questions, even when the answers shed more dark than light."

Dione thought of that as she crossed a long ill-lit hall. A lamp was lit at its door and another at its end, but the way between was dark. She could not hear anything but the hiss of her breath and the pounding of blood in her ears, and the whisper of sandal on marble. The cats were silent. The room was not so large, merely long, more corridor than proper chamber, and yet as she walked she felt that it stretched to infinity all about her.

Her skin prickled. The air was humming with magic, faint yet distinct, like a hive of bees heard from across a meadow. The scent of thunder was strong here. It spoke to Dione of a queen's anger, and the wrath of a goddess.

Instinct more than will raised the wards about her, the protections that she had learned when first her magic grew strong enough to be both a danger and a lure. There were things on the edge of her vision, stirrings, shifts in the shadow, a glitter of eyes. Night's children were always hungry for light, and for the blood of living creatures. Magic called them, for magic promised blood to feed on, and light, even if it were but the pallid glow of a sorcerer's lamp.

Even her guardian shadow had come. He paced behind her, taller than men were in Egypt, jackal-headed, lambent-eyed. Being god and not mere shade, he too fed on blood, but he was its master. Dione felt his solidity, although he drew no breath, nor did his feet make a sound as he trod the floor. If she touched him, she knew she would touch substance, warm like flesh, but strange.

With each step she took, she walked a little farther out of the world men knew. The powers that Cleopatra called on were strong; simple matter yielded to them, and spirit grew weak. Even warded by her own magics and Bastet's cats and the shade of Anubis in the Two Lands, Dione felt the force of blind will buffeting her. It did not care who she was or what she intended. It merely saw her strength and set itself to conquer it.

Even in her sorcery Cleopatra was royal, and accepted no rival. And that was very well, Dione thought, if she used her power as it should be used, and not as a child's fit of pique.

In that bracing mood, she reached the end of the hall at last and set hand to the door. The lock on it was nothing of earth. Dione broke it with a word. That was a challenge, and she knew it; she braced for a storm of fire.

But none came. The room beyond was much as she remembered it, a sorcerer's cabinet full of oddities, some wonderful, some horrible, some merely peculiar. The stuffed crocodile hung still from the ceiling. The owl was a little more motheaten than it had been, the homunculus a shade more wizened in its jar. The mummies of cats and birds and one lone jackal watched blindly from their places on the shelves that lined the walls.

Cleopatra had moved the great carved table, and how she had done that except with magic, Dione could not imagine: it was heavier than any lone woman could shift. Yet she had thrust it toward the wall and bared what it hid: a Great Circle carved and inlaid in the floor. The inlay gleamed in light that came from everywhere and nowhere, sorcerer's light, coldly brilliant. Gold, silver, copper, bronze; pearl, too, that the queen so loved, and a glitter of jewels shaping the signs of the elements.

How like a Ptolemy, when chalk on swept tile would do as well. There was a gate left in it, of course, with a gilded rod to close it, which Cleopatra held in her hand.

She did not look mad or particularly distraught. No wild witch's locks; no gown of rags and tatters. She had put off her court dress for a simple white robe without seam or binding, washed her face clean of paint, and taken her hair out of its elaborate curls and combed it till it was nearly straight. Her feet were bare, her hands and neck clean of jewels. She was like a warrior stripped for battle.

Even so had Dione wrought when the need was on her, even to the circle and the wards at the earth's four corners. It was not something that she did often. Still less in a cold fire of rage, when what she judged right and proper might prove, in a calmer hour, to be grievous folly.

Such conjuring could work either good or ill. Which this was, Dione had no need to guess. The lamps lit at the guardian points were the color of old blood. There was blood in the basin at the circle's center, and blood on the rod with which Cleopatra advanced to seal the gate. Dione's first, irrational fear—that a servant had died for the queen's rage—shrank and fled as she perceived the shape that lay beside the basin. It was a young goat, its coat like black silk, its slotted amber eyes open wide in death.

"Cleopatra," said Dione. She did not speak loudly, and yet the name rang in the silence, breeding a swarm of echoes.

The queen paused.

"Cleopatra," Dione said again. "What are you doing?"

"Go," said Cleopatra in a cold still voice, with no more heart in it than if she had been one of the crowding shades. "I never summoned you. Go, or I cast you out."

"I think not," said Dione. She did not reckon it any greater boldness to cross the queen than to walk in on her conjuring; if she paid for the one, then let her pay for it all. "This isn't the way to confront news you didn't want or expect to hear."

"What other way can there be?" Cleopatra demanded. She had stopped, to Dione's carefully hidden relief, nor did she move to finish the circle.

"You could wait," Dione said, "and see what happens next."

"I waited," said Cleopatra. "And now you see my recompense. Forgotten like last week's fashion, reckoned no more than a dalliance while he disported himself in the east. The moment he came to Rome, Rome devoured him. That creature ate his soul."

"Nonsense," said Dione more strongly than she felt. She understood too well what Cleopatra was saying—what she meant to do with this circle and this blood and this weaving of magics. "What will you summon? Triune Hecate? The Erinyes? The Egyptians' own Eater of Souls? Or all of them? And can you master them, my lady of the Two Lands? They're no commonplace daimons or windy ghosts. Blood alone can't pay their price; a single circle, however prettily drawn, can't hold them unless it amuses them to be held. They'll serve you, true enough, but then they'll bid you serve them."

"How wise you are," said Cleopatra. "How prudent. How perfectly predictable. But what has wisdom won me, or prudence gained?"

"What will this gain you?" Dione shot back. "Furies hounding your rival, Eater of Souls feeding on her liver—that's a pretty picture for a child's tantrum. And I suppose you'll set the dogs on Antony, too, since he was so weak as to yield to her. What then? Octavian has Rome all to himself. Can you coax him into your bed as you coaxed the rest?"

"That," said Cleopatra, "I won't stoop to. What's to stop me from setting the Erinyes on him as well as on his sister?"

"Nothing," said Dione. "Except possibly a small concern for what will happen after that."

"Chaos," Cleopatra said. "Which I can use."

Dione shook her head. She should have known that she could not get the better of Cleopatra in an argument. And such an argument, she on the outside of a Great Circle, Cleopatra on the inside, with a bloody wand in her hand.

The cats were stalking the wand. It wove slightly as Cleopatra spoke, clenched in her fingers. She seemed not to be aware of it. Dione tried to be similarly oblivious. She had considered and discarded leaping to seize the thing. It was dangerous to break even an unfinished circle, more so if the breaker were a mage. The consequences could be worse than if she left the queen alone to work the rest of her magic: setting free powers that had been bound here when the circle was made, laying herself open to the shadows that circled, hungry for blood.

Cats, however, were goddess-born. Magic could not master them. What they could do here, Dione did not know, but she trusted that it would be of use.

She did what she could to help them. "Very well. You don't care what price you pay for your fit of temper. You'll destroy them all with a stroke, leave Rome in turmoil, and maybe—maybe—save Egypt from its yoke. What will you tell Antony's children when they wonder why they lack a father? Will you tell them that you set the Furies on him, and fed his soul to the Eater in the Netherworld? What will they think of you then?"

"A queen does as a queen must," said Cleopatra, no more moved by that than by anything else Dione had said.

"Indeed," said Dione. "And having no soul since it was eaten, he'll not haunt you afterwards. Except maybe in dreams."

"I can make myself forget him," Cleopatra said, "as he has forgotten me."

"Which is not at all," said Dione. "He was married to a Roman woman when you lay with him in Tarsus. Why should it matter that it's a different woman he's married to now, as long as he comes back to you?"

"He won't come back," Cleopatra said, flat and hard. "Fulvia was his wife before he ever lay in my bed. Octavia he took in spite of me. I'll give her spite, and him too, and the worm who wheedled him into it."

"Oh, it is spite," said Dione. "I have no doubt of that."

Cleopatra's eyes were fixed on her. The red-golden he-cat was inside of her circle, oozing on his belly toward the woman and the wand. She seemed not to be aware of him. His sister and his mother had taken station by the circle's gate. They sat like guardian images.

Dione was careful how she breathed, and where she directed her glance. "This demeans you, Cleopatra. Will you enslave yourself to the nether goddesses for a simple fit of jealousy?"

"I am queen and goddess. I am Isis on earth. He was Osiris and Dionysus—and he betrayed me. Gods have destroyed gods for less than this."

"Gods are notoriously petty," Dione said, unswayed by either the grandeur or the simplicity of the queen's utterance. She had gone beyond fear when she entered the queen's chambers. "Goddess you may be, and at the moment you do look like Hera in the face of another of Zeus' infidelities. But you don't know that Antony has even forgotten you. It was a coup, you must admit, to take the woman and gain Rome with her. She's as tedious as her brother, as I remember, but she hasn't his intelligence, or his conviction that he deserves to rule an empire. I'll wager my best silk gown that she bored Antony to tears inside of a week."

"That long?" Cleopatra seemed startled at her own flash of humor; she covered it with a thunderous scowl. "He promised me eternal fidelity. He broke his word. What kind of fool would I be if I let him escape unscathed?"

"He'll pay high enough when he comes back," said Dione.

"No," said Cleopatra. And might have said more, but the sun-cat, positioning himself at last, leaped for the kill. She recoiled from the movement. The wand jerked; he batted it out of her hand.

She sprang for it. He sank claws in her arm. She gasped and flung him away.

The circle of power shattered like glass. Like glass, it fell in glittering shards, shards that cut to the bone.

Dione, warded, still swayed with the force of that breaking. Cleopatra fell. Heedless of splintered magic, and even of the cat who had broken it, sprawled boneless where the circle's edge had been, Dione sprang toward the queen.

She lay white and still, but she breathed: she drew in a breath as Dione dropped beside her, and coughed, and struggled as one struggles in sleep. Dione caught a thrashing hand and held it till it stilled.

The she-cats were licking the he-cat's ears. He stirred as Cleopatra had, but to better effect: stumbling to his feet, shaking his head, licking a paw with fierce concentration. His mother bit his neck gently, a kiss of sorts, as cats would reckon it. He flicked his tail at her and came, a little unsteady still, to sniff at Cleopatra's foot.

"Thou," said Dione in old Egyptian, which was the language she prayed in, "shalt have a dinner of fish, aye, a whole fish to thyself, O breaker of worlds."

"Shall he indeed?" said Cleopatra. Her voice was faint and a little slurred, but its edge was nigh as keen as ever. "I'll dine on his liver first."

"If you can catch him," said Dione, veiling her relief in sharpness. "If I'll let you. What he did was as well done as any cat has ever thought of. Take revenge on Antony in such ways as queen and woman may—I'll even help you. But leave magic out of it. It costs too much."

"Oh, you dare . . ." Cleopatra let her voice die. Dione thought she had fainted again, but she had only closed her eyes to keep her temper from erupting any further. After a while she said, "Someday you'll go too far."

"But not today," said Dione with more relief than she would ever confess. "Now, can you get up? The circle's broken and your spell's all gone to naught, but you've roused half the ghosts in Egypt. We'll be lucky to lay them all before they scatter to plague the city."

Cleopatra looked ready to snap at Dione, but she could see as well as Dione could. All the nooks and corners of that room were murmurous with voices, and every shadow aflutter with wings as of birds, but birds human-headed, spirits of the dead come flocking round the ruin of the spell. There were darker things beyond them, things that even a mage could not quite see.

"Only a cat," said Cleopatra, "could wreak such havoc with a safe and tidy working." She caught Dione's eye and glared. "Safe, yes, as long as I worked the spell, and as tidy as I could make it. Now look at it. We'll be at it till dawn."

"Then we'd best be about it, hadn't we?" said Dione with brisk practicality.

EIGHTEEN

They laid ghosts and bound spirits until the sun rose. Even at that, some few escaped; for months and even years after, Dione heard of a house vexed with a spirit of mischief, or a garden to which no bird would come, or a flitting of shadows through certain quarters of the city.

It was worth the price, she thought on that first morning, as exhausted as she was, with her magic drained to the dregs and her eyes as dry as sand. Cleopatra had come to herself. She would never admit that Dione had had the right of it, but she did not order Dione out of her sight; she helped with the binding, and did not try to compel the spirits to serve her against her rival in Rome. That was as close to concession of fault as she would ever come. Dione was content with it.

Having decided to be sensible and wait and leave Antony to find his own way back to her, Cleopatra settled into a kind of fiercely active patience. She ruled her kingdom. She raised her children. She worshipped her gods, studied her philosophy, honed her magic—though she did not again try to summon the gods below. She took no lovers, though a lesser woman might have done so, matched infidelity with infidelity. Cleopatra was not made so.

Months stretched into years. Selene and Helios grew into handsome children, the dark and the light, the quiet and the boisterous. Their brother Caesarion left the last of infancy and entered the flower of his boyhood as the Greeks would say. Timoleon's voice broke; he lost none of his beauty with his childhood, which cost Dione more worry than she would admit to anyone, even the queen.

There was plenty to do without the distraction of men and their importunities. Cleopatra had determined long ago to make Egypt the richest kingdom in the world. She went about it with a singleminded ferocity, oversaw everything, it seemed, from the least to the greatest, from the laborer's allotment of bread and beer to the prince's quota of taxes.

She waged politics as she might. Herod of Judea, exile and would-be king, came to her for aid against the Parthians who had conquered his country. She sent him to Rome as a gift to Antony: not without irony, for Herod was a handsome young man, a dark sleek smooth-spoken creature with a talent for saying whatever one most wished to hear. Antony, that blunt forthright man, would find Herod alarming, or at least disconcerting.

Of Antony she heard much, and though she said little, she never turned such messengers away. Now he was in Greece, trying something new in his long war against Parthia: sending generals but leaving himself behind, and winning victories as a consequence. Now he was in Brundisium meeting yet again with Octavian, and for once Antony was the victor, the strong one, and Octavian was weak, worn down with futile fighting against Sextus Pompey. Now he was in Greece again with his wife Octavia; he was calling himself Dionysus, and Octavia was his Aphrodite, his goddess and consort.

To which Cleopatra said nothing. Nothing at all.

They were all together on a day of blazing heat, the fourth summer after Antony left Alexandria. The queen had taken a small company—a mere hundred or so—in boats on the lake, where it was as cool as anywhere could be in this season. A breeze played over the water; the children and a fair number of the older folk played in it, while the boats drifted at anchor just off the sandy shore.

Dione, though tempted, lingered on the deck of the queen's boat. A canopy shaded her from the sun. Hebe wielded a fan sprinkled with water from the lake. No one was wearing any more than modesty demanded; most wore much less. Her dress was of gauze and cut in the Egyptian fashion, leaving arms and breasts all but bare.

"A Roman would find us shocking," she observed.

Cleopatra turned her head, lazy as the cat that slept beside Dione's foot. Like Dione, she had chosen to dress as an Egyptian. Nothing else was sensible in this country in summer. "Romans find everything shocking," she said. "If we had any with us, they'd be in armor, or the toga."

Dione paused to watch Timoleon challenge the queen's children to a game of water-war. Others, young and not so young, joined in it, till there were no sides to be seen, only a grand melee.

When she could stop laughing long enough to speak, she said, "I'm missing them still, in spite of everything."

Cleopatra slanted a glance at her. "Them? Or him?"

"Both," said Dione. She could say it with composure by now, after long practice.

"Antony's in Asia again," Cleopatra said.

It was not as abrupt as it seemed. Dione had been wondering if Cleopatra would mention it. It was no secret that the triumvir had left Rome for Athens soon after his wedding, and set himself up there with his Roman wife. From there he had waged his endless war against Parthia, and ruled Asia, and ignored Cleopatra. Nor was it a secret that Octavia had borne him a daughter. When that news came, Dione had braced to turn Cleopatra aside yet again from murderous magic, or from simple murder. But Cleopatra had preserved the icy calm that had been hers since Dione prevented her from calling on the gods below. "A daughter in Rome," she had said, "is not a queen or a child of the gods, but a disappointment. And I gave him a son. Let him remember that; let him ponder it. I can wait."

Dione had thought then and thought now that Antony would do well to fear that quiet more than the fits of rage that had preceded it. "Antony's been in Asia before," she pointed out. "He had a victory over the Parthians, or one of his generals did—enough to give the man a triumph in Rome. Antony didn't see you then, or send you word."

"This time," said Cleopatra, "his wife isn't with him. He sent her home. She's pregnant again, they say—well enough; and she has a pack of children to look after, what with all the breeding she's done and he's done and they've both done together. But he could have gone back with her, or kept her in Athens."

"Romans leave their wives behind when it suits them," Dione said. "They've been doing it since Aeneas left Dido in Carthage."

Cleopatra shook her head. "No. This time is different."

Dione studied her. She had never been given to fancies. Nor was foresight her gift. And yet, thought Dione, she was sure of this.

Dione had no flash of sight, no touch of the goddess' will. She was as blank to prophecy as any common woman. That annoyed her more than she liked to confess. It sharpened her voice, and made her speak more rashly than perhaps she should. "You're still hoping, aren't you? Moping and dreaming like a lovesick girl. What if he never comes back?"

"He'll come back," said Cleopatra. "Whether I'll take him is another matter."

"And why wouldn't you?" Dione demanded, contrary. "He's the god to your goddess. His wandering hasn't changed that."

"They were calling Octavia the image of Aphrodite when he ruled with her in Athens," said Cleopatra. "And maybe she was. But I am more than the image. I am the goddess on earth."

"As he is the god," Dione said. Now she could feel the thrumming in her bones, the power that spoke through her with the goddess' voice. She looked out over the lake, past the warring, laughing children, to the city dreaming in its haze of heat and sun.

"Look!" she said in another tone altogether, but with power in it still, forbidding her to keep silent. "A boat, rowing from the city. Goddess—it's flying!"

If it had had wings like a bird, it could hardly have come more quickly. The oarsmen seemed impervious to the heat. And no wonder, if they were being paid as well as Dione suspected. The man who sat upright in the stern was wearing armor—Roman armor, and a Roman face, one that Dione knew rather well. It was not Quintus Dellius the envoy, who had summoned Cleopatra to Tarsus. This was a different man, and a greater honor: not Antony's errand-runner but Antony's friend, Gaius Fonteius Capito, riding light under the weight of his noble name, and greeting the queen with a smile and a gallant bow. But the errand was the same. Antony summoned the queen of Egypt into his presence.

It was Antioch this time, not Tarsus. Otherwise, as Cleopatra observed, there was little distinction to be made. "He needs me again," she said. "So he comes begging. I'm astonished that he remembers me."

Capito shook his head and smiled. He was a handsome man, much as Antony was, but better-humored. Nothing seemed to trouble him, even the queen's cold stare and colder words. Perhaps they cooled him as he sat in his armor, with a cup of wine in his hand and the sun beating down through the canopy. "He never forgot you, majesty. Not for a moment."

"Not even between Octavia's white thighs?"

Capito did not even blush. "Oh, she's a beauty, I won't lie about that. But she's a bit on the milk-and-water side. Try cutting milk with a knife, Antony said to me once."

"He seems to have done well enough for the past three years," Cleopatra said. "Two children, she's given him now? Or three?"

"One," said Capito, "and one coming, if the gods are kind. You can't fault him for that, surely? A man will do what a man must do, and she keeps the peace between him and that brother of hers."

"Her brother could be disposed of," said Cleopatra. "So, for that matter, could she."

"Rome wouldn't allow it," Capito said. He was smiling still, but that was flat, and final. "Believe me, majesty, when I say that Antony has had you in his mind since the day he left you. Politics kept him apart, and policy dictated that he do what he did to seal his pact with Octavian, but you're the one he thinks of still. Whenever he thinks on strategy, he wonders how Cleopatra would do it. When he's at his ease, he asks us if we remember this and that about you, and wonders what you're doing, and wishes he could see his son and daughter."

"He could have seen them at any time," said Cleopatra, "simply by coming to Alexandria."

"You know he couldn't, majesty," said Capito. He shaded his eyes with his hand, peering into the dazzle of sun. "Are they here? I'm curious myself to see these wonders of the east—the sun and the moon, as you named them, and Rome thought that grand hubris, I can tell you."

"I'm sure it did," said Cleopatra. She beckoned to her maid. "Fetch the children," she said.

In due time they were fetched, damp but decently clothed, Helios in a tunic, Selene in an Egyptian gown. Her black curls and his golden ones were startling side by side, her eyes dark and his blue, but the faces—white reddened by the sun, warm brown darkened to the color almost of terracotta—were strikingly similar. Each had the same level line of brow, the same arched nose even so young, the same determined chin. They looked like Ptolemies, but they looked like Antony, too, and entirely like children who were born to be kings.

"Well," said Capito as he looked them over and they returned the favor. "Well indeed. Not much doubt as to who their parents are. You bear handsome children, majesty."

"Like a mare with breeding but no beauty," said Cleopatra, "I breed beauty in my progeny. Yes?"

Capito laughed. He was well chosen, Dione thought from her refuge of silence. Nothing that Cleopatra did or said seemed to threaten his equanimity. "I always thought you a handsome woman, majesty—and no one is wittier than you. I hope you gave them that, too. Little Antonia is as pretty as her mother, and if anything more docile."

"Poor Antonia," said Cleopatra.

"Mama," Selene said in her clear voice. "Is that a Roman?"

Capito seemed slightly startled that she could speak. Dione did not see why. The child was three years old. She had been babbling without interruption since before her second birthday. That to be sure was early, but Timoleon had been as precocious; it was by no means unheard of.

"Yes," Cleopatra said, "that is a Roman."

"Is he our father?" Helios wanted to know. He was more truculent than his sister, standing with feet braced, scowling at the stranger.

"No," Capito answered for Cleopatra, "young sir, I'm not. Your father is in Antioch, waiting for you to come to him."

"I don't know him," Helios said. "He should come to me. He is only a Roman. I am a prince."

Dione leveled a frown at him. Cleopatra told him to hush. Capito was much amused. "But you are half Roman, and he rules the Romans. You should come to him."

"We could meet in the middle," Selene said. "I'd like to see my father. He's a god, you know. He makes the vine-leaves grow."

"So he does," said Capito. And to Cleopatra: "So they did get your wit, and your pride, too. Antony will be delighted. He's never had much patience with docility—in children or in anyone else."

"But he seems to like it in a wife." Cleopatra stretched out her arms. Selene came to her, and her brother after, leaning one on either side of her, eyeing the Roman warily still. Selene seemed inclined to trust him, but her brother would need better proof than a white smile and a few words of flattery. Even so young, he knew the ways of courtiers.

But Gaius Fonteius Capito, it was evident, knew the ways of kings, and of queens. He spread his hands and sighed. "That I suppose it would be difficult to excuse. He agonized over it, majesty. He came within a finger's flick of refusing to marry the woman. But there just didn't seem to be a better way to secure the peace—and Octavian was adamant. Either Antony married Octavia or Rome split again with civil war."

"I would have said split and be damned," said Cleopatra, "but then I'm only a barbarian and a queen. Antony, with me, had all the power of the east. What are Rome's few legions to that?"

"Rome's legions have a little force of their own," Capito said, "majesty. Still, as you say, between the two of you, there's all the east to reckon with. Antony calls on you to remember that. He doesn't expect you to forgive him, not immediately, but he does ask you to consider why he did it. You might have done the same, if pressed as hard as he was."

"I doubt that," said Cleopatra. "I'll not come to his lure this time. Let him come to me, or never meet at all."

"Majesty," said Capito, "he said you'd say that. He says that he'd have come straight here if that had been possible, but affairs in Asia are too urgent. He says—" Capito leaned forward, lowered his voice. "He says that he's in the east to stay. Octavian has Rome, for a while. Antony will take the rest of the world. He wants you beside him when he does it. He sent Octavia back to her brother; he's had a bellyful of her sweet temper and modest ways. He can't divorce her, you'll understand that, since his marriage to her is the seal of his treaty with Octavian. But in everything that matters, he's your husband, and always will be."

Cleopatra seemed unmoved. "But am I his wife?" she asked of no one in particular. "I don't know that I want to be. No woman can stand without a man, or so the ways of the world require, but I have the greatest refuge of the woman who has been a wife and is no longer: I have sons. Why should I bind myself to a man again, least of all a man who left me lightly and went straight to another woman's bed?"

"Because between you, you can be lords of the world," said Capito.

"Egypt is enough," said Cleopatra. Yet Dione could see how she wavered, how she stiffened herself to resist. She had her pride, and Antony had wounded it to the bone. He would not get her back easily. Still, Dione thought, Cleopatra would go to him. The lure of power was strong. And, more than that, she loved him.

Coarse-humored, wine-sodden, unwitty man—she had chanted that litany all but daily since he left her for Octavia. Yet for all the brutal clarity of her perception, she could not deny, even to Dione, that this man had touched her heart more even than great Caesar. Great Caesar was cold and clever and wise. Love to him was a thing to be used, and Cleopatra had used it as ruthlessly as he had. Antony, the lesser man, was by far the warmer.

Dione watched the queen's face soften. Only a little; only for a moment. But it was enough. She would let Capito beg and wheedle for a while longer, days perhaps, or weeks. But in the end she would yield.

NINETEEN

Cleopatra in Antioch was not the queen who had set herself to enchant the world with her splendor. Splendor she certainly had, she would not have moved without it, but it was Antony's part now to seduce her; to prove that he was turning to her out of more than simple expedience. She came to him not as lover to lover but as queen to ally who might, at a turn of the tide, become an enemy.

This time she did not come to him in her ship. She had herself borne inland from the sea in a golden carriage drawn by milk-white mules, with armed guards about her, and a great glittering tribe of attendants. Caesarion rode at her side, attired as king and pharaoh. Alexander Helios and Cleopatra Selene rode in the carriage with their mother. This was nothing very new to them who had accompanied her all over Egypt. They sat erect as royalty learned to sit, bowing their heads to the multitudes who had come to see the queen.

Antony was waiting for her in Antioch as he had been in Tarsus, on the platform of the tribunal. That was either great confidence, to risk desertion and humiliation again, or else sheer convenience, since this time he had made sure to transact business enough while he waited. Cleopatra had to wait on another embassy, one from Judea.

The Judeans were disposed of quickly, but not quickly enough to appease Cleopatra. By the time she was given leave to approach the tribunal—given leave as if she had been a common petitioner and not the queen of Egypt—she was in no very tractable mood.

She signaled her guards to step back from the carriage. When her way was clear, she rose, taking the hand of her chamberlain and alighting with the grace that she had learned from childhood, grace that Helios and Selene too had mastered, even so young. Standing straight then, with a child holding to each hand, she walked the short distance to the dais and stopped, looking up into Antony's face. Her own was expressionless.

So, for a moment, was his. Then it bloomed into a smile. He rose with dignity mandated by the toga and came down the steps. When they were face to face, he was still the taller. He smiled down at the

queen and regarded the twins with wonder and dawning delight.
"Lady," he said. "Oh, lady. How I've missed you."

Cleopatra raised a brow. "Have you? It hasn't been obvious."

But he was not going to be lured into a quarrel, not here in front
of half the eastern world. He sank to one knee to bring himself level
with his children. They stared; he stared back.

"Mother's angry with you," said Helios.

"Greetings to you," said Antony. "I see you have her temper."

"I'm a Ptolemy," said Helios. "I'm half Roman, too."

"I should know that," Antony said, "since that half comes from
me." He turned his attention to Selene. "Well, little princess? Do you
agree with your brother?"

"I don't know yet," Selene answered him. She slipped free of her
mother's hand and stepped closer, looking him over with care. He
endured her scrutiny with a good will. After a long moment she
reached out to pat his cheek. "I think I like you," she said. "You're
warm."

He drew her to him. She came willingly, even when he rose with
her in his arms. As he stood up, the crowd raised a cheer. He set her
lightly on her feet and raised his son in his arms, holding him high.
Helios, startled, broke into laughter. That delighted the throng to no
end. They shouted till their throats were raw.

Once inside the triumvir's villa, with the crowds left outside with most
of the court and the army, Cleopatra rounded on Antony. It could not
have helped her mood that both of the children had settled happily
in their father's lap, while he fed them bits of cake and honeyed fruit.

He was being willfully dense, smiling at her over the dark head and
the fair, saying warmly, "I've been waiting for this day since I left
Alexandria. Thank the gods it finally came."

"No thanks to you that it did," she said. "How is your wife, my lord?
Has she borne you a son yet?"

"Not yet," said Antony, affable as ever. "Here, try the wine. It's a
new vintage from a vineyard near Caecubum—a little less sweet than
the run of Caecuban, but a little stronger, too."

Cleopatra ignored the cup that the servant offered. "You don't
think I'm going to come tamely back to your bed, do you? Leaving me
for nigh on four years I can almost understand; I know how need can
drive a man. But I won't share you with any woman, least of all
Octavia."

"I didn't think you would," said Antony. "You're not Roman. You don't understand that kind of necessity. I'm not faulting you for it, but I'm not apologizing, either. I stayed with her while I had to. Now I've sent her back where she came from. It's time to take the east in truth and not just in boasts when the wine goes round. Will you take it with me?"

"You were doing well enough without me," Cleopatra said.

"Not as well as I could do with you."

"You have other client kings."

"But only one is Cleopatra."

She frowned. "Why do I feel as if you rehearsed this before I came? Am I so predictable?"

"In some things, yes," he said. "But in others, there's no telling what you'll do."

"I'm not going to give myself to you," she said. "You lost that privilege when you yielded to your necessity"—her lip curled at that—"and let Octavian trap you into a marriage-peace. If you want me as your ally, you'll have to pay for it."

"Fair enough, I suppose," he said. "I won't have Octavia killed, or her brother either."

"This alliance has had enough of blood. I want land now, Marcus Antonius. Give me land enough to make an empire. Make me queen of the east in my own right, even apart from you."

"Just land?" he asked. "Is that all?"

"Rich land," she said. "Land that was Egypt's once, too briefly, and will be again. I know what you need: you need Egypt's ships to keep peace in the Middle Sea, and to guard your back against your so-treacherous fellow Romans. I'll build you ships, and man them for you, if you give me forests enough, and fertile land, and cities that will feed my coffers with gold for the fitting of ships."

"You have Cyprus and the Lebanon," he said. "What more do you want?"

"The Ten Cities," she answered promptly. "The coast of Syria. Iturea inland to Damascus. Cilicia. Even," she said as if she had had to pause to think on that, "Idumea and Judea."

"Not Judea," said Antony. "That's spoken for. The rest . . ." He stroked his chin. "I'll think on it. You're only asking for half the world."

"Perhaps I should ask for the whole of it," she said, "and Octavia's head in a silken sack."

He laughed, which did nothing to improve her temper. "That's what I love about you. You've passion in you, even when you're dickering like a goodwife in the market."

"And why not Judea?" she demanded, refusing to be diverted.

"Because I gave it to Herod," he said. "The two of you were friends, I thought—more than friends, if the rumors are true. What did you do, have a lovers' quarrel?"

She threw the winecup in his face.

There was an enormous silence. Antony sat with wine dripping down his cheeks like blood. And in fact he was bleeding: the rim of the silver goblet had cut his cheekbone. His eyes were pale in that crimsoned mask, a light brown, almost gold, like a lion's. How odd, thought Dione from her place near the queen, that she had not realized this before. Maybe because they were always reddened with wine or narrowed with good humor; she had not seen them opened wide and stark with shock.

He moved. The watchers tensed, looking for him to strike the queen. He did no such thing: he wiped his face, no more, and held the napkin to his cheek to stanch the blood. Then he waited. He would wait, it was clear, until Cleopatra spoke.

Cleopatra spoke with meticulous care, each word shaped entire before she let it go. "You may think as you please. I took him in when he was exiled, offered him help and friendship, protected him from those who would have hunted him down. He repays me now with mockery and contempt. Can he give you ships, Marcus Antonius? Can he defend the sea while you advance, at much too long last, against the Parthians?"

"He can't do that," Antony said levelly, "but he has other uses. I won't give you what belongs to him."

"What of that which he has, which belongs to Egypt?"

"Ah," said Antony. "You want the old empire back in full. Reasonable, from your point of view. But I need Herod. He's a lance in the Parthians' side. He'll yield a little, maybe, if I lean on him, but I won't depose him, or take away the core of his kingdom."

"Then you shall have none of me," said Cleopatra, rising.

He stayed where he was, with his children in his lap. "You'll give up everything for this one small bit of a kingdom that I find useful in my war?"

"It remains useful if it belongs to me."

"No," he said. "You're spread too thin. Herod is there, in Jerusalem, keeping Parthia from breaking out to the sea. His people are as stiff-necked as any men living. They won't serve a woman and a foreigner as they serve him."

"They could learn," said Cleopatra.

"Not the Judeans," he said. He raised his cup to her and drank. "I'll let you ponder it. I'll give you the whole coast of Asia, excepting a few small portions that I keep for my own needs. That's generous, if I say so myself."

"Herod should be disposed of," she said.

"No," said Antony.

Cleopatra paced the state chamber of the triumvir's villa, snarling like a caged lioness. The twins had been pried away from their father and handed into the care of their nurses, and maybe it had taken a little more than mortal persuasion to keep them quiet. Caesarion sat out of his mother's way, curled at Dione's feet. He was as fearless as his father had been; he watched Cleopatra pace, not speaking, seeming calmly interested.

She reached the end of a circuit and spun. "He'll give me what I ask, or I go back to Alexandria. I need him far less than he needs me."

"Maybe," said Dione. She was tired. It was hard work listening to the great ones bicker. She was disappointed, too, though she despised herself for it. There had been a member of the College of Augurs among Antony's attendants, but it was an older man with a leathery bald head and a noble Roman nose, not Lucius Servilius.

Cleopatra paced and seethed, muttered and prowled. Now and then she came back to the worktable, which had maps spread out on it, held down at the corners. The one on top was marked with the lands she wanted. She had marked in red the lands Antony refused to give her. They were few. Judea, of course. Tyre and Sidon, which had ruled themselves for time out of mind—she expressed no objection to that, even in her fit of temper. Most of Cilicia, but he would cede her two cities on the sea, useful places both, rich in timber as in trade.

When the queen's muttering had died to a murmur and she bent over her maps, tracing and retracing the lines of her desire and his, Dione took Caesarion by the hand and slipped away. He was no more reluctant to go than she was, though he was proud enough, once they were out of the room, to claim his hand for himself. "Thank you," he said. "Do you think I might ask cook for something to eat? You may be able to fast through dinner, but I am hungry."

Dione smiled a little wryly. "Of course you may eat. Go, then, and don't mind me. I'm going to take the air for a while, I think."

He paused as if he might have had something more to say, but turned quickly then and trotted off down the passage.

Dione chose the other way, the one that led to a stair and thence to the roof, which as elsewhere in these sunstruck countries was flat and fit to walk and sit and even sleep on. Without Caesarion she felt vaguely forsaken. She shook it off and climbed into the light.

At sea and on the road, one forgot the full impact of cities in the heat. Even in this villa in the high places of the city, the effluvium was inescapable. Dione found that she was holding her breath; let it out slowly. It was not so bad after a while, and there was a tub of roses in bloom near the roof's edge. She plucked a blood-red blossom and breathed its sweetness.

The sun was sinking. Long shafts of light impaled the city, turning it to blood and gold. That made her think of Antony, and of Cleopatra's wine running down his face, mingled with his own blood. Their union in Tarsus and after in Alexandria had been a Great Marriage. Time could not alter that, nor could betrayal—real or feigned—put an end to it. But Cleopatra was not going to make it easy for Antony to win her back.

Dione was tired of thinking about Cleopatra, or Antony, or anyone else. Particularly one who was not even here. She sat on the parapet, stroking the rose absently against her cheek, and stared out across the city. She could not afterward have told what she saw. It could have been bare wasteland for all the attention she paid it.

She came to herself slowly. The rose was wilting in the heat, dropping a blood-red petal into her lap. Her eye followed it of its own accord, but caught on something at the edge of vision. A shadow, the stir of a breath. A presence that neither moved nor spoke, simply stood, watching her.

All her defenses of body, mind, and magic had not even quivered. That made her irrationally angry—and the more when she looked up into a narrow large-eyed face above a toga no longer simple white but bordered with a stripe of deep-dyed Tyrian. So: the senate had snared him at last.

He did not look any more pompous than he ever had. In fact he looked furious, glaring at her as if he had called for wine and been given Egyptian beer. "Marry me," he said.

He said it in Greek. He said it very well. He could not possibly have meant to say exactly that. She was too incensed to ignore such patent fatuity; she said, "What have you been dining on since you left? Hellebore?"

"I am not mad," he said. "I came to offer you a marriage contract."

She rose. This was not anything to meet sitting on the edge of a roof, with a long drop into the kitchen garden. It needed a deep breath, then another, to gather enough of her wits to speak sensibly. "You leave me for almost four years. You send me no letter, no message, not one word. You creep up on me without warning, without even a greeting. Then you tell me to marry you. What else am I to assume but that you've taken leave of your senses?"

"If I did anything foolish," said Lucius Servilius, "it was to leave you when I did, without opening my heart to you."

"What was there to open? Wouldn't any woman in Rome marry into your properties? Especially now you've got that?" Her finger flicked the stripe on his toga.

"Several would have liked to," he said, but not as one who boasted of it. "I nearly gave way to one. Her family was insistent, and she seemed much interested."

"Then why in the world didn't you take her?" Dione asked, exasperated.

"Because you would have set a curse on her when you heard," said Lucius Servilius.

Well for Dione that she was on her feet and not sitting on the parapet: she would have fallen, so swiftly did she snap erect. "How *dare* you think that of me?"

"I saw you," he said. "In a dream. You and the queen in a circle, and vile things crawling beyond it."

"That was the queen," Dione snapped. "I was trying to stop her. She was setting a curse on Octavia."

"Precisely," said Lucius Servilius. "In any case, I realized that I didn't want a maid of fourteen with an estate in Etruria. I wanted a woman of an age to be my equal, with estates who knows where. You do have estates?"

"In the Thebaid," said Dione with the air of one who humors a madman, "and a bit of land on the other side of Lake Mareotis from Alexandria." She shook herself. "You don't want lands in Egypt!"

"No," he agreed. "I want the woman who owns those lands."

Dione's hand stung. She looked down in surprise. She was still holding the rose; its thorns had pierced her palm. She extricated herself with teeth-gritted care, warning him away with a glower. She laid the rose on the parapet, bloodied thorns, falling petals, and all. Then she faced Lucius Servilius again.

She was calmer now, less thoroughly startled. "If you had asked me four years ago," she said, "or even three, I might have considered it—even though a Roman can't legally marry a foreigner. Two years ago, I could have been persuaded. A year ago, you might have been able to woo me, given time and patience. Now . . . I don't want to marry again. I had enough of that with Apollonius."

Lucius Servilius did not look as downcast as she had hoped. "Yes? And how does he fare?"

"Well enough, I suppose," she said. "I haven't seen him or Androgeos since the day before you left. It's been made clear to me that I may continue to look after Timoleon, since he is already hopelessly corrupted, but his brother is to remain pure and unsullied by his mother's indiscretions."

"Has it been as bad as that?"

If he had wept or pitied her, she would have been able in good conscience to slap him away. But he spoke quietly, neither shocked nor visibly stricken, simply concerned, as a friend might be. They had been friends. In memory of that she said, "No. It hasn't been so bad. It was happening before you came to hasten it; once he had the excuse to keep Androgeos away from me, Apollonius made full use of it. I don't suppose you can see why this sours me on the thought of marrying again."

"It wouldn't be that way with me," he said.

"Apollonius didn't begin so, either," said Dione. She raised her hands. "No, don't argue. I'm sick to death of arguments. I had them with Apollonius. I had them with Timoleon when I came to Antioch without him. I had them—"

"Why did you come to Antioch without Timoleon?" Lucius Servilius interrupted her. "I'd hoped to see him. He must be quite the young man by now."

"Timoleon is a student in the Museum," Dione said. She narrowed her eyes. "Stop trying to distract me."

He shrugged and sighed and looked innocent. He could still do that. His face was barely lined; no grey glinted in his hair. He was as beautiful as ever. She wanted to shake him till his teeth rattled.

"I do love you," he said in his soft voice with its suggestion of accent. "If love is never to forget you; to look at any woman reckoned beautiful, and find her plain beside you; to remember every word we spoke together, however brief, however trivial; if that is love, then I've loved you since first I saw you."

"Ah," said Dione. "Poetry. Will you quote Sappho next?"

He flinched, but steadied. "You don't like Sappho?"

"That depends," said Dione. "Occasionally she has something to say to me. 'The moon and the Pleiades have set. I lie abed, alone.' "

"I'm not a poet," he said, "or a quoter of poets. I see the truth, and tell what I see. I love you."

Dione shook her head. She was not denying it, not really, but it was too much, too soon, after too long. And how much she could want it, if she let herself; if she could be such a fool . . .

"You're being very unRoman," she said. "Romans give up love, I thought, when they take their first political office."

"Not all Romans," said Lucius Servilius. "Some of us are almost human. Witness Antony, who loves an Egyptian queen."

"He loves the ships she can build him," said Dione.

"Yes, that is a part of it, but there is more. She's the other half of his self."

That came so close to what Dione did not want to feel, not now, not of this man, that she struck it aside with words edged to wound. "I am not the other half of you. I do not wish to marry again. And even if I did, why would I want you? I don't even know you. You're a stranger I met four years ago, who let rooms in my house for a season. Where is it written that that should predispose me to accept you?"

"Why, nowhere," he said.

"Except in your heart?"

He looked affronted. "I said I was no poet. I may be out of my wits, but I'm an honest fool. May I at least have your leave to court you?"

"No," said Dione.

"Then," he said, "may I be your friend? At least?"

"Why didn't you ask me that first?"

"Because I'm a fool," he answered, "and what's worse, an honest one."

"Well," said Dione. It was difficult beyond words to stay angry with him. He was so like Timoleon, if Timoleon had been a man grown, and a Roman, and no kin to her at all; and she was much too glad of that for her mood's comfort. She held out a hand that was kind enough not to shake. "Dear friend. What a pleasure to see you again."

He hesitated, caught off guard perhaps, or needing to steady himself as she did, to remember what they had been before. That cool distance could be no easier for him than it was for her. But it was all she would take, until she had had time to think. A little slowly, then more surely, he took her hand in his. "A pleasure indeed, my friend. Have you been well?"

Dione wanted to giggle. That was perilous. She fixed her mind on the easy, empty words. "Well enough. And you?"

"Pining away for love of—" He caught her eye. "—Egyptian beer."

She choked. "You *hate* Egyptian beer."

"It's Egyptian," he said. He drew her back to the parapet and sat on it with her, her hand still in his. She tensed to pull away, but he only said, "Tell me everything. Tell me what things Timoleon did to vex you into an early grave. Is he still the very prince of terrors?"

"Well," said Dione, "yes. Do you know where I found him one night? Dancing in a brothel. And once he'd recovered from that, which thank the gods took the best part of a year, he decided he wanted to go adventuring up the Nile. I let him get as far as Memphis before I had him fetched back home. He'd nearly been sold off for a slave, and had started a war in the stews of the city, and was boon companion to a pack of desert bandits. He still gets messages from some of them, and once in a great while they come to visit; they gave him one of their big-eyed little horses, which he rides without a bridle."

Lucius Servilius laughed till the tears ran. "Ah, Timoleon! I did nothing so interesting. A year among the Gauls, true—I was adopted into a tribe, but that was mostly for the hunting, and because I tried to learn a few words of their language."

"And saved the life of a chieftain's son?"

"Of course not. Do I look like a hero in a story?"

She studied him. "Yes, you do, rather."

He flushed just as she remembered, with the same wonderful confusion. "Well, I wish I didn't!"

"I gather your bride-to-be tried to flatter you with something of the sort?"

"Something exactly of the sort," he said, sharp with annoyance. "I thought you'd be more sensible."

"You can't help it that you're beautiful," Dione said.

His cheeks were fiery red. He was in a fair temper; Dione wished she had been able to provoke him so when she wanted to. But that, she thought with a sigh, was the way of the world.

"Never mind," she said. "Tell me about the Gauls. Or would you rather talk about Rome?"

For a moment she thought he would refuse to talk about anything.

But then he softened, even smiled ruefully at himself. "The Gauls, I think. When I was there, I kept writing letters to you, because I knew you'd want to know everything. I have the letters. There never seemed to be a suitable time to send them to you; so I kept them till I should see you again."

"I'd . . . like to see them," Dione said, and why her voice caught like that, she could not imagine.

"Well then," he said. "We came to Narbonensis in the teeth of a gale—sailing across to Massilia, you wouldn't believe . . ."

Dione heard every word he said, but half of her was thinking its own thoughts. It noticed that her hand was still in his; that they were sitting up on the roof where anyone could see; and that she did not care in the least. His face was as animated as she had ever seen it, eyes sparkling as he told her his tales, sweeping her into them with questions and coaxings. It could be, she told herself, that he loved to tell stories—she had seen it before when he was with Timoleon. But he was glad to be telling them to her, heart-glad, as clear as if he had said it.

And she was glad to be here, listening. Not glad enough to marry him, that was preposterous—but to be his friend, yes, with all her heart.

TWENTY

Antony would not yield on the question of Herod. Other, smaller concessions he would grant, but the more fiercely Cleopatra insisted on that one of them all, the more stubbornly he refused. "Would you set an Idumean upstart ahead of me?" she demanded of him as they sat to the evening's feast.

"As long as I need him," he shot back, "yes."

"And yet," she said, "you summoned me like a hawk to the fist. Like a hawk, I must be fed with good meat and plenty of it, or I take to the air and never come back."

"But you aren't asking for hawk's meat," said Antony. "You're asking for the heart of your fellow falcon. We don't feed our hawks on one another, my dear hunter of the air."

"You gave me my sister's head," Cleopatra said. "I don't even ask for Herod's life—only his lands. Which were ours before they were his."

"Long before," said Antony, "and by that logic, I could give Egypt to the Parthians if they demanded it. It was theirs when Alexander took it; or do you forget?"

"I never forget," said Cleopatra.

"That," said Antony, "you certainly don't. What *did* Herod do to you?"

"He holds lands that should be mine."

Antony pondered that. He lifted his winecup, discovered that it was empty. As the cupbearer filled it, flushing with the shame of his mistake, Antony said, "Herod will continue to hold those lands. I need him there, and you elsewhere."

"You may find me in Alexandria, refusing to stir a finger for you."

"I don't think so," said Antony. "I'm offering you half the world."

"Half the world, with a bite taken out of it. I won't eat an apple a worm has bitten."

He grinned and tossed her an apple from the bowl in front of him. She flung it back. He laughed, tossed it out again. Someone else, well gone in wine, whooped and hurled one of his own. Antony's friend Capito diverted it into the midst of the company. With that, the war was on.

Antony's slave was still combing bits of pulped fruit from Antony's hair, long hours later, as Antony sprawled naked on his couch. He was warm with wine and revelry; the strokes of the comb, even when they caught on a particularly tenacious knot, soothed him into a light half-doze. Part of him however was wide awake. He rubbed it idly, without urgency. "I wonder," he said, "if I should call for one of the maids. What do you think, Lysias? The little dark one, or the tall fair one? Or both?"

"Neither," said the one behind him.

He started and half-whirled, floundering in the cushions. Cleopatra smiled a predator's smile. The comb was in her hand; Lysias was nowhere to be seen. "How in Hades—" he began.

Her finger stopped his lips. "Never ask a woman her secrets."

His startlement was passing with soldier-swiftness. He pulled her to him. "I thought you'd never come."

She yielded without softness, lying atop him with her silken gown a ghastly encumbrance between. But she would not move to let him strip her of it. "I have my price," she said.

"The same as always?"

She nodded.

He was trembling with eagerness for her, but his face went hard. "No."

She thrust herself away from him. Or tried. But she had wrought too well. He had her in his grasp. He was strong as Romans went, and that was strong by any measure: big solid muscular man only lightly run to fat. His arms were iron; his face was stone. Until he laughed. "So. There's one place where you can't fight me and win."

"Don't lay wagers on it," she said.

"I'll bargain with you," he said. "You talk. I listen. I decide for myself."

"You've already decided," she said coldly.

"I have, have I? Is that why you've been trying so hard to talk me into giving you everything? I nearly am."

"Nearly," said Cleopatra.

"Are you never satisfied?"

"Sometimes," she answered, "maybe." She wriggled against him till he gasped; then she pulled away as much as she could, an inch at most, but enough. "Give me Judea."

"No," he said.

"Gods. I'm sorry I ever flung that oily Arab at you. He was supposed to make you gag and spit him out."

"Why?" asked Antony, all innocence. "He's charming. And very, very useful."

"The people hate Herod. They despise him. He has no right to his place as they reckon it; he married a woman of the priestly line, but then he slighted her brother, who should have been their high priest. If you don't depose him in my name, his people will do it in their own."

"I'll chance that," said Antony. "He's too useful to waste. And," he said, with a flash of teeth, "he keeps you from claiming too much. I'll give you power, my love, but I won't give you so much that you can challenge me."

"Wise," she said. "After a fashion. You shouldn't have told me you don't trust me."

"I trust you with my very life," he said. "I also trust Herod and his fellow client kings—to look after my interests for just as long as it suits their convenience. Which, I'm gambling, will be long enough.

When you and I sit as king and queen in Persis, on the throne of Alexander and of Cyrus, then I'll give you Herod for a lapdog. Until then, I keep him as he is."

"If we ever get that far," she said, "I'll string him up in his own temple."

"If you want to," he said. "But not yet."

Her breathing was coming quicker. She had been a long while away from him, from any man. When he reached again for her gown, she neither resisted nor escaped. It tore as he rid her of it. She took no notice. Nor, past a brief startlement, did he. His hands wound themselves in her hair; hers were pressed to his buttocks, lifting them as she mounted him.

For a moment, once joined, they did not move. Antony met her eyes. "Now," he said, "I'm home."

She could have taxed him with Herod still. But she was as weary of that, perhaps, as he. When they had taken all the pleasure they might of one another's bodies, and that was a goodly quantity, she said, "I'm not done fighting."

He was asleep. She sighed, frowned, but finally smiled. "Ah well," she said, a little wry. "There's time enough for war; and for love, too. Good night, dear lion of the Romans."

He murmured something that might have been, "G'night."

Her smile widened and softened. She slid down until her head rested over his heart; then, secure in his arms if not in his compliance, she slept.

ACT
THREE

EGYPT AND
THE EAST
36–34 B.C.

TWENTY-ONE

The river was gold, the banks gold, the army glittering bright golden in the light of the rising sun. This was but the outrider of the greatest army in the world, the core of its strength not yet come, and yet it was splendid, utterly. No finer army had ever mustered to march on Asia, straight into the god's burning eye, east and ever eastward. Just so had Alexander gone, until his men quailed and compelled him to turn back, and so, it was said, killed the heart in him.

Antony was a splendid image of the conqueror king. His golden armor was wrought in the likeness of that which lay in the tomb in Alexandria, his cloak scarlet, bright as blood in the morning light. He had even found himself a black horse, a Nisaian charger that champed and foamed and fretted to be gone.

He was not quite as eager as the horse. Unlike Alexander who fled the terrible woman who was his mother—or so the tales said—Antony left behind a woman whom he loved and lusted after. Cleopatra had put on her greatest magnificence and her boldest face to send her lord to the war he had prepared for so long. She was all in silver to stand contrast with his gold, her horse a white mare, her mantle so deep a purple that even in the sun it seemed black.

They stood on the bank of the Euphrates where it was more sand than mud, with the army stretched behind them, waiting for them to give the signal to move. Cleopatra stared out over the broad dun-golden water. Antony stared at her. "I almost wish I didn't have to go," he said.

She darted at a glance at him. "All this trouble and all this expense, and you want to call it off? Don't be a fool, Antony."

He stiffened, but then he laughed. "Always the practical one, my lady. Will you be glad to be shut of me?"

"I could use the time to work," she said.

"Well," he said. "I don't think he was much for farewells, was he? He just up and went."

He meant Alexander. Cleopatra nodded, sharp and short. Antony wavered, then turned toward his waiting horse.

She caught him before he mounted, pulled him round. He held her tightly, but not more so than she held him. "Win this war," she said, soft and fierce. "Conquer Asia; be lord of the world. Come back to me then, and lay it at my feet."

"Always," he said, "my lady of the many lands." He let his hand rest on her middle, that was swelling again with child. "I'll be back before this one is a season old. My word on it."

"Don't bind yourself to that," she said. "Just win. And then come back." She thrust him away. "Now go, or you never will."

He would have lingered, but she had withdrawn, too far to catch without looking a fool. He caught the bridle from his groom's hand and paused a moment to gentle the horse. It paused in its pawing and head-tossing; he swung lightly astride. The stallion whirled under him, half-rearing. "On," he said, no louder than she alone could hear; but after that, clear and strong and—yes—even glad: "On! On to Asia!"

"There's a nice bit of theatre," said Dione.

Lucius Servilius had mounted long since, but his horse was sensible; it knew how long its day was likely to be, and it had seized the opportunity to snatch what grass the army's trampling had left. Dione watched it work its way round a cluster of weeds. The army was forming in ranks, with much milling and shouting and neighing of horses and roaring of camels. It would be a while still before it actually moved.

The two of them were out of the press on the army's edge, not far from the leaders. Lucius Servilius' place was with them, but there was a little time left, if he chose to take it. He was not doing much with it. "I think," he said slowly, "that I don't like all this imitation of Alexander."

Dione had felt that coming for a while. In Alexandria he had been quiet, and quieter as the days went on in feasting, revelry, grand extravagance—but preparation too for war in Asia. He had not taken his old rooms in Dione's house, had insisted on living in a cell of a room in the palace; still, she had seen enough of him to go on with, and he had dined once or twice in her house, with Timoleon to see that they observed the proprieties. Then when they left with the queen and the triumvir for Asia, he had gone almost silent.

Now that it was all done, the war begun, the army gathered and set in motion, he seemed determined to say it all, or as much as he could get into these few last moments. "No matter what your queen says or thinks, no matter how he tries, no matter how many trappings he puts on, Antony is not Alexander of Macedon. He is a Roman. This army is Roman—Roman at the core, where it matters. The territories it gains will be tributaries to Rome. Not to Alexander. And not," he said, "to Egypt."

Dione raised her eyes to his face. He was not looking at her. He was staring, almost glaring, at the golden glitter of Antony's armor, now somewhat ahead of the rest as his horse picked up a prancing canter. "Look at that," he said. "That trumpery splendor. Gold and scarlet, a black horse—Alexander's oxhead stallion was never sixteen hands of Nisaian, not even in Callisthenes' mythmongering."

"Alexander wasn't Antony, either," Dione said. "Antony's a bigger man. He needs a bigger horse."

"Don't be reasonable," he said. "It does impress the masses, doesn't it? The soldiers love it. Good sense is never enough in leading armies. A general needs to put on a spectacle."

"As long as he can fight a war, too," said Dione, "is that so terrible?"

"No," he said. He shook his head, frowning in annoyance. "I just wish he could be more Roman about it, and less Greek. He hasn't worn the toga since he rode out of Antioch. As if, once he sent Octavia back and called for Cleopatra, he decided to go all Greek and forget Rome."

"I don't think so," Dione said, but slowly. "I think he remembers Rome with every breath he takes. But this isn't Rome; this is Asia. He has to take it as he finds it, if he wants to win this war."

Lucius Servilius looked at her for the first time in longer than she could remember—really looked at her, as if for once he saw her clear. He seemed a little startled by what he found. She wondered if she had a grey hair, or a wrinkle that her mirror had been missing. "You aren't Roman," he said.

"I am not," she said stiffly. "I am part Persian and part Mede and part Macedonian and part Greek. In short, I am Alexandrian, and Egyptian, and altogether a foreigner."

He shook his head. "No," he said. "No, I didn't mean it that way. I've been insulting you. Of course you want a new Alexander, not another Roman overlord. Alexander was yours."

"I don't want Alexander," said Dione. "I want Cleopatra—and whatever she has to do in order to keep her realm intact. Even to taking Roman consorts and using them as best she can."

"And turning them into Greeks."

"Am I doing that to you?"

His horse's head jerked up. He relaxed the reins with an effort that she could see. "You have nothing to do with this," he said.

"Except that I wouldn't marry you in Antioch," she said. "Are you blaming my queen for making a Greek of her Roman, because I wouldn't do the same for you?"

He wheeled the horse about. He was a good rider, she noted as one does when one is in crisis: taking refuge in small things to evade the great and painful ones. The Persian in her approved of his light hands on the reins even when he was enjoying a rare and no doubt long overdue fit of temper.

Once he had spun to face the east, however, he did not clap heels to the animal's sides and send him galloping toward his proper place at Antony's back. His horse, recalled from idleness, showed itself as fine as Antony's charger, but less inclined to waste itself in prancing to no purpose. Its nostrils flared, scenting the wind. It snorted gently. It would go, it was saying, if its rider but asked.

"You were . . . reasonable," he said at length, and not easily from the sound of it. "You could hardly accept a man who left you for so long without a word."

"A Roman," she said, "and I an easterner."

"That doesn't matter," he said.

"Yet it matters to you that Antony has done the same?"

"I am not a triumvir. I am not the living face of Rome. Nor do I ever intend to be."

"That's not fair," said Dione.

"No, it's not." He gathered reins. The stallion arched his neck and pawed, once, to express his opinion of the delay. "I never said I was consistent. Or equitable in what I want for myself and in what I expect of my commander."

"But honest," she said. "That you always have been." She paused. "Promise me something."

"If I can," he said.

"Promise that you'll send me word—often, if you can. Don't leave me in silence again as you did when you went to Rome."

He nodded with no hesitation that she could see. "I promise."

"No," she said. "That's not enough. *Promise.*"

He understood, as most men would not. "By my father's shade," he said, "I swear to you, I will not keep silence. I will remember you; and keep myself in your memory."

"And send me word," she said: "letters, messages, spirits on the wind, whatever the occasion needs."

"And if I do all that?" he asked, canny Roman always, even when he was swearing a friend's oath—or a lover's.

"If you do all that . . ." she said, standing beside him as he sat his stallion, pulling him down till he was face to face with her. He stooped without resistance, his mount standing solid, patient. She set a kiss on his lips. It was light, and brief. He tasted of cinnamon.

He straightened slowly. His face was somber, but his eyes were bright. "I wish," he said, "that you had done that months ago."

"So do I," she said. She stepped back before she sprang up behind him and demanded that he take her with him, or stay, or run away, or all or none of them. It was shocking, this rush of pure unreason after so many months of utter and icy reasonableness. And of course it would strike just when he was leaving for goddess knew how long.

She stiffened her spine and called her errant wits to order. They were not eager to come, but she had been their master too long. "Fare you well," she said. "Remember your promise."

"Always," he said. "I'll come back. Will you marry me then?"

"Maybe," said Dione.

He paused. His stallion pawed again and snorted. "I suppose," he said, "that will have to do."

"Just remember," she said, "and come back."

TWENTY-TWO

" 'Lucius Servilius the Augur in Armenia to the lady Dione of the house of the Lagidai in Alexandria, greeting and good health.' " Dione paused in reading the letter aloud to Timoleon. Her fingers were shaking, which was ridiculous. It was only a letter, and nothing of the love poem about it. "See, he says *salve* for the Roman side of it, and *chaire* for the Greek."

"Go on," said Timoleon as Dione paused.

She willed her eyes to make sense of the closely written papyrus. "Well then. Where was I? '. . . greeting and good health. And to Timoleon Apollonides, such greeting as he is best content with.' " That made Timoleon laugh. Dione slanted a smile at him, but kept on reading. " 'I hope this letter finds you well, and enjoying your peace in your city that I have learned to love. When we left you and your queen, we marched north on the Roman side of the Euphrates up into Armenia, which we had been assured was friendly to us, thanks in large part to the exertions of the general Publius Canidius Crassus. We found it to be so, as far as the people were concerned, although the land was as intractable as any I have seen: mountains on mountains, and mountains on top of those, until we came to Caranus that is in the heart of Armenia.

" 'There Canidius was waiting for us with the rest of our army. And such an army—my lady, surely even Alexander in his glory never saw such a one as this. It seemed to stretch for thousands of paces outside of the city—town, you would call it who know Alexandria, but in this part of the world it is a mighty metropolis. Our army stretched it to bursting and filled the fields beyond the walls. By day there seemed no end to it. By night the campfires were like fields of stars. I could stand up on the walls and look down and think that this, it may be, is what a god sees from beyond the spheres of the planets.

" 'But that would be poetry, and I am no poet. It is a great army, the greatest in this age of the world. And every man in it is devoted to the one who leads them. Their loyalty is remarkable; fanatical. Let anyone breathe a word of anything but profoundest admiration for Antony, and he finds himself surrounded by armed and dangerous men, men who would happily die to preserve their commander's good name. When they march by him in review, they cheer till they can cheer no more, and then they hammer spear on shield, raising such a clamor that the mountains ring.

" 'They love him, my lady. They call him splendid, and yet they know him for a man, and mortal: they see him reeling back to his tent from one of his carouses, and laugh and say, 'Ah, so the winegod has him in thrall again.' But then, as men will, they call him god himself, and worship him as they best can, by being willing to die for him. He gives them what they need most: a war to fight and a leader to follow.

" 'And after all, what did Alexander give his own men but that? Antony, like his great predecessor, has a gift for theatre and a talent for the splendid. He learned both, I think, from Caesar—and from Cleopatra. He has been an apt pupil.

" 'So now, having gathered all our forces, we march. The army is enormous, a city crawling over these mountains into Media. Antony means to take Phraaspa, which, not at all incidentally, is the treasure-house of the realm. Our taking it will both strike a blow at the heart of Parthia and enrich our army beyond the dreams of avarice, if not of kings.' "

Dione paused for breath.

"He's very cynical," Timoleon observed with admiration. Timoleon cultivated an air of worldly ennui, except when he was vexing his mother. "So few illusions. He should have been an Alexandrian. He's not half naive enough for a Roman."

"I wouldn't have called Caesar naive," Dione said.

"Caesar wasn't a Roman of the Romans either," he said with the wisdom of youth. "Antony, now—Antony is, Greek clothes and Greek manners and all. They're just trappings. The man is all Rome."

"Perhaps," Dione allowed. She sipped from the cup of citron that was still a little cool from the snow that had been stirred into it— snow from the mountains of Armenia, packed in straw and laden in boats and sent down to Egypt as a gift from Antony to his queen. It tasted wild and a little strange, even through the sharpness of the citron.

She picked up Lucius Servilius' letter again. It was written in parts: he had not dated them, but the ink changed where she had left off, and the writing seemed hastier, as if he wrote in snatches round matters of greater importance.

" 'After some few days' march we came to Lake Matiana, where I saw a prodigy in the evening as we camped by the lake: three suns setting over the long water, one above the other, and that which was lowest was largest, and that which was highest was smallest, and a circle of white fire about them all. It was an omen, we all agreed— common soldiers as well as priests and diviners—but none of us could agree on its meaning. Myself, I thought of Alexander who also, it is said, marched through this country, and he was the greatest of kings and conquerors. The one above him then might be Antony. But if that were so, then why three suns, and not two? Then I thought that maybe the third was Alexander Helios, whom your queen named with such pride approaching hubris. And maybe so; and maybe not, and the gods know more than men can imagine. And certainly as I stood watching, the great sun set, and the middle sun shrank and faded, but the third bloomed like a flower of fire, until it filled the whole sky; and then came the night.

" 'On the morning after the portent, we took the omens in our customary fashion, but they yielded nothing useful. The gods were keeping their counsel. So unguided, but at least not prevented, we marched eastward from the lake. The country is open there, neither forest nor mountain wasteland; and it became abundantly clear that the baggage was slowing our advance to a standstill. The siege engines in particular, which we will need when we come to Phraaspa, weigh down their wagons, and the oxen labor to draw them over the plain. Antony therefore has determined to divide his army. One portion, traveling light, will move on swiftly to Phraaspa and there begin the siege. The rest, which is the bulk of the baggage train and the siege engines, with two legions to guard it, will follow at its own pace.

" 'This is sound enough strategy, as long as the land is friendly to us; the sooner the army itself comes to its target, the more likelihood it has of taking the city by surprise. A full siege might not even be necessary at all, if our men can break in before the engines arrive.

" 'Myself, I could wish that Antony had kept the army together. That slows it to a crawl, but provides less temptation to allies of questionable loyalty—and I do wonder about his majesty of Armenia, my lady. I said so to Antony. He was not quite so rude as to laugh at me, but he made it clear that I should keep to my omens and my books, and let a soldier attend to soldiers' matters. Since I have fought in battles enough, and worn armor and carried a pack till my shoulders are as scarred as a trooper's, but was never a soldier in my heart where it matters, perhaps he has the right of it.' "

Dione had to stop. Her throat was dry; and not only from reading without pause. She drank the rest of her snow-cooled citron.

"Antony shouldn't have divided his army," Timoleon said.

"No?" said Dione. "I don't sense death in this, for Antony or for Lucius Servilius. If there were such danger for them, I would know it. The goddess would tell me." It was not vain hope to say as much, nor was it boasting. There were some consolations in being what she was.

"There are things as bad as death," Timoleon said, unwontedly pensive.

"Hush," said Dione, and made herself go back to the letter. " 'I remain with Antony, who never faults a man for questioning his decisions. Without the baggage we make good speed for Phraaspa, although once we left the plain we found ourselves scrambling again over endless mountains. We crossed into Media yesterday; thus far the land is quiet, its people cowering or fled. Even without our baggage we are a mighty army, and we roll over the land like a long wave, singing as we go, when the mountains give us breath for it.

" 'Up here on the summit of the world, my little apprehensions seem foolish. I understand, I think, why Alexander pressed east and ever eastward. It was not conquest that drew him; it was eagerness, and curiosity—to come to the horizon and pass it, and find what there is to find, new lands, new cities, new races of men. His army failed of its courage before they reached the Stream of Ocean. I can understand that, too. It is a rare man who can leave everything behind but the fire of his spirit, and go where that leads him. I wonder, did Alexander wish, when his army refused to go on, that he had not been a king? Did he think to continue alone, unencumbered, to the world's edge?

" 'But there, I ramble. I am no Alexander, and neither is Antony, convenient though it is for him to assume that image. He has a purpose in this country: to take it for Rome. Once that is done, I doubt very much that he will try to conquer India, too. He knows his own limits. Once Phraaspa's treasure is ours, we have our hand at the throat of Parthia. We have but to squeeze, and the realm is ours. So Antony says, and who am I to contradict him?

" 'Fare you well, my lady, until we return. I will bring you my share of the treasures of Parthia; you can laugh at it if you please, or dress Timoleon's donkey in it, or give it to beggars in the street. I care little, if only I may see you again.' "

"Oh, he is a poet," said Timoleon with only a slight edge of mockery. "Mother, will you marry him? He adores you, you know."

Dione's cheeks were hot. Her frown failed of its effect; Timoleon grinned at her. "And do you adore him?" she asked.

"Well," he said, only a little discomfited, "rather. You should hear some of my friends on the subject of the Beautiful Unattainable. They call him that, did you know? He isn't interested in anybody, woman or man or boy. Except you. It's a little unnatural, but charming enough to set a fashion."

Dione suppressed a sigh. "And I suppose you are the Beautiful Attainable?"

"I should hope not," he said with not altogether reassuring sharpness. "I like to think I have some taste. Mother, *will* you marry him? It would drive everyone wild."

"I'm sure it would," she said. "Don't you have a symposium to go to? An army of suitors to torment?"

"Only three suitors," he said, "and I think I'm going to break their hearts and fall in love with a dancing girl. Don't break his, Mother. I'll never forgive you."

He set a kiss on her forehead and went lightly to his symposium,

which Dione knew for a fact was no such debauch as he wanted her
to imagine. She shook her head. "Even my child orders me about,"
she said.

The goddess-cat, curled at her feet, raised its head and said, *"Mao."*

"Just so," said Dione, but she smiled.

TWENTY-THREE

Alexander Helios and Cleopatra Selene had come into the world in
fire and splendor. Their brother was quiet: quiet the omens of his
birth, quiet and almost brief the birthing itself. Even newborn he was
a solemn child, large-eyed and silent. He never cried.

And yet Dione had no doubt at all that this child, like his brothers,
was born to be a king. His mother named him for the greatest of his
line: Ptolemy, surnamed Philadelphos.

He bore the weight of his name without apparent strain. Dione,
bending over his cradle on the morning after he was born, laid a
finger on his forehead. He stared gravely up, for all the world as if he
could see her clearly. He would be dark-eyed, she thought, but
fair-haired. "You named him well," she said without looking round.

"He belongs to the gods," Cleopatra said from her bed. She was
hardly weary, as easy as this birth had been—blessed, the priests
were calling it, and blessed the issue of it. They wanted it to be an
omen of Antony's victory in Media. So, for that matter, did Cleopatra.

"I see it in him," Dione said. "He shines with it. But it's quiet, like
all the rest of him. He makes me think of summer evenings, and of
cats hunting."

"Danger and comfort both?" Cleopatra sounded amused. "That's a
man for you. Will he look like his father, do you think?"

"No," said Dione. "This one is all Ptolemy."

"Oh, dear," Cleopatra said.

Dione turned. "It's a noble heritage," she said.

"And a great deal of nose," said Cleopatra. She sighed. "Ah well. It
could be worse. He could be a girl."

Dione came to sit on the side of the great bed, tucking up her feet
as she used to do when she was young. Cleopatra remembered: she

smiled, stretching, wincing a little for she was tender still from the birth.

"Do you know," Dione said, "that's three sons you've given Rome and Egypt, and a daughter who will be a queen. I hope you're proud of yourself."

"Am I ever not proud?"

"You know what I mean," said Dione.

Cleopatra nodded. They were silent, companionable, while the baby slept and the nurse rocked him in his cradle. Dione had not slept, but she was hardly tired. Building the world for this Ptolemy had been as simple, almost, as speaking the words. She refused to think that it had been too easy. He was a Ptolemy, that was all. Ptolemies had the world all ready for them, waiting for them to claim it—not like the sun and the moon, who needed a new creation.

It felt, somehow, like a completion. Three sons, a daughter. A son for Caesar, two for Antony, and the daughter for Cleopatra. If others came later, then well enough. But the line of Lagos was secure in Egypt.

Cleopatra's mind had already leaped out of simple things to affairs of state: Dione knew the look she had, the suggestion of a frown. Dione let her do her thinking in peace. She would speak when she was ready to speak.

Dione set her back against the gilded headboard and closed her eyes. She never meant to sleep, but Cleopatra's voice when it came seemed to come out of something she was dreaming.

"Octavian," the queen said. She could never say the name without venom, but that was muted for once, her tone reflective. Dione blinked till her face came clear. It was lost in thought. "I wonder . . ."

Dione caught herself before she slid into sleep again. "What? Has he done something new?"

"No," said Cleopatra, but slowly. "Not new, exactly. Just . . . he makes me think. I despise him. I always will. But have you noticed how he manages, no matter what he does, to hold on to what he has, and to add to it, bit by careful bit? He has no drop of loyalty in him, no honor, no courtesy, not even the simple ability to keep a promise that he has made. And yet, Dione. And yet. What if it's true, what he says of himself? What if he is as great as Caesar was? What if he is greater?"

"Impossible," said Dione. "Caesar had both wit and charm. Octavian has neither."

"Wit is easy enough to come by, or how would courtiers survive? Charm is an empty thing without intelligence behind it. I used to think that both were necessary in a man who would rule. But I begin to wonder. Octavian makes no secret of his belief that he and only he is capable of ruling Rome as it should be ruled—of bringing peace to a state that has known nothing but civil war since Romulus killed his brother on the walls of new-born Rome. What if that belief is truth? What if I've chosen the wrong consort?"

"Dear goddess," said Dione, appalled. "You're beside yourself."

"I am not," Cleopatra said sharply. But then: "Very well. I overstate my case. I could never warm to that cold fish. But as much as I love my lion of the Romans, I know and have always known that he lacks a certain something. Greatness; brilliance of intellect. Ability to rule in peace as well as in war."

"You have that," Dione said. "That's why the gods brought you together. He knows the arts of war. You know the arts of ruling, and of peace. Together you are complete."

"Yes . . ." said Cleopatra, but doubtfully. "I wish . . . gods, I wish that creature had been strangled in his cradle."

"So do we all," Dione said, "and not a few in Rome, as well. Octavian's not a man to invite the love of those who follow him."

"Does that matter, if he can lead them? He has no talent for war at all. But he can connive and intrigue as handily as any eastern prince. And he has no scruples. Not one."

Dione shut her mouth on what she would have said. But Cleopatra said it for her. "You think that there I am a match for him? But, Dione, I do have a scruple—a weakness of the heart. I love Marcus Antonius. I won't share him, and I won't give him up."

"Ah," said Dione, "but Octavian has a weakness, too. He likes to gamble."

"But when he gambles with kingdoms, he only wagers where he can win."

Dione had never been able to defeat Cleopatra in a war of wits. She raised her hands, spread them wide and sighed. "Very well. Octavian is more than either of us wanted him to be. But there's only one of him, and two of you. And he doesn't have Egypt."

"Yet," said Cleopatra. "Or ever, while I live."

Dione was dreaming. She knew it as one does when the dream is a god's sending and not the shaping of mortal mind. It came, the Greek part of her said, from the gate of horn, the gate of truth. But in it she was Egyptian, her winged spirit, her *ba*. Her shape was that of the desert falcon, the bird of Horus, but human-headed, with human wits and will.

She flew on strong wings through the clouds of the dreamworld. Once they thinned and she saw the palace, and the queen asleep, and the children in their nursery: young Ptolemy now a season old, the twins sharing a bed still with their cats, the gold and the silver, and Caesarion in his own chamber with his own guard at the door, like the prince of eleven summers that he was. Dione blessed them with such power as she had. The twins stirred in their sleep, as if they sensed her presence. Ptolemy opened his dark quiet eyes and smiled.

She took that smile with her into the clouds again. A wind caught her, driving her faster and farther than her wings could fly.

The clouds scattered. She sped over mountains like the teeth of Titans, jagged and steep. It was sowing time in Egypt, the rich green season after the Nile's flood, but here it was winter. The peaks were white with snow. The cold cut her to the bone, even in her spirit-shape.

With heart-stopping abruptness, the mountains ended. The earth dropped away to a broad plain, brown with winter. Rivers ran through it.

The wind that had carried her so high now sent her swooping down till she shut her eyes in horror—surely, oh surely she would plummet to the earth. But her flight leveled; the wind softened in-finitesimally. She opened her eyes, trembling. She was flying low, but still far higher than a man could reach. The plain was full of stones, or fallen trees. But did stones smell of blood and burning, and did trees bleed and groan and die?

She had a little volition now, a little freedom from the wind: enough to pause, to begin a long slow circle. Those were men, those shapes on the plain, and wagons, overturned or shattered, and on them all the marks of fire. Still she could see what they had carried, what was left of it: the impedimenta of an army on the march. And those fragments, hacked and charred, had been siege engines; and the pools of blood-red about those were the cloaks of Roman legion-aries, strong men fallen defending their charge.

No, she thought, insofar as she could think at all. This was no true dream. This was nightmare, this image of slaughter.

It would not let her go, though she fought to escape it. The wind, seizing her again, drove her back the way she had come. In merciless clarity she saw men riding on horses, heavy-laden with booty, or driving wagons that had been Roman once, but were now the prize of a traitor's war. The faces of the men who drove the wagons were faces only, to her unaided senses, but the goddess was in her, and the goddess named them for what they were: Armenians who had called themselves friends of Rome, but who had betrayed Rome the moment Rome's army vanished into Media.

Antony's allies in Parthian pay. It was nothing new, nothing shocking in the world of eastern politics. But the coldness of it, the absoluteness of the destruction—two legions cut down, the baggage that they guarded destroyed or stolen—left Dione mute with horror.

Even yet the goddess was not done with her. She prayed to be let go, to be freed from the nightmare, but the wind bore her back yet again, eastward, into a raw grey dawn. The plain rose up into mountains, the mountains of Media. The heart of them, like a tawdry jewel, was a city within walls. An army camped about it.

With the suddenness of dream, she was among the army, flitting down the long straight aisles of tents from campfire to campfire. She went too fast to see men's faces, or to hear what they said. Then she was inside a tent, the largest of them all.

In this hour, so near to dawn, the tent seemed as vast as a palace, and echoingly empty. The few men in it were asleep and snoring in a reek of wine. All but two. They sat facing each other in one of the inner rooms, partitioned from the rest by a wall of canvas. One leaned back in a chair, dangling a goblet in his fingers. The other propped elbows on the table that was between them, and rested chin on fists, and stared blindly into the dark beyond the lamp's light.

Antony set the goblet on the table with a thump. Lucius Servilius started upright. Antony laughed without mirth. "Don't look so gloomy, man. It's not as if the world has ended."

"No?" Lucius Servilius lowered his chin back onto his fists and heaved a sigh. "You can't lay a siege without siege engines."

"We can build them," Antony said. He sounded as if he had said it before, and often, through a long grim day and a longer night.

"With what? And when? Winter's coming. We have to get back over the mountains if we're to get out of here, and fight our way through Armenia. Unless you want to stay here and starve, or freeze to death if the gods are merciful."

"Alexander survived worse than this."

"Alexander had the treasure of Persia to pay his troops."

"So will I," said Antony, "when I take Phraaspa."

Lucius Servilius shook his head. He had been drinking, Dione realized with a start: he who never drank to excess was swimming drunk, and the cup on the table was not Antony's as she had thought, but Lucius Servilius'. Antony had taken it away from him. "You're not going to take Phraaspa. The gods told me so. The gods said get out of here while you still can—before the winter comes and swallows you whole."

"The gods, or a skinful of bad wine? You're taking it too bloody hard, Lucius my lad. You'd think it was you who'd lost your whole baggage train, and probably the war with it."

"No," said Lucius with the obstinacy of the very drunk. "Enough. I've had enough. You aren't Alexander. You shouldn't want to be. You're Antony. You're Marcus Antonius of the Antonii. You belong to Rome. Not Persia. Not Macedonia. Not, *not* Egypt."

"There," said Antony. "There now. I'll get you to your tent. I wish you had your little Egyptian witch here; she's just what you need tonight."

Lucius Servilius thrust himself to his feet. He wobbled dangerously, but his hands braced him against the table. "Don't talk about her. Don't even think about her."

"I don't want her," said Antony with unshakable placidity. "I have one of my own. You need her."

"No," said Lucius Servilius. He kept saying it when Antony came round and propped him up and walked him toward the door. He was still saying it when they came to his tent, one much smaller than the triumvir's and set close by it, with his slave waiting in it, and a brazier keeping it warm, and a lamp lit beside the bed.

Antony tipped him onto the cot and held him down while the slave got him out of his winestained clothes. Dione, hovering in the shadow of a corner, knew full well that she should not be watching, but she could hardly help herself. He was fully as beautiful as she had thought he would be, warm brown all over, and lithe as a boy still though he must be nearly forty.

Once he was stripped he quieted. Antony left; the slave finished washing and tending him, covered him with a blanket and went to sleep on the floor as slaves could, abruptly and completely.

He had feigned to fall asleep while the others were there to see, but once he was effectively alone, he lay open-eyed. The wine was strong in him still, Dione could see that, but his eyes were clear, and bleak.

She must have moved or made a sound. His glance darted toward her, and held.

He could not see her. Of course not. She was spirit and dream. But he was a seer, and he was deep in the power of Dionysus. Who, Dione remembered out of nowhere in particular, had come out of Asia to conquer the west. Why should he not have conquered even this of all the Romans?

His gaze drew her forward. She walked on human feet, in human body. She was, she took note with deep relief, clothed: her gown was Egyptian and therefore covered little, but it was a garment, which was all that mattered. She knelt beside the cot and laid her hand on his cheek. Since this was a dream, she had substance; she felt the warmth of his flesh, the roughness of beard some days unshaven, the flex of his jaw as he tightened it. "Did he invoke you?" he demanded.

"What, Antony?" Dione shook her head. "The goddess brought me. I saw . . . what happened."

He flinched, not much, but enough. "I don't know why," he said, "but it devastates me. I didn't even want this war. I thought it was a waste—a travesty."

"It would have been glorious, if he had been Alexander," said Dione.

"But he isn't!" It was a cry of pain. "He never was."

"It's not the world's end," Dione said. "It's not even the end of Antony. It's a setback, no more."

"No," said Lucius Servilius, as stubborn as ever. He reminded her powerfully and rather absurdly of Timoleon. Which made her think that he could quite easily have fathered that younger of her sons— Timoleon was very like him. Which made her blush furiously.

He did not see. He was caught up in despair. Wine could do that to a man who seldom let it master him.

She stroked his cheek and his brow. He was feverish, a little, and fretful. She could be fretful herself—she had come all this way in a dream, been given substance to address him, touch him, be in every way perceptible to him, and he did not even seem to notice how remarkable that was.

But she, unlike a Roman, had the ability to recognize the absurd. She must not laugh: he would be mortally offended. Since she was after all spirit and not flesh, she did as the spirit prompted, which was to lie down beside him, decorous enough with her gown and his blanket, and take him in her arms. He did not resist her. His arms went about her willingly enough; his head rested on her shoulder above the swell of her breast.

It was very chaste. He did not rouse to her touch, not as a man rouses to a woman. He was warm, that was all. He felt, she thought, as if he belonged where he was. She had not known what that was like. Apollonius was all sharp angles, like lying with a bundle of sticks. Lucius Servilius was not soft, not at all, but his angles fit her hollows. Antony completed Cleopatra: Dione had said that, speaking, she had thought then, of their varying talents. Now she understood the rest of it. It was not only the meeting of mind and mind, spirit and spirit. It was body and body, too.

Could one sleep in a dream? For she slept, with Lucius Servilius' head on her shoulder, there in his tent outside Median Phraaspa, half around the world from the place where her body slept in Alexandria. She slept, and in this sleep within a dream, she dreamed nothing, except peace.

TWENTY-FOUR

Lucius Servilius the Augur woke with a start. He was cold and he was sick, and he was dreadfully, devastatingly alone. He reached for the warmth that had been with him in the night, but it was gone. It never had been. He had dreamed her, that was all: Dione of the Lagidai, lying at his side, cradling his head against her breast.

He sat up very, very slowly. His head stayed on his neck, just. The air in the tent was chill, even with the brazier that his slave was tending. "Gaius," he said.

The man turned, bowing. He was never disrespectful, but never servile, either, and he seldom said anything. He was a Transpadane Gaul, a captive, whose given name was something impossible, with a plethora of syllables. Lucius had given him the most common of Roman names, to call him by; he had shrugged and proceeded to answer to it.

"Gaius," Lucius said again. "Did you . . . hear anything in the night?"

Gaius shook his head. His face was opaque as slaves' faces could be. Lucius considered pressing him, but forbore. If he had heard or seen the visitor in the night, Lucius was not sure he wanted, after all, to know it.

Slowly, with much care for aching head and heaving stomach,

Lucius got himself up and dressed and out to face a siege that could only be futile without engines to break down the walls. Antony was talking of building more, but that would take time. And winter was coming, mountain winter, with snows that came early and hard.

Lucius was warm, for once, with memory that could have been no more than a dream. It sustained him for a remarkable while. Weeks of Antony's resistance to the inevitable.

"We can do it," Antony said. The words were worn with repetition: he had been saying them since the word came of Armenia's treachery.

His commanders had stopped trying to argue with him. This morning they sat wrapped in cloaks against the biting cold, eyeing the sky outside the triumvir's tent. If it did not snow by evening, then Lucius Servilius was no judge of the skies' portents.

Phraaspa sat complacent behind its walls. Occasionally Antony sent a sortie with scaling ladders; his engineers had managed a catapult or two. The citizenry repelled the ladders with contemptuous ease, and ignored the missiles arcing over their walls. They might be getting hungry: they had after all been under siege since summer. But those who appeared for parleys did not look unduly thin or ravaged with famine.

"We can take this city," Antony said. "We'll starve them out or bombard them out—once we get more engines built—"

"Face it, Antony," said Canidius Crassus. "It's not going to work."

They all stared at him. He was the best of them, which not everyone was pleased to recognize. He was also the least given to empty words, which meant that he spoke seldom, and only to the point. He had stayed out of the arguments heretofore, listened in silence or gone to see to things that needed doing.

"Maybe Alexander won Tyre with a siege that lasted through a whole winter," Canidius said. "But Tyre was a sea-city, and Alexander built himself a fleet. And he wasn't trying to do it from the middle of enemy territory. We're losing men every day to raids and ambushes. Our supply lines are thin to nonexistence; we've raided as far as we can, and the country's stripped bare. Now winter's here."

"Winter!" Antony burst out. "Great Hercules, man, it's only Octobris."

"Octobris in Media," said Canidius, "not in Rome, or in Egypt where the sun never hides its face. If we stay here, we won't be alive by spring. We'll be frozen solid, or picked off by Median archers."

Antony's jaw set. "You're telling me to turn tail and crawl back to the sea."

"I'm telling you to make an orderly retreat while you still can. There's bad terrain between here and friendly country, mountains that will be difficult if not impossible to cross if we wait much longer."

"Then we stay here," said Antony.

Canidius took a deep breath as if to summon patience. "Marcus Antonius, if we stay here, we die. It's as simple as that. We're on short rations now. We'll be on no rations by the time winter takes a firm hold. We've got to leave now if we leave at all."

"We're not going to take Phraaspa," somebody said. Lucius was astonished to realize that the voice was his own. He had been thinking it, of course, but he was not like Dione; no god spoke through him. Or none had before.

Antony transferred his glare from Canidius to Lucius. "And who says we're losing the war?"

"All of us do," said Lucius, since Antony had asked. He wondered if Dione felt this way when she said whatever came into her head. It was exhilarating, if a little terrifying, like galloping down a mountainside.

"We are, you know," he said, since he had committed himself—tumbling down the cliff with gleeful abandon. "If Armenia hadn't turned its coat on us, if we had our baggage and our engines, we'd be on our way back by now, with the Parthians' gold in our wagons. We're not accomplishing anything by staying here. And if we make it through the winter and survive till spring, then the Parthian armies will fall on us. You can lay wagers on it."

"One would think," said Antony, "that you had reason to know that."

Lucius laughed. Some of the others were startled: those were killing words, their expressions said. And so they were. But Lucius was not a man for killing. Laughter was easier, and in some ways more deadly. "Come, Marcus Antonius. We'll stay if you bid us stay—we can hardly do otherwise, in enemy country, with winter coming on. But a wise commander knows when to stop; when to cut his losses and get out. The men are still yours, heart and soul, but even they are ready to go home—or at least to Egypt."

"Now I know how Alexander felt in India," Antony muttered. He got up from his stool and paced, growling softly like a lion in a cage.

The others drew back to give him room. He noticed: he snarled at them.

He stopped abruptly. "Gods rot you all. Get ready, then. We're leaving tomorrow."

Lucius knew no triumph at the victory. It was too dearly won. And in any case they did not leave on the morrow: they woke to a howling blizzard that kept them all tent-bound for two days. The men would have been at each other's throats, and there were more than a few fights that stopped not far short of bloodshed, but in the main they were too happy to be getting out of that pestilential place. They called it worse among themselves, for which Lucius Servilius could not blame them.

On the third morning, under a sun that seemed unnaturally warm after such a storm, in the melting snow, they began the long march back to the sea. They were singing; one might have thought that they were victorious after all. They traveled light, with their baggage lost in Armenia. No raiders harassed them, not at first. Media was as glad to see them go, as they were to be going.

The singing died soon enough in the struggle through the snow and then, as the sun went on with its work and the column length-ened on the road from Phraaspa, the deep and sucking mud. At night the mud froze. By dawn it was like iron.

Then the enemy came.

Lucius Servilius remembered little of that long terrible march. Twenty-seven days, they counted, if any had wits to keep the reckon-ing, from Phraaspa to the deep swift torrent of the Araxes that ran between Media and Armenia. Eighteen battles worth the name, un-counted skirmishes, endless harrying from Median horseman and Parthian archers; and what the enemy did not succeed in doing, the land did, and the airs that carried sickness. Men fell where they fought or marched, struck low by fever as often as by sword or arrow.

Lucius lost his horse in the third battle, or perhaps it was the fourth. He made no effort to claim a remount. Others needed them more than he did. He merely had the flux. They were burning with fever or vomiting their vitals in the snow. He put his head down and marched, keeping an ear alert for warning of another battle.

"Lucius! Ho, Lucius Servilius!"

He raised his head. It was almost too heavy to lift, with the helmet weighting it down, but even a dead man, the Egyptians said, must answer to his name. Something huge loomed over him. Slowly he identified it as a man on a horse. Big florid man, big black horse. "Antony," he said.

"Pollux! you look awful," said the lord of the eastern world. Which just then was a rough square mile of Media, with Medians gnawing at the edges. "How sick are you?"

"Well enough to walk," said Lucius. "I haven't had to fall out for a whole hour, I think." He squinted. Antony was gleaming—glowing, no doubt about it, like a cloud over the sun. It must be his armor, which was gold, but there was no sun to strike fire in it, not today. The clouds were full of snow. The first flakes had already begun to fall.

Antony was saying something that Lucius could not quite get his wits around. The next he knew, he was in the air. Then there was a horse under him—and Antony was looking up at him. He looked down at his hands wound in black mane, and past them to Antony's face. "No," he said.

"Balls," said Antony. "You can ride in your sleep, I've seen you. Just don't kick him too far back of the girth. That gets him up on his hindlegs."

"But I'm not—" said Lucius.

Antony was already gone, striding along the line of legionaries, slapping a shoulder here, flashing a smile there. Lucius, mounted on Antony's black charger, could see no decent way to get down. Everyone who was not staring after Antony was regarding him with an expression that was all too easy to read. It was as much as his head was worth to spurn the gift that Antony had given.

He might have essayed it still if the stallion had not taken the bit in his teeth and surged forward. Lucius did not have the grace to fall off; Antony was right, he could stay on a horse no matter what it did. It was one of the few things he did well.

Antony's black horse wanted to be where it was accustomed to be, which was at the head of the army. Lucius, too weak and dizzy with fever to argue, was borne along with it. He could sit upright, at least, and the flux was holding off. He did not think he could have stood any more embarrassment.

And, he thought, if the enemy shot him down while he rode conspicuous in the van, then good riddance to a bad life. Which was needless posturing, as Dione would have told him in no uncertain terms. He could almost hear her say it.

Almost. No warm arms about him now, no warm breast to lie

upon. They were all he wanted, he reflected with the clarity of fever. All he had ever wanted, at least since he saw her on Cleopatra's ship, that day in Tarsus.

If he lived to see her again, he would not let her refuse him. Not this time. Oh, he had been a fool to ask her to marry him, to blurt it out before she had even had a chance to realize that he had come back after the long years away. He should have waited, courted her, won her as wise lovers did, by teaching her that she loved him.

She did. He was sure of it. She did not know it, maybe. She was a little odd, a little cold—her ass of a husband had made her that way, and she was Alexandrian, which made it worse. Alexandrians were strange people, of all nations and none, with a propensity for naming everything and then imagining that they had mastered it. But they knew nothing of aught beyond the name.

Imagine, he thought. A Roman teaching a Hellene the arts of love. How beautifully absurd.

He supposed that he had laughed aloud. No one seemed to notice. There was a skirmish back in the line, shouts and cries, the clash of metal, horses milling and footsoldiers holding what ranks they could while keeping the forward march. Those were all the orders they had: to hold as they could, and to keep on. The army was not to stop, not to engage in battle unless it had no choice.

The snow was thickening, casting a veil across the fight. Lucius wrapped his cloak tighter about him. Fever kept him warm, which was a blessing at the moment. He would almost be sorry to recover, unless he could do it in a villa by the sea, with a certain lady to nurse him and fetch him possets.

More likely she would tell him to stop being lazy and fetch them himself. "Imagine," he said to the horse's ears. "Imagine if I could . . . if she would . . ."

The horse was not interested. The fight was winding down, the attackers drawing away, fading into the storm. He could not see if anyone had died, on either side. Too many had died already. The air was full of ghosts, wailing as ghosts did, hungry for living blood. "But we buried you," Lucius said. "Or tried to. Burned you, at least, and cast earth on your bones."

Ghosts did not care. They had died far from home; they could not find their way back.

"That way," he said, angling his chin in the direction the army was going. But the dead could not hear him through the roaring of the blood in his veins. Some were feeding on the fallen, sucking life from the wounded. He should say something, drive them away. But they were deaf to him, and he was powerless.

A priest and an augur, powerless. How pitiful. But he could not perform the rites from horseback. He could cover his head with a fold of his cloak, yes, and he could say such words as he remembered, but he had no altar, no sacred vessels, no sacrifice. Only his fever and the snow, and the horse under him, plodding with head down, breasting the storm.

The words, once begun, seemed to unwind themselves like thread from a spindle. Half of them had no meaning that he knew: they were as old as Rome, older, formed in the deeps of time for the uses of magic. The rest were bad poetry, nursery nonsense, invocations of gods known not at all outside this conjuring.

He should be afraid. He knew this, dimly. He was affronted, certainly, and with good reason. It was highly improper, this working of magic from horseback without the aid of rite or temple.

Dione would laugh. She thought him a great fool. And while he thought of her, warmth enveloped him that was not fever. Hands seemed to rest on his, small hands, but strong for their smallness. Eyes regarded him, dark and bright at once. "See?" she seemed to say. "I told you you had magic."

"I have none," he said.

She laughed—he heard her, she was there, he was sure of it. "Then where are the dead, my dear idiot?"

"Dead," he said before he thought. "Gone." Then: "There are no ghosts! I was delirious."

"If you say so," she said. She could not be there, floating in the air in front of his horse. Nobody else saw her, or seemed to notice that he was talking to nothing visible. But then the snow was blinding, and there was sleet in it, lashing his unprotected cheeks. He huddled deeper in his cloak.

Dione was certainly an illusion: she shivered not at all, and she was wearing her most shockingly immodest Egyptian gown, the one that showed the dark rings of her nipples and the darker triangle of her sex, barely veiled in gauze, yet somehow more alluring than if she had been naked.

Looking at her warmed him remarkably. He reached for her, forgetting for a moment where he was. His hand met only air, and the bite of sleet.

TWENTY-FIVE

Dione started awake. She had been dreaming the black dream again, the one with the snow and the sleet, and the army dying in it, man by man. That was gone, done, twenty thousand Romans and Roman auxiliaries dead in the snows of Media.

She lay in her bed on the queen's ship, that seemed now as close as a sarcophagus, and as dark, for her lamp had gone out. It rocked as it rode the sea. They were sailing to what was left of Antony's army, that had escaped from Media and Armenia and taken refuge on the coast of Syria. Cleopatra was bringing clothing and provisions for his men, moving at what speed she could, but that was slow: it was winter, and although Ptolemy's birth had been easy, she had recovered less quickly from it than she should. She was not as young as she had been.

Dione could feel her on the edges of her magic, where she always was now. Cleopatra maybe did not know how ill she had been after the Nile's flood had ebbed, an illness that had matched nearly day for day Antony's terrible march through Media. If Antony had died . . .

Dione would not think of that. Not here in the dark. She was not afraid, nor inclined to rise and kindle a light. Still, this was no place or time to think of death.

The warm weight against her knees shifted, rolled, began to walk the length of her body. On her breast it paused, stroking her cheek with its soft cat-cheek, and mewed softly. She folded the cat in her arms. It began to purr.

She was still awake when dawn pierced the porthole, raw and grey. The cat blinked green-gold eyes and yawned, and slipped out of Dione's clasp. Dione sat up, drawing her blankets about her. Hebe was still asleep. Someone else was sitting by the door, a huddle of blankets and tumbled fair hair and eyes that had not seen sleep, perhaps, nightlong.

"Caesarion," said Dione, astonished. "How long have you been there?"

He shrugged. He was growing out of the softness of childhood, coming into an awkwardness of bones and angles, eyes and cheek-bones and strong Roman nose. When he came out the other side, she thought, he would be a handsome man. Now he was simply un-gainly, and endearing in it, though he would have been furious if she had said so.

Hebe had waked at the sound of Dione's voice. She regarded Caesarion without alarm or overmuch surprise. Calmly she got up, smoothed her gown, wrapped herself in her blanket that was also a cloak, and went out as she did every morning, to fetch Dione's washing water and her morning sop of bread in watered wine.

That explained, at least, how Caesarion had got in. But it did not explain why.

"I worry," he said abruptly, when Dione did not say anything, only stared at him. "Mother is so pale. She's been sick so long. Is she going to die?"

"No," said Dione. "She's borne her limit of children, that's all. A woman's body tells her that, if she's lucky, before it can kill her, or even harm her much."

"She's only had four," said Caesarion.

"Four children born alive and strong, and none miscarried, nor any dead in infancy. Few women are so fortunate. But it is enough. The goddess says so."

"Oh," said Caesarion.

Clearly he did not believe her. Equally clearly, he was too well brought up to say so. Sometimes Dione wished he were a little less polite and a little more free of himself. But that luxury was not granted to kings, or to the sons of queens. This small rebellion, this appearance in her sleeping cabin, was almost encouraging. She drew up her knees and nodded toward the end of the bed.

"Here," she said. "Sit down where it's comfortable. Hebe will bring breakfast enough for two, I'm sure."

He hesitated, but after a moment he sat where she bade, and not too stiffly, either. Once he was settled, the sun-and-shadow cat claimed his lap. He received her with a touch of astonishment. "Why," he said, and for a moment he was entirely a child, "she likes me."

"She always has," said Dione. "Now, then. Was it just worry for your mother that brought you here? Or is there more than that?"

"No," he said. "No, that's all. I couldn't sleep. I was thinking, you know. And wishing . . ."

"Yes?" Dione asked as he seemed to want her to.

"I wish," he said, "I could have gone with Antony."

That was a thoroughly boylike thing to want. Dione of course did not say so. She said, "You might have died, or worse."

He shook that off. "Oh, I know that. Mother said so, too. But it was a splendid thing to do, a manly thing."

"Even though he lost his war, and two parts in five of his army?"

"You're a woman," said Caesarion from the pinnacle of his dozen years. "You don't understand."

"I suppose not," she said without embarrassment. "Men make the most horrible messes. Women have to clean them up."

"I'm glad I'm not a woman," said Caesarion.

"Well you might be," Dione said, amused in spite of herself. If he had been younger she would have hugged him, but he was old enough to be prickly about such things. He would not of course show his gratitude. He stayed, that was enough, and played with the cat, and when Hebe brought breakfast, shared it with Dione. By the time that was done, his guards had found his trail. He went with them resignedly, bearing their looks of rebuke with becoming fortitude. A king, Dione had heard said, was the prisoner of his people.

He might be glad that he was not a woman. She was gladder still that she was not a king.

Antony in defeat had come to haven in no great fortress city but in a town called Leuke Kome, the White Village. It was a city now, for his army, even nearly half destroyed, was still a great force. Why he had chosen this place above all others, Dione could not imagine. It was as obscure as any place could be on this coast; and he needed, maybe, to lick his wounds away from the world.

It had a harbor of sorts, enough for some of the queen's fleet. There was a quay, if a wall of stones could be called such, with a wharf extending from it. The town itself was a chalky grey, though Dione supposed that in the summer sun its huddle of huts and houses revealed a hint of whiteness through the grime.

In this poor setting Antony shone with a kind of hectic splendor. The queen came off her ship to greet him, which, her manner said, was concession enough. When he reached to embrace her, she stood back at a cold distance. "My lord," she said. "Well met. I've brought you such provisions as I could gather."

Antony's arms fell to his sides. He did not look particularly crest-fallen, but his face had gone hard. "Well then. And how much money were you able to raise?"

"None," said Cleopatra.

His brows went up. He was not angry, not yet: he had neither flushed nor gone pale. "And why is that?"

"I had no time," she said.

"No inclination, you mean. You had a month."

"Contrary to popular opinion," she said acidly, "gold does not grow in the sand of Egypt."

Antony would have continued the battle, but Dione had gauged the pallor of Cleopatra's cheeks under the artful application of paint. "She was ill," Dione said. "She came as soon as her doctors would let her."

Cleopatra's glare was murderous. Dione cared only that Antony stopped arguing. "Ill?" he asked, as if the word had no meaning.

"It was nothing," Cleopatra snapped. "I had a winter fever, that was all."

"Childbed fever," said Dione ruthlessly. "Your son is well, my lord, and prospering. And so will her majesty be, if she takes care. I'd have kept her home for a while longer, or had her send an embassy to you. But she insisted that she come herself."

"You blazing idiot," said Antony, a snarl that was all love. He had swept Cleopatra up before she could move or protest. Once he had her, she could hardly struggle without losing what dignity she had left. He kissed her, but carefully, and carried her to her boat, and thence to her ship.

There, in the queen's cabin, Dione felt free to leave them. They would continue their quarrel, she knew that, but at least they would do it in the warm.

When she came out onto the deck, the wind struck her like a wall. There were knives in it, edged with ice. Still she was not moved to seek the shelter of her own cabin. She had two cloaks, the outer one lined with fur. And the air was clean.

Someone else was standing by the rail, someone not a sailor. He looked up as she approached.

She hurled herself at him with no more restraint than if he had been Timoleon. He braced himself just in time, or they would both have toppled over the rail and into the icy water.

He clung to her as fiercely as she clung to him. He was all bones and thin skin. She pulled back appalled. "You're burning up!"

"It's you," Lucius Servilius said laughing, though the breath was half knocked out of him. "You make me catch fire."

"Not like that," she said. "You've got a fever."

"It's almost gone," he said—and he with no more flesh on his face than a skull, and his eyes too bright in it, and a flush on his cheek-bones that made her drag him straight back down into the hold. It would strike her, later, that she was doing to him exactly what Antony had done to Cleopatra. At the moment she was too preoccupied to care.

There were medicaments in her belongings, some of which would help him, maybe. She sat him on her bed while she hunted for them. He was protesting, something about propriety, and indecorous conduct, and a lady's bedchamber.

"Cabin," she said, emerging triumphant from the sea-chest with the satchel in her hand. "And here's Hebe, defending my virtue with fire and sword. Hebe, fetch me water, please, as hot as you can get it, and cloths. And wine—I'll need wine. If cook can mull it with cinnamon and cloves, let him do that."

Hebe had no choice but to obey. Neither did Lucius Servilius, though he tried to protest. It might be true what he kept saying, that he was mending, but she did not like the look of him at all.

"If I lose you now," she said, "I'll call you back from the dead, and keep you with me till I die myself."

"What, in a golden coffer sealed with lead and blood?"

"Just so," said Dione. "I'm so glad we understand one another."

"I could wish we didn't," he said wryly. "What it says about me . . ."

"It says that you're starting to see sense." She pushed him down on her bed and held him till he stopped struggling. It was pitifully easy. His strength on deck, in the face of her assault, had been all he had.

"There now," she said when she had him lying down and well covered with a blanket, though Hebe had not yet come back with the water or the wine. She took his hands in hers. They were colder than the wind had been. "You have to be sensible now, because I won't have a husband who isn't."

It took him so long to respond that she wondered if he had even heard her. But then he said, "You aren't going to marry me after all."

"But I am," she said.

His brows went up. "When did you decide that?"

"One night," she said, "when I was in Egypt and you were in Media."

He knew which night that was: his flush proclaimed it. "That was a dream."

"Yes," she said. "And it was real. It showed me what I wanted. It wasn't anything very complicated. Just you."

He lay back as if exhausted, and shook his head. "You're just feeling sorry for me, because I was sick, and I still look half dead. I'm not dying, my lady. I'll be well enough when I can get warm again."

"You will be warm in Egypt," said Dione, "and in my arms." She still had his hands in hers. They were warmer now. She raised them to her cheeks. They curved to fit, as if he could not help it.

"Why—" he began to say.

"You wrote me a letter," she said.

"Oh, that everything were as simple!" He sighed. His lips kept twitching, trying to smile, and he kept trying to stop them. She leaned forward and set a kiss in the corner of his mouth.

He still tasted of cinnamon. He was warmer than he had been in the dream, but some of that was fever.

She would not have drawn back if Hebe had not made a clattering entrance. Dione preserved her calm. Lucius Servilius was blushing furiously. Hebe rolled her eyes and set to work bathing him with cloths dipped in steaming water. Dione, deprived of that pleasure—and wisely, too, if she was not to tax him beyond his strength—coaxed the heated wine into him, sip by sip.

Hebe had brought bread, too, fresh from the oven, with cheese heaped on it. Dione fed him bits of it. For all his protests that he was neither thirsty nor hungry, he drank and ate almost enough to satisfy her. When he would take no more, and was clean and warm and wrapped again in blankets, Dione said, "I'm going to leave you here for a while. You should sleep, and I have things to do. Hebe will watch you. Ask her for anything you wish."

"Will she give me you?"

Dione laughed, for Hebe's expression was eloquent of disapproval. "I'll come back in a little while. Now sleep. When you wake, I'll be here."

"I feel like a child," he muttered.

"That," she said, "you are not. Sleep, my love. Grow well, and grow strong."

TWENTY-SIX

A soldier in winter quarters asked little but to be warm and fed and supplied with the occasional woman, or if his taste ran elsewhere, a willing boy. So much Dione understood from what she had seen of armies. Warmth, Cleopatra had brought in the form of winter clothing; food, too, she had brought, and wine. Women and boys they found, one way and another.

Commanders, however, knew no such simplicity. Antony, with his queen to warm his bed and enliven his councils, grew more grim rather than less.

It came to a head not long after Cleopatra arrived in Leuke Kome. She was better, Dione thought: the cold clean air agreed with her, and likewise her lover's presence, though she quarreled with him more often than not. They were just past one such contention, over what, Dione did not remember. Payrolls, maybe, or Judea. A courier brought a satchel of letters, and one separate from them, that Antony leaped on with a lion's growl.

Dione, behind the queen's chair, was close enough to see the seal. Octavian's. She had seen it once or twice before.

Antony did not open the letter at once. He held it, scowling. "It's something weaselwise again," he said. "I'll lay wagers on it. Slithering out of agreements, breaking compacts, calling *me* a breaker of faith for choosing you and not his milk-faced sister."

"So read it," said Cleopatra, "and get it over."

Antony looked as if he would have argued, but he shrugged and broke the seal. He read in a mutter, too fast to follow—until he let out a bellow that rocked the tent on its poles. "That son of a barracks whore!"

"You flatter him," said Cleopatra, soft after his thunder. "What has he done now?"

It took Antony a while. He was too furious to speak, first, then too intent on finding new depths of invective. Eventually he began to make sense. "We're not a triumvirate any longer. He's got rid of Lepidus. The little rat's been retired to write his memoirs. *And this is the first Hades-reeking word I've heard of it!*"

Dione lowered her hands from her ears. They were still ringing, but she could hear Cleopatra well enough. "Maybe there's another letter in the bag, consulting you on the matter."

"You know there isn't." Antony stalked through the tent, the letter still clutched in his fist. "He thinks, because he's got Rome, that he has everything. But he doesn't. He has nothing. Nothing but spite."

"You know you despise Lepidus," said Cleopatra, "and only found him useful to preserve the fiction of a triune power over Rome. That's long outlived its usefulness. Can you fault Octavian for tiring of the pretense? At least he let the man live. He could have had him killed."

"How do we know he didn't?" Antony raked fingers through his hair, casting the careful curls into disarray. The thin spot on top was clear to see, but for once he seemed not to care. "It's not that he got rid of Lepidus. It's that he did it without me. We're supposed to rule autonomously, yes, each in his own sphere. But matters that affect the triumvirate—those were for all of us to settle."

"Don't tell me it surprises you in the least."

"What does that have to do with it?"

Cleopatra shrugged. She had been rifling through the satchel while he spoke. She plucked out a letter from the many. "Here's one from Octavia. Shall we see what she has to say of all this?"

"No," said Antony viciously.

Cleopatra ignored him. "Well," she said as she read. "Well, and well, and well."

He snatched at the letter, but she eluded him, reading as calmly as if he were not there at all. "By the dog!" he swore at her. "You're as bad as Octavian."

"Certainly I am not," said Cleopatra. "Such tender regard she has for you. 'My dearly beloved husband, greetings and health. The children are well and missing their father. Young Antony in particular bids you remember him and a certain promise you made him—' "

"Let me see that!" Antony won the letter this time, because she did not trouble herself to resist. "Great gods! She's sending the boy to me. What is she trying to do, seduce me with my own offspring?"

"Probably," said Cleopatra. "Read a little further. See what she says. She's coming to Athens as soon as the weather allows; she's bringing you money, clothes for your troops, provisions—"

"—seventy ships, and two thousand picked soldiers." Antony was reading both letters at once, eyes flicking from one to the other. "He owes me twenty thousand, damn his eyes. And what can I do with seventy ships, without men to sail them? Every man I've got who can run up a sail or grab an oar is already spoken for in one of your ships. He's fobbing me off with the tail while he keeps the whole ox. Listen to what he says: 'Rome celebrates your glorious victory and triumphant march from Media. We, meanwhile, do as we can in your shadow. Our forces are depleted, our numbers too low to permit the full payment of the men owed you. You will however be pleased to know that such forces as we have, we direct toward the war in Illyria, thereby winning new lands for Rome and keeping Rome's soldiers from becoming a burden on Rome's resources. You of course have the wealth of Egypt at your disposal—we wish you most well of it.' " He stopped, growling in his throat; then spat. *"Pah!* He makes me sick."

"So," said Cleopatra. "He's claiming a victory for you. Wise of him, since he has to keep Rome quiet."

"If I've won a victory, then the sky is green and the sea's as dry as sand." Antony held up Octavia's letter and shook it, rattling the parchment. "Now listen to what *she* says. 'The Senate has been so generous to us, my dear husband. Why, only the other day it voted both you and my brother statues in the Temple of Concord and in the Forum, and if that were not enough, granted you both the privilege of dining in the temple with your wives and your children. Is that not a lovely gesture? When you come home, my dear husband, we must all go to thank the senate and the goddess Concord, whose harmony rules us all, and break bread under her gracious eye.' " He flung the letter to the floor. "The senate! That was Octavian's fine hand, or I'm a Parthian. He'll never let Rome forget, not for a heartbeat, that I have a Roman wife and Roman children—and that I left them for you."

"So," said Cleopatra with a fine show of indifference, "go back, then, and leave your Egyptian whore. It won't be the first time. Or, very likely, the last."

Dione was sure that Antony would take a fit, his face was so blackly livid. But he stayed on his feet. He even spoke coherently, which she would have thought beyond him. "No," he said. "No, madam. My choice is made. They may not know it yet, not to be sure of it, but for me there's no going back."

"Even if she'd given you a son, and not a second daughter?" Cleopatra inquired.

No one else would have dared to say such a thing, and stand within reach of his fist while she said it. But he would not strike his queen. Cleopatra knew that as well as she knew her own limits. She rose in the silence of Antony's wrath and recovered the letter that he had cast away, and smoothed it on the table. "Are you going to go to her when she reaches Athens?"

"No," Antony said.

"Maybe you should," said Cleopatra. "If you want to keep on pretending that you're married to her, after all, you have to keep up at least some appearances. It would discomfit Octavian terribly to have his predictions go unfulfilled—for you can be sure, my lord, that he expects you to slight his sister and remain with me."

"I had all I could take of her," said Antony, "when we were in Athens before. I'll let her go there—she likes it, and it will keep her brother in suspense for a little while longer. But I won't join her. I've spent my last day in her so-proper company."

"Propriety can be a spice," said Cleopatra.

"Not to me," growled Antony.

Dione had heard all she cared to hear. She was not needed, in any case; she had only been there because it was warmer than waiting outside, and the queen had wanted an attendant of both rank and discretion. She slipped away, slowly lest she should be wanted, but no one even seemed to notice.

Just outside the tent, she nearly tripped over someone who was sitting in the wan sun. It was a child, a boy of about Caesarion's age. He leaped to his feet. He was bigger than Caesarion, heavier-boned, with a broad pleasant face and a great deal of brown curly hair. His eyes were a very light brown, almost amber, under level brows. They were a little startling, and they reminded Dione strongly of someone else altogether.

"Don't tell me," she said, "that Octavia sent you here with her letter."

He seemed somewhat taken aback. "Lady?" he asked in good Latin. "Do we know one another?"

"You don't know me," Dione said, "and I apologize for it. My name is Dione; I serve the queen of Egypt. And you, I trust, are Marcus Antonius the younger?"

"They call me Antonillus," he said. "Or Antyllus, if they're Greek enough."

"Then I shall call you Antyllus," she said. She glanced back at the tent and sighed. "I don't know if you should go in yet. Your father has no idea you've come."

"Is he with . . . Her?"

He said it just that way: as if he spoke of a goddess, or of a power below. "He's with Cleopatra," Dione said. She came abruptly to a decision. "Here, you look cold, and you must be hungry. These are your guards, yes?" she asked of the two men shifting uneasily from foot to foot and looking as if they wanted to drive her off but did not quite dare. "Tell one to come with us. The other can stay here and, in a little while, send word to Antony that you're in the cooks' tent with Lady Dione. It's warm in there," she said, "and Antony's cook does astonishing things with honey and spices."

Antyllus was a trusting child: he nodded eagerly and went with her in happy disregard of his guardhounds' snarling. They were making a great deal of sense, if any had been necessary. How did he know this woman was one of Cleopatra's servants? How could he trust her? She could be set to feed poison to Antony's eldest son, who must surely be a rival to the queen's own sons.

Antyllus heard not a word of it, or if he did, chose not to notice. Antony had that facility, too, to hear only what he wanted to hear.

The cooks were delighted to wait on their commander's son, new come from Rome and patently in need of good feeding. Antyllus had his father's brilliant smile matched with a charmingly ingenuous manner. He did not, Dione was interested to notice, share Antony's passion for wine. Maybe he was only too young. He did not cavil at the jar of snow-water, but took it with the rest of the heaping platter and carried everything into a patch of sun.

It was warm today, warmer than it had been in days: almost warm enough to be comfortable without a cloak. Dione, thin-blooded Egyptian, kept hers wrapped about her. Antyllus flung his aside as he ate. He had the voracious appetite of all young things, and very pretty manners—better than Timoleon's had been at that age.

When Antyllus had taken the edge off his hunger but was still filling in the corners, Dione saw Caesarion making his way toward them down the avenue of tents. The sun in his hair made it seem more golden than it was. He was dressed like a prince, which was not always the case, and followed by a pair of guards in the royal livery. Dione thought he looked very handsome.

Antyllus, beside her, bristled like a dog. "What in the world is *that?*" he demanded, making no effort to keep his voice down.

Dione raised a brow. Antyllus did not know her, however, to take the warning, and he was young and male and Roman. He went on with splendid disregard for Caesarion's ears. Maybe he thought the stranger would not understand Latin. "Oh, my, just look at him. He's adorable. He looks like my stepmother's lap-dog."

Caesarion halted. He seemed oblivious to Antyllus, bowing in Dione's direction and saying in Greek of insulting purity, "Lady. Well met. Isn't it a lovely warm day today?"

"Lovely," said Dione with an edge of irony.

"Yes," said Antyllus, who clearly understood Greek. "He is lovely, isn't he? Is that perfume he's wearing? And eyepaint?"

In fact Caesarion was wearing neither. Dione had no time to say so. Caesarion said, "I see you're vexed with a stinging fly. How did he attach himself to you? He looks very ill-bred. Is he some soldier's by-blow?"

Dione suppressed a sigh. "Where are your manners, Caesarion? Ptolemy Caesar, greet Marcus Antonius the younger. Antyllus, greet the king of Egypt."

But Antyllus was beyond such easy recall. "King? That? He looks like the King of Armenia's dancing boy."

"Bithynia," said Caesarion through gritted teeth—in Latin, too, with an accent not much worse than Antyllus'. "My father, they say, danced between the sheets with the King of Bithynia. Can't you even get your insults straight?"

"*You* weren't fathered by any Caesar," Antyllus shot back. "Who got you on Cleopatra? One of the stablehands?"

"I can see you're Antony's get," said Caesarion, sweetly poisonous. "He's coarse in his cups, too."

"La-di-da," sneered Antyllus.

Dione thought of stopping the battle before it started in earnest. Antyllus' one and Caesarion's pair of guards were glowering at one another, ready to defend their charges. She could command the Egyptians at least in Cleopatra's name; surely they would suffice for a pair of boys in full strut.

On the other hand, she reflected as she got out of the way, boys, like tomcats, had their own laws.

It was Caesarion who leaped first, Antyllus who reeled back. Caesarion was the smaller, slight and wiry as his father had been; Antyllus had his own father's bulk, but that was not necessarily an advantage. A smallish boy who was a prince learned early how to do battle with larger opponents.

Even at that, Antyllus was big for his age, and once he had recovered his wits, he showed that he knew how to use them. He was a canny fighter as well as a substantial one.

They rolled in the dirt like dogs. One or both of them was snarling in remarkably canine fashion. Their guards would have waded in, but Dione stopped them. "No. Let them fight it out."

They might have argued, but they had been boys once—none too long ago, in the case of Antyllus' guardsman. They yielded, but kept a close eye on the fray, as Dione did. It would never do for either of this pair of princes to suffer serious damage.

Dione knew the moment when the fight turned. Caesarion was on the bottom, being drubbed soundly, but wriggling hard enough to render Antyllus' position precarious at best. With a sudden wrench Caesarion overset his adversary. He paid for it, and quickly: Antyllus caught him in a chokehold.

There was a breathless pause. Dione tensed to leap.

Caesarion laughed. It was a strangled sound, but genuine. "Oh, sir! You are good!"

Antyllus was grinning himself through the remnants of a scowl. "You aren't so bad, either. Yield?"

"Never," said Caesarion.

"Well," said Antyllus in honest regret, "then I'm going to have to thump you."

"I'll thump you back," said Caesarion.

"With what?" Antyllus demanded.

"This!" said Caesarion. Dione never quite understood what he did. It was something like a snake's twist, and something like a cat's oozing out of a collar. He was sitting on Antyllus' head, while Antyllus thrashed to no effect. Then he was on his feet, staggering, filthy, and grinning vastly. "Yield," he said.

"Not though I die," said Antyllus.

Caesarion whooped. "Oh, I like you! Here, get up, clasp hands. Nobody else has given me as good a fight."

Antyllus got up stiffly, but his grin was as wide as Caesarion's, and he took the handclasp with evident pleasure. Still, he looked Caesarion up and down, and doubt was written clear in his face. "You're as dainty as a girl. You ought to be a pushover."

"That's why," said Caesarion. "And being Caesar's by-blow."

Antyllus nodded, understanding. "But you're a king. The lady said so, and other people told me—Ptolemy Caesar is king of Egypt, but his mother rules where it matters."

Dione held her breath. But Caesarion chose not to take umbrage.

"Being king doesn't count for much when you're settling territory in a boy-pack. It didn't count for anything with you."

"Well," said Antyllus, "but I'm a Roman."

"So am I," Caesarion pointed out. "Or half of me is."

"The other half's the king," Antyllus said. "It masters the whole."

"You're clever, too," said Caesarion. "Your father isn't. Not with words, much, though he fights well. And my mother loves him."

Antyllus sat where he had been before Caesarion arrived, on the ground beside the cooks' tent. With grand disregard of his ruined finery, Caesarion sat beside him. "My mother's dead," Antyllus said. "My father says she could have been a queen if she hadn't been a Roman. I don't know if he loved her, or she him. We don't talk about such things in Rome. They were a useful match, that's all. Till she went too far. She died of shame, they say. I think she died of frustration."

He spoke dispassionately—thoroughly like a Roman. Caesarion, who was half a Hellene, laid an arm about his shoulders. "There. I'm sorry for that."

"Don't be," said Antyllus fiercely, but without hostility. "Octavia sent me to try to bring my father back."

"Oh, I knew that the moment I heard your name," said Caesarion. "Are you going to try?"

"I don't know," Antyllus said. "Probably. I promised her I would."

"He'll stay with us," Caesarion said with sublime certainty. "You can, too."

"Your mother would allow it? I'm a rival to her own sons."

"But you're Roman," Caesarion said. "You can't be king in Egypt."

"And there is no king in Rome." Antyllus nodded as if he had explained everything. Maybe, in his mind, he had. "If I can't talk him round, I'll stay. Octavia is very good to us. But she's *good*. You know?"

"I know," said Caesarion. "You never quite forget how good she's being."

"Exactly," said Antyllus. "And you know what's even worse? She pats me on the head. And calls me her darling boy."

Caesarion gagged expressively. Antyllus' nod was equally expressive, and very sharp. "You know what else she does? I'll tell you . . ."

Dione smiled to herself. She would have to get them both cleaned up and fit to be seen, but not right at the moment. They were doing too well as they were.

TWENTY-SEVEN

Caesarion came back to Alexandria arm in arm with Marcus Antonius the younger, friends and brothers in spirit, and given no more to fighting than anyone might expect of boys who were raised to be princes. It was a great relief to their parents—not least to Cleopatra. Antyllus would do no more luring of his father to Rome than strictest duty bade him.

On a day of soft sunlight and full spring, Dione went to the palace in search of Lucius Servilius. She found him after a half-hour's hunt, and the small sun-and-shadow cat with him. He was reading a book in the queen's winter garden. The cat was drowsing at his feet, poured out in a patch of sun. They looked equally at ease, and equally content.

Lucius Servilius was recovered from the fever that had beset him in Media. He was still thinner than she liked to see him, and still somewhat pale, but his brow as she kissed it was cool.

He smiled at her. He had been doing that often of late; it made her giddy to see him. As if, she thought, she had been a featherhead of a girl and not a woman of a certain age and a certain rank and a fair quantity of experience in the world. None of it mattered when he looked at her as he was looking now. No one, his eyes said, had ever been more beautiful than she; no one more desirable.

That was nonsense. But it was very difficult to be sensible when Lucius Servilius was refusing to be any such thing.

"Tomorrow," he said, laying aside the book. She sat on the bench beside him, not touching. It was pleasure close to pain, to be so near and yet so distant. She savored it for the sweetness that was in it, for the knowledge that in a little while she could move that last tantalizing inch, and touch hand to hand.

And tomorrow, tomorrow night . . .

She swayed. His face filled her vision, white with terror. "What—" she began.

"You're ill," he said. His voice was tight.

"No," she said. "No. I—" But she stopped. Love was an illness, the poets said. The breath coming short; the throat locking shut; the sight going grey and then dark. The hammering of heart in a breast grown suddenly too small for it. Fear, panic terror, conviction, all at once, that she could not do this. She was not worthy. She was not able. She could not—

"Dione," said the voice that she should know best of any in the world, yet now she did not know it at all. Its accent was strange. Its timbre was different. It sat deeper in the throat; it had not the sing-song cadence of Greek or the clattering swiftness of Egyptian. "Dione," it said. "Lady, love, sweet friend, don't go away from me."

It was not pathetic, though it pleaded with all its heart. It had the arrogance that was born in all Romans, however gentle they might seem to be. It made her bristle.

Her sight came clear. Lucius Servilius was holding her hands. His grip was like an anchor to the world. "I almost turned coward and ran," she said.

"But you aren't a coward."

"No." She shivered, though the sun was warm. "Now I understand the terror of Pan who rules in the wild places. Panic terror. It's white, like bone. Red, like blood. It's almost beautiful."

"Stop it," said Lucius Servilius. "You're scaring me."

She tried to smile at him. "You see what you're getting, dear Roman. Are you sure you want it?"

"All of it," he said without hesitation. "Even the things that frighten me."

"Oh, not those," said Dione.

"Even those." He raised her hands to his lips, kissed each palm, held them together between his own. "I did know what I asked for. I had all those years, you see, to understand it, and to decide that I wanted it all. Priestess as well as woman. Goddess' voice as well as wife."

"I won't change," said Dione. "I'll still belong to the goddess. Apollonius didn't understand that. He thought he could alter me once he had me—diminish me, take the goddess out of me. No one can do that. Not even you."

"I won't," he said steadily.

"You're still afraid of the goddess' voice in me."

"Then I'll have to learn not to be."

She shook her head, not to deny him, not at all. "I do love you. But can you really take all of me? Can any man?"

"I can try," he said.

He was so brave, to say such things and mean them. She found that she could not care that later he might regret every one of them. He meant them now. That was enough.

She bowed her head. "Tomorrow," she said. Tomorrow they said the words. Tomorrow they finished what they had begun in Tarsus.

TWENTY-EIGHT

"This is preposterous," Dione said. She had been saying it over and over.

"Nonsense," Cleopatra said as she had been saying since she came to fetch Dione out of the chamber in which she had been resting—hiding, to be more precise. The rest of the women, servants and courtiers, priestesses and friends of the queen and the queen's friend, were laughing as they bathed the bride. They were supposed to consecrate her maidenhood, preparing her to become a woman—blessing her with their greater wisdom. As if she were either young or a maiden. As if she even wanted to be.

"And why we have to pretend," Dione said stubbornly, "I can't understand. Everybody knows this isn't my father's house, this is your palace. And the house I'm to be carried off to is my own. It's all profoundly ridiculous."

"It's a wedding," said Cleopatra. "Don't I stand in the place of your parents, may they rest in the peace of Osiris? Haven't I the right to bestow you on the man I can pretend to have chosen for you? Not," she added in a different tone, "that I would have thought of it if you hadn't done it yourself, but he is a good match for you. And so lovely to look at. Everyone's jealous."

Everyone was giggling and lifting Dione out of the bath, drying her with scented cloths, smoothing and oiling every reluctant inch of her. It had not been like this when she was married first. Oh, there had been the nuptial bath, the feast, all the rest of it, but she had gone to them as a lamb to the sacrifice. Now she was merely impatient. She wanted it over. She had wanted it quiet, solitary if possible—but Cleopatra would not hear of that, and Antony had been loudly dismayed. They wanted a proper wedding, whatever the principals might think.

Still, she thought, it was not too unpleasant to be fussed over, pampered and made beautiful. They all said she was that, but she had never felt it, even staring at her mirror of a morning. Her face was simply her face, her body her body. Now they were making it something to notice. Greek beauty for a Greek wedding, with much jesting at the modesty of the gown, and mock protestations that she should marry as an Egyptian, in the sheerest of Egyptian gauze.

"No, no," said the queen. "Modesty is the best spice of all. It lets a man dream."

The women sighed. Those who were married looked wise; those who were not, yet, looked eager and a little afraid. Dione wanted to comfort them, but she had no comfort for herself. What in the gods' name was she doing?

Marrying a man, Cleopatra would have said, if Dione had been fool enough to speak aloud. Cleopatra always saw to the heart of things.

Marrying a man. Dione clasped that thought to her as she was dressed, her hair combed and anointed but left free as if she had been a maiden. It would be bound up later, when she was a married woman. Again.

She must forget that. She must remember only this, this rite, this man.

Cleopatra, with the most deft of the maids, draped the bridal veil over Dione's head. It fell softly, like sleep; faintly cool where it brushed her cheeks and her arms. It was Coan silk the color of flame, so that the world seen through it was tinged with gold and red. Like fire, like blood. Like the heat of the flesh.

Robed, veiled, cleansed and scoured clean, Dione was borne out to the feast. The women were as relentless as the goddess, and as irresistible.

The halls were full of light. There was music, singing of high voices, laughter. She heard Antony's exuberant roar, the titter of courtiers, a silence that she knew, somehow, heart-deep, belonged to Lucius Servilius.

She could not touch him or even stand beside him, but must face him across a cold length of floor, first for the sacrifices, then for the feast. Everyone made a game of keeping them apart. He was one center of quiet, she another. She could wait, she told herself. She was not a trembling girl, nor yet a wanton, to fling herself across the hall and into her lover's arms.

She ate, she supposed, and drank. She did not notice. It was difficult to do in a veil, easier to give it up and sit immobile, hands folded in her lap, and wait for the others to finish.

Lucius Servilius was picking at his own array of plates and bowls and cups. The teasing was merciless, and monotonous on the subject of lovers too eager for one another to care for more mundane sustenance. It was supposed to be good luck to have one's ears burned with ribaldry. Antony was very good at it, and very ingenious. So, not too surprisingly, was Cleopatra.

Dione wished they would stop. Vain hope. It would only get worse—and her son was there, and Cleopatra's children, listening to all of it. Not that it mattered so much for Timoleon; he was a young man. But Caesarion and Antyllus, and the twins nodding but still fiercely awake, could hardly be edified by what they were hearing.

The princes looked rather bored. Timoleon had the expression he wore when he was studying something from all angles and committing it to memory. He would make something of it, Dione knew. Dione only hoped it came later rather than sooner.

The feast dragged on interminably. Dione drank enough wine to make her dizzy, but not enough to put her to sleep. The twins were curled on their ends of the great wedding couches, Selene on the women's couch and Helios on the men's, sound asleep. Caesarion's head nodded on Antyllus' shoulder.

Timoleon was flushed and full of wine, and getting truculent. "Say *what* about my mother?" Dione heard him say, rounding on a young man with more mouth than sense.

Cleopatra saved them all the diversion of a brawl. She rose from beside Dione and held out her hand. Dione stared at it for a moment, bewildered, before she remembered what she was supposed to do. She got up with a start, with little enough grace. The noise had died down. It was almost quiet, a quiet full of eyes. Men's eyes: the women were all on Dione's side of the room, the men opposite, staring at her.

She raised her hands to the veil. It felt suddenly comforting, like shelter in a storm. Taking it off would lay her bare to any wind that blew.

She shook off the thought. The veil slid in her fingers, seeming to resist her, but she was stronger. Its flame-colored curtain slipped away. The world was a strange white-and-gold place, the air cool on her cheeks, redolent of wine and sweat, perfume and flowers.

A long sigh ran through the hall. It was always so at the unveiling of the bride. Even if they all knew her from daily custom, the veil made her a stranger; on the other side of it she was a new thing, and beautiful no matter what her features, because she was the chosen one.

Dione saw only one face amid the blur, narrow, olive-skinned, crowned with wilting flowers. It was rapt, the eyes all dark, as if he dreamed awake.

The silence broke in a new uprising of clamor. Servants ran in with torches. The music turned wild.

Men and women leaped up from the couches. The women caught Dione up, bearing her toward the door and the carriage that waited to carry her to her husband's—her own—house. But the men, laughing, cut them off.

That was not part of the rite. Dione was affronted, then astonished. The men were fighting—no, they were charging through the women, the women shrieking in fear both real and feigned. Dione gasped as someone seized her from behind. But she knew that touch, those thin strong arms. She twisted in them. "Lucius—!"

He swung her onto his shoulder. He was laughing, she could feel his body shake, but he had breath enough for words. "This is the Roman way. Antony's idea. Fight a little. It's allowed."

She was fighting more than a little, by instinct. This was ravishment—abduction—outrage.

Lucius Servilius could not carry her the whole way to her house, not though he had been as strong as Antony. He did manage the distance to the carriage, which was impressive enough. He was breathing hard but still firm on his feet as he laid her on the cushions, gently enough when all was considered. She was too breathless with shock to speak. He was barely settled himself, and Antony beside him with a lurch and a groan of axles and much mirth, when the white mules sprang into motion. Dione's head snapped on her neck. Lucius Servilius' arm braced her. She shrank from it, but infinitesimally.

The men were disgustingly pleased with themselves. The women were plotting revenge, with Cleopatra their ringleader.

Dione, trapped in the carriage, drew her veil over her face and slid as far to the side as she could, and simmered. Neither Lucius Servilius nor Antony seemed to notice. Snakes, she thought. Frogs. No, mice. Romans would make wonderful fat mice for Bastet's cats to hunt.

Her magic was there if she chose to call on it. It was hot round the edges, like her temper. She held it off, not out of any charity for Antony's bully-boys, but because mice could lose themselves too easily in Alexandria's streets.

They were singing the *Hymen Hymenaie,* with the verses that were

meant to make a maiden bride blush till she wept. The torches
burned bright in the dusk. The stars were coming out one by one, the
evening star most splendid of them all.

Io Hymen Hymenaie, Hymenaie Hymen!

The women were singing, too. They sang in Greek, and the men,
Dione realized, in Latin; were they all Romans, or did they only wish
to be? The city paused to watch them pass. Wedding processions
were nothing so uncommon, but few were led by the queen of Egypt
and her Roman consort.

Io Hymen Hymenaie, Hymenaie Hymen!

The carriage lurched over an uneven paving stone. Lucius Servilius
swayed against Dione. She braced without thinking, and when he
swayed back with the movement of the carriage, she found herself
swaying with him. She stiffened. His face in the torchlight told her
nothing. He was not even looking at her. He was listening to something that Antony said in his ear, nodding and laughing.

Io Hymen Hymenaie, Hymenaie Hymen!

Her hands clenched into fists. *Over,* she willed it all. *Get it over.*

Her house was not even her own. It was full of flowers and lamps and
people. Lucius Servilius carried her out of the carriage, limp and
unresisting but unhelpful too, and over the threshold, and set her
down to a roar of acclamation. "Luck!" they all cried. Some of them
were flinging something that rattled as it fell: fistfuls of nuts, some
gilded, some not. "Luck!"

At the blessing of the hearth, when Dione was welcomed into her
own house as if into a stranger's, Cleopatra took the place of the
mother-in-law as she had taken that of the father of the bride. It was
no more absurd than any of the rest. The house seemed amused, if
anything. The servants were either grinning like fools or weeping for
the sheer damp pleasure of it. It was raining nuts and dried dates and
raisins and figs, which the children scrambled for. It was purely
untidy.

Lucius Servilius was beside her again. His hand held hers. She felt
cold in his clasp, distant, no part of him at all. Her eyes were wandering among the faces that crowded so close.

One of the men in the middle ranks looked familiar, but she could
not place him. He was thin, tall, mouse-haired: a young man, weedy
still as he got his growth, with a furze of unfashionable beard.

Dione stared at him for long moments before a name came to her.
"Androgeos." And, in pure amazement: "Androgeos!"

He could not have heard her. She could not hear herself. Her elder son—here, at her wedding, when she had not seen him in five years and more, not since Lucius Servilius first came into her house.

She wanted to fight her way through the crowd, find him and shake him and demand to know where he had been for so long, what he had been doing, why and how he had come. But the force of the rite, embodied in Lucius Servilius's clasp, was too strong.

He drew her with him through the house—dragged her, it might be, but her feet had a will of their own, and that was to follow where he led. The others flocked behind, singing the marriage hymn, the epithalamion—the bedding-song. They sang of love and of lust: the two were womb-kin, gentle and fierce, mild warmth and searing heat.

She did try to stop. She did try to say why she wanted to. "Androgeos—I need to know—how—"

No use. Weddings left no time or place for grown sons of older marriages.

At the door of her bedchamber, she was allowed to stop. The world spun on for a moment. It turned her to face the crowd in the passageway. She did not need, this time, to be reminded; her hands were on the veil already, lifting it, letting it fall to the floor. That was a great success: the men laughed and whooped. Lucius Servilius swept Dione up and carried her inside, and kicked the door shut.

The quiet was abrupt, if not quite absolute. They were singing again outside. They would sing all night in the corridor and under the window. Some would try to get in, or at least to peer through the shutters. But Dione had had curtains hung over the windows, thick curtains, too thick for any eyes to see through.

Within was lamplight and a scent of perfume, rare essences mingled for lovers' delight. The bed was spread with new sheets, strewn with flowers. There were blessings on it that needed the eyes of magic to see, and a murmur as of music in the air: sweeter music than was coming from without, and stranger. No mortal breath awoke it, no earthly instrument.

A very earthly voice spoke through it. "You look furious," said Lucius Servilius. "Did somebody say something to get your hackles up?"

"Said," said Dione, "no. Did, yes. How dared you grab me and carry me off like that?"

"It's how it's done in Rome," he said without overmuch repentance.

"In Rome they part the bride's hair with a bloody spear, too. How barbaric do you think I am?"

"Utterly," he said, "and not at all." He sat on the bed and began to unlace his shoes. "You look interesting when you're angry: as if you'd like to hiss like a cat. Do you know, I've never seen you in a temper before?"

"Are you going to divorce me over it?"

"Not yet, I think," he said. His shoes were off. He stood up again and started on his toga, doing it carefully, the proper way, instead of flinging it down in a heap.

The sheer prosaic casualness of him left her speechless. He should have been standing tongue-tied, or else trying to rip off her clothes and ravish her where she stood. Not acting like a husband of many years' standing, no more discomfited by his wife's presence than if she had been one of the slaves.

Partly for defiance, partly to see what he would do, she lent a hand with the toga. It was enormously long and very heavy. They were companionable, almost, smoothing and folding it, laying it on the clothes-stool. He seemed more slender without it, more graceful, but no less Roman.

Dione smoothed the parcel that they had made, running her hand from clean white wool to the purple stripe. It felt different, smoother, more finely woven. "I don't think I know you at all," she said to the stripe, but mostly to Lucius Servilius.

"Do you regret this, then?"

She looked at him. He stared back, dead calm. That was how he made himself strong, she knew as clearly as if he had told her. He schooled his face to stillness, and willed the rest of him to follow. "Yes," she said. "I've been regretting it. How could I have married a foreigner, and a Roman at that? I must be out of my mind."

"I'll release you," he said. His voice was calm as his face, as dead to emotion. "Do you want to take the bed? I'll take the floor. Unless you'd rather go out now and tell them it's off."

"Oh," she said. It was all she could say, for a long count of heart-beats, before the rest found its way out of her. "Oh, you *idiot!* You—you Roman! Of course I don't want to call it off!"

"But," he said, "if you want—if you—"

His stammer was back. That was reassuring. She had been afraid for a moment that he was going to be stubborn. She laid hands on his shoulders, in part to shake him, in part to hold him steady. "What I want," she said, "what I wanted, is, was, to have you. Just you. Without all the rest of this mummery."

"But the mummery makes it real," he said. He was holding himself in: his face was cold again. But under her hands he was trembling. With anger, maybe.

"It is real," she said, "with or without the bawdy verses and the raisins sticking to my shoes. The floors will never be the same."

"They'll come clean," he said.

His hands rose, came to rest on her hips. They felt comfortable there, holding her as for a dance. Strange how she could feel the heat of his body from nigh her arms' length apart. It made her breathless, a little, but not so much as to keep her from saying, "I didn't like being abducted."

"I won't do it again," he said.

She narrowed her eyes. He did not look as if he was joking. "Promise," she said.

"I won't abduct you again," he said, "unless you ask me to."

"Not likely," said Dione.

"Still," said Lucius Servilius. "One never knows."

She shook her head. "And you call me incalculable."

"Oh, I'm eminently calculable. I'm a Roman."

"No," said Dione. He seemed too far away, suddenly. She moved closer. Her heart was beating: she could feel it under her breastbone, under her breasts in their Greek girdle.

It had not been like this with Apollonius. He had stared at her till she wanted to crawl under the bed and hide. Then he had told her to lie down. She had done it because she was too cowed to do anything else. Then he had put out the lamp and got in with her, pulled up her skirt and done what men do. Or so her mother had referred to it. What men do was painful and rather embarrassing.

Dione had learned since that not every woman thought so. For many it was a pleasure, and one they sought as often as they could.

She had not been thinking very hard about that. She wanted this man near to her, wanted him living in her house and dining at her table and keeping Timoleon in as much order as that young man would ever permit. Marrying him meant that people would stop frowning at her for it—or mostly. There were still too many who would frown because she had married a Roman.

She could ask him not to take her as a horse takes a mare. He might even agree to it. They were friends first, after all. He could have slaves if he wanted them, or women of the court. Though he never had, that she knew of. Maybe he did not care for coupling, either, though that was hard to credit in a man. Which he was. She had seen enough of him to know that. He was not a eunuch.

She opened her mouth to say something, she was not exactly sure what. He covered it with a kiss. She went stiff, but only briefly. Kisses she could endure. They were pleasant. Even Apollonius', though his lips were wet. He had chewed cloves before he went to bed with her. Lucius Servilius preferred cinnamon. He tasted of wine, too, and of honey.

It seemed more comfortable to move closer still, touching body to body. Her arms fit round his neck, his round her waist.

He smiled at her. She could not smile back. He smoothed her hair out of her face, and paused. "What, love? Are you afraid?"

For some reason that made her want to cry. He was startled and visibly dismayed, but capable enough for that. He held her till she stopped, and went on holding her, stroking her hair. "There," he said. "There."

Abruptly she struggled out of his clasp. "Stop that! I'm not a child."

"I should hope not," he said.

She glared across an expanse of floor grown suddenly immense. "Then stop treating me like one."

"Well then," he said. "Come here."

She was going to refuse. Truly she was. But her body had its own opinion in the matter. It slid back into his embrace. Nor did it resist when he unclasped the brooches that fastened her gown at the shoulders. It slipped down, baring her breasts. They tightened in the cool of the room. It was winter, after all, and night, and even with a brazier the room was chill.

Moving softly, as if she were an animal and he had no wish to startle her, he unbound her girdle. She wanted to stop him, but her hands would not obey her will. Instead they ran down his sides to the hem of his tunic. Even as her gown slid down to pool at her feet, she got the shirt off him, easily, for he helped her with the best will in the world.

"Oh," said one of them, or maybe both. "Oh, you are beautiful."

He was blushing. So, from the feel of it, was she. They were like a pair of maidens—and he forty if he was a day, and she not so much younger than that. "Have you ever—" she tried to ask. "Have you—"

He nodded. He looked angry.

"With women?"

She thought for an instant that he would hit her. Then he laughed as one does who is trying not to be mortally offended. "Of course, with women. What do you take me for?"

"A man," she said, meaning to apologize, but unable to find words that would do.

"A Greek." He was still trying to be light about it. "I am a foreigner, aren't I?"

"Yes," she said. His shoulders were beautiful, olive-colored, wide and smooth, a little too sharp where the bones were, but time and feeding would take care of that. She ran her hands along the plane of them. He shivered lightly, not with revulsion, she did not think. No, not at all.

His own hands rose to touch her breasts. Her shiver was stronger than his, and some of it was fear. He seemed to know it: his hands stilled, curved softly round her, warm and quiet. He was always quiet, was Lucius Servilius. She could not recall that she had ever heard him raise his voice.

"You're afraid of me," he said.

"No," said Dione.

"You are," he persisted. "What did he do to you, that stick of a husband? Did he beat you?"

"No!" She almost pulled away again, but that would have been monotonous. She stayed where she was. "He was always respectful of me. Sometimes he remembered to ask me—if—"

"If you wanted him to couple with you?"

That was as close to coarseness as she had ever heard from this proper Roman. It startled her enough to be honest. "If he was hurting me."

"He *did* beat you." Lucius Servilius looked, for a moment, like a stranger: a stranger who could do murder.

"No," she said, gripping him hard, making him look into her eyes. "No, he never beat me. He never even raised a hand, no matter how exasperating I was. It was just . . . I'm not made right. I can't seem to get any pleasure from what men and women do."

There. She had said it. She steeled herself for his revulsion, or else for his denial.

He gave her neither. He said, "He didn't think of you at all, did he? He just went in, did his duty, went out again. And he got two sons on you. Gods, what a fool that man is!"

She could hardly contradict that, since she was of the same opinion. But she said, "I do love you. I want to be near you. If you want—if you would have pleasure—I don't mind, really I don't. It would make me happy to see you happy."

She had made him angry again; angry enough to thrust her away from him. "Hercules! You sound exactly like Octavia."

"You've lain with her?"

He looked startled, and then more angry than ever. "No! Antony has. And told me about it after. Do you think it can make me *happy* to see you lying there like a fish, suffering this inconvenience so that I can have a few moments' pleasure? I could pay a woman in the market to give me that much."

This, Dione could see, was going to grow into the kind of quarrel that would break them both. She was half minded to let it. The other half of her had had enough of this, both quarrel and impasse. It launched her at him, bore him back and down—fortunately on the bed, or they would both have had bruises. He was too astounded to struggle.

She had no skill. She had some knowledge and a great deal of fear, but she was past caring about that. She knew where everything went. He was no eunuch, most certainly, and startlement had not wilted him by much—not at all, once her hand was on him.

It was not so bad, if she set herself to do it. It hurt at first—she was tight and small, like a girl, and never mind that two living children and two more who had died, had come out that gate. But after a while it stopped hurting.

She had never had a man in her arms, moving as she moved, as her body wanted to move—not holding her down, or making her bend over while he came in from behind. It was like a dance. Parts of it were awkward. They did not know each other yet, not this way.

Yet, she had been thinking. As if there would be more of this.

As if there could not.

It was different when one wanted it. When the other looked at her and saw her, herself, Dione, and not the reflection of himself in her eyes. "Beautiful," he said. "Beloved."

Words, even such words as these, were a distraction. She lowered her mouth to his. That brought them together in every part of them, within and without. Hearts, too, beating hard, measure to measure. The dance, that had begun slow, awkward, painful perhaps for him as for her, went quicker. But not too quick. Not yet. There was something . . . there was . . .

Almost she pulled away. Almost. This—this new thing—it was—

More words. There were no words for this. Poets, who thought there were, were fools. Idiots. Babblers of nonsense.

He would never understand why she laughed, if she laughed now. And yet, maybe he would, he of all men who were. She let it out, a great whoop, bigger than the whole of her, bigger than the world.

It stopped the singing without. It began a whole new singing within.

Io Hymen Hymenaie, Hymenaie Hymen!

And, more to the purpose: *Io triumphe!*

ACT
FOUR

ALEXANDRIA
AND ATHENS
34– 32 B.C.

TWENTY-NINE

At last, triumph. Victory in Armenia, revenge for the lives lost in the war against the Parthians, joy and more joy from end to end of the eastern world.

Or so Cleopatra willed it, and Antony her consort. A full year he had prepared this new campaign, then gone out with somewhat less pomp than before, but to considerably better effect. He took Armenia and its king and its queen and their sons, and the wealth of their kingdom. It was not as great a treasure as he would have won had he taken Phraaspa, but still he seemed to be swimming in gold—the merest eddy, he liked to say, of the Parthian flood that soon he would win.

But that would wait for another year, another season of war. Now he celebrated his triumph.

He came out of Asia like Dionysus in his glory, driving his royal captives before him. Their chains were of gold, heavier than lead. Antony behind them rode in a chariot of gold, and golden horses drew it, bright rarities that he had found in the stables of the Armenian king. They came, it was said, from somewhere deep in Asia. Their coats were like beaten gold, their manes bright silver; gold and silver their trappings, set with a dazzle of jewels.

Now and for once Cleopatra awaited him while he came to her, seated on a throne of gold, arrayed in gold, till the eye fled all that brightness and took refuge in the shadows of Isis' temple. The goddess' image rose behind the queen, robed as was the queen: Isis in stone, Isis on earth, cold marble and living flesh, goddess and woman together in this one glorious moment of the world's time.

Antony drove his chariot right into the temple's precinct, its gold-shod wheels rattling on the tiled floors. His captives halted before Cleopatra. The children were weeping, but silently, with set faces. Their mother tried as best she could to comfort them, weighed down with chains as she was: kneeling in front of Cleopatra, drawing them to her and holding them as if she could protect them from the shame of their defeat.

Armenia's king, however ignominiously deposed, stood tall in front of the Egyptian queen. By custom he should bow down before her. But he would not. He was too proud.

One or two of the guards moved to force him down, but Cleopatra raised a hand. "No," she said. "He was a king. He never knew aught but pride. Now pride is all that he has left. Let him keep it, if it comforts him."

"One day," said the captive king, too cold for venom, "you too will be led in chains in a Roman's triumph."

"Not I," said Cleopatra. "I would die first." She beckoned to the guards. "Take him away. Keep him under your protection, but treat him well. Feed him if he wishes it. Remember that he is royal, and he was a king."

She could afford to be generous, Dione thought. She was queen, and triumphant, and wealthier than ever. The festival went on seemingly without end, one long bacchanalian revel, the Triumph of Dionysus. The height of it saw a mighty throng gathered among the colonnades of the Gymnasium, staring up in awe at the images of divinity on earth. Golden thrones inlaid with silver were raised high above the crowd. The two highest stood side by side, and in one the living Isis, in the other the new Dionysus, Osiris on earth, lord and victor in the Two Lands. Below them on thrones lesser but still of surpassing magnificence sat the children of gods.

Caesarion, eldest of them all, was king of Egypt as his mother was its queen, wearing the two crowns, the red and the white, and bearing the crook and the flail that had marked the pharaoh for years out of count. But Alexander Helios wore the garb of another realm altogether, the trousers and the richly embroidered coat of the Parthians, and he wore the Mitra, the tall crown of Persia, and the guards about him were Armenian, attendants once of the fallen king. His sister Cleopatra Selene, as if to balance his kingship of the east, wore the crown of Cyrenaica that was west of Egypt, that had been half a Roman province, half a dependency of Crete. Now it was hers, given her as another child might be given a nursery to play in.

To the youngest, to Ptolemy Philadelphos whose name was nearly larger than he was, went the kingdoms of Syria and of Lesser Asia, the lands that Alexander had conquered first when he rode out of Macedon. The child was decked like a Macedonian king: purple cloak, broad-brimmed hat adorned with the ribbon of the diadem, guard of big fair Macedonian soldiers such as had marched with Alexander himself.

Cleopatra, above them all, had named herself Queen of Kings, and her eldest son the king of kings, lord and master over his brothers and his sister. He bore it well enough. What mattered more to him, and to Rome, was the decree that Antony had published, proclaiming him the legitimate and acknowledged son of great Caesar. That was a slap in Rome's face, and most of all in Octavian's: deliberate, calculated, and brazen in its boldness.

It was only the truth. He pointed that out, when it was all over and he could be himself again, Cleopatra's son and Antyllus' brother-companion and Dione's fosterling from his childhood. King of kings he might be, but the Queen of Kings ruled well enough for herself, a fact that did not appear to embitter him overmuch. He could be a boy as other boys were, hunting birds in the marshes round Dione's house on Lake Mareotis, riding one of the golden Armenian horses in races with Timoleon's Numidian mare, sitting of an evening in the colonnade while the breeze blew in off the lake. The summer's heat was gone a month since, the air cooling as the sun sank, but it was pleasant still, and quiet but for the calling of birds on the water.

"I am my father's son," Caesarion said. "Now even Rome has to admit it, as it did when my father was alive."

"It's not Rome we have to worry about," said Timoleon. "It's Octavian."

Caesarion shot him a dark glance. He bore it with serenity that he seemed to have learned from his mother. He did look like her, if she had been a tall young man in a foppish gown, green shot with silver, distressing to Roman eyes—and well enough he knew it. Lucius Servilius was sure that he had worn it expressly for that purpose. Timoleon was deeply pleased with his mother's marriage, Lucius believed that, but he was never one to care for affection when he could be outrageous.

Timoleon was being sensible enough in spite of the ridiculous robe and the garland of lilies on his crimped black curls. For Timoleon. He said, "Ah well, Octavian has Caesar's property in Rome, but you have his name—and his power in the world, several times over. Caesar was never a king of kings."

"In Rome, they abhor kings."

Lucius should not have said it. It slipped out under the force of his own pent-up emotions, days of them, weeks, months. The Egyptians stared at him, even Dione silent on her chair with its carved footstool. Caesarion's expression was the one he feared, or should fear, most.

It was not angry as it well might have been, nor even surprised. "Is that what you think of me?" Caesarion asked.

"No," said Lucius. He was telling the truth. "You are Caesar's son. I see him in you; but you are your mother's too. And through her you are a king."

"And her you despise."

"No," Lucius said again. "I admire her greatly. But I know her. Rome . . . Rome knows only the eastern witch, the monster of nature, the queen of Egypt who seduced Caesar, who seduced Caesar's friend, who raised Caesar's son to be a king."

"I never understood why Rome hates kings," Timoleon said. "Is it because your old kings were so inept? Or because your people have such a talent for carrying grudges?"

"Both," Caesarion said before Lucius could open his mouth. "Romans never forget a slight, and never forgo their vengeance. Even over hundreds of years."

"How silly," said Timoleon.

"As silly," Caesarion said, "as hating the Persians still, three hundred years after Alexander conquered them and made them his servants."

"I don't hate Persians," Timoleon said. "I'm part Persian myself."

"Rome hates kings," Caesarion said, "because Rome hates any single man who may presume to set himself over it. Even the dictators can rule only for half a year. Marius, Sulla, Pompey, Caesar—they all found ways to explain away their assumption of power. Words, titles that created a polite fiction. But we call ourselves what we are. Rome will learn to endure us, or Rome will fall."

Lucius shivered in the soft air of evening. "There, sir, you show yourself for what you are. And that is not a Roman."

Still Caesarion was not angry, or not that he would let Lucius see. "I'm half a Hellene. I'm all a king."

"Therefore Rome will never acknowledge you."

"It will learn," said the son of kings. He did not even say it with arrogance: it was a fact, simple and incontrovertible.

"No," said Lucius, whose stubbornness came out of everywhere and nowhere, out of frustration that he had not even known was there until it burst full-grown into his consciousness. He tried to soften it. "Well, and maybe they'll accept you—as a foreign king, no ruler of theirs. But Antony sets himself up as a lord of the eastern world. That, they'll never forgive."

"Romans can never bear it that we're civilized, and they only wish to be," said Timoleon.

"We would say the reverse," Lucius said. He rose abruptly. "Please. Excuse me. I'm not well. Something that I ate . . ."

"Something that you said," said Dione in the room they shared in this less frequented of her houses. It was larger in fact than their chamber in Alexandria, as all this house was larger but lesser, because it was far out by the lake, away from the city, and the other was in the city proper. She did not sound angry with him, but then she seldom did.

He regarded her as she lay on the sleeping couch, banked in cushions of silk as soft as her skin. She wore a coverlet wrapped around her, and her hair was free, flowing over her shoulders and down her back, but there was nothing wanton about her. She looked as young as her son, and gravely intransigent.

"Something that I said," he agreed. "I was about to commit mortal offense against the king's majesty."

"And you hadn't already?"

"I wasn't going to give him time to decide I had." He sat on the clothes-stool to pull off his shoes. "I think I'm glad Antyllus didn't come here with us, though the children gave us trouble and to spare for it. He would have agreed with me—and him, Caesarion could happily have thrashed. Or tried to."

"Such stiff necks you Romans have," she said. Her small odd cat came stepping delicately over the coverlets, patted her cheek lightly with a paw, and went on about its inscrutable business. Dione's hand went to the cheek that the cat had touched, resting there. Her eyes were dark, blurred, as they were when she was half asleep, or seeing visions.

But she did not speak for the goddess tonight. She sighed and said very much in her own voice, "I think Antony knew—and that's why he kept Antyllus with him, and never mind what he said of the child's education in matters Roman. You're not the most opaque of men."

"I haven't been as obvious as that," Lucius said, shocked.

"Sometimes Antony doesn't need the obvious, to understand," Dione said. "Always when you don't want him to see. Or Cleopatra saw for him. *She* has Argus-eyes, as a goddess should."

That made too much sense to argue with. Lucius drew a weary breath. "So the whole world knows what I think of this 'triumph' in Alexandria."

"Not the whole world," said Dione. "Antony understands, I think.

He's Roman, too, however Greek he may have allowed himself to become."

"If he were Roman, he would never have affected the manners and estate of an eastern king, or allowed his children to be called kings."

"Of course he would," said Dione. "A Roman is pragmatic first of all, and a Roman of his ilk hungers after power. If he has to play at kings to have it, then play at kings he will, and take care for Rome's objections later, when he has answers ready."

"So much you know of us," said Lucius, bitter enough to hurt.

But she was never wounded by matters of state. She saved her heart for the deeper things, the things that mattered to her: woman-things, magic-things. She held out her arms. "Come here, beloved despiser of kings. Do you care if you never understand us, as long as you love me?"

"Yes," he said. But he came to her arms, because they were warmer than the night, and because they were hers.

All the reticence that had troubled her on their wedding night was gone now, and well gone. She kept her modesty and her delicacy of manner, but she had passion and to spare. When she had spent it, and his too, they lay in spreading quiet.

He had almost forgotten the vexation of kings, and even the power of Roma Dea. Dione's head lay on his shoulder, her hair scented with an oil that she favored, that was mostly roses, with something under that, sharp yet sweet. She played with his half-flaccid penis, but not enough to raise it again. Something about her—the feel of her in his arms, the rhythm of her breathing—made him ask in sudden concern, "Beloved? Are you well?"

"Most well," she said. But there was a catch in it.

His heart stopped, then started again. "You're ill."

"Oh, no," she said. "I'm not ill at all."

"Dione—"

She tilted her head back so that he could see her face, foreshortened with nearness, all eyes and pointed chin. She looked half elated and half terrified. "I'm going to have a baby."

She sounded surprised. And how could she be, if she had known it for as long as women did before they troubled to tell their men?

So much he managed to think. Just so much, before the full force of it fell on him like Pelion falling from Ossa—and how in the name of Typhon he had happened to think of that, only the gods below could tell. "You—" he said. "You—are—"

"I'm pregnant," said his wife, sounding mildly affronted. "At my age. It's indecent."

"Then you don't—want—"

And what he thought, what he felt, he did not know. Not yet. He could not.

She neither rose nor flung him away from her, but in her expression she did both. "Of course I want this baby! I'm just taken aback. I wasn't even sure till today. I thought I was dreaming, or being ridiculous. But I reached for my magic this evening, to quiet our young cockerels, and there was no doubt about it. It's gone."

"What in the world does that have to do with—"

She was remarkably patient, considering. "We who are the goddess' servants, or her flesh on earth . . . we lose the most vexing of her gifts when we bear her children. Hers, you understand, because they have magic. Cleopatra was like this with all of hers. I was luckier, or unluckier if you like. I had only sons; and sons in my line, unlike Cleopatra's, are not chosen by the goddess."

"Then," he said in sudden fear, "how can you defend yourself?"

"There," she said, patting him as if he had been one of her offspring. "There, be comforted. The goddess defends me. Her mantle is all about me—it's too thick even to let my magic through. And the more fool I, for not realizing it until tonight. I'm nearly three months pregnant, as close as I can reckon."

"But—" he said.

"I said, I was refusing to admit it. Women do have interruptions in their courses, you know. Especially as they reach a certain age. I'm young for it, a bit. But not so much. And magic does odd things to us who have it."

"You don't lose magic as you lose—that?"

"Oh, no," said Dione. "We gain it, immeasurably. The goddess makes us strong than we've ever been."

"Ah," said Lucius, rather faintly. "I see what I have to look forward to."

"But not for a while," said Dione. "Not at least till I've borne and nursed this child. The goddess willing," she added, breathing a prayer with it.

"Do I have any say in it?" he inquired.

She blinked her great dark eyes at him, gravely and honestly astonished. "Why, of course you do. It's half your fault the child exists at all."

"I mean," he said, "that it's mine to decide, once the child is

born—if the child is born, if such fortune is given us—whether it may
live or die."

"No," said Dione. "If you were any other man, married to any other
woman, yes, that would be so. But this is the goddess' child."

"I could contest that," he said.

"I hope you won't," she said, as serene as ever. "Apollonius got to
choose twice—fortunately those were both boys. If he hadn't agreed
that they should live, I would have been most unhappy. And rebellious, probably. Almost certainly."

He looked down into her face, so beautiful and so foreign, and
sighed.

She frowned. "Lucius? Are you angry with me?"

Of course. She could not see, any longer. She was like any other
woman.

But she was not. She never could be. He traced the line of her
cheek with a fingertip. "No, my love. I'm not angry. I'm only . . .
surprised. And glad." And he was, he truly was, who had never lain
so, while a woman, his wife, told him that he would be a father. It was
ineffable. It was terrifying—no wonder she had looked so afraid.

He tried to say it all, but he was no more a poet now than he had
ever been. He could only say, "Glad, yes. Glad beyond words."

"Even if it's a daughter?"

"Another Dione?" He smiled. "I could hope for that."

"Or it could be another Lucius Servilius," Dione said. Her hand lay
on her belly, that showed no sign yet of the child inside it. She smiled
as his own hand came to rest over hers: a smile that shook a little, but
was brave enough, considering. "Boys are such a nuisance. But a son
like you . . . yes, I could manage that."

"May the gods bless him. Or her, if such is their pleasure," said
Lucius.

Dione's smile was all the blessing he needed for himself. For the
child . . . the gods would provide. He would trust them, for this while
at least. Was this not their child as much as it was his?

THIRTY

Antony's friend Plancus danced before the cream of the court, painted blue, crowned with reeds and wearing a fish's tail. The cream of the court, swimming in wine as Plancus pretended to be swimming in water, sang—sometimes even on key—the verses that accompanied the dance. Plancus was Glaucus the river-god. The court was itself, Antony's own and most favored fellowship, his Inimitables, Roman faces mingled with Greek, all flushed with wine and feasting.

Cleopatra's gown was all pearls, a moon-bright shimmer from her shoulders to her feet. Her hair was plaited with pearls, pearls in her ears and on her arms and her fingers. She was as fabulous a creature as the noble Roman writhing naked and blue-bodied and fish-tailed on the floor. Antony, leaning on her shoulder, seemed almost prosaic: his chiton was merely cloth of gold, and his cloak, flung over the back of the couch, a mere and earthly lionskin with the head shaped and tanned to be a helmet. He had wine-goblets in both hands. One was his own. The other was the queen's, from which he fed her sips of the best Caecuban. He had exchanged cups once, for a jest, but she had known in an instant: he drank his wine barely watered, she watered it well and prudently and not at all like a proper Macedonian.

The Inimitables in full cry were audible clear down to the palace gate. Lucius Servilius the Augur had heard them as he came, arriving late and excusable enough in the middle of Plancus' spectacle. There was a couch near the door, a place of so little honor as to be almost insulting, but he was not in a frame of mind to care for trifles. He accepted wine from the servant, let a plate be filled for him, took out his napkin from the fold of his toga and laid it before him and set himself to be, if not convivial, at least polite.

That was difficult, considering Plancus. That a Roman of his rank danced at all was scandalous. Painting oneself blue like a Hyperborean savage, putting on a fish's tail, and acting the part of a minor god, went utterly over the edge.

"You look like a Vestal Virgin in a brothel," said Antony, sitting on the couch beside Lucius and helping himself to one of the untouched confections on the plate.

"I'm that obvious?"

"I know you," said Antony. "How's your lady? Is she well?"

"Very well," Lucius said, rather glad to change the subject, "but a little out of sorts. She wants to have the baby and get it over."

"Don't they all," Antony said. He leaned back on his elbow, thoroughly at ease, watching the entertainment that had succeeded Plancus: a much more sedate consort of musicians on flute and lyre. "You think I'm going too far."

Lucius shrugged slightly, reached for a sugared almond, ate it. It was too sweet for his taste. He sipped the wine, which was watered as he liked it.

"And this of course is no place to discuss it," Antony said, "even if you would. Yes? But what better place? No one's listening unless he has a right to; and everyone here is trustworthy."

"You think so?" Lucius tried a cake. It was made of almonds, too, with honey. Dione would have liked it. He would try to remember to bring her a napkinful.

Antony's gaze had wandered to Cleopatra. She had a companion on her couch, a lion-cub of a boy, big for his years and strong, but still young enough to blush when one of the naked Egyptian slave-girls walked past him with her tray of sweets. She offered it to him, bending, her tawny breasts swaying. He took a sweetmeat at random, hardly knowing where to look.

"He'll be a man soon," said Antony with pride. "Look! Isn't he a Roman among Romans?"

"And Greeks," said Lucius, "here. Everyone's calling him Antyllus now. How Roman is that?"

"Just as Roman as I say it is," Antony said, showing for a moment the steel behind the smile. "He's quicker-witted than I am. He thinks better on his feet. This is the place for him to hone that—this court, where he's safe but where he has to watch every step, and learn every turn of the courtier's dance. My queen teaches him everything she knows; so does her son."

"Caesarion," said Lucius. "Where is he tonight?"

"Studying the stars," Antony replied, "with a gaggle of philosophers. They asked Antyllus, but he said he'd rather come to the revel. He's my son in that. The stars do as they will. A man's mind is best turned to the things he can master."

"Such as wine, and fishes' tails?"

Antony laughed heartily. "Just so! And queens, old friend. And kingdoms."

"There are those," said Lucius, "who say that the queen is ruling you. That she leads you by the nose, and that sunk in a winecup."

"Of course they say that," Antony said. "They're listening to Octavian. It would serve him all too well if I drowned in a winejar, or expired in my queen's arms. He'll hasten it if he can, kill my reputation in Rome at the very least, and make my name a laughingstock. But I'll laugh last, Lucius Servilius. Be sure of that."

"I wish I could," Lucius said.

Antony clasped Lucius' arms in a sudden, powerful grip. His fingers were warm and solid, rock-steady in spite of all the wine that must be in him. "Be sure of it," Antony said again. "This game is mine, Lucius Servilius the Augur. I rule my queen, and not she me. No matter what they say in Rome—or in the back streets of Alexandria."

Lucius looked into the amber eyes. The words were easy to read as the protest of a man whose woman has him wrapped about her finger, but the eyes were not the eyes of such a man. Lucius was a little startled to see the strength there. He had let himself grow apart from the triumvir, caught up with his wife, her son that he had made his own, all the affairs of a man of substance in this foreign and yet familiar city. Of Antony he had seen little save at a distance: the eastern king on the golden throne, the chief of the Inimitables in his wash of wine, the lover and consort of the Egyptian queen.

This was all of them, but it was Antony too, Marcus Antonius the Triumvir.

Lucius was not sure that he was comforted. This was power, and power went its own way. Whether that way was Rome's, or Egypt's, or simply Antony's—he could not tell. He did not have Dione's gift of seeing into a man's heart. His gift for reading a sheep's liver, a bird's flight, was of little use here in this scented and wine-reeking hall.

"Octavian wants what Octavian wants," said Antony, still grasping Lucius' arms. His grip was just short of pain. "If what Octavian wants serves Rome, then that's a coincidence at best. What I do here *is* Rome, no matter what the trappings. I've taken the East in the name of Roma Dea. I'll hold it, and my son will hold it after me."

"Son?" asked Lucius. "Not sons?"

"My Egyptian sons are kings in the east," said Antony, "but my Roman son is my heir in Rome."

"Caesar did much the same," Lucius observed. "He left Rome to his nephew."

"The more fool he," Antony said. "He knew what that boy was. He'd have done better to leave everything to Caesarion—though Rome would never have stood for that. They've already made Cleopatra into a monster."

"Maybe," said Lucius, "he thought Octavian could carry on as he began. And maybe he knew what you would do as soon as he was out of the way—seek out Cleopatra and the alliances she had to offer. Maybe he wanted exactly this: contest to the death, and victory to the strongest."

"Or maybe he wanted nothing once he was dead but to be remembered—no matter who took Rome after him."

"Maybe," said Lucius. "He was—is—the Divine Julius. Who can fathom the mind of a god?"

"They say I'm a god myself," said Antony with a flash of teeth. "I can't say I feel it much, except when I'm in my queen's bed. Then I'm lord of the world."

"What, not even when you play the sun on your throne, with your children like moons about your feet?"

"That's spectacle," said Antony. "It gives the people something to talk about, and Rome something to be scandalized by. Rome loves a scandal. I'll give it all it wants—and then I'll give it Octavian on a platter, with a pomegranate in his mouth."

"Unless, of course," said Lucius, "he gets you on his platter first."

"That's the game," said Antony as if he relished it. "That's the challenge. Remember what Alexander said when he died, when they asked him whom he was leaving the kingdom to. 'To the strongest,' he said. That's all. 'To the strongest.' "

THIRTY-ONE

"There's strength in waiting," said Cleopatra, "as in rushing headlong into battle."

"Most of war is waiting," Dione said. She sighed. She was very pregnant, and very tired of being pregnant. It had taken a major rebellion to persuade her servants, suddenly become her masters in the matter of whether and how she exerted herself, to let her travel in her litter to the palace, and there be carried into the queen's presence as if she had been a queen herself, and an infirm one at that.

Even the queen had tried to coax her into the bath where she might, Cleopatra insisted, be more comfortable. Dione refused. She was not comfortable in the bath. She was not comfortable anywhere, and would not be until this baby was born.

At least, with Cleopatra to talk to, she could take her mind off her burgeoning belly. Not that Lucius Servilius failed to do the same. He was very good at it, but he was out in the city with Antony, overseeing the building of a new hospital. Cleopatra might have been with them, but she was, she said, more pleased to enjoy a quiet hour with a friend. "Which we seldom have, these days," she went on. "Everything is going as splendidly as any of us could wish—except perhaps Octavian. But it tends to be rather hectic."

Dione nodded. It was safe to do that. Less safe to say, "Everything is going as Antony wishes. Even that pirate Sextus Pompey, dead and burned and out of mind. What of you?"

"Antony's wishes are my own," said Cleopatra. She said it without irony, but she added, catching Dione's glance, "No, I haven't gone soft! We're allies—in heart as well as in politics. Would he do what he does, I ask you, if he cared only for Rome?"

"He cares for Cleopatra," said Dione. "And for Rome. But most of all for Antony."

"Well, and I look after Cleopatra first, however devoted I may be to my consort. And Cleopatra is Egypt. Egypt profits from its alliance with these Romans."

"*These* Romans," said Dione.

"You married one," Cleopatra pointed out.

"So I did," Dione said. "He's not a king, nor minded to be one."

"Antony will be king only as far as it suits him to be, for the enhancement of Rome's power—and of his own."

"And you allow that? You depend on it?"

"I build on it," said Cleopatra. She left her chair as she could do when duty did not chain her to it, and prowled the room with its fine tiles arranged to form images: beasts, birds, the waters of the Nile as it flowed from Nubia to the Delta. As she moved from a river-horse in reeds to an ibis stalking its prey, she said, "Egypt needs Antony. Antony needs Egypt. There is no separating the two."

"Then if Antony falls, then so falls Egypt," said Dione.

Cleopatra spun. "How can Egypt fall? Octavian stumbles and staggers in his feeble attempts to equal Antony's feats of arms. Rome is nothing but what its rulers make of it. Parthia waits for us to rise up and destroy it. The world is ours to shape as we will. And we *will*. I know it. The gods tell me so."

Dione, whose goddess was silenced by the child growing in her belly, could only shake her head. "Then I'll be your chorus, and warn you of hubris."

"Ah," said Cleopatra. "Like the slave at a Roman's triumph, who stands at his ear throughout and whispers, 'Remember, thou art mortal.' "

Dione had seen Caesar in triumph, and the slave whispering into the ear that seemed barely to hear, still less to heed; she had seen Caesar dead with his body full of wounds. She said, "You are mortal. Even you, who are Isis on earth. All flesh must die."

"But some die later than others." Cleopatra spread her arms. "See what we are. We will die as all men do—but no one will ever forget us."

"Such grandeur," said Dione. The baby kicked; she winced. "Ah! Boots of iron, this one has: a regular little legionary."

Cleopatra laughed. She never seemed to mind being brought back to earth, particularly by such distractions as this. She approached the couch on which Dione had been laid. "May I?"

Dione nodded. Cleopatra laid a hand on her belly and smiled as the baby rolled under the touch.

"Soon," said Cleopatra.

"Within the week, I think," Dione agreed. "It's early, a bit. But not too much. Remember when you hated me for never swelling, and you were like a river-horse when the twins were born? Do you feel vindicated now?"

Cleopatra took Dione's hand in hers. "You're no river-horse. A fish, maybe, smooth and sleek: a dolphin for sailors to wonder at. They bear their young alive, did you know? One of my natural philosophers saw one off Delphi, a queen attended by a court of her fellows, and when the baby was born it swam after her on its cord, singing."

"Singing?" Dione asked.

"So he said," said Cleopatra.

"Such tales," Dione said, but she smiled. "It's good of you to entertain me when you could be doing something more interesting."

"Such as laying cornerstones for hospitals or listening to endless squabbles over taxes?"

Dione conceded the point. "Still," she said, "I'm poor company for a queen."

"I don't recall that I was any better when I was bearing my young ones," said Cleopatra with a hint of sharpness. "Allow me to give you this much at least, since you won't let me send any of my women to help you with the birth. Won't you reconsider?"

"Hebe has a gift for midwifery," Dione said: "a magic, I would say. She's all I need for the birthing of the flesh. That of the spirit . . . do your women have such power? Can they shape the world about a child who belongs to the goddess?"

"Some could," said Cleopatra. "So most of all could I. Are you asking me to do it?"

"If you will," said Dione.

Cleopatra's eyes glittered with exasperation. "Three times you did it for me, and you can imply that I won't gladly return the favor? It's little enough for you to ask for."

"But I had to ask." Dione almost smiled. "Now I'm content. And I'm not afraid at all. I was terrified with the others. Does that mean anything, do you think?"

"Probably not, except that you've borne two alive and lived. You know how it's done."

"Do I? Timoleon was the last, and he's a man already. I embarrass him, I think. I should have had delicacy not to have a baby at an age when he could be making me a grandmother."

"Not quite yet, I hope," said Cleopatra. "Though he's not over-young for it, I grant you that. Does he favor men too much, then?"

"Not that I've noticed," said Dione. "He's chasing after a girl in the city now. Hetaira, fortunately. He seems to have a gift for avoiding the respectable ones."

Cleopatra laughed. "May my own sons be as wise!"

"Your sons have never given you a moment's anxiety," said Dione. "I could almost envy you."

"Ah, well," said Cleopatra. "He's not debauched, you know, or particularly rebellious. Just . . . outspoken. And inclined to go where he pleases, with whom he pleases. Do you know what he said the other day to the king of kings in Egypt?"

"Well," said Dione faintly, "no."

"He told Caesarion that it would do him good to misbehave for once, and to stop being, as he put it, such a perfect little plaster godlet. Caesarion was absolutely speechless."

"I can imagine," Dione said. "Those two have always found one another incomprehensible."

"No," said Cleopatra. "No, I don't think so. They understand each other very well. They may not approve, mind you. But they do understand."

Dione found that she could smile at that. She had her serenity back, or as much of it as she could manage, this far along in pregnancy. Pregnancy did not encourage serenity, not really; more a kind of bovine complacence. Fighting it was most of what made her testy. She did not like the way her mind kept sliding into a fog.

"Timoleon," said Cleopatra, still musing on the subject, "is a law unto himself. It's a wonder he's not more dangerous."

Dione, for some reason, was not alarmed. She should be, no doubt of it. But if Cleopatra meant Timoleon harm, she would not be speaking of him so honestly, with such evident affection.

"He has no ambition to be a king," said Dione, "or to be a god's voice, or anything but a young man of the world. Even in the womb he was like that: in his own way, focused. Do you remember? He didn't cry when he was born. He wrapped the world about him and was content."

"Much like my Ptolemy," said Cleopatra. "Strange as it seems to compare a youth so volatile to a child so self-contained. He frightens me sometimes."

"So do all children," said Dione. "They're born of us, but they're not part of us. They go where they will."

"Men, too," said Cleopatra. "And husbands." Her face was pensive. Without the vivacity of eyes or smile, it was quite homely, and pure Ptolemy. Dione thought it beautiful in what it was. "I do let Antony rule, because it suits me, and because he does nothing that I can wholly disapprove of. You could call it harmony, I suppose. Or convenience."

"Expedience," said Dione. "That's the word you want. It's expedient to yield to him. He listens to you, I notice that. Sometimes he even does as you suggest. But he won't divorce Octavia. He won't make you his undisputed wife."

"Yet," said Cleopatra.

THIRTY-TWO

The birth-pangs began as Dione returned to her house from her hour with Cleopatra. She knew what they were, but she kept quiet. She did not want people to fret.

Toward evening her waters broke. Hebe by then had divined the reason for Dione's quiet. She saw Dione to her bed with an air of grim satisfaction, drove everyone out but the servants whom she had chosen herself and the messenger who would go to the queen when Hebe judged it was time, and set about her work. Which was, chiefly, to make Dione as comfortable as possible, and to wait.

By morning of that night—the first night—the pains were coming close together, but the baby was not about to oblige them. Dione, whose sons had both come with commendable dispatch, was too much in control of herself to be afraid, but she was hoarding her strength. She even tried to sleep, or at least to doze.

It was not proper to want her husband there for this most female of all female things, but she did want him, desperately. Enough to ask, and to be startled when Hebe nodded. The maids were shocked. The recipient of Hebe's stare ventured to remonstrate, choked on it, went on the errand.

Lucius took his time in coming. Dione would have been angry—her temper was as short as her intervals of rest, and getting shorter—but he looked so tired, unshaven, rumpled, obviously dragged out of sleep and not in a bed either, that she simply held out her arms. He hesitated, then embraced her carefully, trembling with the effort of not crushing her to him. She knew: she felt the same.

She ran her fingers through his tangled hair. "Why, my love. Did you fall asleep at your worktable again?"

He nodded. He tried to smile. He was pale under the fine dark olive of his skin; he looked gaunt, though he had not been that since he came back from Phraaspa. It was worry, and first fatherhood. It made her want to smile, but a pain snatched the smile away, and her breath with it.

When she could breathe again, he was clutching her in something close to panic. "There," she said. "There. It's nothing. Only child-birth."

"It's *you,*" he said.

"And it's all your fault, too." She was laughing a little, but he was too scared to laugh with her. "Hold me," she said.

He was glad to do that. But he could not do it all day; he had things to do, she knew that very well. She made him go and do them. He half dragged, half ran—half hating to go, half dreading to stay.

The room was very empty without him, even as full of people and pain as it was. The pain went on. It did not seem to get anywhere. There was a rhythm to it, a pulse like a heart, as regular and as relentless. But this pulse, when it stopped, would bring not death but life.

Lucius Servilius remembered nothing of what he did that day. He supposed that he did something, and that some of it was in the city. Otherwise he could not explain Antony's presence in the room in which he received guests, or the legionary at the door, standing as legionaries knew best to stand, like an image cast in bronze.

Antony, with tact that few would have credited, was saying little, and that easy, light: commentary on the wine, on the carpet, on the fresco that Lucius had had painted as a gift for his wife. It was done in the Greek style but in Egyptian colors, as brilliant as the light in that land of everlasting sun. It showed a woman in a colonnaded temple, making offerings upon the altar. The goddess' image lay beyond the field of the painting, but her shadow stretched along the floor, meeting the woman's shadow, that rose into living substance. The jackal-head of the protector god was both predatory and benign, its eyes sulfur-colored, its teeth long and white as it smiled.

"Most unusual," Antony said. "Isn't that the god they have here, who does Mercury's duty in guiding souls into Hades?"

"Anubis," said Lucius. "Yes. He's a guardian spirit of my lady's house." He did not add that he had seen the god himself, smiling in shadow, when his wife was in one of her goddess-ridden moods. When he was allowed into her chamber he had looked, but the shadows had been merely shadows without substance. That disturbed him, and never mind logic or plain reason. He would have been happier by far if the guardian had been there for her.

Perhaps it was as well that it had not. It was, after all, a guide of the dead, as Antony had said. Its absence might be a good omen.

His shoulders ached. He had been straining for all these hours, most of them not even aware of it, to hear her voice in the deeps of the house, or better yet, the cry of a baby as it greeted the world. But there was only silence. That women screamed in childbirth, he had always known, and thought to be invariable. Dione, it seemed, preferred to do her suffering in silence. It was like her. It was maddening.

Something bumped against Lucius' hand as it lay on the arm of his chair. He started, gripped without thinking, stared at the brimming cup. "Drink," said Antony. "You're worried dry."

Lucius shook his head. "No. That's no solace for me."

"Drink," Antony said again, quietly, but his voice had the crack of command. Lucius had obeyed before he knew what he did. Antony sat back and nodded, satisfied. "You're better off a little addled, believe me. This is the worst waiting in the world."

"Worse than waiting for a battle?"

"Infinitely worse." Antony raised his own cup and examined the designs engraved in the gold: words, Dione had said when she had the cup made. Lucius did not remember what they meant. Something like a prayer for the inebriated, or a poem to the god of the vine. Antony, Dionysus on earth if one believed the Egyptians, said reflectively, "I wasn't here when Cleopatra's three were born, but I remember Antyllus' birth. He was my first. I didn't love his mother, I'll tell you that, but right then it didn't matter. She was doing battle for me, to give me an heir. And I the soldier, the commander, the friend of Caesar—there wasn't a damned thing I could do but sit and wait. That's what women do every time we go off to war. Makes you think, doesn't it?"

"It makes me think that women endure altogether too much for their men," Lucius said. Sitting was suddenly unbearable. He pushed himself to his feet, abandoning his barely touched cup. But he was not a pacer of floors as some were. Once he was up, he simply stood, swaying a little, hands clenched into fists. "Great Jupiter! What if I've killed her?"

"Down, lad," said Antony easily, no alarm in him at all. If anything, he was amused. "She's borne two living children already, little thing that she is, without the least trouble. This one's taking its time, that's all. They do sometimes. It's nothing to worry about."

"The last time was eighteen years ago," Lucius said, uncomforted. "What a young woman can do, in her youth and her strength, can kill a woman nearer forty than thirty."

"And is it polite to say so?" Antony asked. "She's one of the great beauties of Egypt—and she'll still be beautiful when she's sixty. She *will* be, Lucius my lad. Believe it."

Lucius shook his head. Antony leaned forward and set the winecup in his hand again. He stared at it, thought of pouring it out on the floor. But Dione would be furious if he ruined her good carpet. He drained the wine in a burning gulp, set the cup down with a sharp click of metal on wood, and whirled as the door opened at the legionary's back.

Legionaries did not blush. It was a matter of honor. But they could be severely disconcerted to be caught off guard—and by a pack of children, too.

Caesarion led, with Antyllus looming behind him, nigh as large as the legionary. More startling were the ones who followed them: a pair of twins, dark and light, leading between them a small solemn prince-ling—Alexander Helios and Cleopatra Selene with their brother Ptolemy, under the guardianship of a pair of young men. Timoleon, Lucius knew very well indeed, but the gangling youth behind him was a stranger.

"What in the world—" Antony began, quite evidently as disconcerted by the invasion as Lucius was, but struck less than speechless.

Caesarion ignored him and strode directly to Lucius. "Come with us," he said, as imperious as ever a king in Egypt could be. "We need you."

The rest of them, from Ptolemy the prince to the brown-haired, gangling stranger, fanned out like bravos in an alley, with much the same expression of unshakable purpose. "I'm not carrying any money," Lucius said, which was the first thing that came into his head.

Timoleon laughed. Of course he would understand: he was a regular young rakehell by all accounts. "No, stepfather, we're not out to shake you down. Will you come or do we have to drag you?"

"Where?" Lucius asked.

The invaders glanced at one another. It was dawning on Lucius that the stranger might be one of Dione's. The elder son, whom he had not met: the one whose father kept him close and never let him loose. Androgeos, that was his name. What was he doing here now of all times?

"He had to come," said a clear small voice. Ptolemy Philadelphos was staring straight at Lucius with eyes that could see through stone, let alone the thin cup of a man's skull. "He's his mother's flesh, too.

When she has need this great, he knows. He stops pretending he doesn't."

"She isn't dying," Lucius said fiercely. "She's taking a while, that's all. She's had children before."

Antony's words, repeated like an incantation, a spell against fear.

"Of course," said Androgeos primly, "this may be complete idiocy. But one never knows. And, for all that anyone may think, I do value my mother."

"Does your father know where you are?" Lucius demanded of him.

He looked briefly uncomfortable, until he covered it with stiffness. "I am not answerable to my father for every breath I take."

"In Rome," said Antony mildly, "there are many who would argue that." His glance took in them all. "Maybe I can see why the lady's offspring are here in their phalanx, but dare I ask what brings the royal auxiliaries?"

"Need," Selene answered with as little shrinking as any of her siblings. "Mother sent us. There's a company of the palace guard outside. She'd have come, too, but she had to stay where she was. To anchor it, you see."

Lucius did not see. He doubted that Antony did, either. Neither of them had opportunity to say so. Selene had Lucius by the hand, tugging him toward the door. "There's not enough room here. Come quickly. Time's short."

He dug in his heels. Selene nodded to Dione's sons. They were both taller than Lucius, and strong, stronger than he might have expected. Silly of him. Timoleon spent his days in the gymnasium, whatever he did with his nights. So, it seemed, did Androgeos. They had both learned the trick that legionaries had of marching a man where they wanted him to go, and not a thing could he do about it but march or be dragged.

They did not take him far. Just to the dining-room, shadowy now in the night, with its couches thrust back against the walls. Its lamps sprang into light as they all came in, and no hand upon them, no earthly fire to kindle them. Lucius could not say that he was surprised. There was more raw magic in this army of children than in the whole College of Augurs in Rome.

Antony had followed, he noticed distantly, with cups and winejar. He set his burdens down in a corner and found a couch to sit on, interested, perhaps a little bespelled. Though maybe he had seen such things before. He lived with the royal children, and with their mother, who was a mistress of magic. Dione was much quieter about her oddities. She knew how uneasy they made Lucius.

None of these children cared for his discomfort. They arranged the couches in a circle as if for a banquet, but no servants brought in the feast. Lucius found himself at the head of the hall, where he would have been if he had been the host. "You," Caesarion said, "are the west. Remember."

He was the east, then, opposite Lucius, and Ptolemy Philadelphos the north, and Cleopatra Selene the south. The others filled the half-directions. Timoleon was on Lucius' right, Androgeos on his left, Alexander Helios and Antyllus facing them. Antony remained outside, as if he had no part in whatever rite this was.

"You could stop it," Lucius said to him.

He shrugged, a broad Roman shrug with hands and brows as well as shoulders. "I'm only a god on earth. I've got no magic worth mentioning."

Nor have I! Lucius wanted to protest, but that would have been a lie. He did have magic. Dione said so. He knew so. He wished he could forget that it existed. He had been doing that very well since he became a married man.

"Your nonsense is slowing us down," Caesarion said coldly. "Do you really want your wife to die? Keep on like that."

Lucius started as if the boy had struck him.

"You could be a little more tactful," Antyllus said to Caesarion. "He's terrified for her, as who wouldn't be? And we haven't exactly been explaining anything, just dragging him about."

"There isn't time to explain," Caesarion snapped. "He should know."

"He's a Roman," said Antyllus. "He needs explanations."

"You didn't," Caesarion said. "Enough. He's here. If he can help, good. If not, we'll just use what he's got, and never mind the niceties."

"Oh, you're a cold one," said Timoleon. "Mother would be horrified."

"Your mother won't be alive to feel anything if we don't stop yattering," Caesarion said. It was not coldness that made him so merciless, Lucius could see that perfectly well. It was fear. He was terrified for Dione's sake.

That, more than any words, told Lucius what he needed to know. He cut across the beginning of their quarrel. "He's right, Timoleon. You can tan his hide later. What am I supposed to do?"

He knew better than to hope that Caesarion would praise him for coming to his senses. The others clearly thought that it was about time; all but Timoleon, who grinned in what was probably meant to be encouragement. He had a great number of teeth, and they were all very white.

Caesarion's voice thrust him back into the moment, and the deep anxiety that went with it. "Just be here," he said. "Do what we do. Has Lady Dione told you how she builds the world for children who are born with magic? She did that for this baby when it was conceived, which was a mighty thing to do, but very dangerous. The worst danger is now. The baby will try to take the world she made and make it again as it sees fit. We can't let it do that. It will strip the souls right out of her."

"But—" said Lucius.

"No questions," said Caesarion fiercely. "Just follow."

But Lucius had his own stubbornness. "How is anyone ever born with magic, if it takes this much to accomplish it?"

Caesarion looked ready to spit with impatience, but he answered, after all, and as fully as Lucius could have asked for. "Our whole line, both branches, is exceptionally difficult about sharing anything to do with the gods' power. Fortunately we know how to deal with that. I just wish . . ."

He trailed off, but Ptolemy finished it for him. "We all wish she hadn't given this baby quite so much. She wasn't thinking. She was just loving. Loving you, and it because it's part of you."

"So I *am* killing her," Lucius groaned. "I knew it. I knew from the moment I—"

"Stop it," said Caesarion. He stretched out his hands. "East," he said. "I am east, where the sun rises. The gods are brighter here. The light is strong."

The rite had begun. Strangely, it calmed Lucius. Dione dispensed too much with ritual, wielded power unadorned. Not so, it seemed, these children of hers and of Cleopatra's.

"South," said Selene, her voice soft and pure. "I am south, where the Nile rises. The gods are deeper here. The earth is strong."

There was a pause, a thrumming in the air. From that, Lucius took the words that he must say. "West," he said, shaky at first, but then growing steady. "I am west, where the sun sets. The gods are wilder here. The air is strong."

No one paused to approve, but he felt the relief that sighed through them all.

The rite went on. "North," said Ptolemy. "I am north, where the sea flows at the feet of Egypt. The gods are swifter here. The water is strong."

So they built the wards that were the world. But that was only the beginning. Their circle enclosed emptiness: a void that should be . . . something.

A birth. A child. An end to pain.

"East," said Caesarion. "The rising sun. Amon-Re, Apollo, Mithras, light and splendor: a soul is born to you. A child is given to you."

"South," said Selene. "The earth's breast. Taweret, Lucina, Mother Ge and Mother Isis and all goddesses who bring life into the world: a child comes. Breathe life into its bones."

Lucius opened his mouth, but Ptolemy spoke, forestalling him. "North," said the child. "The waters' flowing. Father Nile who becomes one with the Great Green, Neptune, Poseidon Earthshaker, lord of horses: a child is born. Fill its blood with the water of life."

Now they waited. Now Lucius must speak. But what he must say, what his heart bade him speak . . . he could not.

He must.

"West," he said, word by painful word. "Power of air, but power too of darkness. Land of the dead at the back of the Two Lands. Osiris, Hades, Pluto who is lord below: a woman labors to bear her child. Close your gates to her. Open the gates of her flesh. Let the child be born. Let there be no price, no life in return for life."

There are always prices.

The air was full of whispers as of shadows. In a chamber on the other side of the house and yet somehow within this circle, a body struggled, stripped of name, of consciousness, of aught but the will to thrust the child forth. But the child refused. It clung to the dark and the warmth. It wanted them. That wanting was a whole world.

The circle was empty still, and yet it quivered with visions. Lucius saw a green field full of flowers, and shapes moving on it, shapes like men, but glowing faintly like clouds about the moon. Then there was darkness, a flare of light the color of blood, a gate—it was blood-colored, darkness-colored, but in honest light he feared it would be white, the color of bone, the color of ivory. Something crouched in it, something like an animal, but what beast was ever triple-headed?

He gasped. The darkness quivered like an image in water. The beast reared up. It had but one head after all, but terrible enough, the scaled deadly snout of a crocodile, rimmed and battlemented with teeth. Its body was vaguely like a jackal's, vaguely like a lion's. It was somehow more frightening than the triune horror that had preceded it.

"That is the Eater of Souls." The voice was Alexander Helios', the boy sitting next to Lucius though Lucius had thought him farther down, on another couch. He seemed perfectly calm. "It's waiting for its dinner. We won't be feeding it; no, nor Lady Dione, whatever she thinks. She's trying to give up. Can you feel her? She thinks she can just walk out of her body and leave Hebe to cut the baby out of it, while she goes off to the Field of Flowers. She's forgetting Eater of Souls, and the judgment. She'll fail. She's abandoning life too soon."

Lucius was beyond horror, and beyond fear. It was as well, he thought dimly. Paralysis accomplished nothing.

He was jealous, rather, that this child should know so much of Dione, and he so little. But that was his own fault. He had only to look inside himself where his heart was. Her presence there, once so strong, was barely perceptible; her strength was shrunk to a shadow. There were things that Helios had not spoken of, perhaps because he was too young to know. Woman-things. The baby's fighting had torn her. She was bleeding where she should not be.

The beast at the gate yawned, baring its armory of teeth. He resisted the urge to show it his own feeble human weaponry. Teeth were not a man's best defense. Wits were.

If he could go in to her, physically shake her, *force* her to remember her strength . . .

She was past that, or her maid would have done it. Hebe was a strange creature, incalculable in most ways, but of this Lucius was certain: she cherished her mistress. Whatever skills or sorceries she had, she wielded them now. But they were not enough.

Nothing was enough.

He shook off the thought. That was despair. He had an army, if he could use it. Children, yes, but such children. Some of them were gods, or thought they were. There was even Antony, keeping his prudent distance, and Cleopatra in her palace, praying, chanting, whatever a goddess did when she was trapped in flesh and her kinswoman had need of help.

All of that, and they could not coax one small infant into the world.

He laughed, sharp enough to hurt. The children were staring at him. "Listen," he said in his ordinary voice, as if this were calm daylight and he were tutoring them in their Latin. "See what terrors we've made of the simplest thing in the world. What after all is simpler than birth? Everything is born. Everything dies, too, but not tonight. This is a very stubborn child I've begotten. We've all been trying to conquer it by force, but force, as anyone knows who knows my lady, is the last and worst way to move the truly obstinate."

He paused. None of them said anything, which was a miracle of sorts. Even Timoleon was unwontedly somber. His insouciance ran no deeper than Caesarion's coldness.

Lucius nodded as if they had spoken. "Well then. How quickly do you think we can seduce a baby?"

"That's disgusting," said Androgeos. But then he said, "We should make the world look more worth living in than the womb."

"So," said Lucius. "And is it?"

Androgeos nodded without hesitation. "It's dark in there. Dull. How can anyone prefer that to the sun on the Pharos in the morning? You know how it shines, so white it blinds you, and the sea is blue-blue-blue, and the ships come in from everywhere, some with their purple sails, and some with white, and some striped red and gold, and once in a while a green sail against the blue water and the white tower."

"Why," said Timoleon, "you love them." He was not mocking his brother, Lucius did not think.

Androgeos shrugged, brusque with embarrassment. "I like to look at them," he said.

Timoleon nodded. "I don't suppose it's quiet in the womb, any more than it is in the sea. But there's more to living than that. There's music. The aulos, the lyre, weaving in and out of one another. The trumpet calling men to war or actors to the games. The drum that beats like a heart. The singer's voice—one of the queen's eunuchs sings as surely the gods must sing, so high and yet so strong, but at such a price . . ."

"Think," said Caesarion, "how it is to swim in the water of life: warm, yes, but monotonous beyond words. How can anyone refuse the touch of silk, or the sifting of sand through fingers, or even the stab of pain? Pain is life. So is pleasure. Do you remember, Antyllus, how we played in the snow at Leuke Kome, the day it fell out of the sky? It was cold, but soft, and when it melted and ran down our necks—" He shuddered, but he laughed. "You were shrieking like a girl."

"I was not," said Antyllus with dignity. "You were." He grinned at him. "Do you remember how it tasted? It tasted like cold, and like the sky. It even kept that when we cooled our wine with it, through the wine's sweetness. We had roast boar that night, that Antony killed in a hunt in the snow. We were all ravenous; our stomachs were growling like dogs. I'd hate to have missed that for any comfort of the womb."

"It smelled," said Timoleon, "like Elysium. So did the perfume the queen brewed up from the ghosts of flowers. There were roses, I remember, and jasmine, and just a touch of heliotrope, not enough to be sickening, but enough to give it richness. Imagine not wanting to be born, or to discover what it is to use one's nose."

Selene wrinkled hers. "Not everything smells wonderful."

"Even stench is worth living for," Timoleon said. "It's alive. It changes. It doesn't cling to the same gate and the same safety, till the gate and the safety fall down, and the mother is dead of her child's selfishness."

"Softly," said Lucius. "Carefully."

Timoleon's glance was rebellious, but he subsided. It was not often, Lucius thought, that that young gentleman lost his composure.

"Now," Lucius said, "remember. Simply that. Remember what life is."

He had expected at least some of them to argue. But either they had reached the same conclusion, or they saw no other hope. He had no surety that it would do any good at all—that there was anything that could help, not after so long.

He must not think of death. He must think of life. That, to him, was Dione in her quiet that was not really quiet at all but a studied stillness, a veil over a heart both tender and passionate. He could still see into the circle, and into the eyes of the creature there, the one the children called Eater of Souls. Those eyes dared him to despair; mocked him with their certainty that all life led only to death.

But there must be life before there could be death. He wrought an image of Dione as he remembered her best, standing on the deck of Cleopatra's ship as it sailed into Tarsus, dressed as a nymph and as beautiful as any goddess. But it was not the beauty that had drawn him; it was the way in which she had looked at her son, half stern, half struggling not to laugh.

That must come again. This youngest child must know what its brother had known. It was too young yet, too blind, too ignorant of anything that life meant. But it would learn.

He had never prayed as hard as he did now, never shaped his will so strongly, to lure this progeny of his into the world. It resisted with all the force of its ignorance.

"Remember," Lucius said to the young ones about him. *"Remember."*

The air felt as it did before thunder: vast, lowering, full of terror. The Eater of Souls grinned with all its myriad teeth.

In Lucius' heart, something stirred. It felt like hope. It had a shape: Dione herself, rousing as if from sleep, stretching, looking about with blurred half-conscious eyes. "What——?" she said.

"Dione," Lucius said.

She turned to him as she always did when first she woke, smiling, reaching drowsily, drawing his face to hers and kissing him.

No, she was not there at all. And yet she was. Her lips were warm and cool at once. He was clasping her to him, and yet somehow he was inside of her, riding the wave of pain that crested endlessly and would not break.

Break, he willed it. *Curse you, break.*

"No," said Dione, inside of him, outside of him. "That's how a man would think. You were wiser before. We coax it. We lure it. See."

Like a gate, yes. Locked, and barred within. But the bar was flesh, and flesh could yield.

"So," said Dione. "Come, child. It's been long enough. Come out and see the sun."

There was pain beyond belief, beyond words to speak. And then—— there was not. It was gone. The wave broke and poured out on the shores of the world.

THIRTY-THREE

After so much struggle, it seemed almost anticlimax to look at the small red crumpled thing in Hebe's arms. "A daughter," said Lucius Servilius. "I have a daughter."

Hebe grinned enormously. Lucius, trapped still in a fog of unreality, peered into the infant face. It was rather shockingly ugly. "Am I supposed to think she's beautiful?"

"Of course not, idiot," said a voice he had never expected to hear, not so soon—not, in the deeps of his fears, ever again. Dione smiled at him from the bed, gaunt with exhaustion but somehow triumphant. "Newborn babies are dreadfully ugly. One wonders how anyone manages to keep them alive long enough for them to become presentable."

Lucius would have sprung upon her, but Hebe was in the way, thrusting her burden at him. He recoiled, only to find himself with an armful of swaddlings and a baby in the middle. "Little monster," he said to her. "Little murderer. I should hate you."

She opened eyes that were far too young yet to see. And yet they seemed to look at him, and to know who he was, and what he did there: the wisdom of utter newness to the world. They were blue as all infants' were, but they would be dark soon, as dark as her mother's.

Hate was not what roused in him as he met stare with stare. Not even resentment for what she had done to her mother. She had only been doing as instinct bade her, clutching at the only safety she knew.

Gently, almost fearfully, he laid a finger to her cheek. It was impossibly soft. She turned toward the touch, blindly, lips moving in the first instinct of any newborn thing.

"You had better give her to me," said Dione. "She needs the one thing no man can give her."

Lucius laughed, startling himself, and laid the child in her mother's arms. She fit there far better than she had in his wobbly clasp. His heart was too full to let him speak. He watched her find the breast that she had been seeking, and attack it with impressive strength.

Dione winced, but she smiled. "She's strong. Too strong for me to manage by myself. But I'm the first comfort she knows. She'll remember."

Fear stabbed anew. "You're not well," Lucius said. "At all. Are you?"

"I'm perfectly well," said Dione calmly. "I'm not going to have much milk this time. I knew that before she was born. There are prices, you see. She is strong, and she will live—I've been promised. Do you mind very much if I call her Mariamne?"

He had meant to call her Servilia, which she would have been in Rome. But he said, "Mariamne she is."

"And you've taken her up," said Dione. "You've acknowledged her. Not that I doubted it. Still . . . one never knows."

He did not remember any such thing. Hebe had thrust the child into his arms, yes—but he could have thrust her back. That would have been all the law needed, to refuse the child, to order it exposed and thus disposed of.

He shuddered. He could never have done such a thing, not after he had fought so hard to bring her living into the world, from a living mother.

Dione's eyelids were drooping, but her smile did not waver. Lucius leaned forward and set a kiss on her brow. She was cool, no fever, but no cold of death, either. Still smiling, still nursing their child, she slipped into sleep.

The nurse whom Hebe found for Mariamne was a quiet young woman, an Egyptian who had lost a child the day before Mariamne was born. Lucius would have objected to the hiring of a free woman when they could have purchased a slave, but he was still riding the euphoria of new fatherhood. He could be magnanimous. The woman seemed clean and respectable, and she had had some training in the temple. "I suppose we'll have to hire the husband, too?" he asked Dione.

"We already have," said his wife. "He's assistant to the overseer of our estate on Lake Mareotis. Hebe saw Tanit there and thought that she might do for a nurse, if she was willing. Which she was. It's sad that she lost her baby. It would have been useful for Mariamne to have a milk-brother of an old Egyptian family."

Sometimes, thought Lucius, the machinations of the women in his own household were quite out of his reckoning. Since that was the universal lament of the men he knew—married or unmarried, it never seemed to matter—he kept quiet about it. He said, "Tanit was to be a priestess? Is she magical, then?"

"Oh, she was a priestess," Dione said. "She still is. I was one of her teachers, years ago, when I lived in the temple. She's very intelligent and greatly gifted in the magical arts."

"Was it even a coincidence that she had a baby so close to your own time?" Lucius asked, mostly of the air.

Dione answered him calmly. "Probably. Though with the goddess, you never know. Mariamne could be very difficult. She's the goddess' child; she needs a nurse who can manage her. If I tried to do it myself, she'd be impossible—she'd drink too much magic, and not enough sense."

"You are an enormously sensible woman," said Lucius.

"Now I am," Dione said. She smiled at him with a touch of wicked-ness. "I married a Roman, after all."

He shook his head, unwilling to laugh, unable quite to maintain his stern expression. "And our new wetnurse looks so harmless, too, like a brown mouse. You are all mighty deceivers."

"No," said Dione. "We're quiet, that's all. Except when it suits us to be splendid."

And when it did suit them, thought Lucius, they were the most splendid people in the world. Yes, even his modest wife in her white gown, wearing no jewel but the emerald he had given her to wear on her finger, the day after Mariamne was born.

He should not be thinking what he was thinking, that he would very much like to get her out of the gown and into bed—not so soon. By the slant of her glance, she was thinking it, too. They both had to settle for a decorous kiss: decorous at least in its beginning. When it began to grow warm, Lucius ended it. That was not easy, not in the least, but this much one could say for a Roman: he knew how to be prudent.

And never mind how much he wanted to damn prudence. He valued this woman too much. "When it is safe," he said to her. "Then . . ."

"Then," she said, "we'll be scandalous beyond belief. Waiting will only make it sweeter."

He had his doubts of that, but those were his baser nature speaking. He resisted the temptation to kiss her again, chastely, on the forehead—chastity would not have lasted long—and bade her a slightly breathless farewell. She, as always, was serene. "The queen's coming later to see the baby. Will you be home for dinner?"

"Of a certainty," he said. "You'll dine with me?"

"If you wish it."

Such formality; such a polite dance, as if they were spouses of convenience. But her eyes were laughing. He left her before he could forget all good intentions.

Cleopatra approved of this latest addition to the house of the Lagidai. Mariamne seemed to approve of the queen. She allowed herself to be held in those capable arms, and stared fascinated at the queen's eardrops, small cascades of pearls set in gold.

"I'll have to give her pearls, I see," said Cleopatra. "Mere gold won't do for her."

Since the queen's birth-gift to the child had been a golden coffer full of such playthings as a young child would cherish, wrapped in the title to an estate outside of Memphis, Dione did not see that pearls would add much to it. "You'll spoil her," she said.

"Of course I will," said Cleopatra. "I have to be strict with my own. With my kin I can indulge myself."

That was logical. Dione felt much the same with Cleopatra's tribe, without whom Mariamne might have been born alive, but Dione would not have lived to see it.

She shivered. She did not, at this particular moment, want to remember the dark and the pain. She would remember the moment of light, the baby's cry, the flooding of her magic until she brimmed and overflowed. It had caught in an eddy, a swirl of knowledge: she would have no more children. This battle had ended it for her.

She could not say that that was grief. Regret, perhaps, that she would not be giving Lucius Servilius a son, since Romans valued sons so highly. But when he looked on his daughter and she saw not even a flicker of disappointment, she knew that it would be well. He had even let her name the child, nor quarreled with the name she gave her: Mariamne, or Meriamon in Egyptian, after the founder of her house in Alexandria.

Some things had a rightness, and Mariamne's name was one. As Cleopatra returned the child to the nurse's arms, Dione sighed faintly. The queen lifted a brow. "Tired?"

"A little," Dione admitted. "Still. But I'm not ill. I'm very well, in fact."

"The children are dragging a bit, too," said Cleopatra. "You have a strong one here. A strong nurse for her, too, I notice."

The nurse did not raise her eyes. She was giving Mariamne the breast, seeming all drowsy-serene, but Dione could see the shimmer that was on her, the whispered words of guide and guard. Tanit was taking no chances even with her charge so young.

Wise woman. Dione smiled. "One learns with experience," she said. "We won't have another Timoleon, I don't think. This child will learn self-control in her cradle."

"Children have a way of surprising us," said Cleopatra. She was smiling, albeit somewhat wryly. She stretched out on the couch opposite Dione's and drew a long breath. "Ah, it's a pleasure to be somewhere quiet."

"The revels began early today?" Dione inquired.

"Actually, no," said Cleopatra. "Antony's over at his hospital again, and his Romans are at maneuvers or out hunting. But the world does crowd one, if one is queen. Here there's space to think."

"Even though I could fit my whole house into the royal baths?"

Cleopatra laughed. "Trust you to remember that! Yes, you were wise after all to insist on your own house. I should visit you more often. You and your Roman—you've found a gift for peace."

"Hardly," said Dione, "with Timoleon flying in and out. Though he's actually calmed down a bit. I think he's in love with a hetaira from Phyllida's establishment. She hasn't milked him dry yet, for a wonder, and he didn't give her his Numidian mare when she asked— but then he's more in love with the mare than he's ever been with a woman. Should I arrange a marriage for him, do you think? Or should I let him play a while longer?"

"Oh, let him play," said Cleopatra. "He never does any harm, for all his pretensions to outrageousness. He's quite steady underneath, you know."

"Oh, I know," Dione said. "He just has to try things. At least he hasn't magic to make him dangerous."

"You think he has none?" asked Cleopatra. "I think he has a great deal. It's quiet, that's all. Unspectacular. A gift for people, and for curiosity, and for pulling people up short. No one but you has ever been able to get round him."

"And I have to labor mightily at it," Dione said. "So you call that magic, what he has. I call it a gift for being Timoleon."

"That's magic," said Cleopatra.

Dione had occasion to remember that after Cleopatra left. Tanit had gone to lay Mariamne in her cradle, since she had fallen asleep at the breast. None of the servants seemed to need Dione for anything. Timoleon was in the gymnasium as usual. Lucius was out about his business.

She felt oddly alone, and oddly free. She thought for a moment of going somewhere frivolous—was on the verge of acting on it when Senmut the house-steward peered round the door. "Lady?"

She suppressed a sigh. She was needed after all, and probably for something suitably dull.

But Senmut said, "Lady, a visitor for you. Shall I send him in?"

His expression promised something extraordinary. Her heart beat a little faster, no matter why. "Yes," she said. "Yes, do admit him."

The visitor came slowly, which gave her time to call for wine and refreshment. When at length Senmut bowed him in, she had arranged herself in as dignified a fashion as she might, and was pretending to read from a new book that Lucius had brought her from the Museum. The words on the papyrus meant no more than a march of ants across a floor.

She looked up from them into a face both familiar and utterly strange. The last time she saw it so close, it had been a child's. Now it was a man's, with a soft unfashionable beard that actually rather became it, and a big knobby-fingered hand that took hers and clasped it with sudden, bruising tightness.

She did not wince, did not even feel the pain. "Androgeos," she said with her most carefully cultivated calm. "What a pleasant surprise!"

His frown was still the same, faintly puzzled and more than faintly annoyed. So was the loose-jointed way he moved, dropping to the chair beside her couch, still holding to her hand. His voice was deeper than his father's, without the reedy overtone. "Mother," he said. "I've never called you that, you know. It made—makes—him very angry."

That was more like Timoleon than like the Androgeos she remembered, this propensity for beginning conversations in the middle. "I saw you at my wedding," she said. "I wanted to say something, but there was no way—and in the morning you were gone."

He blinked rapidly as he always did when he was nervous. "Father wanted to forbid me, but I said I had to go. He should have been glad that you were finally becoming respectable, instead of muttering about foreign conquerors. You looked very handsome that night. You still do. He treats you well?"

"Very well," said Dione.

He nodded. "I can tell. People like your husband. He's civilized, for a Roman. He understands responsibility. He must be very good for my brother."

"Your brother does rather rein himself in when Lucius Servilius is about," Dione conceded.

"It's well for a boy to have a man to look up to," said Androgeos from the pinnacle of his very young manhood.

Dione offered him wine, fruit, a bowl of cook's spiced apples in honey. He looked too twitchy to accept, but he always had adored spiced apples. It was almost painful to watch him eat, taking prim small bits but taking them with deceptive speed, as a cat will, preserving its dignity while it satisfies a potent hunger.

"I am . . . glad to see you," Dione said with some difficulty: her throat was tight.

He blinked more rapidly than ever. "I've seen you. Now and then. And heard about you. And I was there when the baby came. You won't remember. We all—we had to—I couldn't stay away. Father doesn't know. He thought I was visiting a friend. You won't tell him, will you?"

"Certainly not," said Dione. As if Apollonius would give her the opportunity, who had not seen or spoken to her since he condemned her out of hand for keeping company with a Roman.

"You're angry," said her elder son. "Of course you would be. He's treated you badly. He always has."

"By his lights," she said carefully, "he's done the best he could with a very poor bargain. He always both wanted and needed a wife like Laodice: quiet, modest, and unburdened with any greater concerns but those of his care and comfort."

"I suppose I'm a bad seed," said Androgeos. "I can't be entirely his son. I keep having to come back to where you are, and be sure you're well, and sometimes just know you're here. That's what I came to tell you. You almost died with this baby. I couldn't let that happen."

"And you didn't," said Dione. She swallowed. Her throat ached with trying not to weep, but it was wonderful to have to do that: to be sitting here, looking into this face that she had bidden farewell to years since. She had told herself that he was not her son; that he was his father's; that he was lost to her.

It was almost too much to bear, that he was not lost at all, merely withdrawn out of deference to his father.

"You worked magic," she said, "for me. Even you. How that must have cost you!"

He stiffened, misunderstanding her. "I had to. Even if you hated me for it. You were *dying.*"

She reached for his hand again where it clenched on his knee, coaxed the fingers open one by one, wove her own with them. It was a strong hand, all bones and wire. "No, love, no," she said. "I wasn't laughing at you. I was marveling. You who seemed almost to hate the part of me that belonged to the goddess—you came to help when I needed you most. That makes you the strongest of all my children, because it never came easily; it was never a simple thing for you to accept."

"You're my mother," he said, sullen still, but at least he would speak to her. "I do my duty to my father, but I owe you a debt, too. He may want me to forget it. I never could."

"Lucius Servilius would appreciate you," said Dione. "He understands duty, and debts."

"I know he does," Androgeos said. "I see him sometimes. He's not unlikable, for a Roman."

Dione's heart stabbed with sudden, unreasonable temper. Lucius Servilius had seen and spoken to her son, and had never told her.

Androgeos, who could sometimes be perceptive, caught the flash of anger, and understood it. "The first time or two, he didn't know who I was. I was just another young stranger from Alexandria. After the baby was born we met properly, but I asked him not to tell you. It might hurt you that I couldn't come and see you. Father was in a terrible temper about everything then. He's calmer now, and I'm a man after all. I make my own decisions."

"You've grown up." Dione kissed the hand in hers, remembering when it had been no longer than her smallest finger. Now it engulfed her small hand. "When you can, give him my regards. I don't bear him any ill-will. He's only done as he judged best—it's not his fault that I don't fit anywhere into his philosophy."

"You don't fit into mine very well, either," Androgeos said. "But blood's strong. I remember you said that once to my father. I thought you were wrong then. I was an awful fool."

"You were young," said Dione. She paused. She was calmer now. The tears were less insistent; her heart had slowed a little. "I don't think I mind almost dying, if it brought you back home."

Androgeos was almost Roman in his lack of humor. He regarded her with formidable severity. "Father is right about one thing. You have no understanding of either dignity or propriety. But," he added after a brief pause, "you are my mother, and I do value you. May I visit you occasionally?"

"Often, if you like," said Dione. Her heart was full again: she could barely breathe. "You can show me how to be dignified, and how to be proper."

His eyes narrowed. "You're laughing at me again. Father says you're the most exasperating woman in the world."

"He's right," said Dione. "He learned how to resist me. I thought you had, too."

"He's not your son," Androgeos said. "My bood is corrupt, I told you that. I'm teaching myself to forgive you for it."

"Oh, do," Dione said. "Do it frequently. Have you met your sister? Would you like to?"

He looked so horrified that she almost took pity on him. But he said with commendable courage, "I should see what almost killed you."

"A baby," his mother said. "That's all."

Androgeos did not believe her. Not till he saw the small sleeping creature in her cradle, touched her with the half-fearful, half-fascinated air of the young male presented with a newborn child, shied in open terror from the invitation to take her in his arms. "No!" His voice cracked, and for a moment he both looked and sounded like the child he had been. "I'll wake her up."

"True," said Dione, much amused.

"And this is the great dark thing that nearly rent your souls from your body." Androgeos shook his head. "She's so small."

"Babies are," his mother said. "They grow. Visibly, sometimes."

"I remember," he said. "Timoleon was as little as this. But noisier."

"Timoleon has always been outspoken," Dione agreed. "Mariamne keeps her counsel."

"She's this young, and you can tell that?"

"Mothers know," Dione said.

He was as arrogant as all young men are, but he knew surety when he heard it. He nodded, still fearful, growing perhaps a little bored. Dione forbore to be disappointed. Timoleon adored his sister, but Timoleon was Timoleon. Androgeos had other matters on his mind. He was like his father that way.

It was enough that he had come; that he would come again. Dione had not even known that there was a gap in her world till she saw this son of hers filling it. It righted a wrongness. It made the rest complete.

THIRTY-FOUR

In the year after Mariamne's birth, Dione did what she had never done before: she left the queen to her wars and her politics, and remained in Alexandria. She was simply, for once, Dione who was married to Lucius Servilius the Augur, who was mother to Androgeos and Timoleon and Mariamne, who was priestess of Isis and voice of the goddess in the Two Lands.

That voice was not silenced, but neither did it compel her. Whether she had earned her peace or had merely been granted it by the goddess' whim, she knew no more vexation than the little ones of every day, such as any woman knew who had the charge of a household. It was a marvel and a delight. It felt, in its center, like the calm before a storm.

For all her studied quiet, she was not oblivious to the happenings of the great world. Antony was still stalking in wary circles round his Parthian war, never quite ready to mount the invasion. Cleopatra was at his side, rumors said, from dawn till dawn again.

But the great rumor, the one that overwhelmed them all, was that Octavian had settled enough of the west to be able to turn at last toward the east, and on the man who ruled the east. There had always been war of words between them, exchange of barbed courtesies, dislike never quite pointed enough to be called hate. Now they were like the combatants in a satire, exchanging blow for blow with vicious glee. Antony a drunkard, Octavian a gambler and a spendthrift; Antony a pursuer of women wicked or wedded, Octavian the keeper of mistresses on every hill in Rome; Antony a god indeed, Dionysus the Devourer, and Octavian a toady to his divine uncle, in whose name he perpetrated endless offenses against Roma Dea. Antony had luck, sneered Octavian's partisans, and luck had given him a queen for his bed. But Octavian's luck was greater than his: luck like a lesser god, a daimon of good fortune, and Antony rightly was afraid of it. To which Antony replied that he needed no daimon when he had Isis herself to protect him, and Isis on earth to stand at his side and bless him with her presence.

So did children quarrel. But when those children were lords of the world, the world did well to be wary.

Worse than these follies, in Dione's mind, were the wilder things, the strokes of prophecy and counterprophecy. Antony or Octavian, either or both, was savior or destroyer of Rome, of the lands about the Middle Sea, of the world. A lifetime ago a mad praetor had sung of a woman who would sail out of the east to cast Rome under her feet—now the mad and the less than mad were singing it in the streets of Rome, though it was death to be caught, death even to read the book in which the prophecy was written. The name they set to the prophecy was Cleopatra's own, with Antony her consort, her master of slaves. They called her the Woman, the Widow who had slain her brother-king, She who conquers, ruler of kings—mockery of the title she had taken at Antony's triumph, or homage to it, depending on who told the tale. And Antony was the Lion, the Consort, Heracles come again; he would rule or destroy, conquer or enslave, be god or god's plaything in the circles of the world.

Cleopatra's letters laughed at the depths to which Octavian's followers would sink, and the heights of absurdity to which they forced Antony's own partisans to rise. Dione sensed no dread of such mere and windy words. *What is real,* wrote Cleopatra, *is power. And the power is ours. We rule the east. Let the upstart dream that he rules the west. When my lord is ready, that dream too will end, and Rome will know in truth what Antony is.*

Antony was a soldier, Dione thought, and a lover of pleasure, and close enough to a god—Dionysus, Heracles, it mattered little which—to be a worthy match for the queen of Egypt. But what he was beside Octavian—that, she did not know, and the goddess was not telling. The goddess kept secrets when it suited her. Or maybe Octavian's luck blinded even Mother Isis.

Good luck or ill. Dione could not tell. She kept vigil in Isis' temple, not once but thrice, because of the uneasiness in her bones. She dreamed, but the dreams were the simple follies of sleep: Timoleon married and father to a child even more of a hellion than he was, Mariamne turning men into sheep and herding them in the hills of Attica, Lucius Servilius sacrificing one and reading a poem in its liver, something grandiose about a child and a flock of Muses and the Golden Age.

Maybe it was simply guilt that she was happy, and at peace, and far from Greece, and thus from Cleopatra. Even so, the longer she went on, the less she could stop gnawing on her unease. She hid it from the children, who seemed oblivious. Lucius Servilius was more difficult, but she could distract him with kisses, or with some new feat of Mariamne's: her first tooth, her first step, her first and utterly precocious word.

The goddess-cat from Tarsus, no longer in first youth but lively enough for a whole scramble of kittens, had had her latest litter in Mariamne's cradle, three sleek tawny creatures like the temple cats of Egypt, and one small mottled oddity the image of herself. That one, even before its eyes were opened, showed a predilection for crawling up Dione's gown meeping, clinging to her shoulder with its plethora of claws. It was on one of these occasions that Mariamne, watching her mother peel the small monster from her sorely tried flesh, proclaimed gravely, "Cat."

"Cat," Dione agreed with reasonable aplomb.

Mariamne nodded. She was as quiet as Cleopatra's own youngest, but unlike him she had no compunction about vouchsafing a smile. She smiled now, and laughed as the kitten's mother tickled her nose with its tail. "Cat," she said. "Cat, cat, cat."

A prodigy, surely, Dione mused, but nothing so remarkable in this family of hers. The kitten refused to go back to its mother. It wanted Dione, loudly, with all its claws clamped on her gown, since it could not have her unprotected shoulder. She sighed and let it stay. It was old enough by now to be weaned, just. Certainly its mother did not object to its adoption of her servant. Perhaps she looked forward to an honorable retirement, now that she had a successor to live in Dione's shadow.

The kitten was still attached to Dione's gown when, much later, she went out into the city. Mariamne's first word had been duly reported and exclaimed upon in the house, and she had obligingly repeated it until all the servants and both her brothers had heard it, even to Androgeos on one of his visits. Lucius would hear it tonight when he came back from the Museum. He had been asked to teach there, which was a great honor: philosophy, and something of mathematics, in which he had a gift. But he would reckon it a greater honor to enjoy his daughter's favor, and to hear of her accomplishment.

The thought warmed her through the cold of her anxiety. There was no reason for this restlessness, no base for the fear. The city was quiet, the air serene, warm with spring slipping softly into summer. She had called for her litter but chose to walk instead with the bearers for guards and Hebe for company, and as she passed the gate, Timoleon in robes and insouciance. It took a sharp eye to see how quick his breath was coming, and to deduce that he had heard his mother leaving and run to catch her.

Timoleon at almost twenty was alarmingly beautiful, and all too well aware of it. He could hardly avoid it, with people remarking on it wherever he went. But it did not matter as much to him as perhaps it might. His preoccupations lay in other directions. His hetaira, of course, and wine-parties, and vexing and being vexed by his elder brother. And, lately, acquiring and reading volumes of rather abstruse philosophy. It was interesting, he said. Particularly when it contradicted itself.

At the moment he did not look very philosophical. He looked determined, and mildly startled when Dione did not challenge his presence. "Aren't you going to send me back?" he asked as they started down the street.

"No," Dione said. "Should I?"

Timoleon tilted her head as if in reflection. "I suppose not. You might need me."

"And what do you think I'm going to do?" Dione inquired.

"Something that I can help you with," Timoleon answered.

Lucius would have said that Timoleon had mastered his mother's art of being perfectly and exasperatingly opaque. Dione shrugged and sighed. "Maybe you can. In any case I welcome the company."

Timoleon inclined his head, as gracious as any king, and walked beside her in the circle of guards, through the crowds of Alexandria.

The queen's absence made little difference to this greatest of cities. The palace was quiet, its banqueting halls empty, the revelries stilled while the heart of the court beat elsewhere. The rest of Alexandria went on as it had since Alexander founded it, pouring out the wealth of Egypt, pouring in the wealth of the world.

It would go on, Dione knew with a shock of clarity. No matter what became of them all, Alexandria remained. It was older than any human creature, and greater, and its life was its own.

That was comfort of a sort, even at its true center, which was not the palace but the marble and gold of the Sema, the tomb of Alexander. Dead, he lived, more legend now than man.

The guards at the gate knew Dione and bowed as she passed. She wondered briefly as she sometimes did, what it was like to spend one's life guarding the dead in a city of the living. Ordinary, probably, if one lacked imagination: a door, a duty, people passing in and out to look on the king on his bier of crystal and gold.

Since Dione had not announced her coming, no one had cleared the hall for her. There were people coming and going, sightseers either gazing dropjawed at the spectacle or professing to be unimpressed. Some of them were noisy, with children who ran about and shrieked. The kitten in her cloak dug in claws, horrified. No one shrieked in Dione's house, except the odd servant when Timoleon tried a new mischief—and he had not done that in rather a while.

As if the thought had touched him, Timoleon looked about with a slight curl of the lip. "Shall I dispose of them?" he asked.

At least, thought Dione, he had asked. Such was progress. Aloud she said, "No. No, let them be. They've as much right to be here as we."

Timoleon's brows raised. "We are Lagidai. They are rabble."

"I see you've grown up arrogant," said Dione mildly.

Timoleon was offended, but he laughed at the jest, such as it was, and moderated his expression; the disdain was barely visible. Dione led him and the rest of the escort toward the bier. The crowd was thickest there, peering at the figure in the crystal.

Dione did not need to see it in order to know what was there. She

knew the face as well as she knew her own; better, maybe, since she
was not given to long contemplation of her mirror. She had long since
imagined for herself what he was like in life. Not as he was here,
frozen still, mummified, flesh dried and sunk in upon the bones, but
vividly alive, ever in motion, swift turn of head, flash of eye, words
spoken in the rapid light voice that all the tales told of. He had never
been a quiet man, or a placid one.

That was all gone. Here was only the husk, the shell empty of its
soul—or souls as the Egyptians perceived it, the *ka* that was the
body's image, the *ba* that was its winged spirit, the lesser shades that
made up the living self. Most of him was gone where all the dead go,
whether to the Field of Flowers or to the Greeks' Elysium. If his *ba*
had lingered as they were said to do, swift falcon-form, human-
headed, she had never seen it. Perhaps the throngs of people had
driven it away, or perhaps, being Alexander, and Amon's son, and
near enough a god to make no matter, he had taken all of him when
he went, and left nothing to wander the earth.

Dione had not come to talk with him. If she could have been so
presumptuous, she would have come at night when the dead were
more at ease, and when the Sema was empty, its gates barred on the
silence and the solitude. She had come in daylight because the goddess wished it, and because she wished to consider what was here.
Alexander, king of Macedon, archon of the Greeks, king of Asia,
pharaoh of Egypt, Great King of Persia. He had built an empire but
left no heir with strength to rule it when he was gone. When he lay
dying, when his people asked him who would rule, he had given
them no help, no clear guidance at all; merely murmured a word that
might have been Krateros, who was his general, or *kratistos,* which
was "the strongest."

Of course it had been most convenient to believe in *kratistos.* The
wars thereafter had lasted for a whole lifetime of men, and ended in
a patchwork of empires both petty and not so petty, and the king's
body stolen by his friend, his general, his half-brother some said, and
taken into Egypt, and kept there. Cleopatra was descended from that
general. Dione was descended by adoption from that general's
brother.

Slowly the crowd thinned about the bier. Dione moved toward it.
The king lay as he had lain for so long, gleaming in his golden armor,
in his crystal prison. "What would you think," Dione asked him, "of
us who rule where once you ruled? What would you say to our queen
who is all a Hellene, yet who sees herself as queen of Egypt, and who

looks to be queen of all the lands you conquered? Would you admire her? Or would you find her reprehensible?"

"He'd like her," said Timoleon, startling her a bit, for she had forgotten that there was anyone with her. "He liked bravura; he understood women who were queens. His mother was one."

"His mother was a virago."

"So's Cleopatra," Timoleon said. "I admire her for it. She's magnificent."

"So she is," Dione said wryly. Timoleon had done her a favor: had brought her to herself and cleared her mind. She laid her hand on the crystal. It was cool, almost cold. Life hummed in it, memories, visions of people who had come and gone for three hundred years. It could have been dizzying if she had let it. She calmed it with a word and a gesture, a movement of hand across the shimmering stone.

People were staring. She let them slide from her awareness. Someone would tell them who she was; or not. Her guards were large enough and formidable enough to prevent incidents, and she had Timoleon. Timoleon as a weapon was surprisingly effective. He could wield his white smile quite as potently at the dagger at his belt.

"Tell me," Dione said to the man in the crystal. "Why can't I be blindly happy? What makes me want to fret and pace and look for omens in shadows on the wall?"

"You don't need to ask him that," said Timoleon. "It's you. You're afraid somebody will take it all away."

"No," Dione said. "No, it's something more. The goddess wants me here. Why?"

"To see," Timoleon answered promptly. "To understand something."

"What? That Alexander is dead? That Antony's no Alexander? That Cleopatra could be, but no woman is that much a fool?"

"You've known all that for years," her son said. "Maybe you're supposed to understand that the queen's on top of the world; that she can't lose, not as she is now. Not unless death takes her."

Dione shivered. " 'Remember,' " she said, " 'thou art mortal.' "

Out of the corner of her eye, she saw Timoleon's nod, heard the clear young man's voice that had something—more than something—of the goddess in it. "Hubris," Timoleon said. "The pride that provokes the gods."

"But they are gods," said Dione.

"So was he," Timoleon said, laying his hand beside Dione's on the sarcophagus. Two hands so much alike, one smooth with youth, one showing the first signs of age: flesh thinning, growing dry, sinking about the bones. It was like a little death, a hint of what all men came to, and all women, too, who walked living on the earth.

"Even gods die," Dione said.

"Certainly," said Timoleon. "They have to make room for those who come after."

Dione looked from her son who was so much like her, to the tiny cat curled in the fold of her cloak, who was the image and likeness of its mother. "But not exactly," she said, trusting Timoleon to understand. "Things change. They grow less, the poets will tell you."

"Certainly they are different. Would you rather have Alexander than Cleopatra?"

"No," Dione said. "Not at all."

Timoleon nodded as if there were no more to say. But there was, if Dione could find a way to say it. She turned her eyes to the crystal between their hands. Shadows stirred there, shapes, images half-seen, half-understood. Cleopatra's face under a crown of gold. Antony in his armor with his face hidden, but there was no mistaking the bulk and the solidity of him. Ships on the sea. Fire burning. Legionaries; cloaks the color of blood. A man in white—a toga, no mistaking the awkwardness of that, or its perverse dignity. He was young, frail, long neck like a bird, mouth pursed tight, eyes narrowed as if he calculated the worth of every obol in every purse.

He seemed to look into her face and to frown, puzzled, perhaps annoyed to be so spied on. She did not flinch. She needed to see him whole. But he was too clever for her, or for the goddess who gave her these eyes to see. He drew his toga over his head, veiling his face, sinking into a blur of white that was the dazzle of lamplight on Alexander's breastplate.

But he could not conceal his name. No, not he. Not Gaius Julius Caesar Octavianus. Caesar Octavian. Caesar's heir.

Dione blinked. The world came into focus. Her fear was gone, but she was more restless than ever. Yet now it had a focus.

"I have to go," she said.

Her guards bowed, turning toward the door.

"No," she said. "Or, yes. Home first. But then I must go."

"To Cleopatra?"

Dione met Timoleon's eyes. They were wider even than usual, and unwontedly grave. "To Cleopatra," she said.

"And then?"

"And then," said Dione, "whatever the goddess requires of me."

THIRTY-FIVE

Dione, returning home from the Sema, found affairs much as she had left them, and Lucius still out about his business. Mariamne was awake and calling for Timoleon. He, her devoted slave, had to do as she bade him, which was to teach her to walk by holding to his fingers and taking step by step into his waiting lap. She thought it a marvelous game.

Dione was diverted, but not conclusively. There were things that she could set in train, preparations familiar from other departures but grown stiff with disuse. She began them, but left them to find their own way. She came as close to cowardice as she ever had. She shut herself up in her workroom behind a wall of accounts, and stayed there while the day waned.

Lucius Servilius found the house in a mild uproar when he came home, somewhat later than usual and feeling guilty for it. That guilt kept him from asking why everyone was so busy. He did ascertain that it was not a crisis with the children—that was relief. Perhaps he had forgotten that they had guests for dinner; but the dining room was dark, and a table was laid in his study as always when there were no guests and Dione was otherwise occupied. He did not need to think that she was rebuking him for tarrying so long over a disputation of scholars.

Guilty or no, he was hungry. He ate the excellent dinner that his slave Gaius brought him, drank the wine—the new shipment of Caecuban, a very good vintage and rather strong. When he stood up, he realized just how strong; he should have watered it more liberally than usual.

He was not tipsy, he assured himself. He did have more courage to face the wrath of his wife. He went in search of her.

When he found her he almost laughed. All that fretting, and she had simply forgotten the time in one of her periodic attacks on the accounts. She was deep in them, hunched over the worktable with stylus and tablets. There were rolls of papyrus everywhere. He picked his way through them, not making any particular effort to be quiet, but she seemed unaware of him.

In a clear space just out of her reach, he stopped. She made a note on a tablet, stabbing the wax with her stylus, a swift, angry motion that was utterly characteristic of Dione afflicted with finance. After a pause she picked a pen, dipped it in ink, made a neater and less forceful annotation on the roll in front of her. There was a spot of ink on her cheek; her hair was coming out of its matronly knot. She looked no older than the princess Selene.

She finished with the pen, laid it down, turned back to her tablet. Lucius, mischievous, reached for the pin that held her hair in place. The pin slipped out; her hair tumbled down her back.

She spun like a cat. Her expression was startled, and vividly furious.

Lucius grinned, unrepentant. "Good evening, madam," he said.

He watched her remember her usual calm, putting it on like the mask it was. There was an edge to it still, that set his nape to bristling in sympathy.

"I'm going away," she said. No greeting, no inquiry after his lateness or the reason for it, simply the flat announcement.

He preserved his serenity as best he could in the circumstances. "We're leaving? When?"

"I am. As soon as I can get passage."

"Where?"

"Wherever the queen is. Greece, I think. Athens."

"She summoned you?"

Dione shook her head. She was shivering, looking small and cold and yet so fierce that he dared not touch her.

"The goddess." Lucius' voice was flat. "She remembered you again. She might also have remembered that you're not a beast of burden or a footsoldier, to go wherever her whim drives you."

"But I am," Dione said. "I am her creature. I go where I must go."

"Why now?" he demanded. "What's happened?"

He was too strong, he knew that as soon as he spoke; pressing her too hard. But there was no calling it back. Dione stiffened against him. "Nothing. Nothing's happened. I just have to go."

"There must be a reason," he said.

"I have to go," she said. He had never seen her look so sullen. As if, he thought, she wanted a quarrel.

He was above that, he hoped. He drew a long breath to steady himself, and said, "If there's no reason, then why not wait until you have one? Your goddess has left you alone this long. She can keep on doing it for yet a while."

Dione shook her head. "You don't have to go. I can go. You can stay. You're happy here. Or you can go to Rome. It doesn't matter. I have to go to the queen."

"You are babbling," he said. He meant to be light, but even to himself he sounded severe, like a father with a fractious child. He tried again. "Come now. Something has happened, hasn't it? Have you had a vision? Or are you just feeling guilty that you've been here and happy, and the queen is in Greece? She's happy there, I'm sure. She has Antony beside her; she has the world in her hand."

"You don't understand me at all," Dione said. She thrust herself to her feet. He barred her escape; nor did he move to let her by. "Please let me go."

"First," he said, "tell me why you want a quarrel."

"I don't want a quarrel. I want to eat my dinner. Then I want to sleep. And in the morning I want to find a ship to take me to Greece."

"You don't want to go to Greece," he said, "or you wouldn't be blaming me for existing. Stay here in Alexandria. The queen will call for you when she needs you. Then you can go in all good conscience, and in one of her ships, too."

"Let me by," she said, low and tight.

"Dione," said Lucius. "You're being ridiculous. Is it Apollonius? Has he been at you after all, for marrying a foreigner?"

"You are just like him," she said with venom that took him aback. "You want me to stay and wait on you, and forget my queen and my goddess. Will you divorce me if I go? Will you try to take my children from me?"

"Dione!" The pain in his voice struck her: she recoiled. He seized the advantage. "Dione, my dearly beloved wife, I would never divorce you for being yourself. I only question the suddenness of your decision, and the reasons for it. What are you running away from?"

"To," she said. "I'm running to. Stop being so bloody rational."

"Someone has to be," he said. His temper was slipping its leash. In a very little while he was not going to care what he said, or what harm it did. "Why are you attacking me? What have I done to you?"

"I'm not attacking you. You're refusing to believe that I have to go."

"I do believe. I'm asking why."

"Because I must."

"That's not a reason," Lucius said.

"It's all you'll get." She advanced a step. "Let me by."

After a moment he moved aside. If she tried to force her way past him, he might lose his temper for a fact, and strike her. He had never struck a woman. He did not mean to begin now.

As she brushed by him, he asked of her, "Why? What have I done to earn this?"

She would not answer. She had never meant to quarrel so, for no reason in the world but that he was there, and she was in such a mood as she had never been in, not even when she defied Apollonius' threat to divorce her. It was as if there was a daimon in her, a spirit of ill-will that cast its eyes on her husband whom she loved above all men, and whispered, *Roman. Foreigner. Stranger to anything that is in Egypt.*

She should turn back before she passed this door, cry his pardon, make them whole again. But she could not. She had gone too far before she thought, out of her workroom and into the room she slept in. She barred the door. He had a sleeping-room of his own, though he never used it. Let him do so tonight. She needed to calm down, she told herself. She had to subdue the daimon by herself, before it made matters any worse.

He had not tried to command her to stay in Alexandria. He had reasoned with her, that was all. She was reasonable herself when she was in her right mind.

But not tonight. Strict reason told her that she should book passage for them them all, even the baby, and have done. Cleopatra would welcome her gladly. Antony would be delighted to see his friend Lucius again. Timoleon would gain a respite from his round of symposia. They could make an excursion of it, a tour of the isles of Greece, with Athens as its culmination.

She could not make herself do it. The thing that was in her, the dark thing, wanted to be where Cleopatra was. It did not care what harm it did in getting there, if only it was swift.

Alone, she could take a cabin on the first ship that would carry her, and be in Athens in a handful of days. Encumbered with husband, children, servants, all the impedimenta of a woman of family, she might wait weeks before she found a ship, and weeks before they were all mustered to take passage on it.

Lucius Servilius did not even want to go. He had settled in Alexandria. He was comfortable there. It irked him to be uprooted by a woman's whim, which for all his protestations was exactly what he thought of it. She could tell. He was as transparent as the crystal of Alexander's sarcophagus.

If she quarreled now, if she thrust him away from her, it would be that much easier to leave him while she did her duty to the goddess. That was the reason behind her unreason. That was why she had shocked him so, why she had shown him anger when he had every right to expect affection.

It was better, she told herself. He did not want to be dragged all over Greece in Cleopatra's train. He could stay here, teach in the Museum, keep Timoleon in hand, even—and this wrenched at her—watch Mariamne grow from infant into child. She would leave him that, as she had not been willing to do when the husband was Apollonius and the child was Timoleon.

Alone. To be alone in the world, with no one but her goddess and her queen . . .

"Why?"

She whipped about. Her heart thudded. Never mind what she had known, but been too much a fool to think of: that her rooms looked on the garden, and it was a simple matter for a man to walk in. The doors were never locked, merely fastened with a latch.

He stood just within the door to the garden, in his Greek robe yet looking utterly and incontestably Roman, his black brows meeting over the high bridge of his nose. "Why are you doing this to yourself?" he demanded.

"Get out," she said. "Leave me alone."

"No," said Lucius Servilius. "Not till you start making sense. You're trying to drive me off. Why? Is there something a Roman shouldn't know?"

"No!"

"Then why?"

She turned her back on him. She did not hate him, no, she could not, ever, but oh, if only he would go away. "I need to be alone."

"But you aren't. You have me. You have the children. You have a household. What madness is on you that you'll abandon it all at a moment's thought?"

She seized on that in something like relief. "Mad. Yes, I'm mad. The goddess possesses me."

"That's too easy," said Lucius.

She spun. "Will you stop that?"

"I can't help it," he said. "You won't let me. You want this battle, Juno knows why."

"Because," said Dione. She felt as if she were falling. "Because I can't—let—"

"Because you can't let me be unlike Apollonius? I have to divorce you too, so that you can serve your queen?"

"No," she snapped, called back to herself, with her feet on solid earth and her temper long out of its leash. "I can't let you be killed, or be forced to betray your Roma Dea."

Truth, she thought, dizzy again. Truth was pain, and worse if it dawned late.

He did not seem stunned by it, or even alarmed. "So. It's coming to that. Antony and Octavian, I suppose. Parthia was always a side issue, no matter what Antony thought. The real war was between the two Romans."

"And Cleopatra," Dione said.

"Cleopatra who was Caesar's lover, who bore Caesar's only living son."

Dione's lips pressed together. This was not relief, to know that his understanding was so swift and so complete. She did not want him to understand. She wanted him to quarrel, break with her, stay safe in Alexandria while she sailed off to Athens.

"And how safe would I be," he asked, reading her as he sometimes could, not even knowing what a gift it was, "if Antony lost, and Octavian found me here, gone over to the enemy?"

"Safer than if you were in Antony's army, fighting against him."

Lucius shook his head. "War has honor, and men who fight in it are given pardons."

"Sometimes."

"More often than not, if those who fight are Romans of the senatorial class. I've proved my allegiance already by lingering so long in the east, and by marrying you. I won't be safe at all if Octavian comes riding over the bodies of the slain."

"Don't say that," Dione said swiftly. "He won't. Antony will win, and Cleopatra. But there is war coming, I feel it. I don't want you in it."

"Is that your choice to make?"

She glared, furious again, and past caring if they mended the quarrel. "I can try."

"You failed."

"Bloody Roman."

"Damned stiff-necked Hellene." He tossed his head as if to prove the flexibility of his own neck. "Pollux, woman! You'll drive me mad."

"I don't care," she shot back, "as long as you're safe."

"I'll decide what's safe and what isn't."

"You will not."

"I—" His mouth snapped shut. "Gods. We sound like a pair of squabbling children."

She refused to laugh. She would not be so suborned, or so distracted. "I want you to stay here," she said. A little plaintively maybe, but she was not above wringing at his heart if it bent him to her will.

"I should stay and be safe, when you are daring war in Hellas?"

"You should stay and protect the children, while I do as my goddess bids me."

He shook his head, as stubborn as she could ever be. "It's a mother's first duty to guard her young, a husband's to guard his wife. If you can't stay, then neither can I."

"But the children—"

"Timoleon is a man grown. Mariamne . . ." There he paused, and she almost dared to hope that he would falter, but he was only searching for the words to say it. "Mariamne needs her mother, surely, but she has her nurse, and she has her brother—brothers—to look after her."

"Her father would serve her better," Dione said.

"He can't," said Lucius Servilius, "if her mother can't do it herself."

"I can't," said Dione with rising desperation. "I *can't* take her into what I see."

"Then leave her to her brothers, or send her to the temple. Her nurse is a priestess; she's half of them already."

Dione shook her head. Tossed it, rather, between the pain and the pressure of the goddess' will on her. "I can't—I want—"

One long stride and he was on her, folding her in his arms.

She did not want that. She tried to fight free, but he was too strong. She gave it up, rigid in his clasp, refusing to complete the embrace. He did not seem to notice. His hands moved on her back, seeking the knots, working them out one by one. "Beloved," he sighed into her hair. "Oh, my beloved. I could hate your goddess for what she does to you."

"She doesn't care," Dione said.

"Good. She'll not blast me for saying it."

She tilted her head back, glaring. He stared gravely down. "I wish you wouldn't be so difficult to fight with," she said.

"I can't help it." Nor did he look very apologetic. "In the morning I'll get us a ship. One of Antony's couriers should be coming in in a day or two. It should take us aboard, between your rank and my senatorial privilege."

"I don't think—" she said. "I don't know—if it's as soon as that—"

She was contradicting herself. She knew it. So did he, but he did not remark on it except with a lift of the brow. "We'll have a little longer with the children before we go. And they'll be safe. The temple for Mariamne, I think, after all. They did well with you; how can they do less with her? Timoleon will do very well as steward for our affairs. It's time he had a taste of responsibility."

"So reasonable," she said. "So sensible. I hate you."

The corner of his mouth quirked up. "No woman ever likes it when a man is rational. It happens so seldom, you see. It takes her by surprise."

"Oh," said Dione, half exasperated, half provoked into laughter. "Oh, you are impossible!"

"No," he said. "You are. But I love you. And think—what an adventure, just us two, as if we were new-wed children."

She did think. It was terrifying. And if the war came—when it came—and he died in it—

"Later," he said. "Later, for the fear. Now is for love."

No, she tried to say. But he was too strong. Or she was, in her heart, where against all sense and thought and foresight, she was singing.

THIRTY-SIX

Antony and Cleopatra in Athens stood at the pinnacle of the world. Dione's fears here seemed but shadows, half-memories of a dream. She was welcomed, feted, treated to the gentle and the not-so-gentle mockery of those who thought they understood very well why the queen's friend and kinswoman might appear so suddenly with her husband at her back and no children to be seen. Antony certainly believed that the two of them had fled dull duty for the diversions of the court. Cleopatra professed to believe it.

Rumor had the queen disliking to dwell in Athens in the very house to which Antony had brought Octavia and lived with her for years as man and wife. Truth saw her triumphant over the memory. Few in Athens professed to remember the Roman woman once the queen of Egypt had supplanted her. It was conquest; it was victory. Cleopatra, queen and goddess, ruled Athens as she had ruled in Alexandria, with the force of her wit as well as her wealth. Athens, like Alexandria, knew well the rule of intellect, or wished to believe it did.

Dione had never been before to this city that claimed so much for itself. It was old, but never as old as Memphis or Thebes. It was beautiful, though she thought that Alexandria was more lovely than Athens could ever be. It was proud, but then all great cities had their pride. Its claim to be the city of wisdom in the name of its virgin goddess, struck her as grandiose and faintly absurd.

Lucius laughed and called her an incurable Alexandrian. He loved the city, loved to climb the rock of its acropolis and walk among the temples, to wander the alleys of the lower city or to make the journey to the Piraeus, the harbor that was Athens' window on the world. Without the cares of household and family, freed from his responsibilities in the Museum, he was a different man, one whom sometimes she barely knew. This must be the young Lucius who had studied philosophy in the venerable grove of the Academy, this man who smiled more often than he spoke, and who was always finding new places to wander and to explore.

She did not often go with him. Wives in Athens kept to their houses, went out veiled on the rare occasions when they went out at all, and lived as Parthian women were said to do, locked in seclusion that their men reckoned an honor and a privilege. Only the women of less respectable stripe, the hetairai, went about as women of every rank did in Egypt.

Cleopatra, being queen, did as she pleased. Dione was not a queen. Dignitaries' wives would receive her, but they made it clear that they expected her to live as they lived, shut up in walls, whether of their houses or of their litters and carriages. They were invariably dull, ill-read, concerned only with their husbands and their children and their small family squabbles that swelled with boredom into great wars and conquests. The husbands, erudite as Athenians were known to be, witty and clever and wise, still found Dione's presence a discomfort. She was too clearly a respectable woman, too disturbingly an educated one. They did not approve of her.

She could not complain to anyone, least of all to Lucius. He thought that she chose to let him go where he would, and to stay in her rooms in the villa that Antony had found for them, except when she attended the queen. She had willed this, had forced it on him. Her pride refused to betray regret. She was glad at least that Lucius was happy; happier here, it seemed, than he had been in Alexandria.

She would reflect that happiness. She would smile and be charming, and go where she was allowed to go, and wait on the goddess' will. It had gone quiet again once she arrived in Athens, as if the coming here had been all the goddess wanted, or all she needed of her servant.

No shadow lay on the lord of the Romans or on his Egyptian queen. All their fortunes were splendid. Rome itself, or the greatest part of Rome, had come to wait on Antony: a full half of the Senate and even the two consuls, the men to whom in law belonged the right and power to rule in Rome. That they were Antony's partisans and always had been, and that their election had been decided years since when the triumvirs parceled out the empire and its offices, did not matter. What mattered was that they were here, in Athens, in Antony's camp. The city was full of senatorial togas. Greece, which heretofore had seen little of consuls in their full and present power, saw those noble Romans escorted on the slightest errand by a guard of lictors with their fasces. Axes bound cumbersomely in bundles of rods were poor weapons enough, but as symbols they were potent. They signified Rome.

Antony's triumph in Alexandria had been a glory and a splendor. This visitation of Roman notables, austere as it was compared to the magnificence of Cleopatra's eastern state, was a subtler victory, but its import was profound. Rome's senate itself had divided and half of it decamped into the east.

Nothing like it had ever happened before. Octavian held Rome itself, but he had no assurance that the portion of the senate that remained was his, or simply not Antony's.

Antony could have taken Rome. His senators urged him to consider it. But, being Antony, he never moved till he was ready, and seldom took thought for haste. He was comfortable in Athens. He was mustering a fleet, training armies, entertaining his guests in grand style.

This, Dione told herself, was what the goddess had sent her here to see. Rome had fallen into Antony's lap. He had only to claim it in its own Forum, and it was his.

His, and Cleopatra's, once Octavian was disposed of. The thought of Octavian was a constant irritation. It had become a jest at Antony's banquets: they toasted Caesar's nephew and wished him happy among the shades, or they mocked his prim manners and his secret extravagances. They all knew, or declared loudly that they knew, what they would do when Octavian was fallen and they were lords again in Rome.

In the full bright sunlight of his glory, in front of the cream of the senate and the two consuls, Antony proclaimed the end of his alliance with Octavian. He divorced Octavian's sister, named her no longer wife and consort. Cleopatra was not with him when he did that, meeting with the senate in the hall that the Athenians had cleared for them. She knew better than to deepen a wound; and she was not universally loved in Rome, even in this part of Rome that had come to wait on Antony.

"Of course it was inevitable," she said to Dione while the men had their meeting. Lucius Servilius of course was among his fellow senators; Dione wondered if he was surprised, or if he had been expecting this for as long as she had.

Cleopatra went on through Dione's abstraction. "Once Octavian proved himself Antony's enemy, the marriage was an inconvenience to say the least. I can't condemn my lord for dragging it out as long as he did. After all, there might have been a reconciliation."

Dione regarded Cleopatra under lowered lashes. "And you tried to work a great magic, a demon to destroy her, when first you heard of the marriage."

"That was before I was sure of my position," said Cleopatra calmly, with neither guilt nor shame that Dione could discern. "Antony is mine. This decree is for the world's ears. I knew the truth of it years ago."

True enough, Dione thought. "So you've forgiven him."

"No," Cleopatra said, still calm, and quietly implacable. "I don't forgive. I win my wars. I choose to be gracious in victory."

"Now you're his only wife," Dione said.

"And so shall I remain," said Cleopatra, "until we die."

Dione felt the truth of that: felt it in her bones, and in the shiver of her skin.

Lucius Servilius the Augur sat at the feast of the senators, three hundred couches in a vast hall, so vast that the one feast was apportioned into several. Each circle of couches touched on the circles about it, an interweaving of honor and precedence, each with its army of servants, its musicians, its dancers, its more exotic entertainments. They

celebrated the end of Antony's alliance-by-marriage and the beginning of a new Rome, a Rome that was as much itself in the acropolis
of Athens as it was on the seven hills of Rome.

Antony was still calling himself triumvir, though Lepidus was
deposed and Octavian had discarded the title. Like the meeting of the
senate and the decree in proper form, it was a shadow, an image
imposed upon the truth.

Which was that Antony was not a Roman. He had not brought
Cleopatra to this feast, any more than he had brought her to the
meeting of the senate. But her presence was strong, her memory
distinct. Rome would not call her a wife; the law forbade it. But wife
she was, and consort, and queen. And Antony, in all but name, was
a king.

Lucius' couch was so positioned that he could see the ring of
couches over which Antony presided, and the man himself in the
place of honor. They had crowned him with laurel in the senate; he
wore the crown still, though it had begun to droop. His toga had
slipped down over his shoulder. He let it, not caring now for dignity,
expansive with wine and good fellowship. He laughed at something
someone said, a deep glad sound with undertones of a lion's roar.

His circle was liveliest of them all. No surprise in that to anyone
who knew Antony. He could make men laugh, and make them love
him, too.

Lucius, whose circle was one of the quieter ones, made up as it was
of youngish senators with an inclination toward philosophy, let the
conversation blur past him and watched Antony at his revels. He had
done so oftener than he could count; for years, through war and
peace, in Greece, in Asia, in Alexandria. Even in Rome, though that
was long ago.

Antony was holding his years well, as well as he held his wine. His
body was a little thicker, his hair a little thinner, than it had been
when first he summoned Egypt's queen to Tarsus. His color was a
little higher, the wine a little stronger in him, making his laugh louder,
his gestures broader, than they might have been. He was still a
handsome man, a strong man, a leader of men.

Lucius' heart shrank tight and small. Here was half the senate of
Rome. Here were the consuls in the pride of their office. Here was
Antony, to whom they had brought their honor and their loyalty, or
at least their fear.

Here was not Rome. These walls, this earth, were Athens—were

Greece. This air was strange. The powers that rode it were alien. They were not of Rome, nor did Rome know them.

What moved in him had nothing of justice in it, and little of fairness. He knew no guilt that he had taken to wife a foreign woman, and that against the laws of Rome—yet he could condemn Antony for doing exactly that. Not because Antony had done it—Lucius understood love, and inevitability—but because Antony wanted power in Rome. Lucius wanted no power, only peace. His marriage was no threat to that, or ever to his city.

He looked at Antony and knew a deep and tearing revulsion. This was not Rome. This was not what he wished to rule him in the name of Roma Dea. None of it: senators drunken or sober, consuls hanging on Antony's every word, Antony himself the center and the focus. Antony, who had made himself a king in the east. Antony, who played at being Roman, but who had always chosen the east, and Egypt.

Oh, to be sure, Antony fancied that he remained faithful to his own city, that he betrayed nothing that mattered to it. But the east had conquered him. He had taken to its ways, assumed its dress, become consort to its great queen. Even this feast was Roman only in that the feasters affected the toga. Much of the conversation was in Greek, and all of the entertainment.

Lucius rose. No one asked him why he was leaving. At a feast where the wine ran like water, people were always coming and going as nature commanded. There was that, yes, and a knot of senators eager to talk of he cared not what—the war in Illyria, he supposed, or the latest gossip from the Palatine—but he escaped.

The whole city celebrated Antony's freedom from the pact with Octavian, a pact honored, as the wits remarked, far more in the breach than in the observance. Antony had provided the wine and the dole of bread to the masses. The rest they supplied for themselves. Joy for its own sake, and little enough understanding of the occasion for it.

Romans would have understood. Yes, even the least of them.

Lucius was homesick—sick with longing for the city that he had left years since and without regret.

Antony would come to Rome in the end. He must, if he expected to rule it. But that was far less than comfort. Antony in Rome would mean the end of Rome that was. He would not linger there. He would claim it, set proxies over it, return to his heart's home in the east.

And Lucius could not bear to think of it.

He wandered the streets of this foreign city, jostled by its crowds, borne along in singing, shouting processions, knocked hither and yon till he hardly knew where he was. He lost his toga somewhere, and gained a mantle that reeked of garlic and of some lurid scent. By some miracle he retained his purse and its contents, such as they were: a handful of drachmae, an obol or two, and an amulet of Bastet that Mariamne had teethed on.

Sometime toward morning, somewhere about the Piraeus, he stopped. The wind was blowing, bearing a fetor that was Athens and a sharp cleanness that was the sea. A woman was singing in a language he did not know, sweet and plaintive yet with an edge of anger. He looked about him. It was dark but for a torch that lit the door of a tavern. There were no stars, no moon, only night.

"This is not Rome," he said in Latin, which was defiance of its own. "This is the east. And the east has conquered Rome."

ACT
FIVE

ACTIUM AND ALEXANDRIA
31–30 B.C.

THIRTY-SEVEN

The setting sun, half veiled in cloud, shot long shafts of light across the Gulf of Corinth. The water was gold on black, gold tinged with blood and the silver of the waves' crests in the wind that blew out of the west. In the harbor below the fortress walls, the fleet rode at anchor, masts up but sails furled, secured against the coming of the night.

Antony stood on the wall. His cloak was wrapped about him, for the wind was cold. It was his whim tonight to forget splendor, to wear simple clothes and a plain cloak and be but another sightseer on the wall. His guards, indulging him, kept their distance. Those few of his friends who had come with him were unusually quiet.

Cleopatra, clad in like simplicity, stood armlinked with him and gazed out over the water. The sun shone full in her face, etching its lines in gold, but she seemed hardly to notice. Light, her manner said, was her element. She was smiling faintly. What had she to fear? War was coming, yes. Rome had slid round the fact of the matter, that Octavian dueled with Antony for Roma Dea's favor. That could not be thought of, no, nor admitted. Therefore Rome had found a pretext, cobbled up an enemy out of its own fears and blindnesses, and called it Cleopatra.

Rome had declared war on Cleopatra. Not on Antony, of course not. But Cleopatra was Antony, and Antony was Cleopatra. Any thinking being knew that.

Rome's alleged enemy was unperturbed to be the object of such condemnation. She leaned lightly on her consort's arm, weaving her fingers with his as a girl might do, strolling on the seawall of a pleasant evening. Her voice when she spoke was soft, with laughter in it, but what she said, no simple woman would say. "It cannot but go well, I think. The eastern sea is secure behind its line of fortresses. The enemy can do nothing but stand on the shore in Italy and snarl at us."

"From Corcyra to Cyrenaica," Antony mused. "Yes, we've secured this end of the Middle Sea, and well enough. But Octavian might be up to a bit more than bared teeth. He's got an army, I'm told. And ships."

"Such ships as we have?" Cleopatra shook her head. "Oh, no. Rome is mighty in its legions, but it has never been comfortable on the sea. And we in Egypt—we who are Hellenes have been sea-peoples since the dawn time, and we who are Egyptian have sailed in boats on the Nile; lived in them, sometimes, for the pure joy of riding on the water. No Roman fleet can match us."

"Maybe," said Antony. "But they've got Agrippa, too. He's a better admiral than any I know—even yours, my lady of Egypt."

"Even the greatest of admirals needs ships to command," Cleopatra said. "Maybe we're not invincible. But strong: we are that. And we will win this war."

"Gods willing," Antony said. All once and rather startlingly he smiled. "We've waited a long while to come to it, to challenge Octavian face to face. How much longer, do you think? Should we leave our defenses and go west, and take the war to Italy?"

"Let him come to us," said Cleopatra. "We have the whole of the east at our backs, and Egypt's wealth to sustain us. Let him leave his own lands behind, his lines of supply, everything that he needs to come home victorious."

Antony nodded. They were not saying anything they had not said often before, until it had become a ritual, a conjuration almost, to assure their victory. Sometimes it was he who reminded her that their best strength was on the sea and in the east, and that Italy was best left until they could take it uncontested. Italy mattered little enough, except that it held Rome, and Rome was the prize for which they all fought.

This would be their battleground, this eastern sea.

"So it was," said Antony, "from the beginning. The east is the key. Alexander knew. So did Caesar. So, for that matter, did I—but I thought that it was Parthia. But it wasn't. It was Greece and Egypt and Asia. Rome can't have empire without them. It needs their wealth, their granaries, and their people."

"Ships, too," Cleopatra said. "There's no sea-power without ships."

"I remember," said Antony, "how you came to me in ships, like a goddess on the sea. I was furious—you'd upstaged me. But Jupiter! you were magnificent."

Cleopatra laughed. "I was shaking where I sat. You could have put me off, insulted me, forced me into concessions I never meant to grant—anything but what I wanted you to do, which was to take me as your ally."

"And more?"

She smiled out across the sea. "Maybe," she said.

"I didn't see any 'maybe' about it. I saw that you meant to have all of me that you could get. But then," he said, "I had the same thought myself."

They laughed together warm, comfortable, in harmony as in fact they rarely were—there was always something, some matter of state, to put an edge in their amity. Tonight, as they waited for their war to come to them, they were happy. They watched the sun go down, and lingered as the stars came out one by one, though the chill of sunset in spring had turned swiftly to cold. They simply wrapped their cloaks about one another and tarried, cherishing the moment, the mood, this peace before inevitable war.

The messenger came in the grey light of morning, wet with the rain that had begun to fall. His face was blue with cold, for the rain was edged with ice.

He tried to bow gracefully at the feet of the queen and the triumvir, but stumbled and fell on his face. His words seemed to come up from the earth. "Methone, lord, lady—Methone has fallen."

Amid the gathering of commanders, petitioners, hangers-on of the morning audience, someone gasped. The rest stood frozen in silence.

Antony might have been stone for all the response he made. But Cleopatra kept her wits about her. "What? Methone has fallen? How can that be? Fool, to think you can lie to us. Who paid you? Octavian? He can't have given you much; his purse is full of spiders, every wag knows that."

The messenger lifted himself to his knees, struck to courage, and even to temper. "Lady, I don't lie! The Lord Antony's fortress at Methone, that looks west to Italy—it's taken. A fleet came across, fell on it when no one was expecting, and seized it. King Bogud the Mauretanian, who had the command—he's dead. The rest of the garrison is killed or captured, or gone over to the enemy."

Antony was speechless still, staring like a blind man into an endless dark. Dione had seen such an expression on the face of a man about to fall down in a fit, but he remained in his seat, seeming not even to breathe.

"Who did it?" Cleopatra demanded, her voice gone harsh with shock. "Who commands the Roman fleet?"

"Agrippa," the messenger answered. "Marcus Vipsanius Agrippa."

"That toad." They all started: Antony had spoken at last, like a lion's growl. "That miserable excuse for a man. What's he doing taking my fortress?"

"Probably the same thing he did in taking care of Sextus Pompey," said one of the senators who still lingered about Antony's camp—Ahenobarbus, who had been consul last year, but was no longer: that office was given over to Octavian, and to someone else whom Dione did not know, except that he had a poisonous hatred of Cleopatra. Ahenobarbus' voice was dry. "He got rid of that sea-pirate, and handily, too. We should have expected Octavian to use him against us."

"We did," said Cleopatra. "What we never expected was for him to take one of our strongholds with hardly a fight. What was Bogud thinking, by the gods? Did he turn traitor, or merely coward?"

"Neither, lady," the messenger said. "It was so sudden—we had no warning, no preparation beyond what we were doing as a matter of course, nothing, before they were on us. King Bogud led the fight; he was one of the first to fall."

"Fool, then," Cleopatra said, "and worse than fool, to leave his troops without a commander."

"We weren't expecting such an attack," the messenger said. "None of us was. Not even you, lady. They were supposed to be weak; they couldn't even collect their pay, we heard. They'd sail up, see how strong we were, and run crying back to Italy. But they were the strong ones. They hit us with everything they had."

"Therefore," she said, "they have nothing more to bring against us. It's a blow, I admit it. Methone's crucial. It sits right on the sea-road between us and Egypt—and Egypt's where our supplies are. But we'll take care of that. My lord?"

Antony started as if roused from sleep. "What?" He shook himself so hard that his cuirass rattled. Some of his shock seemed to pass with the shaking. He was still paler than Dione had ever seen him, his ruddiness lost in a greenish pallor, but his eyes had lost their blank look. He was thinking again, planning, snapping out orders with a general's swift competence. Troops mustered and sent to Methone; ships called out; the whole army set on battle footing.

But it could not be done in a moment, and he was caught, as his soldiers would say, flat-footed. His troops were not precisely out of training, but they had lost their edge with long idleness. His ships were ready, but their crews needed to be called to order out of the dockside taverns. The army had been prepared to frighten a weak enemy with its mere numbers. It had not expected to find the enemy strong, or his strength applied so swiftly, to such devastating effect.

"May the Furies hound Agrippa," Antony snarled. "May vultures eat his liver. Gods damn him for a competent man!"

"Luck," said Cleopatra. "Don't forget luck."

"Octavian's famous fortune?" Antony shot back. "The daimon that I'm supposed to be so afraid of? Should I tuck my tail between my legs and run now, while I still can?"

"Oh, stop that," said Cleopatra. "That was a lucky blow—shrewd, too. Agrippa knows his business. But Methone's only one fort, and we have a whole line of them, with all our power behind them. He's won one battle. It's a long chance yet that he'll win the war."

Antony scowled, but he could see the sense of what she said. "Curse it, that's all. He caught me with my wick half-dipped. I should have expected it. I should have *known*."

She could hardly deny that. She said, "Now you know. Now you're warned. The war's begun—and you're going to win it."

"Gods grant," said Antony.

The gods granted that Agrippa should secure his victory at Methone, scour the lands about it, and advance as far as Sparta—and there gain another victory, this one without a blow struck. Eurykles, who was lord in the warrior city, had never been a friend to Antony—the triumvir had slain his father for piracy. He went joyfully over to the enemy. But worse than that, he took with him one of Antony's own, the commander Atratinus, and made Agrippa master in Sparta.

That was bitter, but more bitter still were the ravages of Agrippa's ships on the sea. They harried the supply-ships from Egypt, the great wallowing grain-carriers and the merchanters bearing wine and lesser delicacies, spices, honey, dainties to sweeten the tempers of Antony's troops. More sank or were captured than sailed safe into port past Methone.

"I could stand it," Antony's friend Dellius said at dinner one day when the ships had come in, but only half as many as expected, and half of those half-laden, or taken and stripped of their cargo and then let go to mock the army. "I could stand it, I really could, to drink this Greek vinegar, if I didn't know that Octavian's pet page was swilling down the best Caecuban. That hurts, you know. Octavian's page has no palate for wine at all. *He*'d drink this dreadful stuff and think it good enough for a god."

"Well, and so it is," said Antony, grinning and draining his cup. The rest of the gathering laughed, but the laughter was tight, and faces pinched with discontent. They were not hungry, not yet; Greece perforce was feeding them, since Egypt was prevented. But they all saw famine in Agrippa's harrying of the fleets—and none of theirs had been able to stop it. Antony could not defend his whole line of fortresses and still dispose of Agrippa. That was exactly what Agrippa hoped he would do—and leave the whole of Greece open to Octavian.

"This isn't so bad," he said, filling his cup again. "It tastes like a ship's bottom when it's not sour enough to curdle honey, but there's something to be said for ship's bottom. Solid, you know. Rounded. Lots of substance."

"So's Octavian's page," sighed Dellius. "And he's loaded with Caecuban."

Now that the war had come, Dione was lifted out of her months-long sulk. For sulk it had been, missing her children fiercely, watching Lucius draw away from her by slow but perceptible degrees, and seeing no purpose in it, no need of her presence. The war was won before it was even begun. Octavian was weak, penniless, ill-supported in Rome. He would fall. How could he not?

But Methone's capture, Agrippa's stranglehold on the army's lines of supply, changed things. It showed Antony's confidence for the hubris that it had been. It sharpened the edge of their waiting, made victory seem less a surety. This, the goddess had foreseen. This, she had wished Dione to witness. She would speak when it was time. Dione knew it, a knowledge that filled the empty places, drove out her ill temper, settled her into a watchful silence.

She was almost happy, drinking sour Greek wine, eating what the queen's cooks could glean, waiting for the latest messages from the war. Octavian had landed an army in Corcyra, the runners said, and taken it as Agrippa had taken Methone. Corcyra was north of Antony's camp at Patras; Methone was south of it. The pattern was clear for her to read. Octavian and Agrippa would, if they could, close in and crush their enemy.

Their enemy had troubles enough without them: sickness, hunger, slow wearing away of spirit such as comes with siege. And yet they had not seen the invaders, had done nothing but wait, send out scouts and skirmishers, and hold what they had, as they could, while the earth of their confidence crumbled underfoot.

"This strengthens us," Antony said. And truly he looked well. He was drinking less, eating less; he had been out and about in the army and among his fortresses, making them strong against attack. Dione could not see any wavering in him, or any fear for the outcome of the war.

"We've had setbacks," he said, "surely. We deserved them. We got too cocky. But we're the stronger still, and we've got the greater numbers and the better fleet. We'll lure the enemy in, and then we'll take him."

He had come on Cleopatra and some of her women by the harbor, where they had come to greet a handful of ships that had run Agrippa's blockade. He was in armor, not his golden parade splendor but good solid bronze and leather made for use. An aide held his horse for him while he walked the quay with his queen.

"No ships yet," said Cleopatra. "I hope to the gods they weren't attacked again after they were sighted off Zakynthos. We need the corn they're bringing."

"No wine?" Antony asked, but his tone was light. He sighed. "Ah me. I'll live with the stuff they're feeding us now. They put pitch in it, I swear. It tastes like a mouthful of pinewood."

"Yes, there's resin in it. It's vinegar underneath." Cleopatra frowned out to sea. "There's a new plague in the west camp. Men are coughing themselves to death. They're saying it's Octavian's luck and Apollo's arrows, killing them for daring to oppose the one true heir of Caesar."

"It's more like staying too long in one place and taking too much time to fill in the latrines," Antony said. "Comes of having so many who aren't Roman—they don't understand Roman efficiency."

"I am not Roman," Cleopatra said, calmly enough but with an edge of ice.

"You're not a Syrian conscript, either," he pointed out. "They'd live in their filth like dogs if the centurions didn't watch them every instant. It's no wonder they get sick. I'll see about more sanitation details. Gives the men something to do, if nothing else."

"We could move," she said.

"No," said Antony. "Not yet."

"But soon."

"Soon," he agreed. He brushed her cheek with his finger. "There, love, buck up. We miscalculated, we surely did, but we'll fix it. You'll see."

"I hope so," said Cleopatra.

*   *   *

The ships never did come in. Agrippa had taken or sunk them. Even the queen's following went on half-rations, which was still, to be sure, enough for decent comfort. They were not hurting, not yet. Not as they had on the road from Phraaspa.

Lucius Servilius' mood waned as Dione's waxed. He could see that she was happier, which would have been a paradox, but he knew that she had been feeling worse than useless. It made him feel guilty, which made him cross. He was not the one who had insisted on going to Greece. He would joyfully have stayed in Alexandria. Away from this long slow eroding siege. Away from the truth that he had seen in Athens, that Antony had made himself alien to Rome.

In truth Antony seemed more Roman here, commanding his troops, ordering his war, leaving aside his wine and his silks and his Greek revels. And yet his army was far more eastern than Roman, his legions filled with men who had never seen the seven hills or smelled the reek of Tiber in the morning. Rome—and Octavian—had been refusing him Roman troops. Necessity had forced him to recruit in the east.

Necessity, because he would not take the battle to Italy, would not go back to Rome and face Octavian on their own home ground. His reasons were good, Lucius could not contest that. War in Italy rent the heart of Roma Dea. War in the east settled matters where no harm could be done to Rome herself.

Yet Antony's war had taken him out of Rome, made him other than Roman. His men were strangers, his tent full of foreign voices, foreign faces. He shared his bed with an Egyptian queen. She held his heart; she sat in his councils, and ruled them as much as he.

Lucius liked Cleopatra, insofar as she could be liked—she was the sort of woman who inspired love or hate, and seldom anything between. But she was not his queen. He did not accept her rule over aught that he did.

He could say none of this to Dione. They met, it seemed, only in bed, and then they made love in silence and went to sleep, or more often of late, just went to sleep. He used to wake and find them wound in each other's arms. Now he would be stiff and alone on one side of the bed and she on the other, curled with her back to him and her cat in the hollow of her middle. If he tried to touch her, she shrugged him off in her sleep, or woke and stared at him as if he were a stranger.

To be sure, once she was truly awake, she always smiled and came to his embrace. But there was a distance between them.

He wondered if she felt it. He never quite managed to ask: proof enough, at least in his mind, that they had grown apart.

He lay awake through long nights, with the lamp flickering on the tent's walls, and watched her sleep. She never looked unhappy. Quite the opposite. She had an air of a creature sufficient unto itself, needing no other to complete it, alone and content.

Had she been like that when he first saw her? He thought not. She had had her son with her. Never till she came to Greece had he seen her without a child in her shadow. This perhaps was Dione as she had been before she married Apollonius, Dione who had been Isis' priestess from her childhood, voice and servant of her goddess. She reminded him of her cat, small and sleek and self-contained.

There was room for him on her edges, she made that clear to him. But he did not want her edges. He wanted her heart.

He was, he thought, rather too much like Antony for comfort. But Antony did not want a priestess from Alexandria. Antony wanted Rome.

THIRTY-EIGHT

Lucius Servilius the Augur took the omens in the morning, a month to the day after Antony's army had left Patras and come to Actium. Actium because Octavian had come there from his conquest of Corcyra; because Agrippa had driven Antony out of Patras and then out of Leukas with his ships and his land forces, and Actium was Antony's last refuge north of Leukas and south of Corcyra.

Antony was still stunned by his reverses. He had expected to hold Patras, or at least Leukas. Agrippa had been too strong, and too clever by far. Now Antony must hold Actium, or he would lose his war.

"But we haven't lost yet," he had said to Lucius while they waited for the sun to come up. "Give us some good omens, to show the troops what's what. We're holding here, aren't we? We've kept Octavian from taking the other side of the strait. We'll burst out all at once, see if we won't, and drive the enemy yelping back to his den."

Lucius had not said anything then. There was nothing he could say that Antony would want to hear. Omens came as omens would. He was not a man who could feign them, or lie about their import.

Now he stood by the altar in the camp, with the sun glaring straight into his eyes. The priests and the acolytes had sung the hymns one by one in proper and prescribed order, without error that would have compelled them to begin all over again. The sheep waited dumbly for its sacrifice. It did not even move as he approached it. Its blank amber eyes seemed dead already, empty of either will or intelligence.

He curved his arm about its throat. Its fleece was soft, washed snowy clean and scented with incense. There were garlands about its horns. One trailed over Lucius' hand, a spray of yellow flowers like little suns.

One swift sidewise slash opened its throat. The blood's fountain was beautiful as always, the purest and most splendid of reds, brighter than any fuller's dye. An acolyte caught it in the golden bowl, and spilled none—good omen there for Antony, if he chose to see it as such.

Lucius made the cuts as the rite prescribed. It was bloody work, but swift; he had done it often before. His knife did not pierce the gut: good omen again, and relief, to be freed from that stench. The organs were as they should be, none missing, none marred by deformity. It was altogether a perfect example of a sheep. Precisely the omen Antony had asked for. Precisely what the army needed to lighten its leaden heart.

And he stood silent, bloodied to the shoulders, staring at his perfect sacrifice, his impeccably correct omen, and knew it for a lie. The gods mocked him—mocked them all.

He knew then how Cassandra felt when one of her prophecies came upon her. The tightness in the skull, like a storm building. The surety, the absolute certainty, that what she was about to say was true, but that no one would believe her.

His audience grew impatient. He saw them stirring, heard them muttering. The priest nearest him hissed, sounding for all the world like an angry goose. "Psst! Wake up! Or are you sick?"

The man's concern was genuine, if short of patience. But Lucius could not say what the gods, grinning their skull-grin, willed him to say. They knew the truth. They knew that he saw it. They were much amused.

"No," he said, but faintly. He was swaying. The earth had lost its solidity. The gods—the gods could lie.

His fellow priests thought that he was taken ill. That was omen, too, he thought with a small surge of satisfaction: ill omen, and truth. But the priests were quick to cover it. One of the others spoke the augury as the gods designed it to be spoken, the lie, the deception, the promise of their enemies' defeat.

Lucius was well. Too well. He saw too clearly. Like Cassandra, like Dione when the goddess possessed her.

He let the priests lead him away from the altar, half carrying him. He had no power to resist them. They washed him clean in the water sanctified for the purpose, relieved him of his bloodstained vestments, helped him into his more ordinary clothes. They tried to comfort him with assurances that if it was another of the plagues that beset the army, it was a mild one. Let him eat a little, rest, be quiet for a while, and it would go away.

But no amount of food or rest or quiet would banish the truth. The gods lied. And he knew it.

Actium was not the place Antony would have chosen to confront his enemies, and certainly he would never have chosen to stand at bay there, separated from the great bulk of his fleet, with enemies closing in to south and east and north. He had chosen the place for one of his fortresses because it stood at the gate of the Ambracian Gulf: good harbor for ships, and protection for that part of his fleet which he had stationed in this one of his line of defenses. Leukas' tall stark-sided isle stood southwest of it, a loom on the horizon, a day's march away at legionary's pace. Between the isle and the camp lay a waste of stones and sun-scorched green, rising eastward to the mountains of Akarnania. West was the sea, and north was Greece, a wall of mountains veiled in cloud.

Octavian stood between Antony and Greece, at the north gate of the strait as Antony stood to the south. He had no skill in warfare, everyone knew that, but someone had been wise in choosing this place for him to camp. The north was defended by its wall of mountains. The south offered a plain level enough for a battle, if battle there was to be. And the strait itself, held with even mild strength, kept Antony's fleet bottled up, with Agrippa's ships prowling the sea just beyond, alert for any escape.

"We'll wait him out," said Antony in the council of his commanders. "He thinks he's got me locked in a vise, but I have two things he doesn't have. I've got water where I can get at it without risking my neck. And I've got safe anchorage for my ships."

"Water's close enough," Ahenobarbus said, "and he's got a harbor he can use unless it storms—and it won't, not in this season. And he's got more ships than you have, now he's trapped you away from most of your fleet."

"So I fight him on land," Antony said. "I can get into Greece, and I can outmatch him with the troops I've got there."

Ahenobarbus shook his head. He was ill—they all were, these days, with one plague or another. He was not young, but he had been vigorous when this war began. Now he looked weak and old. "You think to outwait them: muster your armies, strike Octavian's legions, let Agrippa's ships wither and drop away. Wise. Sensible. It may work. But I'm tired, Marcus. I'm sick; sick of fighting, sick of waiting, sick of living so far away from Rome."

They were all silent, staring at him, or at their hands, or at the maps spread out on the table. They knew every line of every map; every hope and every chance, whatever any of them could expect their enemies to do. They had the better general. They knew that. Ahenobarbus knew it, admitted it.

"But this isn't Rome," he said: Lucius' thoughts to a word, and not only Lucius'. "Marcus, I'm sorry. I can't keep on. You're not going to Rome when this is over—don't try to make us think you are. You're going back to Alexandria. You're choosing the east, and your eastern queen."

"You can't be sure of that," Antony said, carefully calm, but his nostrils were white and pinched.

"I'm as sure as I need to be." Ahenobarbus pushed himself to his feet. "I think I'd better go."

Antony sat still at the table's head. No one quite dared to meet his eyes.

Suddenly Antony laughed. It was almost genuine; almost merry. "Oh, go, by all means! Your mistress is tired of waiting, isn't she? Go back to Rome; give her a kiss for me. Tell her I'll claim a kiss of my own when I come home."

Ahenobarbus dipped his head. Maybe it was only weariness. A storm of coughing seized him. He waved away all those who tried to help; steadied himself, turned his back, walked out of the tent.

Antony's voice was loud in the silence. "Make sure we send his baggage after him. He'll be wanting those clean tunics when he visits his Lalage."

No one laughed. No one said anything at all.

*   *   *

"What happened?" Lucius wondered aloud. "What turned it about so quickly?"

Dione had been spreading coverlets on the bed. That should have been Hebe's task, but Hebe was prostrate with a fever. For a while she had been like to die, but now, Dione had assured Lucius, the maid would recover, the gods willing. He rather missed her dark presence at this evening ritual, her eyes that seemed always wary, as if she had never learned to trust him. But he trusted her implicitly. She would die for her mistress; she was furious now that she could not rise from her pallet in the room without, had glared terribly when he came in.

She could of course hear him through the thin walls of the tent, but he fancied the illusion of privacy. Dione finished making the bed and straightened, sighing a little. He tensed, but she looked and sounded well enough. Maybe her goddess protected her from the sicknesses that ran rampant in the camp.

"We're losing the war," Lucius said. "That should be obvious to anyone with wits to understand. But how? We had everything. We had numbers, money, strong places. The other side had a good admiral, a miserable general, no money, and no walls to hide behind. What happened?"

"Luck," Dione answered. "Fate. The gods. Hubris, too. Antony was too sure of himself. He let too much get past him, and waited too long to stop it."

"Cleopatra could have seen," Lucius said. "Could have got him moving."

Dione did not bridle at that, but he heard the snap in her voice. "Cleopatra did exactly what she thought was best for Egypt."

"But not for Rome."

"Why should she care about Rome?"

"Because," he said with careful patience, "Rome could devour her alive. Rome *is* the power in this world now."

"Not necessarily," said Dione. "Antony is still strong. And Antony is the other half of Cleopatra."

"So Rome says—and hates her for it."

Dione sat on the bed, upright like a carving in an Egyptian temple, hands on her knees. She was beautiful in the lamplight, beautiful and distant. "What Rome thinks matters very little to Alexandria."

"It will when Octavian marches his legions through the gate."

"He won't," Dione said, but her voice was less firm than it should have been. "Cleopatra will prevent him."

"I hope she can," said Lucius. "The gods are giving us false omens now. What else will they do to us for their amusement?"

"*Your* gods," she said. "Maybe they give you omens for Rome, that Rome will conquer. They would want that. But we have our own gods, and those will protect us."

"Pray to them," he said.

She regarded him steadily, as if he had been a stranger whom she must study, lest he be a threat to her. "Why do you stay, if you believe that Octavian will win?"

"You can ask that?"

She nodded, though the question had not been looking for an answer.

He was shaking. He could not stop it. "I remember honor, and loyalty given. I remember friendship."

"Does Roma Dea care for any of that?"

His head shook. "I married in the east. I'll never repent it, or revoke it. How can I fault Antony for doing what I did, with the same god-born inevitability?"

"Antony in doing it defied Rome, which he would master. You simply pleased yourself. A citizen can do that. A ruler should not."

Lucius' thoughts to a word. They were bitter, coming from Dione in that soft, dispassionate tone. As if she did not care. As if she had never loved him, or been his wife. "I won't desert. No matter who else has."

"Plancus," Dione murmured, "nobleman and buffoon, and Antony's friend. He was one of the first to change his loyalties. Ahenobarbus—he died, you know. He never had that kiss from Lalage. The fever killed him. Dellius is wavering. He used to admire Cleopatra to the point of worship, but that has gone sour. The sweetness cloys; the splendor is brass. Even gods-on-earth should be wary of daring too much."

Lucius stared. The goddess was speaking, the mother of gods in Egypt. "But," he said. "It fell so fast."

"Great glory," Dione said, "swift fall." She sighed. Her head bowed. When she lifted it, she spoke for herself again, but a little cold still, remote. "If you have to go, then go. I know what Roma Dea is to you. It's tearing your heart to pieces."

He could not bear it. If she had railed, raged, been as reasonably unreasonable as any ordinary wife would be, he could have shouted back, and quarreled, and left in the heat of it. This understanding, this serene acceptance, left him no armor and no weapon. He was naked in the soul, and he hated it.

"I've seen it since Athens," she said, further devastating his defenses. "Since Alexandria, even. You were repulsed by what you were seeing. You wanted Rome back—Rome as you perceived it, uncorrupted by eastern luxuries. No matter that that dream was vain when the first Scipio was a child. It was yours. You cherished it. You still do. And now the gods lie when you try to prophesy for Antony. If the gods themselves are making game of him, how can you stand by him?"

"I have been his friend," he said, forcing out each word. "I have served him as best I could."

"Now you can no longer serve him. So go. Octavian will welcome you as he's welcomed all the rest of Antony's distinguished defectors."

"Deserters."

"Is it desertion to return from the paths of error to the arms of Roma Dea?"

He came within a breath of striking her down. Only a thread of restraint held him; that and her cool dark eyes fixed on his face. "You are mocking me."

She shook her head. "I'd be the same if it were Egypt calling me. But you don't want me to understand, do you? You want me to fight with you. I'm too tired. I've got too much to do."

Somewhere behind that face was the woman who had loved him, she said and he believed, with all her heart. He could not find her now. This was the foreign woman, the priestess, the goddess' instrument.

And yet she was his wife. "If we pack now," he said, "we can be gone by dawn."

"You can," she agreed.

He heard that. He refused to understand it. "Octavian will treat you well. He's a purse-mouthed little priss, but he knows the uses of diplomacy. I'll make sure he doesn't ask you to do anything against Cleopatra."

"He won't be able to," she said. "I'll be with my queen wherever she goes."

"You are my wife," said Lucius Servilius.

She nodded once, but she said, "I am the goddess' voice. And the queen is the goddess on earth."

"We're going together. I can't have you here, being defeated—wounded, raped, killed—"

"That's not your choice to make," she said, still cool, still calm, but her face was white. "I know you have to go. You've been hating every step of the way since Athens. Roma Dea wants you and will have you. But she is no goddess of mine."

He stood, she sat in silence. This was impasse, both pure and terrible. Like, he thought, Roma Dea herself.

"May the Furies curse your vision," he said at last. "I promised you that I'd never abandon you. And I won't."

For the first time her serenity cracked. She stretched out a hand, drew it back. "You can't do that. You'll gnaw yourself to pieces."

"I promised," he said stubbornly.

"I release you from your promise."

"No."

"You have to go. Your goddess needs you."

"Then come with me."

"No."

And so they came again to silence. There was no resolving it. Lucius felt the teeth rending at his heart. Rome was on the other side of the strait. This was Egypt, and Egypt's following. The very air here was wrong, scented with exotic unguents, the perfumes of the east. He gagged at it and nearly vomited.

But this was his wife, sitting on the bed, staring at him. This was the place that he had chosen. He would stay in it, though it killed him—and though she hated him for it.

He spread blankets on the floor and wrapped himself in them. Dione did not try to stop him. For all he knew, she slept the night long. He barely closed his eyes. The pain in his heart was too great.

He would endure it. He had made his choice long ago. He would stand by it.

THIRTY-NINE

All through that long burning summer Antony waged his war in the marshes and the barren heaths of Actium. Now the struggle took itself out to sea against Agrippa's fleet; now it surged inland as he swept the towns and villages for men to fill his legions and to row his ships, for those whom he had already were falling sick and dying in the cesspit and malarial marsh that was his camp. Once he even went out himself. He had sent Dellius to muster land-forces in Macedonia; he took half his army northward behind, while Sosius, the commander of his fleet, broke out of their trap in the gulf and ran full on Agrippa's ships.

Sosius almost won. Almost—and broke free. But Agrippa was too strong for him.

It had been a clever plan, worthy of Antony's generalship: escape by land, escape by sea, reunite the two forces and fall on the enemy from without. That left Cleopatra and half the army, and much of the fleet, in Octavian's trap, both bait and diversion. But the effort failed. Agrippa would fight, and strongly. Octavian would not. Antony coaxed Octavian's cavalry out by threatening his water-lines, but Antony's own horsemen turned round with their commander and went over to the enemy.

But Antony refused to be beaten down even by such a blow as this. He called in all his commanders, left guards and guardposts lest the enemy attack, but summoned the heart of his strength to the heart of his camp. It was the month that the Romans called Sextilis, when the heat is heaviest, and the Dog Star burns the days away to the slow cooling of Septembris. Long months of encampment here in this bleak place, where no water ran but from the sea, had bred a stink that rivaled the worst of Rome in the worst of summer. Soldiers sweated themselves raw in their armor. Princes sweltered in the robes of their dignity; the few senators who had not gone belly-crawling back to Rome or to Octavian, drooped under the steaming weight of their togas.

Antony had put on his parade armor. Its glitter was hard and bright under the canopy that his servants had raised to give shelter against the sun. He who was the ruddiest and fullest-blooded of men looked paradoxically cool; his face was sheened with sweat, but he seemed to be in no discomfort. Some of those gathered looked sidelong at Cleopatra, who sat near Antony in a chair no more elaborate than anyone else's, and thought they knew what protected him. She wore Egyptian dress, supremely practical in such weather, with a glorious pectoral of gold and lapis, and her own hair in the many plaits of an Egyptian noblewoman. She might have been made of stone, for all the notice she took of the heat.

Antony had received the first comers on his feet, and stayed so until the last stragglers hurried in: Dellius in an impeccably arranged toga, face haggard but carefully shaven and powdered, with one or two of his friends. Once they were greeted and settled, with wine to drink— raw Macedonian stuff, drinkable if one were parched with thirst, and strong enough to dull the senses if one drank a cup unwatered— Antony scanned all their faces. Some met his eyes direct. Others were intent on the wine or on one another. Someone coughed, a deep, racking sound.

"So," said Antony at last. "There's more of us than maybe Octavian thinks, after all the changes of heart we've had. Is anybody going to be leaving tonight? If you are, speed it up. Leave now. I won't take care of you the way I did with Iamblichus and Postumius—unless I catch you after this meeting is over."

No one said anything. Iamblichus of Emesa and Postumius the senator had been too slow and too obvious about going over to Octavian; Antony had had them executed as an example to the rest. It had not slowed down the exodus that anybody knew of. But it dampened moods now, if indeed they could have been damper than they were already.

Antony nodded to himself. "We're all in this together, then. We're at the end of it."

"Surrender?" someone asked—someone well back in the assembly, which probably gave him the courage to say it at all.

Antony did not erupt into wrath, although he spoke quickly to quell the faintheart. "We're nowhere near surrender. Octavian's got us in the pincers, sure enough, but there's still a hundred thousand of us and three hundred ships. We can't stay here much longer, let's face that. We're short on supplies. We've got people from inland bringing us grain for our bread, but we can't get much out of them— Greece is picked bare as it is. Much more recruiting for our ships and there won't be anyone to bring in the harvest."

"And yet," said Sosius the admiral, "without oarsmen the ships don't fight."

"Without food, the army doesn't stay alive to fight," Canidius Crassus said sharply.

They glared at one another, sea-commander and land-commander, until Antony came between them with a gentling hand. "There now, you're both right, and that's the trouble. We're bottled up here, being eaten away bit by bit, by fevers, by hunger, by heart-sickness. We need a battle, and that's just what Octavian doesn't want to give us."

"So we force it on him," Canidius said.

"We tried that," said one of the senators. "All it got us was a rash of desertions and a drubbing at sea."

"We'll try it again," Antony said. "They won't be expecting it, maybe, so soon. They know we're desperate, but they also think I'm the sort who dithers till it's too late for anything. Let's let them keep on thinking so—for a few more days. Then we hit them with everything we've got."

"To what end?" demanded a prince from somewhere in Asia Minor. He had a small company of archers and a great air of importance. "What do we want? Just to get out? To do any damage?"

"Both," Antony answered promptly. "As I see it, we've got two choices. We've got land-forces and we've got the fleet. We can't get all the soldiers on the ships, and we certainly can't fight with that many men on board, getting in each other's way. We tried to use both at once, but it didn't work. It took too much coordinating in too little time."

"So what do we do?" asked Canidius Crassus. "Abandon one force or the other? Leave the land-forces to slog back through the enemy's lines while the fleet runs for Egypt, or forget the fleet and fight our way out by land?"

"We can guess which one you'd choose," someone muttered.

Canidius glowered in the general direction of the voice. "Well, and doesn't it make sense? We're outnumbered at sea. And we don't have a sea-general—whereas the enemy does. You're no Agrippa, Antony, and you know it. But you're ten times the general that Octavian could ever be. You won Philippi with brains and luck and good fighting. You can win Actium, too, or wherever else you can draw Octavian to fight."

Antony nodded slowly. "And we can get reinforcements in Macedonia and Thrace—there's still pickings to be had there, and they aren't fond of Octavian."

"No," said Cleopatra. Her voice was like a trumpet-call, clear and
hard and cold. People started at the sound of it; gaped at her who had
seemed as immobile and nigh as lifeless as a carven image. Now she
was alive, bending forward, her face fierce and her words sharp and
to the point. "You can't win a land battle now, no matter how good
a general you may be. A general needs troops—and you have none.
A hundred thousand, you said? I doubt you'd count half that if you
reckoned up all the sick or the wounded or the simply unfit to fight.
You'd have to take them north, since the enemy holds the south too
tightly: up through the mountain passes when they're barely able to
crawl from the winejar to the privy and back. And tell me, how do
you expect the fleet to escape if there are no soldiers to do the
fighting once the ships engage?"

She rose. She was not overly tall, but she knew how to tower over
tall men, and she did it now. "Now suppose you simply abandon the
ships, forget them, let them surrender or be destroyed. Forget for a
moment that any ship lost to us is a gain to the enemy the next time
we have to fight him. Just think of what you can do once you've made
that break for Macedonia. How do you think you'll get back to Asia
or to Egypt, where most of our strength and our allies are? You're
bottled up there no less than you are here."

"But there's more of Macedonia," said Canidius, "and it's rich country. We could regain our strength there, get morale back up, be ready
for a whole new war."

"Could you? Or would you find yourselves captives of a turncoat
king, while Octavian seizes everything south and east of you?"

"Now see here," said Canidius, forgetting in his temper that he
addressed a queen, and not politely, either. "When you're fighting a
war, the first you think of is who's fighting it—who's got the better
general. At sea, that's Agrippa. On land, that's Antony, and no question about it. Antony at sea isn't going to win anything that Agrippa
doesn't let him have."

"That," Antony said mildly, "is a bit insulting, you know."

Canidius' mouth snapped shut. He glared, not at Antony but at
Cleopatra.

She stared levelly back. "We risk much less by breaking free in
ships than we do by taking the army through the mountains. We can
man the ships with the pick of the land-legions, preserving them at
least instead of losing them in the passes—and losing all of the fleet.
We can load, what, four or five legions on the ships? And there are
seven more to be had in Syria and Cyrenaica. Break out of this trap,

claim those legions and the rest of our fleet, sail to Egypt and mount our defense from there, and we stand in better case than we ever would in Macedonia."

"But first," said Canidius, "you have to break out. You have to get past Agrippa. Land battle's a sure thing. Antony can't lose it unless he trips and falls flat on his face. At sea we're outnumbered and outadmiraled."

"Of course Antony can win the land battle," Cleopatra said impatiently. "But then what is he to do? Lose half his army in the mountains, and lose the rest when Macedonia decides Octavian's gold has a brighter sheen than Antony's? Maybe he won't win the sea-fight as fast or as easily, but he has more to gain at the end of it—and more chance of escape if he loses. The legions won't leave Syria and Cyrenaica until he commands them. And Egypt won't turn on him. I am Egypt," she said, drawing herself up, "and I tell you now: while I live, I shall never surrender to Gaius Octavius."

She was splendid, standing there, speaking in absolute belief and absolute truth. But Canidius Crassus was long inured to royal magnificence. Cleopatra's fault, that, and past mending, even if she had cared to try. "Let's be honest, then, madam, and never mind the posturing. We can't win where we are. The best we can do is strike a blow and get out. I say we strike that blow on land, because that's where Antony has the advantage."

"And I say," she countered swiftly, "that we strike it at sea, where we don't need to win—simply to break free and claim the forces that have been denied us, and find a better and stronger place from which to wage the war."

A mutter ran round the gathering. Some looked at Canidius and nodded. Some looked at Cleopatra and growled, but that growl was agreement.

She was not trying to make them love her. She had given that up, if she had ever wanted it all, before they camped at Actium. It had cost them: lost Plancus, lost Ahenobarbus, lost too many other allies both greater and lesser. If they thought her haughty beyond endurance, then so they must. She could not be other than she was, and that was queen and goddess.

Canidius resisted her still, with purely Roman obstinacy. "Land battle is a surer bet. We *can* win that—and bring up morale into the bargain. Running out by sea on Egyptian ships isn't going to help our men's spirit at all."

"Most of our men by now are Egyptians and easterners," said

Cleopatra, "and they would rather be alive and morose than dead and content."

Canidius looked into her face. "It's down to that, isn't it? The army isn't even Roman any more."

She drew breath to speak, but Antony forestalled her. Very gently he asked, "Do you want to leave, Publius Canidius?"

Canidius jerked as if struck.

The regret showed in Antony's face, in the darkening of his eyes. But he had to say the rest of it. "She's right, you know. Your way loses us the sea beyond recovery, and most of the army too, the shape it's in. I know what I'm facing in Agrippa. I'm not happy about it. But if we can just get past him, we can grab those legions and run for Egypt. And Egypt is strong enough for anything Octavian can throw at it. Egypt's ours, Publius Canidius: heart, soul, and grainbasket."

Canidius shook his head, resisting any compulsion of logic or practicality. "Maybe we need to cut ourselves loose from Egypt, too. Make our own way, fight our own wars, be Romans again."

"Die nobly on Octavian's sword," said Cleopatra. "You will, you know, beyond any question, if you try to make for Macedonia. There simply isn't enough there to fight a war with. A battle or two, yes, but then the enemy rolls over you."

"But," said Canidius, "we've got Antony. They don't have anything to compare with him."

"Antony alone is little enough when all of Rome is massed against him."

Antony, wearying suddenly of being spoken of as if he were not there, said, "I'm glad you're loyal, Publius Canidius. Gladder than maybe you know. But let's be practical. Wars need men, and men we've got if we take the sea route. It's risky, yes. They can see everything we do, perched up there north of us in their vultures' nest. They'll do their utmost to stop us. But we can fight our way out. *Out,* you understand? We don't need to win. Just to escape. Winning's for later, when we're not shut up like mice in a trap."

Practical, thought Lucius Servilius. Utterly practical, and Roman to the core—but Antony's commanders yielded to him as to an eastern king. Save for Canidius, those who would have argued—marked by the glitter of eyes and the clenching of fists—bit their tongues and were silent. The easterners, of whom there were more than he had thought possible, bowed down and murmured their acquiescence. Many would try to fade into the landscape once the fleet had sailed.

Others would fight on the ships—archers in particular. The horse-men at least had some hope of escape.

As the council dispersed, Lucius found himself walking beside Dellius. That clever man's expression was as grim as Lucius' own must be. For once he was neither smiling nor waxing witty. He greeted Lucius with a word or two. Lucius, undertaking strenuously not to notice Dione in Cleopatra's shadow, returned two words or three.

They came from the shelter of the canopy into the full and brazen heat of the sun. The sky was white, blinding. But Lucius felt some-thing, a shifting in the air. He shaded his eyes with his hand, peering out over the dazzle of the strait. "Storm's coming," he said.

Dellius raised a brow, a little more like his urbane self. "Really? Is that a prophecy?"

"A feeling in my bones," said Lucius, refusing to be angered. He did not know that Dellius was mocking him: the man always sounded mocking, even when he was serious.

"Maybe you're seeing battle," Dellius said. "You know who'll lose, don't you."

It was not a question. Lucius did not feel obligated to answer.

"This is the end for him," said Dellius. "He knows that. He's keep-ing a good face on it, but after this he's a hunted man. Roma Dea has chosen Gaius Julius Caesar Octavianus, she alone knows why. Even I can feel it, and I'm no seer."

"No," said Lucius. "Merely a practical man."

Dellius smiled slightly. "Practical, yes. I'm going for a little sail tonight, to take what breezes there are. Would you like to come with me?"

Lucius' stomach clenched. This was the moment; this was the choice. He had not been given it before—it had been each man for himself, and rightly so.

He smiled. "Thank you," he said. "Thank you, but I have an en-gagement. With my wife. You understand."

Dellius did indeed, or thought he did. He was not contemptuous, that Lucius could see. "Ah," he said. "Well. Give her my regards."

Lucius inclined his head. Dellius walked away, shoulders straight, head at its wonted, jaunty angle.

He knew everything, Lucius thought. Every turn of the plan, every strength and weakness of the army. He would take it all straight to Octavian. That was treason, treason indeed, not merely desertion or abandonment.

And Lucius said nothing, did nothing. Watched him go, and turned, and went to the duties that waited.

Roma Dea silenced him. He told himself that. He knew that he should go with Dellius: sail with him and throw himself on Octavian's mercy. But Dione was here. He could protect her at least, when it came to the end of things. She might never speak to him again, might hate him till she died, but she would live. She might even escape.

The gods would decide it. Her gods or his. Or both, dicing on the table of the world. She was but a voice, he but a pair of eyes. They had no right or power to intervene.

Sophistry. Cowardice.

He turned back against the waning tide of the exodus from the council tent. It was still enough to hinder him, what with those who must be greeted, and those who wanted to stop and talk. By the time he reached the inner wall, it was deserted. Antony had gone to rest, the guard said. No, he was not seeing visitors. Yes, the good senator might come back later, but he might or might not find Antony disposed to speak to him.

The man winked. Lucius was to consider what Antony was doing in there, closeted with Cleopatra.

Lucius debated pushing past the guard, but the man was big and armed and clearly determined to allow his general an hour's peace. "There's something he has to know," Lucius said.

"You can tell him later," said the guard.

So, thought Lucius. And would there be a later?

The gods knew what they wanted. The air was full of them, their whispers, their mocking eyes. He yielded before them.

FORTY

Dellius was gone, crept away in the night as so many had done before him—but none had taken as much knowledge as he had. Cleopatra would have sent troops after him, or a binding of terrible curses, but Antony restrained her. "We don't have time for that," he said, "and they'll have guessed anyway what we have to do. Let's just hope we do it fast enough to get out."

She might not have yielded to counsel so reasonable, but she could see how effective her troops might have been against Octavian's walled fortress-camp on its crag, and she had no strength to spare for a working great enough to destroy a man within that camp. Not if she was to defend what could be defended, and help them all to break free of Actium.

Antony burned every ship for which he could find no rowers: a few of the lesser warships, and the great wallowing tubs of the transports. There was a bleak glory in it, pouring out the casks of oil upon each deck, into each hold, then running from ship to ship with torches, a long stream of fire that pause as it touched oiled wood, hesitated, and suddenly, mightily, roared up into heaven.

It was a sacrifice of fire, a hecatomb to the sea-gods. After the first wild flames had faded, the victims settled to burning steadily. The smoke of their pyre was rich with the scents of burning pine and cedar and cypress. The heat of them, even in smoldering ruin, was fierce. It seemed to suck the sun dry, to drain the sky of its brazen clarity. Clouds rolled in like cold smoke.

As the blackened and skeletal hulls burned down to ash, the wind began to blow. It was little enough at first, a breeze off the sea, with salt in it, and damp. But it grew, and kept growing.

As it swelled to a gale, the rain came. The wind drove it, battering it against the ships both burned and whole, rocking the latter on their moorings. It lashed men's faces. It crept through the crevices of their armor. It seeped into their tents, where they huddled, swearing, gambling away the next ten years' pay, cheated of either battle or escape.

Cleopatra faced Antony in their tent, in the gathering of the most trusted commanders. She was haggard, weary as she had seldom been before. "No," she said. "This is nothing that the enemy has made, or I could stop it. I have tried. The gods only laugh."

Antony's laughter was as bitter as the gods' must have been. "They were late, weren't they? Too late to keep us from burning the ships. But not late enough to give us our battle. Still," he said, "this may be a blessing of its own. Sosius, how fast can we get everybody loaded and run out under cover of the storm? Agrippa's battened down somewhere, you can bet on that. This could be just the break we need."

"Yes," said Cleopatra swiftly. "Yes, I remember what Caesar told me, how you ran through Pompey's fleet in the teeth of a gale, and brought his troops to win him a victory at Dyrrhachium. He never forgot what a feat that was—or how well you accomplished it."

They all looked at one another in dawning hope. A few even smiled, began to nod.

But Sosius shook his head. "Can't do it. The wind's blowing from the west—straight down the gullet of the strait. We'll never sail through, let alone round Leukas and head to sea. Unless, lady, you can give us an east wind instead?"

Her eyes glittered at the hint of insult, but she kept her temper. "The gods who drive this wind are greater than I. I can cloud the minds of our enemies, at least enough to get us free of the strait, but the wind is more than I can master."

Dione, quiet as always in the queen's shadow, watched how the commanders watched her, how easily they laid the blame on her for all their own folly. Even those who had admired her were become her enemies through the slow bitter months of the war. She was Rome's enemy, their eyes said. Therefore she was theirs.

Clever, so clever of Octavian to make war on Cleopatra and not, explicitly, Antony. It gave the Romans the excuse they needed to serve Antony but to despise his Egyptian queen. She was the cause of this war, was she not? Without her they would not be here, hungry, wet, filthy, and trapped.

Without her they would have lost the war when it began, for lack of ships and provisions and pay for their troops. But they did not want to think about that. They did not want to remember that they were deeply in debt to a foreigner, and a woman at that.

Dione was not bitter. She was too tired. They had done everything, she and the queen and the queen's priestesses, to ease the blow of Dellius' desertion, and then to turn the storm aside. The former might have succeeded: they would know when, if, they came to the battle. The latter had failed utterly.

"Let us pray," said Antony after the pause had stretched to breaking, "that the wind changes, and that, if we can't escape under cover of storm, then we have fair weather for fighting. We'll take the sails, don't forget. Tell the men, if they need telling, that we'll be needing sails to go after the enemy when he's beaten. No use to let them know we aren't fighting just to win—we're fighting to get out and stay out of this trap."

No one spoke, either to agree or to argue. A commander who expected to win a sea-fight did not carry the sails on his ships but left them safe in harbor. They were heavy; they got in the way. Ships that fought for sure victory, fought stripped of aught but men and weapons. Sails were for the defeated, and for flight.

Dione wondered how many of the men on the ships would understand what the sails' presence meant. Most of them would, she suspected. There was little that a commander could keep from his troops: soldiers and sailors learned early to read their officers. And defeat tainted the air; it darkened the sun even when it shone, and pierced through the stink of the camp, straight to the hearts of the men who lingered in it.

Some of that was Octavian's doing. He would use every weapon that he could, and some of his priests were skilled in calling out the dark things, ill dreams and sicknesses of the soul. Cleopatra had worn herself thin protecting Antony from the brunt of that sorcery. She had not been able to guard the whole of the army, nor had her priestesses. Least of all Dione, who could not even keep her own husband from falling into despair.

That itself was despair. Dione banished it with an inward word, a turning of the spirit. Tonight again she would sing the spells, call on the gods who were as weary as she. Tonight and every night that she must, until they were free. She did not ask or expect that they be victorious. Only that they win through to Egypt, where their souls could rest, and restore themselves, and return strengthened to the war.

Four days the storm howled out of the west. Four days: and Sextilis ended, not in searing heat as it had begun, but in damp cold, and Septembris began.

At dawn of the fifth day, Antony's men stumbled from their tents and looked about in dim astonishment. The roar of the wind was gone, likewise the hiss and lash of the rain. The clouds fled away eastward. The sky over the sea was clear and pale. But for the waves that battered the shore still, as if they could not give up their hatred of the land, the earth was quiet.

They had little enough time to marvel. Drums and trumpets roused every man who had not yet waked. Signals ran from end to end of the camp. Today it would begin. Today, at last, Antony would have his battle.

As soon as the rain stopped and the clouds began to break, Antony had summoned his commanders and held his last council of war. That was done by the hour before sunrise. They all knew what they were to do: which of them would embark on the ships, which would remain in camp under Canidius Crassus.

Canidius' task was simple enough to describe, however difficult it might be to accomplish. If Antony escaped without a clear victory, Canidius would retreat through Macedonia and thence into Asia. The fleet's strategy was more complicated. Lucius Servilius was not sure that he understood it completely—but then he was afraid that he did. He knew how the winds blew at Actium, and little though he knew of ships, he could see what Antony was doing.

Sosius' squadron would take the left, Antony with his admiral Gellius Publicola the right. Cleopatra with sixty ships, merchanters most of them, and a few warships, was to take refuge behind the center. She would escape first, if she could. The rest would follow.

And Antony—Antony on the right, where the wind blew best and strongest past midday—would win free unless the gods were truly minded to destroy him, but Sosius would have a bitter fight. It was a practical plan, certainly. It was also a coward's.

All the senators who remained, and Antony's friends, would be with him on the flagship. Lucius, too, since he was as distinguished as anyone else. "Unless, of course," one of his erstwhile friends purred, "you would prefer to accompany her majesty. Your wife will be on that ship, yes?"

If Lucius had been even half a decade younger, he would have knocked the idiot flat. But he was a man of respectable years and impeccable breeding, and he was above mere insult. At least, he thought, until he could take vengeance in a properly civilized fashion. Have the babbler arrested for election fraud, perhaps. That was always a safe gamble among Romans.

Ah, indeed, he was grown cynical. He almost smiled at himself. Dione had told him, when she would speak to him, which was not often, that the enemy had magics, too, and those were dark ones, shaped to sap will and spirit. He would blame his ill humor on that, then, and not on his own inner war.

Antony's tent was so placed that he could look straight up at Octavian's camp on the cliff, on the other side of the strait. Lucius knew every stone and crenel of that walled fortress, every glitter of bronze or iron in the armor and weapons of its guards. Yet there was an enduring fascination in staring across the water, and knowing that there was the enemy in clear sight, yet there was nothing, nothing at all, that Antony could do to remove him. What Lucius could do about it, he knew very well. He could do as Dellius had, find a boat and row across and walk up to the gate, name himself for a senator if his toga's stripe was not sufficient evidence, and be welcomed with open arms. Or, if not with open arms, at least with civility, and without the inconvenience of shackles and a prison cell.

Too late now. Morning was coming fast, and the gulf and its strait were full of ships. The men who would sail were forming ranks, preparing to board. Those would who stay behind either took guard stations or broke their fast while they could. Shrieks and squawks told of a tentful of camp followers rousted out and sent packing. The latrine detail marched to its post, singing a dreary song that was, if one listened, quite scatologically funny.

Lucius bit down on laughter—hysteria. He was going to fight in a battle for which he had no heart at all, and on the wrong side at that. His armor was ready, his weapons sharpened, his slave Gaius waiting to help him with both. But he lingered. He had no reason to love this place, every reason to loathe it, yet it was familiar. Its sewer stink— moderated by four days of rain—had become almost companion- able. Out there on the sea was clean air, open water albeit full of hostile ships, and with luck, escape. But that was not certain at all, and this was: the long dull siege amounting, in the end, to nothing.

Little as he liked to admit it, he tarried in part because Dione, in leaving, would have to walk past him. He had not seen her in days, since before the storm began. She had been living in the queen's tent, sleeping there, working magics that left their mark on her. She was thin to transparency yet full of light, like a lamp in a dim room.

They had not slept together since—he could not remember when. The first night he had slept on the floor, whenever that was. After that, he had spread a pallet and she had taken the bed, until she began to spend nights with the queen. Or in the queen's tent, at least, since Cleopatra had by no means stopped being Antony's lover. When Lucius saw Dione, she seemed a stranger, with her foreign face and her foreign ways and her air of remoteness from gross humanity. She belonged entirely to her goddess and her queen. There was no room in her heart for a mere Roman.

The last stragglers wandered out of the commander's tent, deep in thought or in conversation. Cleopatra still had not come out, nor any of her women with her. She would be saying farewell to Antony now, while there were few to watch and whisper. They would not speak again, not as lovers speak, until the battle was done.

Lucius had to go soon or he would have no time to arm himself before his ship sailed. Still he loitered, glowering up at Octavian's promontory. "And why," he demanded of the air, "would Roma Dea have chosen him, of all men that she could choose?"

"Because," Dione said, "she wants an empire, and empire needs an emperor. Antony's not clever enough to manage it without setting Roman teeth on edge. Octavian, I think, is more subtle—and more palatable to Roman taste."

Lucius did not either start or whip about. He was accustomed to her sudden appearances. Timoleon was fond of them, too. Timoleon was an appalling young man, but Lucius missed him. He missed them all, even dour Androgeos.

But most of all, and in her living presence, he missed Dione.

She was no warmer or more approachable than she had been in the queen's shadow. It was enough, it seemed, that she had come near him at all, still less addressed him.

He considered indulging anger, but she would only smile at it. That much he knew of this mood of hers. He stilled himself instead, made himself as cold as she. "There is always the possibility of empire without Rome."

"Yes," she said, "if Octavian dies. Perhaps he'll die today. Then Antony has the victory, regardless of the battle's outcome."

Lucius narrowed his eyes. "Is that what you've been hatching?"

Her chin rose a fraction: her only sign of temper. "If it were, would I tell you?"

"Once," he said, "you might have."

She shook her head. Beneath the cold mask she looked faintly sad. "Some things no Roman can understand. Or should."

"Such as you?"

Her head shook again. Suddenly, and this time she did startle him, she took his hand. Her own was cold and small, like her voice when she spoke. "Please, Lucius. Please stay alive today. Promise me you won't get yourself killed."

"Even to spite you?"

She responded neither to the dark side of that nor to the light. "Promise me."

"I can't promise not to die. Battles aren't like that."

"Just don't try," she said.

He wanted to take her face in his hands—no, the whole of her in his arms—and cling. But that would break both of them. He raised her hand to his lips and kissed the fingers one by one. Her eyes were wide, dry, filling already with her goddess, but for once she kept a little for him. "I won't try to get killed," he said. "Though I may—not—"

"If you have to surrender," she said, cutting him off, "do it. Don't think of me. Promise me that, too."

"You're asking too much," he said.

"Promise," said Dione.

"And what do you promise me?" he demanded of her.

"I promise," she said. Her voice faltered. "I promise not to die. If I can help it. And to—wait—if you can—"

Why, he thought in dim amazement, she was not cold at all. It was all a mask.

But before he could speak, act, redeem anything that he had done to her since they came to Actium, the queen's voice came between them, calling to her priestess. Dione started, pulled away from him. He tried to catch her, but she was gone, running to her duty and her queen.

She had promised him everything. He had promised only half of what she asked. The other half . . .

He ran as she had run, away from the truth, and from the terror that was in the truth. Toward Antony's flagship; toward the morning and the battle.

FORTY-ONE

Sea-battle sounded splendid when the poets sang of it: the clash of mighty ships in the deep water, vast outpourings of blood and fire, noble speeches, deeds of daring, glory for the victors and death for the vanquished.

The truth was nothing so elegant as a march of hexameters. For one thing, it was slow; snail-slow. Most of it was waiting, waiting for the wind to come up, for the ships to crawl into position, for one side or the other to make the first move.

"Lovely day for a battle," said one of the sailors near Lucius Servilius, cheerfully, while Antony's flagship made its ponderous way to its place. And truly it was delightful. The storm had washed all the cruel heat away. It was a bitter-bright morning, cool and crystalline,

with but the lightest whisper of a breeze. The sea had quieted with
the sun's coming; now it was calm. Such a day in Alexandria would
have brought them all out in boats on the lake, fishing and bird-
hunting and swimming.

Lucius had nothing to do but stand under the canopy on the
flagship's deck and watch the slaves who manned the map. That was
a great circle of wood painted blue, with a whimsy of dolphins and
a wave here and there. Small wooden ships sailed on it. Some,
golden-prowed, stood for Antony's. Those with black prows were the
enemy. There was a wooden crag with a wooden fortress on it,
representing Octavian's camp, and a carved headland that was
Leukas isle, and the curve of the land round the strait to Actium and
thence into the gulf of Ambracia.

It was strange to see the world reduced as a god would perceive
it, and to look up and see it as it was: a dazzle of sun on the water,
the dip and surge of oars to the beat of the drum, the stately progress
of ships out of the gulf and into the open sea. On the south shore their
own camp looked sturdy yet somehow dilapidated, its walls lined
with men in bronze and legionary scarlet, cheering them on. Generous, that, from troops who had been effectively abandoned and must,
once the ships were out, make their own way home.

The fleet was a brave sight, rowing out of its long confinement.
Two hundred and thirty ships, from the triremes to the mighty tens
that were like battlefields set afloat. Sailors had told Lucius that these
were not ships, not such as a true sea-rover loved; these were war-
engines, built for no other purpose than to lock sides with the enemy
and give space for the legionaries to fight. Behind them sailed Cleopatra's grain-ships and her merchanters, and her glittering flagship,
with here and there a dart of swift liburnians.

The enemy could not possibly fail to know what they did or how
they meant to do it. Yet Octavian made no move from his rock, even
to vex their passage. For any other man the temptation might have
been impossible to resist. Octavian had even, it seemed, kept most of
his men from lining the walls and shouting insults as the fleet sailed
beneath.

"No sense of humor," said Antony with evident regret as the flagship passed the crag and slowed, preparing to pick its way through
the sudden shallow beyond. "I'd have had a line of men on the wall,
bare-arsed and farting the trumpet-signals for the fleet."

Lucius held his breath. Fortunately no one volunteered to get up a
chorus.

*   *   *

Antony meanwhile had turned his attention out to sea. The water that had seemed so broad and open and empty in the early morning was now barred by a wall of ships. Agrippa was waiting.

But Antony had expected that, and planned for it. What he wanted was closer in: Octavian again, safe in his walls. "Come out," Antony willed him. "Come out, damn your prim little eyes, and fight."

But Octavian would not. He was safe, he had his great admiral to do his fighting for him, he would stay precisely where he was, and wait for Agrippa to bring him his victory.

"And then he'll claim it for himself," Antony growled, "call it *his* triumph, and flaunt it through Rome. But not while I have anything to say about it."

Agrippa's fleet made no move to attack as Antony's ships moved out of the shallows and into their positions. None had gone aground, not even the massive tens. Those, and the rest of the largest ships, took the flanks. The left—the south—was Sosius'; the center, its line slightly and alluringly thin, belonged to two younger commanders, Insteius and Octavius, whom Lucius barely knew; and on the right, the northward flank, was Antony, with Publicola his admiral. Cleopatra hung back. Her ships were not to fight unless they must; they served another purpose.

Lucius glanced down at the map. The gate of the strait had twin posts, the rocky promontories called Scylla and Parginosuala. Antony's fleet curved out from these in a doubled line like a child's drawing of a simple bow, with Cleopatra's ships the arrow, aimed at the west and freedom.

And now, having taken the places that Antony had ordered for them, they waited. Octavian made no move from his aerie, Agrippa's ship-wall did not stir. Even the wind was stilled. The sea flattened to a mirror reflecting a whole fleet reversed, masts plunging into the blue sea, hulls floating on the rim of the sky.

In that breathless pause, even fear was silenced, and apprehension stilled. Those men who would take it were given wine then, much watered, to slake their thirst and give them strength. Lucius took a cup, sipped at it while the sun seemed to hang overhead. Without the breeze it was hot, although it lacked the hammering heat that it had had before the storm. He sweated in his armor; thought of shedding it, but that would not sit well with either the troops or their commanders. A man wore his armor in a battle, even if the battle consisted of standing for hours on end on a ship's deck while nothing happened, not even a ripple of air on the water.

Slowly at first, and so subtly that he did not even notice it, the air changed. Sea and sky, that had blurred into a single softness of blue, divided as if by the slow cut of a knife. Little by little the horizon came clear. Just as it stood black and distinct, a breath of coolness brushed Lucius' cheeks. The wind had come in from the sea.

Antony, who had been pacing the deck till the pounding of his steps felt like the beating of Lucius' own heart, stopped and turned on his heel. "Good," he said as if to himself. "Good! Now see if you can hold off from the fight, dear Marcus Vipsanius Agrippa." He turned toward the signalman, who waited as always, alert to his command. "Now," he said.

The fleet that had stood still so long, at last began to move. The left wing, having farthest to go round the mountain-wall of Leukas, lowered oars first and advanced. Antony, whose wing would move when the left was under way, stood poised, eyes fixed on the enemy's right. "Close," he willed it. *"Close."*

But it would not. It backed water; it retreated before Antony's ships.

Antony muttered something soft and thoroughly rude. His own ship surged under him. The center too was in motion, the slaves at the map scrambling to keep every painted ship in position and matching the movements of the living battle.

They were all backing water, all of Agrippa's ships, and not too clumsily, either. Drawing Antony out of cover. Setting him up for the slaughter.

He laughed to himself as he glanced from map to sea and back again. He had the fewer ships, but also the larger, and he had had them strengthened with great beams banded with iron. He could batter his way through. Only let them give him enough water, enough room to get up speed. Oars first, then—as the wind freshened and veered to the west of northwest as it did every fair day off this cursed strait, and bless the gods for it—the sails that waited, ready to run up at the word of command.

Not that it could ever be that easy. The enemy was Agrippa, and Agrippa could see everything that Antony could, and act on it faster. It was a gift. Antony could be generous and admit it. He had the same gift on land: an eye on every chance, and a talent for knowing what to do in the heat of a battle.

This sea-fighting was unendurably ponderous, like a war of tortoises. Antony, who could move units of his legion as easily as counters on a board, looked at ships on the map and knew nothing but a fierce impatience. It was Sosius who kept him quiet, who guided him with a word or a tilt of the head when he was ready to climb down off this floating tower and *march,* by Hercules, straight across the bloody sea to bloody Octavian and strangle him barehanded.

He was not about to let anyone see how frustrated he was becoming. He had made his choice. He could have fought a land battle, and fought it his way. He had settled on the sea, and he would live with it, win, lose, or black impasse.

Agrippa's fleet had stopped backing water. There was a pause as they rearranged the oars—looking like nothing so much as an army of millipedes—and then at last, with a beating of drums, the enemy surged forward.

The two fleets closed. Missiles that neither side had wanted to waste while they played chase-the-rabbit began to fly from the catapults mounted on the decks. Some trailed streamers of fire. The rest were plain lead shot and ordinary stones, more than deadly enough to flesh and bone and timber.

Antony's face ached. He was grinning from ear to ear. Now, at too long last, he had a battle. Maybe he could not win it; maybe he could only hope to escape it with his skin intact and his fleet not too badly battered. But it was infinitely preferable to no battle at all.

Octavian hated battles. Antony hoped that he was loathing this one cordially. "Sick to your stomach up there, are you, prim-and-priss? Shitting good Roman bricks till you can see it's over?"

Someone else picked it up—one of the wags among the senators, Antony forgot his name offhand, bad politics as Caesar would have said, but Antony never had been Caesar. "Let him shit enough and he'll build himself a whole new city. What d'you think he'll call it? Cloaca Victoria? Kakopolis?"

"Oh, that's *indelicate!*" another of them warbled. "He'll call it Nikopolis, of course. For his victory that Agrippa got him all by himself."

"Victory over what? His voiding bowels?"

And round it went, while the fire flew and the ships closed, until the first prow rammed the first side, caught and grappled, and men fought hand to hand at last as men were meant to fight, even floating on the sea.

* * *

Dione stood on the deck of the queen's flagship, just behind the throne. It had always been her rightful place, but she had seldom claimed it, settling instead for the greater comfort, if lesser honor, of edges and shadows. But today she needed to be close to the center of things.

Cleopatra wore robes of gold and a golden diadem, a Hellene to her finger-ends, and a queen. If she were captured—and she might be, if all her calculations were awry, if she failed to do her part as she had planned it with Antony and his admirals—she would show herself royal beyond any question. She had pride to protect. She was, after all, the Enemy of Rome.

Dione wondered if, beneath her robes and her gold, Cleopatra was as cold at heart as Dione herself was. The enemy's will that sapped their own, the dark thing that came out of the camp on the crag, beat stronger, the more of the fleet rowed past the rock and into the open sea. It was a thing of dank caves and empty places, droning chants, old blood—strange in Octavian's ordered and practical world. But he would use whatever he found convenient, if only it won him an empire.

Cleopatra, with the priestesses in their circle about her, sustained the ward over as much as of the fleet as they could. That, while the battle held off and the sun shone strong on the calm sea, was all of it. They could not bring light to souls that had none, that was beyond their strength, but the imminence of escape, the surety of battle, served better by far than any magic.

Neither Dione nor Cleopatra, nor anyone else, had asked what would happen if the circle broke—or if Cleopatra escaped but Antony did not. Dione hoped that, once past the crag and on the sea, they would find the enemy's sorcery weaker. But it did not seem to be so, while the long hours stretched and the battle forbore to begin.

Still, the enemy's power grew no stronger, which hinted that they were taxed as sorely as the priestesses were. Within as without, in soul as in body, the war stood at impasse, with neither willing or able to advance.

When the wind came and the ships moved at last, the circle drew taut. Now if ever the enemy would press the advantage. But no blow struck; no darkness veiled the sun. The wind blew as it did every day, freshening with noon, shifting round to the direction from which it could fill the sails and bear them past Leukas and away out to sea. Nothing hindered it, or caused it to falter and die. The gods who had sent four days of storm upon Actium were weary, or had bent their malice elsewhere.

Cleopatra's fleet held aloof from the battle. Certain of her people, young and not so young, yearned to send their ships against the enemy, but her orders were firm and not to be disobeyed. They would not fight. That was not their purpose. They were to wait. Wait, and watch.

It was clear before them and yet impossibly distant, set apart from them by the expanse of water. It might have been a game, or an entertainment for the queen, a mock sea-battle in a palace pool. Agrippa's smaller ships swarmed round Antony's great wallowing monsters, tormenting them as jackals might torment a wounded lion. Enemies chose their targets, which either strove to evade or closed eagerly with boarding-bridges and grappling hooks. Lead shot, stones, fire-missiles flew from ship to ship. Arrows fell in a thin, deadly rain.

It was ungodly noisy: shouts, screams, the thunder of hull striking steel-shod hull, and the battlefield song of metal on metal. Even in the gilded calm of the flagship Dione smelled smoke, burning wood and tar and flesh, blood, the stench of voided bowels as men fell to terror or to death.

Some of those about her had taken refuge in vials of scent. Dione refused. So too did Cleopatra, though her priestesses burned incense on their small altar, trying to overcome the reek of battle with the sweetness of divinity. Cleopatra's fists were clenched on the arms of her throne. Her eyes burned as they scanned the battle, scanned it and scanned it, conjuring order out of murderous confusion.

The wind grew stronger, and the battle with it. Ships grappled together rocked in the swell. One, burning, careened into one of its fellows; the men aboard the latter labored frantically to thrust themselves free, while on the other side of them an enemy galley closed for the kill.

On Cleopatra's flagship the sailors that had been idling by the rails, watching the battle and laying wagers on it, leaped into sudden motion. Dione had not heard the signal—the battle filled her head. She watched blankly as the sails ran up, royal purple rimmed with gold. They had faded, she noticed. They were the color of amethysts, and the gold was wan like a winter sun.

Much of the battle clustered southward, and some of it north where Antony's flagship was, distinct with the golden lion on its prow. In front of Cleopatra's ships was a surprising quantity of clear water. There was fighting there, yes, but scattered.

The queen's trumpeter blew a long ringing blast that echoed down the fleet. The sails filled with the swift strong wind.

Cleopatra sat immobile as she had sat since the battle began. She did not turn her face toward the furious fight that centered on Antony's flagship. She did not speak, though there were mutters of cowardice and sorcery and worse.

Her fleet held the wealth that she and Antony had gathered together. She, in her person, held Egypt. She at least must escape to begin the war again, but in a place where she and not Octavian was the stronger.

Dione had heard every argument, every resort to logic and sense. Cleopatra the queen had agreed completely with Antony the general that she must escape as soon as her way was clear—and that the enemy must be tricked into giving her an opening. Cleopatra the lover had cried aloud in the deeps of the night, "But what if you die? What if you can't break loose and follow? What will become of me?"

"You'll take revenge," Antony had replied, "and make sure our sons rule after me."

Dione wondered if Antony was as sure of himself now. That wonder was the frame on which she hung the end of her working, the last weaving of the wards that would protect the fleet while they fought their way out. He *would* keep faith. He *would* win free.

A sigh ran through the gathering on the deck. Dione realized with a start that there was no battle in front of them, only open water. And—she glanced back. No enemy rowing after. Not yet. They were all engaged by the broken center of Antony's fleet, that had been set in place for just this purpose: to open the way for the Egyptian ships, and to close it to pursuit.

They were not safe. Not yet, and not truly till they found harbor in Syria. But they were free. They had broken out of Actium.

Antony's fleet was bitter beset. The enemy that had stood flat-footed while Cleopatra sailed scatheless away, fell on the rest of her allies with all the greater ferocity.

In the air over them, swelling out of the clear sky, a storm broke: lightning, thunder, lashings of rain and white-gleaming hail. Squall, Dione's logic said. But her eyes looked to Octavian's rock, and her magic stretched outward, seeking. It should have met a wall, a shining rampart against the dark. The wall was there, but it was no fortress. It was as thin as silk, and like silk gone to rot, it tore. Her touch, meant to test if not to strengthen it, rent a great hole in it. Within were the dark things, hope lost, victory compromised, faith broken in despair. All of them aimed like a catapult bolt, straight at the gleaming bulk of Antony's ship.

She flung herself at it. Too little, too late—too light, alone, to do more than turn the bolt aside. It nearly destroyed her. She recoiled by instinct. Every thought in her mind was for the ship, and for the men on it—man. One man. And not Antony, though she remembered him dimly, as in a story. Lucius was on that ship. Lucius was full in the path of that sorcerous onslaught. And he had the eyes to see it, the mind to comprehend it—but never the strength or the skill to ward it off.

He would try. She knew him too well to think he could be prudent. If he died—

She could not know. All her magic was gone, driven out of her by the glancing blow of the enemy's weapon. She had only mortal eyes, mortal mind frayed and tattered, mortal body tumbling bonelessly to the deck of Cleopatra's ship. She tried to speak. Tried to warn, to bring the circle together.

But those who were aware were as shattered as she, and the rest were powerless. One helped Dione to a stool and coaxed her with wine full of spices and something stronger, that wrinkled her nose and made her turn her head away. The priestess persisted, gentle but determined, until Dione had choked down a swallow or two. Then the child let her rise, though she staggered, stumbling to the rail. In that little time, the battle had dropped far behind. It was but a shadow on the sea now, a flicker of fire, a cloud of smoke rising till the wind took it and scattered it.

Much, she thought, like Antony's army, and Antony's war. She was not even bitter. Her grief was too strong.

Lucius Servilius saw the Egyptian fleet break free and escape. As slow as sea-movements could be, once Cleopatra's ships raised sail they made impressive speed. Not even one of them fell behind to be taken and boarded.

He had time to loose a sigh—but no more than that. Agrippa's ships had broken long since through the guard of lesser craft and fallen on Antony's flagship. It was good sense to strike for the head and hope the body would follow. It made for a ferocious fight.

He was no better than Antony after all. He needed to strike, to kill something, and never mind whose side he was on. When the enemy boarded, he was waiting. He had a sailor on his right hand, armed with a grappling hook and a mad grin, and a legionary on his left, grimly efficient even standing still. Not bad allies for a man who had no country. No wife, either. She was gone, back to Egypt where she belonged, and well for her that she did it.

His heart, he discovered somewhat to his surprise, was light. Dione was safe—her goddess would guard her, now that she was away from this cursed place. He had nothing in the world to do, no task to perform, except to keep this ship from being taken too soon.

He was aware, in his skin more than anything else, that Antony was drawing back away from the fight. As long and wide as the flagship was, it was too much for any one ship of the enemy to overpower all at once. Another had come up behind—no, that was a lion's head on the sail, it was one of Antony's, hovering off the stern as if it had lost its courage.

"Lucius Servilius!"

He glanced over his shoulder. Antony's eye was on him. The triumvir's head cocked slightly toward the stern.

Lucius chose not to understand the summons. The first wave of enemies had come boiling over the joined rails and the boarding-bridges. One launched himself straight at Lucius, short sword drawn back to stab him in the belly. He stabbed first, felt the catch and give as his blade slipped under the breastplate and thrust home. The man convulsed and died.

His skin felt the fading of Antony's presence. It was slow to begin with, like a sea-battle. Then as urgency caught it, it ran as swiftly as a man can run, down the length of the long ship and over the side, into the waiting galley. The sails ran up even as the galley backed water away from the flagship. It caught the wind and ran.

Lucius laughed, breathless. He stood on as fierce a battlefield as any he could remember, and his commander—the field's commander—was gone, run away to safety with his Egyptian queen. Lucius rather hoped that Antony succeeded. Roma Dea might reside with Gaius Julius Caesar Octavianus, but Marcus Antonius had a grandeur of his own, even in flight from the battle he had wanted. Even leaving his fleet to save itself as it could, as he had left his army: work of a coward, or of a general whose first duty was to survive and to win the war—however badly he lost this battle.

Lucius Servilius fought, for if he did not fight he would die, and he did not want that. He had rather a tenacious attachment to life, even life that had lost both focus and savor. He was aware that something strange had fallen on the fleet, a thing like a shadow but less substantial, that whispered of hopelessness and of surrender. He shrugged it off. His mind could conjure despair all by itself; it did not need a trumpery magic to encourage it.

He fought till his sword broke. He found another, but it was dull, good for little more than hacking at the men who seemed to come in endless swarms from everywhere. He had seen a wounded river-horse fallen on by crocodiles in the reeds of Lake Mareotis. This fight made him think of that. The massive victim, armed with blunt teeth and brute strength but little else. The myriad attackers, slashing, tearing, rending the great beast to pieces, devouring it alive.

He dropped the useless sword. There was a spear nearby, but it was in a man's hands, and that man was aiming the point at Lucius' throat. Lucius smiled. Death would be good enough now. It would let him rest.

The spearman squinted at him as if attempting to set a name to his face. He could not imagine why. He had never seen the man before in his life. Some last impulse toward self-preservation led his hands to reach for the spear. It swung round and knocked him down but not, alas, out.

He lay ignominiously on the hard deck, with a spearbutt resting on his breastplate. "Yield?" the man asked in fairly cultivated Latin.

He asked, Lucius took note. And politely, yet. Lucius considered rudeness in reply, but he had been brought up too strictly for that. He sighed. "Well then. Since you ask, I yield."

His conqueror looked relieved. He was a young man, a touch too ornately armored as a military tribune tended to be, but the spear was businesslike enough, as was the hand that he offered. Lucius took it, let it pull him to his feet. Why not?

"You're all right?" the boy asked.

He seemed to frame everything in questions. He had a doting father, Lucius surmised, and an adoring mama, and more money than he would ever know what to do with. Still, he seemed to know how to fight. For the sake of that, Lucius spared him the edge of sarcasm and answered honestly. "Tired, that's all. Sick of fighting on the wrong side."

"And then the queen's leman turned tail and ran," the boy said, sympathetic. He looked about. So, for lack of other occupation, did Lucius. The battle was still going on, but less fiercely than before. There were other men with prisoners, and altogether too many dead.

"I think you've lost," the boy said.

"Probably," said Lucius. "Do you mind if I sit down? Just for a moment. Then I have to see Gaius Octavius, if he'll speak to me. Or Agrippa." He could not keep his lip from curling at the name. No one, as Antony had often said, liked Agrippa. He was very much in the order of a necessary evil.

The boy frowned. "I'm not sure—"

"Never mind," said Lucius. Suddenly he was very dizzy. He sat down more quickly than he had meant, and less comfortably. He could not understand why. That was not his blood coming out of his side. Was it?

Not that it mattered. Much. "See Octavian," he said. "See . . . Agrippa. See . . ."

The boy's voice, when he was excited, soared up as shrill as a girl's. "Surgeons! *Surgeons!* The senator—his excellency—"

Well, thought Lucius with a small shiver of amusement. And he not even in his toga. How had the child known? Was it someone he should have remembered from Rome? Some neighbor's brat? A relative? Cousin—nephew, Juno help him? Ah, family. If family it was. If it could matter, which it did not. The dark was lovely, warm and deep. He fell happily into it.

FORTY-TWO

Actium was lost—there could be no question of that. Cleopatra had escaped without harm, even with the vexation of a determined pursuer, the Spartan Eurykles, who betrayed a distressing reluctance to forget his vendetta against Antony. They beat him off, seized the wind and left him far behind, shrieking like a gull. "I'll have your head! You killed my father! I never forget!"

They took no more notice of him than of a stinging fly, nor troubled to remember him once they were out of his reach. They had other and greater worries: the fleet's loss, which was certain by the time they reached Taenarum, the third day out of from Actium. Forty ships sunk, the rest surrendered.

But Canidius Crassus' army had escaped from its cesspit of a camp and made for Macedonia. Cleopatra kept that hope, though Antony had lost all—battle, hope, desire to fight on. For all the three days of their escape from Actium, he had sat in the hold of the queen's ship, in the dark, not speaking, not moving except to drain cup after cup of wine. He was sodden with it, but still and furiously lucid, the lucidity of despair.

Something in him had broken when he fled from his beleaguered fleet. Dione feared—but could not be certain—that she had caused it: that her striking aside of the enemy's sorcery had spared the flagship but struck Antony himself as he escaped on the smaller, lighter ship. But she could not know. The goddess' power in her was coming back slowly, as a well fills with water after a drought, but it was not strong enough yet to be sure. A man could break by himself. A strong man, long tempered in war, made stronger by defeat as well as by victory, could turn brittle at the last and shatter.

He was Roman. He sat in an Egyptian ship, in the care of an Egyptian queen, surrounded by her slaves and her treasures. Dione knew what had broken Lucius Servilius: the knowledge that what he served, while he served Antony, was not Rome. How much worse might it be for Antony if Roma Dea, great goddess tyrant, had laid him bare to himself, and persuaded him that he had betrayed her?

Dione did not know the truth of that. Antony spoke to her no more than he spoke to anyone else except the cupbearer, and that only to demand more wine.

From Taenarum, once they had rested a little, they sailed toward Egypt. But as they rode the sea, a small ship, sailing swift, brought word. Canidius' army had surrendered. There had not even been a battle, except at the bargaining table. Antony's Romans had had enough. They wanted a rest; they wanted what was due them, the honorable retirement, the bit of farm in Italy, the rewards of peace after years of war. Antony could not give them that, not while Octavian stood between. But Octavian was master of Italy—and he would promise anything that would win him this war.

The dispatches were apologetic. *We're sorry,* one of them said. *We did the best we could. But we can't see settling down to the quiet life beside the Nile. We're Romans, after all. We've got Italy in our bones.*

It was one more blow to Antony's spirit, one more proof that he had turned his back on Roma Dea.

Then came word that only added to his despair. Scarpus, his legionary commander in Cyrenaica, had gone over to Octavian. Antony had no refuge, then, short of Egypt—and Scarpus on his tail, looking to confirm his new allegiance with a battle. That woke Antony a little, enough to emerge from his winy stupor and take a portion of the fleet to Paraetonium. There, in that waste of sand and sun and stone, he mustered enough display of claw and fang to send Scarpus scampering home.

Cleopatra had no particular desire to immure herself in that bleak desert, but she would have done it if Antony had clearly needed her. He drove her off as much with pretension of returning health as with the pointed observation that, if she did not defend their backs with her royal presence, Egypt would take itself over to the enemy. That was counsel of despair, certainly, but it was true enough. Alexandria, ever volatile, needed her there, and her firm hand on its neck, or it would run, and drag the rest of Egypt after it.

Therefore she left Antony to his contest of wills with Scarpus and returned to her own city. Antony followed her there soon enough. He had driven Scarpus off, but it was not a victory, not really; the luster of it wore thin and vanished almost before it appeared. He sank again into gloom, took his cupbearer and his army of winejars and retreated to a tower in the harbor. From there he could look out on both the city, which could betray him, and on the sea, from which Octavian could come to destroy him. In his black humor he called the place the Timonium, or, as he liked to put it, the Grouchery.

The Whinery, Cleopatra preferred to call it. She had caught none of her consort's despair. She refused. If Antony would not conquer, would not even exert himself to prevail, then she would do it herself. She laughed at the lying tales that her spies brought from Octavian's camp. Cleopatra, the story went, had betrayed her lover and run from Actium. Her lover had run like the coward he was, abandoning all his loyal followers, out of lust for his Egyptian queen. Canidius Crassus, meanwhile, had betrayed his army and fled, while that army fought valiantly to a noble defeat.

Lies, every one; the fabrications of a man desperate to claim everything for himself. She scorned them. She sent her own message, in her own fashion. She proclaimed a festival in Alexandria, a celebration not of defeat that had been, but of victory that would be.

She did it quickly, too quickly for most minds to keep pace. Dione's certainly did not. She had come home to a house that echoed with emptiness, even as full of her children as it was, with Timoleon proving himself a good steward, and Mariamne home from the temple to greet her mother, and all their slaves and servants, and their deep gladness to have her back again. There was one who did not welcome her, one who would not come back. She did not even know if he lived—if he had come alive from the battle at Actium.

One night in that cold and lonely bed sufficed to tell her what she should have known from the beginning. She could not stay in this house, not without Lucius Servilius. She took little but her maid and her daughter and her daughter's nurse and such small necessities as the child needed, and sought Isis' temple. She was there, settled, woven into the pattern of duties and ceremonies, before her sons even knew that she was gone.

And she was there when she received the news of the queen's festival. It was time, the queen proclaimed, that the people knew in truth that Egypt's succession was secure. Therefore they were summoned to a grand gathering, a rite of passage: the entry into manhood of the two princes, Ptolemy Caesar the king of kings, and Marcus Antonius the younger. Caesarion would take the rank and station of ephebe, a youth on the threshold of manhood. Antyllus would assume the *toga virilis,* the garb and the honor of a man in Rome.

"Oh, she has gone mad," Dione said when word was brought to her. She had been deep in a rite that brooked no interruption, a conjuring for the protection of the Two Lands. She was weary to collapse and ravenously hungry. Above all she needed food, and then sleep, a good day's worth.

But this could not wait. She let Hebe persuade her at least to bathe and take a bite or two of bread. Then, still damp from the bath, her hunger barely blunted by the single small loaf, she braved the dazzle of sunlight and the crush of people in every street and byway. No matter how hastily the queen might declare a festival, the common folk always knew, and flocked to it.

She should have taken a litter, which would have had the advantage of guards, and therefore of weight to throw against the crowds. Alone and clad as a simple priestess, with only her maid in attendance, she had no more authority than a leaf in a flood. She had to go where the crowd went. That, fortunately, was in the direction in which she needed to go. It was not nearly as fast as she liked, but short of conjuring up a phoenix to bear her on wings above the press, she could not manage any more speed than the current of people allowed.

In sight of the palace but still distressingly far away from it, the flood began to slow and clog. Dione, with Hebe clinging grimly to her girdle, managed to make her way through the crush of bodies. A space here, a waverer there, a surprisingly long clear space along a wall—but then the crowd was thicker than ever.

That in itself should have told her that she was too late. But she was past the edge of exhaustion and into a realm in which nothing existed but stubbornness. She must come to Cleopatra. Therefore she would.

She fought her way as far as the gate. There, by the goddess' mercy, was a clear space, a bit of stair and a column to which she could cling as she peered over the heads of the crowd that packed the great court within.

At the far end stood the platform that went up for festivals, and there was Cleopatra all in a blaze of gold, on her golden throne. Caesarion sat at her side, his throne for once equal to hers. He wore armor, all gold, and a cloak of deepest Tyrian dye. Dione could not see his face; it blurred with distance and with the dazzle of sunlight.

In front of the queen and her son the king stood Antony in a white toga, and Antyllus. The boy, Dione noted with a small shock of surprise, was as tall as his father, though not yet as broad. They looked remarkably alike. Antyllus stood straight and proud in a white tunic as his father spoke words that Dione could not hear, and then draped him, with the ponderous dignity that marked all Roman ceremony, in a toga so white it shone.

The light stung Dione's eyes to tears, blurring everything into a pattern of white and gold and purple. "No," she said. "Oh, no. Why did you do it? How could you?"

She said the same, long hours later, to Cleopatra herself. By then she was so far past exhaustion that she was perfectly lucid and even steady on her feet. She had stayed by the pillar through the whole of the rite, the speeches, the hymns, the entertainments. At long last the sun had begun to sink, and the crowd ebbed toward the city and the promise of feasting at the queen's expense. The queen herself feasted in the palace among her court, and since it was the day on which both her son and her consort's son had become men, she poured wine for them with her own hands, and played the servant. But everyone knew that they, as all men were, were her devoted slaves.

Dione was not there to see. When there was room enough to walk away from the court of the ceremony, she walked, entering the palace as freely as any priestess might who wore the white robe and the golden collar of Isis. Some of the guards recognized her and called her by name as they bowed to her. The rest simply bowed, even the Romans. That was courtesy to the goddess' servant.

She was waiting when Cleopatra left the feast. The queen had taken time to undress, to be bathed lightly, to retreat as was her custom to the room in which she kept her best-loved books and her favorite couch and such comfort as a queen could know in her own palace.

Dione, seated in a chair in which she had sat often before, looked up at the queen's coming. She could not find it in her to smile, though Cleopatra greeted her with unfeigned delight. "Dione! Where have you been keeping yourself? I've missed you."

Dione shook her head, discarding the need for greeting, and said what she had come to say. "Why? How could you have done what you did today?"

Cleopatra stiffened, but she did not pause in bringing out the wine and the cups, the sweets in their box, the bowl of fruit and small sweet cakes that was always here, waiting on her pleasure. When she had arranged them on the table, she reclined on her couch and took up her cup of wine, but did not drink from it. Her eyes rested on Dione's face. "You look dreadful," she observed. "Are you ill? Have you been delirious?"

"No," said Dione. "You don't look any madder than ever. What possessed you to raise those children from boys to men? What made you do it now?"

Cleopatra turned the cup in her fingers, seemed to realize what she was doing, set it down sharply. A drop of wine escaped the rim and spattered on the table. She ignored it. "It was time. Caesarion is sixteen years old; Antyllus is nearly that. They've both sprouted their first beards, or haven't you noticed?"

Dione had not, but she forbore to admit it. "You shouldn't have held this festival. You should have waited."

"Until when? Until Octavian could hold the razor to take Antyllus' beard, and then use it to slit his throat?"

Dione shuddered so hard that she nearly convulsed. "Yes," she gasped. "Yes, that's just what he'll do. Don't you understand? Boys who are sons of enemies are only boys. Men who are sons of enemies—men are enemies themselves, and fair prey. You've killed those children. Can't you feel it?"

Cleopatra's face went white. "I have not. I am not going to lose this war. Our people know now that the succession is secure: mine in Egypt, Antony's in Rome. That will bind them to us as nothing else can."

"You didn't need to do it now," Dione said. "It was impulse, wasn't it? It was desperation. You didn't think it through."

Cleopatra's voice was as cold as her face. "It was necessary."

"You've been killing people, too. Getting rid of anyone who stands in your way. Building yourself a wall of corpses to fight behind. Do you think it will help? Will Roma Dea give way to you, even for a blood sacrifice?"

"Roma Dea and I are not on speaking terms," said Cleopatra.

Nor, if this went on, would Dione be with Cleopatra. But Dione had come to speak, and speak she would, even if she died for it. Which she well might. Cleopatra in this mood was a cold, still, dangerous creature, like the cobra that reared up on her crown. "Killing traitors is a queen's prerogative, yes. But setting her sons up to be killed is pure folly. And you have done that. If Octavian wins the war—and he could, my lady, he well could—he might, for Rome's sake, spare Antyllus. But not Caesarion. Caesarion is too strong a rival. And you just made him stronger. You made him a man, and subject to a man's vengeance."

"He is a man," said Cleopatra, "and a king."

"And dead, if Octavian gets his hands on him." Dione stood. Her knees wobbled alarmingly, but she set her will on them and steadied. "You never should have done this. Both of them are still young for the burden of manhood. Caesarion could have had another year, Antyllus another two, or more. Now you've forced them to it, and made them targets. I'd double the guard on Caesarion, if I were queen, and watch his every move, and taste every bite he eats, every drop he drinks."

Cleopatra seemed too full of fury to speak, but Dione read words enough in her eyes.

Dione sighed. "I hope you can win the war—or else win Octavian over. He's coming, you know. I hear him. He's marching into Egypt."

"Does the earth groan under his tread?"

That was mockery, but Dione answered it as if it had been honestly meant. "Well, no. Not till he comes to the Two Lands. They don't want him. The rest of the world has already given way to him."

"But not Egypt," said Cleopatra. "Never Egypt."

"That's bravely said," said Dione. "Guard your son and your husband's son. They're dead else."

"Oh," said Cleopatra, "I will. Have no fear of that."

She seemed to have mastered her rage, and to be thinking through it. Dione had hoped for that. Enough that she ventured to say, "You might think of alternatives."

Cleopatra's eyes glittered, but she spoke mildly enough. "Running away? Again?"

"If necessary."

The queen nodded slowly. "I've thought of that. You didn't think I had, did you? But I've considered utmost defeat. If that happens— and the goddess forbid that it does—Octavian only thinks that he rules the world. There's the whole of the east beyond his reach. Media—we have allies in Media, did you remember? Antony may never have been friends with the Medes, but Egypt has been, and remains so. Helios will marry the king's daughter. Helios' mother may find refuge at need.

"Or maybe," she said, "even farther than that. India? Or should we go west, do you think? Would Iberia welcome us? Could we rule at the Pillars of Heracles, and be queens of the sunset sea?"

Ah, Dione thought. How she dreamed. Grand dreams, as befit a queen. "I should like to see India," she said.

"And so you shall," said Cleopatra, "if I lose this war. But I won't. Even if I have to take Octavian to my bed—I won't lose this war."

FORTY-THREE

Octavian was coming. They had had a reprieve, but without great hope that it would last. He had tarried to secure Greece and Syria; then, as he poised to leap on Egypt, Italy called him back. His armies were in revolt. They wanted to be mustered out, to be paid, to be given the lands and comfort that they had been promised. He could give them none of that. His coffers were chronically bare, and worse now that his forces had grown so much with Antony's deserters.

But he knew, few better, whose coffers were filled to overflowing, whose wealth was legendary. He had declared her Rome's enemy. Now he had to defeat her, or win her over. He needed her riches, and the riches of Egypt.

So had Caesar, and she had used him as he used her, in open reciprocity. So had Antony, and Antony she had loved, still loved, and fought for to the utmost of her capacity. For him she gathered all the resources that were hers to command, called in every debt though it broke or slew the one who owed it, brought it all together in the safest place she could think of: in the great shrine and tomb that she had built near Isis' temple. She meant to rest there when she was dead. Now it housed the greatest treasure in the world, the greatest perhaps that had ever been. Not Croesus himself could rival it.

And Octavian, knowing this—as who could not, for Cleopatra could never keep such a secret—came on her as a crocodile comes on his prey: arrow-swift, arrow-straight, direct to Egypt. Herod of Judea, whom Antony had valued so highly and Cleopatra hated so much, proved Antony's value false and Cleopatra's hatred well judged. He cast in his lot with the enemy. He opened the path for Octavian to tread.

Cleopatra tried to turn the war aside. She was canny enough for that, and who knew? It might work. She sent an embassy to Octavian where he had landed in Phoenicia. She would abdicate, she said, in her children's favor. She offered him the crook and flail of the Two Lands and the diadem of the Ptolemies. He kept those and sent her envoy back, but gave no answer.

The second time it was Antony who sent the offer of terms, in the hands of a noble ambassador: Antony's son Antyllus, stiffly proud with the honor of his position, but stiff with terror, too. He knew that he could be killed if Octavian was of a mind to be vindictive. He was to buy clemency and a safe retirement for his father—dishonor, surely, but Antony was past caring for honor or even appearances. What Cleopatra said when she heard of what he would do, no one knew. They kept it between themselves, behind a barred door in the Timonium. Antyllus went out unhindered by the queen, and even with her blessing on his head. He came back lightened of the money that he had taken, but unburdened with Octavian's reply.

The third envoy was Cleopatra's again, her children's sweet-spoken tutor, to repeat her offer of abdication and her request that her children be allowed to rule. He too brought back no response, but Octavian's movements were answer enough. Each embassy found him closer to Egypt.

And then, on a fair summer morning, the message came that they had all dreaded. Pelusium was fallen. Egypt's gate was broken; the enemy had come in.

Cleopatra, who had been calm even through Antony's fits and follies, Octavian's insults, the myriad betrayals and desertions, lost her temper at last. Pelusium's governor had left his wife and children in Alexandria, where the queen's presence would keep them safe. The queen sent men to them, men with swords, who cut them down where they stood. The eldest child, who fell last, was still asking when the sword pierced her heart, what these great tall armored men wanted, and why they looked at her so fiercely.

When the heads and hands were brought to Cleopatra, she regarded them without expression. She had seen their like often enough before. If she knew any glimmer of remorse, she suppressed it. This was war, war to the death. It left no room for mercy, or even for justice.

Antony, faced with the immediate threat, turned from despair to a kind of wild gaiety. His Incomparables changed their name to the *Commorientes,* the fellowship of those who would die together. It was the name of an old comedy, and fitting, he thought, for the players in this comedy turned tragic. He had been going to win it all and be king. He had won much, that was true, but he was losing it with every step that brought Octavian's legions closer.

And yet he felt lighter of heart than he had felt since he sailed away from Actium, shut up in the queen's ship and closing his ears to the din of battle that faded as the wind freshened. On impulse, soon thereafter regretted, he sent a man to Octavian, bearing a simple message: *Let the queen be and I'll fall on my sword.* But Octavian was infinitely predictable. He did not reply. Antony hoped that he was disconcerted, if only for a moment.

When Octavian was within a day's march of Canopus on the eastern edge of Alexandria, Antony called his troops together—they were still loyal enough, he took note, though their mood was sour at best—and took them out to fight. Canopus had been a favored retreat once, where he had gone with Cleopatra to take the breezes off the sea. It was an armed camp now. And Octavian came on.

He seemed to have forgotten his old reluctance to join battle. Antony doubted that he had acquired the taste for it. He was hungry for other meat: for the treasure piled in Cleopatra's tomb and in the shrines about it. For that he would do anything, no matter how distasteful.

"Prim little penny-pincher," Antony muttered, studying a map of the town while runners ran in and out bearing word of Octavian's every move. Antony had his own troops dispersed to meet the enemy, some round the fringes, others advancing through the broad paved streets.

One of the runners clattered up on horseback. "Fighting!" he gasped. "Real fighting by the hippodrome—cavalry, their vanguard, we can't seem to—"

Antony leaped up from his stool. "Publius! My horse! Caecilius! Blow the *Arm and Mount!*"

It was not Publius who brought the big black, but Marcus. Marcus' expression was eloquent. Publius had gone walking toward the enemy. Antony did not trouble to care. He swung from the ground to the stallion's back—still limber enough for that, by Hercules, whoever might call him a fat and broken old man—and clapped heels to the broad sides. Marcus yelped as the horse dragged him along by the reins, then fell back as Antony got them in hand, spurring toward the scent of the fight. The pick of his cavalry pounded behind him, as eager for it as he.

What grand irony, too. A cavalry engagement by the hippodrome. Octavian's horsemen had driven off Antony's foot-soldiers and camped, damn their arrogance, right there on the field where the young bloods liked to race their horses. Only about half of them were still mounted. The rest of them were busy digging the ditch that marked the camp's perimeter. Antony fell on them with a roar and a whoop.

Now this was fighting. It was fast, it was fierce. One mad charge into the middle of the new-made camp, then a flurry of fighting hand to hand. Antony's men outnumbered Octavian's, and were better mounted, too, on fresher horses. They captured the enemy's mounts, all but a few that escaped, ridden or unridden, and killed a good few of the enemy, and drove the rest clear back to the main mass of the army, which was still hovering on the town's edge, wondering where to go next.

That whole long line could have charged Antony's small company and annihilated it, but they seemed as nonplussed to see him as the vanguard had been. He laughed, light wild laughter that rang loud in the startled silence. "Octavian!" he bellowed. "Ho, Gaius Octavius! What say we end it now? Single combat, right here, all or nothing, and winner take the spoils."

Silence, as usual. Antony shook his head. "Octavian, my boy, you're getting monotonous."

There was a stir in the ranks. After a moment a man walked out. He was small, slight, dressed in armor that seemed too big for him. His voice had a wheeze in it: another of his endless catarrhs. Still, it was clear enough. "Surely there are plenty of other ways to get yourself killed."

"Well, certainly," said Antony, "but how many of them take you with me?"

"You do have a point," Octavian said, dry and precise. "No, thank you. Why don't you charge my army? That will do the job nicely, I should think."

"No, thank you," Antony echoed him, mocking in his politeness. "I'll hold out for slightly better odds." He kicked his horse up onto its hindlegs in the cavalryman's salute. Even as the horse came down to all fours again, he wheeled it about. His men were on their way already, leaving him behind. He laughed—why be angry?—and spurred after.

Antony rode his black Nisaian right into the palace, into the hall where the Commorientes were sitting to their dinner, and leaped down with a clashing of armor, right at Cleopatra's feet. He was grinning like a boy. His horse snorted and pawed, wreaking havoc with the priceless tiles of the floor.

"Good evening, my lord," Cleopatra said calmly. "I gather you had a pleasant day?"

"Marvelous," said Antony as a slave came to lead the horse away. Some of his daintier comrades held their noses at its parting gift. He laughed at them. "Stallions, you know. They stake their claim wherever they go."

"Rather like men," Cleopatra observed. She held out her hand. He took it, reclining beside her, armed and sweaty and horse-reeking as he was. She betrayed no revulsion. He was happy; he had won a victory, however small, and found his way out of the black mood that had beset him.

It was a fine feast, one of the finest that the fellowship had had. The food was superb, the wine sublime, the entertainment lavish and delightful. Cleopatra's wit sparkled with rare brilliance. Antony's earthier humor had even the exquisites laughing. They forgot the empty couches, the battles lost, the enemy camped among the villas of Canopus. Later they might die together. Tonight they lived and were glad.

Dione woke from uneasy sleep. She had been aware dimly, as in a dream, of the revelry in the palace. It had a fierce brilliance even from so far, the laughter of a brave man in the face of death. Fortunate for them that they could laugh. The rest of Alexandria huddled in the dark and tried to shut out fear. The enemy was at the gate. Tomorrow he would break in or be driven back. Either way, people would die.

The Commorientes were still at it, though it must be nearly midnight. She heard the music as clearly as if she had been in the hall, a shrilling of pipes and a throbbing of drums, and the chanting of voices, high and piercingly sweet.

She started up on her pallet. That was no dream-music, no half-awareness of a revel that went on out of her mortal hearing. She heard it clear. It was in the temple—no, in the street.

She clutched a shawl about her and ran, barefoot and bareheaded, through the murmurous darkness of the shrine. Other shapes ran with her, ghostly in the gloom, but real enough as one caught at her hand. "Mama. Mama, what is it?"

Mariamne, wide awake and clinging to her nurse's hand. Dione hissed her to silence and led her, with the gaggle of priestesses, to the temple's porch.

The street was dark. The stars shone, soft with summer. Nothing moved there, not even a hunting cat.

But the music was distinct, the voices chillingly clear. Dione knew their measure. She knew the song they sang. *Euoe! Euoe Bacchai!*

In the still night, in the breathless quiet, the storm of sound swelled and slowly faded as if a great throng had passed.

Alalalai! Euoe! Euoe Bacchai!

And yet there was nothing to see. Only the voices. Voices that passed away out of the city, passed into the east, toward the Gate of the Sun: toward Octavian in his camp at Canopus.

"Mama," said Mariamne, drowsy and a little fretful. "Mama, why did the god go away?"

Dione shivered. Tanit's eyes were wild. The other priestesses clung together. One of them was weeping: hysteria, and she knew better, but clearly she could not help it.

Dione said what had to be said, what they all had to face. "Yes, the god has gone away. Dionysus is gone, departed from our city."

"Then we've lost," Tanit said.

"No," said Dione. "Not yet. Aren't you forgetting something?"

Tanit looked blank. So did all the others. It was Mariamne, the infant, the child who should have been too young to understand such things at all, who said, "We still have Mama Isis. She'll take care of us. But I wish the god hadn't gone."

Dione swung her daughter up into her arms. The child was a warm weight, sleepy, blessedly free of the fear that chilled Dione's bones. "So do I, little minx. Oh, so do I."

FORTY-FOUR

On the last day of the month that Julius Caesar had named after himself, at the last stroke of midnight, Dionysus departed from Alexandria. At dawn on the kalends of Sextilis, as mild night gave way to steaming day, Antony's fleet sailed from the harbor of Alexandria, striking eastward against Octavian's ships. Antony's army, and Antony with it, held position between the hippodrome of Canopus and the walls of the city.

It was a much smaller army than he had left, riding laughing into Cleopatra's arms. Much smaller. So small that, as he came back in the dark before dawn, having slept little if at all, he thought himself deluded, or mocked by a god.

Daylight showed him a camp laid out like every Roman camp from Parthia to Ultima Thule: straight lines of tents, pathways both greater and lesser, commander's tent in the middle, wall and ditch about the rim. That ditch had been dug and that wall raised for a mighty army, a confluence of legions. It enclosed a scattering of tents, the scorchmarks of numerous cookfires, and his own tall tent with those of his own guard about it. And, in their place, and still intact as far as he could see, the cavalry with their horses.

The bright mood of the night lingered. It made him laugh as he looked about at the ruin of his war. He could well see where his army had gone. Octavian's forces seemed to spread from horizon to horizon, a forest of spears as the poets would say, and a rampart of shields. He knew the legions numbered on those that were closest. Last night they had been his own.

His men came out to the call of the trumpet, infantry and cavalry both. They dressed ranks well enough, in order correct, but none of them would meet his eyes. Afraid, he told himself, or embarrassed for their fellows.

He mounted his stallion and rode down the pitifully short line, then up again, and stopped. "Well," he said. "We'll put up such fight as we can. Take a few with us down to Hades."

Time was when the cheering at such a speech would have shaken the earth underfoot. At this, he received only silence. Someone shuffled his feet. Someone else coughed. One of the horses snorted and tossed its head with a jingle of bit.

"You've been loyal," Antony said to them—horses, too. "The gods will remember that."

"The ones who left the city last night?"

Antony could not see who had spoken. He answered as if it had been all of them. "Just one. Just Dionysus, who comes and goes as he pleases. The rest are with us yet."

No one responded to that. He could feel the gloom that lay on them. It wanted to capture him, too, as it had at Actium. Later, he promised it. Now he had to fight.

He nodded to his trumpeter. The man hesitated, which he would not have done had there been more men to call to the march. But as Antony waited, he raised the trumpet to his lips and blew. Not a brave call as such things went, but enough. Antony's army marched forth to meet the enemy.

Who waited, massively still, in a great half-circle that trapped him between his camp and the city wall. Bad tactics; miserable. But only if he wanted to win.

"No orders," he said to the men behind him. "Just do what you can. Make me proud of you." And to the trumpeter: "Now."

The trumpet sang the charge. Antony gathered reins, set spurs to his horse's sides. It bunched under him, half-rearing, and lunged forward.

The silence behind him was profound; unnatural. Antony's horse slowed under the influence of it. He glanced back. None of his men had moved. The cavalry were cavalry no longer: they had dismounted, were drawing back toward the city's walls. The infantry at least had shields up and spears in position as if to advance. He hauled his horse about and rode at them, roaring. "March! *March!*"

They broke in front of him. Broke ranks, dropped shields, and ran.

Antony sat his horse in the middle of the battlefield. He was all alone.

When Cleopatra came to Tarsus, his people had deserted him, too, and left him to feel the dreadful weight of solitude. But that had been glorious in its consequence. This was bleak ignominy.

He kicked his mount back again toward Octavian's army. It had not moved, had made no sound. "Are you daft?" he shouted. "Give me a fight!" Nothing. Not even the gleam of eyes in the blank helmets. "Cowards! Arselickers! Eaters of shit! Come out and *fight!*"

None of them would. He could fling himself on their spears. They would not care.

"No," he said. "No, that's too easy." He hauled his horse about yet again and flung it toward the camp.

All the fighting men were gone, but his slaves were there still, watching over his tent. They came out as he rode up. He sat his heaving horse and curled his lip. "What, you aren't grabbing the main chance, too? Go on, take it. You'll be dead soon enough. At least die on the right side."

Most of them needed no more encouragement than that. They ran wide around him as if he could strike them in passing. That saddened him, even in his mood of perfect despair.

Two lingered still. One was his body-slave, Eros. The other was one of the queen's people, now that he took time to notice. He sprang down from his horse, let it go, not caring where it went. It wandered a bit, sighed, dropped its head and began to graze.

"Well?" Antony said to the queen's man. "Does she have a message for me?"

"Yes, my lord," the eunuch said, trembling. "I mean, no, my lord. My lord—she—"

The creature's face told him what he dreaded to know. But he wanted to hear it in words. "What? What does she want?"

"She can't—" the idiot blubbered. "Lord, she can't—she's dead."

"Of course she's not dead," Antony said perfectly reasonably. "How can she be dead? She hasn't lost yet. She's still got Egypt."

"My lord, she died. She said—she said tell you—death is better than Octavian."

Antony stood very still. Yes, she had said that. Jesting, he had thought, with much raillery about the boy's wet lips, clammy hands, and undersized member: none of which Antony had ever had.

Still, how like her to make a decision all at once and stick to it. How like to her to make sure she did not live to see him beaten, or to see Octavian in his place, occupying her bed, sharing her throne.

He was perfectly empty, and perfectly calm. He said, "You, whatever your name is. Go back to the palace. You're safer there." He did not wait to see if the eunuch obeyed. "Eros, come with me."

Eros, faithful servant, was weeping soundlessly. Antony slapped him on the shoulder. "Here, stop that. Come inside."

It was dim within, but light came through the opened flap. All the familiar things were there, the map-table, the camp stools, the cot in the alcove, the stand for his armor. He kept the parade armor in the palace; here he kept what he had on, the armor made for use. He unbuckled his swordbelt and hung it in its place.

Eros, starting into motion, reached for the fastenings of the cuirass. Antony waved him off. "No, no," he said. He drew his short sword and held it out. His hand trembled no more than did his voice. "Take this. Kill me with it."

Eros stared. "My lord—"

Antony thrust the hilt into the slack hand, clamped the fingers roughly about it. "Stab me. You know how. I've shown you often enough."

"No," said Eros, weeping. "My lord, please."

Antony struck him across the face. *"Do it,* damn you."

The slave stared at the sword in his hand; stared from it to Antony. His eyes went wild. Antony braced himself. Now, he thought. Yes, now.

Eros dipped suddenly, braced the hilt on the hard-tamped ground, and fell on the blade. Quite literally fell—leaped, for a fact, and with admirable aim.

Even at that, he took a while to die, mewling with the pain, vomiting blood.

"Damn you," Antony said. His eyes were burning dry, or he would have wept. "Oh, damn you."

Eros' convulsions slowed and stopped. The stench of voided bowels was abrupt and convincing. Antony closed the slave's eyes—curse him for a loyal idiot, why could he not have killed himself after he killed his master?

The sword was buried deep in the slave's body. Antony tried to draw it loose, gagged as it caught on something—bone, gristle. He had another sword. It was not the one he was fondest of, though it had been a gift from Cleopatra. Its hilt was ornate, chased with gold.

It would do. He brought it from its chest. His movements were deliberate, but without weakness or hesitation. He had been thinking of this, if truth be told, for a long while. Before Actium, even, in the darker nights. He had known how he would do it—not the easy way, commanding a slave to spit him, but the way of the honorable vanquished. Brutus and Cassius had done it at Philippi, and so atoned for the murder of Caesar.

Now it came full circle. Would Brutus consider himself avenged? Octavian would feel cheated—he liked to gloat.

All the more reason to do it and get it over. Without Cleopatra, after all, Antony had nothing. She was Egypt, and with her death he lost it: all its wealth, its fields of grain, its ships and its sailors.

Antony took his time in preparing. First he took off his armor, to make it easier. Then he laid his cloak on the ground, to spare the fine Egyptian carpet that Cleopatra had given him. He braced the sword's hilt as Eros had, with attention to the angle. It would hurt—like fury, he knew. He had seen the faces of men who died this way. But he had never taken much notice of pain.

He knelt. The sword's point touched his breast just below the heart. He should say something, he supposed. Orate. Pray. But who would listen? Certainly not the gods. They were too busy laughing.

He shrugged slightly. Gathered body and mind. Set his teeth. Thrust.

The pain was blinding, overwhelming, unbelievable.

And it went on. It did not end. Blood—there was blood everywhere. His limbs were numb. But his soul clung stubbornly to his body.

"Sweet merciful gods."

Antony turned his head. It felt like moving the world.

Someone was standing over him, staring down, looking so comically appalled that Antony could have laughed. But laughing hurt, oh, gods, it hurt.

The man dropped to one knee. Antony squinted. After a while a name came to him. "Diomedes. Come to invite me to her funeral?"

The queen's secretary gasped. "What in the world— My lord! Oh, she'll grieve, she'll grieve, to see you like this."

Antony frowned. "She's dead."

Diomedes shook his head so hard it must have rattled. "My lord, she lives. She is well—but sad, grievously sad, and when she discovers this . . ."

"So the little beast lied." Antony did laugh this time, though it cast him on the edge of the dark. Yes, let him fall, let him die.

But the gods were not so merciful. He retained enough awareness to hear Diomedes say, "She wants to see you, for you to come to her. Oh, thank goodness I brought my two brawny slaves. They were supposed to look after me you know, fight off footpads, wandering armies . . . Oh, dear. We'll need a litter—and how we're to get you up there—"

Diomedes was a babbler, but he got things done while he yattered on. The shift from floor to litter was more than Antony's fortitude could bear. He could scream, or he could lose consciousness. For pride he chose the latter.

FORTY-FIVE

Cleopatra saw Antony off in the dark before dawn. He was past any hope of winning, she knew that. He could acquit himself honorably, and would, being Antony. She would guard herself and her children as she could.

Helios, Selene, and Ptolemy had a refuge prepared long since: Cleopatra had betrothed Selene to the Prince of Mauretania. He was but a child, and his father the king was not a pleasant man; but he was strong, in will as in armies, and his word was sacred to him. He had promised to protect the children entrusted to his care. Cleopatra could trust that he would—inasmuch as she trusted anything in the weak and turning world, and more than she trusted Media's king, whose daughter had been promised to Alexander Helios. Yes, Mauretania would serve them best. They would live, no matter what came of this war. They might even prosper.

None of the children wept as she bade them farewell. All, even the youngest, understood what was happening. She had never believed in shielding children from hard truths, and these children were the gods' own. She could not have hidden anything from them even if she would.

Parting from them was almost easy. They would be safe, she told herself. Caesarion—Caesarion her young king, whom she had raised to manhood with her own hands—for him she saw nothing, not light, not darkness. Nothing.

He had put on coarse common clothes like a tribesman from the desert, his fair hair hidden beneath the headdress, his handsome Roman face—so like his father's—dirtied and darkened to help in its concealment. His one companion, his tutor Rhodon, roused a quiver of anxiety. The man was big enough, and trained to fight; he had been a soldier before he turned philosopher. But he was a Thracian, white-skinned, blue-eyed, redheaded, as unlike a man of the desert as human creature could be. The dusty robes only made him look the more outlandish, and hence the more noticeable.

This parting was supposed to be private, but that was never possible in a palace. People would come and go, slaves with duties, priestesses on errands—Dione mute in a shadow as she liked to be, and in the light beside her, the younger of her sons. The adversity that had struck the kingdom had done nothing to dim Timoleon's sheen. He was as beautiful and feckless as ever. As he felt Cleopatra's eye on him, he smiled. "You're thinking the same thing I am, aren't you, majesty?"

"And what am I thinking?" Cleopatra asked him.

He cocked his head at Rhodon, who was trying to wrap the end of his headdress about his face. "That great gawk of a scholar isn't going to fool a blind man, let alone a Roman soldier. Let me go."

Dione gasped.

Cleopatra had no compassion to spare. She studied the boy—the young man, in fact; he must be twenty at least, though his beauty made him seem younger. Half the women in Alexandria were in love with him, she had heard, and most of the men. He had grown a beard of late, hoping perhaps to start a fashion. He did look remarkably rakish and barbaric.

"I've been among the tribes," he said. "I can get us horses, keep us fed, win us through wherever you want us to go. Deep in the desert—Numidia, Libya, even Arabia. No Roman can find us there. We can even carve a kingdom, if we've a mind."

"That is a very bold *we*," said Caesarion.

Timoleon grinned at him. "I've been named a prince of a tribe west of Memphis. You'd have to earn that."

Caesarion lifted his chin. "I am a prince and a king."

"Not in the desert," said Timoleon. "Not yet."

Dione found her voice at last. "Timoleon—"

"Yes, mother," he said before she could go on. "Yes, it's dangerous. Yes, we could get killed. We will get killed if we stay here. I'd rather have a fighting chance."

"You are not in danger," his mother said. Her voice was soft and might seem cold, if one did not know her.

"Of course I am," he said. "And Caesarion is dead the minute Octavian walks through the palace gate. I'll get him out and keep him safe, if anybody can."

"But," she said, "nobody can."

"We can try," said Timoleon. He kissed her lightly, insouciantly one might have thought, but Cleopatra knew him better than that. He was one of the gods' children, one of their best beloved: one of those whom they favor with a gift of madness. It was sane for what it was, and quite enchanting.

"Goodbye, mother," he said. "We'll send you word from the kingdoms of the desert. And when we're kings, we'll come for you and make you a queen."

"I don't want to be a queen," Dione said. "I want you alive."

"I'll try to stay that way," said Timoleon.

"And I," Caesarion said, not to be outdone.

"Go," Cleopatra said. "Quickly. Before the enemy comes."

The look Dione flashed on her was pure hatred. She did not care. She was doing as she must—protecting what she could. She did not ask or expect that she be loved for it.

For herself too Cleopatra had prepared a refuge: the strongest place in Alexandria, the treasure-house that was also her tomb. The upper story was yet unfinished, but the lower floor was built like a fortress. Once she was inside, with the gates sealed, the only entry was through a single window up above. An army would be hard put to attack through that; even Octavian would have to work to get at the glory of treasure that filled the foundations, lined the walls, lay heaped on the floor.

It was a house of gold. Unlike Alexander's tomb that for all its glittering ornaments was bare of real treasure, even the catafalque stripped to fill a king's empty coffers, this great half-finished tomb and shrine contained the wealth of an empire. The eye glazed on it, blinded by surfeit, till gold seemed as common as lead, and jewels no more precious than glass.

To Cleopatra it had stopped being a lure long ago. She who had presided over banquets clad in nothing but a net of pearls strung on golden wire, whose great gift and skill had always been to heap up wealth wherever she went, walked through the coffers piled one on the other, the bolts and bales of silk and finest linen, the rarities of the sculptor's and the painter's art, and took no notice of them. The inner chamber, the vault of the tomb with its empty bier, had space to move in, and to live in if one must. There was a couch, one of the more practical treasures, and a table, and chairs of priceless woods gilded and inlaid with gems. Lamps on stands, gold and silver and bronze, stood all about, many of them lit in honor of her coming. Her ladies Iras and Charmion, and Mardian her eunuch who had been with her since she was a child, were waiting. They had the fixed, faintly angry expression of those who would die if they must, to keep a thing they valued: the queen herself, and all she stood for.

It made her a little weary. She had shut off the weaker emotions when the war turned against her. Letting Caesarion go, knowing how little chance he had, even with such a guardian as she had given him, had stripped the last vestige of softness from her heart. She was all hard now, all royal.

A whole flock of people like frightened geese had tried to follow her into her refuge. She got rid of most. Some she sent on errands; her secretary Diomedes, with his rattling tongue but his keen mind, she sent to Antony, to bring him when his sham of battle failed him. A few she let stay, even when the gates were shut and the workmen moved swiftly to seal them behind a wall of mortared stone. There was still the upper window—she glanced up at it. Dawn glimmered there, casting a faint illumination on the unfinished gallery, the scaffolding that had been left behind and would, perhaps, never be taken away.

She went to the chair that was most like a throne, which happened to have cushions on the seat, and a carved and gilded footstool. Charmion brought her wine, which she did not want, but she indicated that it be offered to the others. None of them accepted it. Dione, whose manner had always been modest but who managed nonetheless to carry herself as one who yields to no will but her own, sat as Cleopatra had, with her dark maid behind her. Her daughter Mariamne, Cleopatra knew, was safe in Isis' temple; the priestesses would protect her with their lives if they must.

Cleopatra knew a brief, fierce envy. All of her children were gone away. Even the one who was not the child of her body, but whom she cherished as if he had been—Antyllus had not come when the rest were brought to her, nor did she know where he was. With his father, she hoped, or taking it on himself to escape while he could. Octavian would be no more merciful to Antony's grown heir than to Caesar's kingly son.

"Oh, he's not dead yet," Dione said, her soft voice uncanny in the faintly echoing space. "He thought to spare your tears, and to keep to his rooms. He asked me to tell you that he'll be well. He's Roman, after all. Octavian can't punish him for being loyal to his father."

"Can't he?" Cleopatra sighed, letting the bitterness drain away. "May the gods protect him, since I no longer can."

Dione bowed her head. The others were silent. Cleopatra preferred that silence to determinedly cheerful chatter. It was oppressive, but empty conversation would have been worse.

The light in the window strengthened. A shaft of sun stabbed through, made its slow way down the wall.

Just past noon by the sun's angle, a shadow blocked the light. A voice called out. "Majesty?"

Cleopatra found herself on her feet.

"Majesty," said the voice—Diomedes', unwontedly steady. "Your lord has come."

Cleopatra had never heard Diomedes speak briefly, still less in that flat tone without the affected warble. Her heart, that she had thought truly hardened, proved her false: it shuddered and went cold.

There were scrapings above, voices trying to be quiet, a lurch and a curse as a man pulled himself through the window. A big man, but not Antony. Diomedes had edged out of the way along the gallery. Something slid through the opening, something long and flat.

Cleopatra gasped. A bier—they had him on a bier.

She was there, standing below the gallery, as the two slaves and Diomedes brought him down. He looked shrunken under the military cloak, his full cheeks gone slack, their ruddiness drained to a grey pallor.

But he was not dead. That was sweat on his brow, new and cold. Fever? Had he suffered the ignominy of illness, and so fallen without a blow struck?

He roused to the touch of her hand on his cheek. He felt her anger, too. He grinned at it, or tried: it was more a grimace. "They told me you were dead," he said. His voice was as wan as his face.

"They lied." Cleopatra did not like the feel of him at all. He was too cold. Cold that crept through her, too, as her wits—her lethally quick wits—told her what he must have done.

Before he could stop her, if he could, she twitched the cloak down over his body. He had taken off his armor. She noticed that first. Because what else there was to notice, what screamed at her with blood-red urgency, was too terrible to face.

They had tried to bandage him. It had kept him from bleeding to death, for a while, long enough to be alive when he came to her. The bandages were soaked through. The goddess knew what he was like inside. Numb, she hoped, with excess of pain.

"Oh, you fool," she said. "You bloody impulsive fool."

He nodded somewhat ruefully. "I should have waited, I suppose.

Shared the moment with you. But there didn't seem much point. Since, the way I was told it, you'd gone ahead without me."

"You know I wouldn't do that."

"Really?" He coughed a little, but his body stiffened with the pain of it. He muttered a curse that resolved into a command. "Wine. Give me wine."

It was the eunuch Mardian who brought him the cup, who held it to his lips while he drank. He did not drink much. The eunuch took the cup away again. His smooth cheeks were wet.

Antony coughed harder this time, with visible pain. "Damn, lady," he said when he could speak. "I'm dying." He sounded annoyed, and not at all afraid. The rest came quickly, almost too quickly to catch. "Look. Take care of yourself. There's a man close by Octavian—we weren't friends, but he's trustworthy. Proculeius. Gaius Proculeius. Get him to help you."

"I can help myself," said Cleopatra.

Antony shook his head. "Stubborn to the last, aren't you? And the last it is. Imagine it. And here I thought we were immortal."

"In all ways that matter," she said steadily, "we are."

He groped, found her hand. His eyes were dimming, his fingers icy, but he had strength still to raise her hand to his lips. "You were always magnificent. I . . . well, I made do."

"It was enough," said Cleopatra.

He smiled. "Kiss me," he said.

"Importunate," said Cleopatra, but she bent. His lips were as cold as his hands. His breath, strangely, was sweet, with a hint of spices. Myrrh, she thought with the remoteness of perfect grief. Myrrh for mortality.

She felt his souls passing one by one: the flutter of wings, the whisper of air, breath mingling with hers as he sighed, and shivered a little, and died.

Very, very slowly she straightened. Her heart, that should have been emptied, was full. He filled it. She touched fingers to her lips. Cold, yet beneath them a living warmth.

"Oh," she said to the darkness, and to the glimmer of gold within it. "Oh, my lord. Caesar was a wonder of the world; but you, my lord—you I loved."

FORTY-SIX

Antony was dead.

It seemed an impossibility, like a mountain's falling, or a god's dying. Dione saw the exaltation that was on Cleopatra, knew it for what it was: grief transmuted into a kind of defiance. This the tragic actors tried for but never quite approached. It needed the edge of truth, and the soul of a queen.

Cleopatra turned slowly. She was perfectly sane, so sane that she could only be mad. "Dione," she said in a voice as gentle as it was implacable. "Dear cousin and friend. Bear a message for me."

Dione did not ask as she was expected to—did not wish to know the name.

"Go to the victors," said Cleopatra. "Go to the one Antony spoke of. Not the one who calls himself Caesar; the other. Proculeius. Tell him that the lady of the Two Lands would speak with him."

Dione considered arguing. Considered what could happen once she had been got rid of—what was in Cleopatra's eyes, dark and bright at once.

But the queen said, "I won't kill myself before I see him. Bring him to me."

Dione bowed, not too deeply, as cousin bows to royal cousin. "Majesty," she said.

It was not difficult for Dione to climb down from the window, with Hebe behind her, guarding her back. There was scaffolding enough, and a rope that the workmen had left. The wonder was that no one had thought to rob the tomb before the queen walled herself up in it. But there had been guards, and distraction enough from the armies outside the walls.

Those armies were all one great army now, and they had marched into the city. The city made no effort to resist them. They were too many. And, Dione thought, the city was too weary with war and too cowed by the gods' abandonment. Only the deaf and the dead had failed to hear the passing of Dionysus.

There were Roman Eagles in Alexandria, come not as guests of the queen but as conquerors. The tramp of their hobnailed boots was loud in the hush of the streets. Their arrogance made Alexandrian pride seem modest. They owned the world, and they knew it.

She could not in fairness hate them. It was their time, that was all, as it had been Alexander's before them, and Persia's before that, down through the long years.

Octavian had gone straight to the palace, as she might have expected. His men were already on guard at the gates, and Cleopatra's people were who knew where: hiding, fled, gone over to the enemy. They did not see a lone priestess and her dark soft-footed maid. Dione made sure of that. Another small magic led her, directing her feet through familiar passages gone all strange, chambers full of foreigners, loud irreverent voices calling in the gardens and across the roofs.

It was not, for all of that, a sack. They were moving in, that was all. Romans had a habit of that. Even a night's camp was built like a stronghold, as if they meant to remain for generations.

In the hall of the throne she found what she was seeking. She was surprised not to see Octavian sitting on the great golden chair. That was empty. Soldiers stood about. There were togas, plain and senator-striped. They were all gawking like sightseers, even the ones who had lived long months in this palace when they were Antony's loyal friends.

Only one of them seemed at ease, unawed by the splendor about him. Dione had seen the coins and the portraits. They flattered him, but not overmuch. He was smaller than she had expected, and thinner, with an extraordinarily long neck and a surprisingly attractive face. His nose was long, yes, his mouth prim, his chin narrow and pointed. But one thought that if he smiled, or even relaxed those tightly pursed lips, he might not be ill-looking at all.

She was staring. She lowered her eyes. In any case she was not sent to him. One of the men about him had to be Proculeius, but she did not know which. So many Roman faces, so many voices speaking Latin in that hall which had known for so long the music of Greek. They made her dizzy.

One face of them all, she knew. A narrow face, dark, brows knit over large dark eyes. Her own eyes drank it in before her mind mastered them, wrenched them away. She must not know him. She must not see him.

Proculeius. She must conjure the name while she still could. The name bespoke the man. That was the wisdom of Egypt.

But the name in her heart was Lucius Servilius, and it was to him that her feet led her—veering in the last instant, coming face to face with a pleasant ordinary Roman who started and stared. "Proculeius?" she asked.

His hand flicked in a gesture that she remembered from the legions: averting evil. His face, being closer to the cultivated mind, mastered itself first. "Lady," he said.

Now they were all staring. None could have seen her enter; she had been working that magic still. She delivered her message in the clear cold voice that came to her when she was most shaken, like the goddess' gift. "Gaius Proculeius, the queen would speak with you."

The Romans looked at one another and then at their commander. Dione refused to follow suit until his voice compelled her. "What? She doesn't want to see me?"

She kept her head up, according him no respect. It was a small vindictiveness, but it was the best she could do. "She wishes to see Proculeius."

"Then she shall," said Octavian. It was an empty generosity. No one had asked him for it, no one wanted it.

Dione looked him up and down, so that she would remember him. All that she had heard of him, all that she had seen in what he did and said and wrote, came together and fixed. She liked him no better than she had before. But she said, "You are an emperor. A king, no; you lack the warmth. But you can rule a world."

Octavian looked flustered, which must have been a rare thing for him: it made him angry. She watched with interest as he took himself in hand. "Are you a seer, then?"

"I am the goddess' voice in the Two Lands," she said.

"Then can you tell me—"

She cut him off. "The queen is waiting. Come, sir."

Proculeius waited to be given leave, but Dione observed no such niceties. He had to hurry a bit to catch her. Another man came after him, one of the armored officers, and high up from the look; Dione had never paid much attention to such Roman fripperies as military rank. "Gallus," said Proculeius in some relief. "Good. Lady," he added hastily, "you don't mind . . .?"

"She only wants to see you," Dione said, "but if you feel safer, then yes, bring a guard."

It annoyed Gallus to be called a mere bodyguard when he was obviously so much more. Dione did not care. Let the Romans know what they were in the eyes of Egypt. Conquerors, maybe, but upstarts nonetheless, hardly fit to set foot on floors where kings had trod.

She did not take these men to the window and thus into the tomb. It would be enough for them to speak to Cleopatra through the grille that the masons had left in the door. She left them there, contemplating their position. They, as she had wished, were oblivious. "Lady," said Proculeius hesitantly. "Majesty."

The ladder was where she had left it. Hebe helped her to set it in place, and climbed up behind her. She was still nimble, which was rather gratifying; it was long years since she had seemed to spend more time in trees than in her chambers.

The tomb was dark after the bright sun, and seemed deserted until her sight came clear. Diomedes and his slaves were gone. There were only Cleopatra's three servants, and Cleopatra herself by the door, speaking with the men outside. She was laughing at something that they had said: bright, bitter laughter. "Oh, do tell me another! You know as well as I, what Octavian is afraid of. He thinks I'll burn this whole house of treasure, and cheat him of it and of me."

The answer was indistinct. It seemed to be in Gallus' voice, which was deeper and somewhat rougher than the other's. Dione moved toward the queen.

Something scraped behind her. She whirled. Men—men coming down the stair from the window.

She had left the ladder up. Too late to curse herself for it. The army that startlement and shadows made of them, resolved into a mere three men, Proculeius and two more, who must have followed in spite of her.

She had no magics ready, not even a weapon. Still she did her best to stop them. They set her aside as lightly as if she had been a child, and ran for the queen. Her servants were no more use than Dione had been.

The Romans seized Cleopatra. Steel glittered in her hand: a knife. Proculeius wrested it free.

She stood in the hands of his two servants, ruffled but deadly calm. "So," she said. "No Roman is to be trusted."

"You are the enemy of Rome," said Proculeius stiffly. "I take you prisoner in the name of Roma Dea, and of Gaius Julius Caesar."

"Caesar is dead," said Cleopatra.

Proculeius did not reply to that. "Epaphroditus. Guard her." The larger of the two servants nodded. Proculeius raised his voice. "Gallus! Tell Caesar. We have the woman."

Not even a queen, Dione thought. Only a woman. In outrage, and because it no longer seemed to matter what anyone said, she inquired, "Do you really care that you have her? All he wants is the gold. He's always out at pocket, Octavian is. What will he do when he's gambled this away?"

"That will take him a while, lady," said Proculeius dryly. He had wit, for a Roman. In another world she would have begun to like him. He faced Cleopatra. "Lady, can I trust you to wait while I fetch Caesar?"

Cleopatra raised a brow. "I can hardly do anything else, can I? If you're going out, will you fetch the embalmers, and such things as they need to attend the honorable dead?"

Proculeius seemed startled. He must not have seen the bier, or the shape laid on it, with the military cloak drawn up to its chin. He walked toward it as if drawn, and stared down into the still face. The jaw was bound up, the eyelids weighted with golden coins from the hoard. There was no beauty in it, but no horror either, to Dione's eyes.

But Romans had a great fear of death, even as often as they were given to falling on their swords. That was a kind of defiance of terror, cowardice that masked itself as bravery. Proculeius turned away abruptly, grey-faced. "I'll send the embalmers, majesty," he said thickly. "I am . . . sorry to learn of your loss."

"Would you have been as sorry if he had been executed at Octavian's command, as a traitor and an enemy of the Romans?"

Proculeius had no answer for that.

"You may go," Cleopatra said with dignity, as if she had never been taken prisoner.

He went. That much power she still had.

Proculeius' departure seemed to lighten the air in that closed place. It still smelled of death, and of the cold metallic scent of gold. Cleopatra returned to her chair. She walked as one who holds herself straight by effort of will—who will not, adamantly will not, be defeated.

"Epaphroditus," she said abruptly. "That is your name, yes?"

He nodded. He was blushing: young, then, in spite of his bulk, and somewhat taken aback to be guarding a captive queen.

"Epaphroditus," said Cleopatra, "will you allow me a few moments' modesty? I'd like to receive my conqueror in more suitable attire. Might you, do you think, stand guard over the window, to make sure I don't escape, but keep your back turned while I dress?"

Dione watched her carefully. There was something frightening about her calmness.

Cleopatra saw; she smiled. "Dear cousin. It's time you left, I think. Your husband is with Octavian, yes? He'll see that you're safe from reprisal."

"He is not my husband," Dione said in a thin, tight voice.

"Of course he is," said Cleopatra. "You love him with all your heart. But he, being male and therefore a fool, thought that he loved Rome more. He's sorry for that now, I'm sure."

Dione shook her head. Her eyes were full of tears.

"There now," said Cleopatra, rising, coming to her, wiping them away. She let her hands rest on Dione's shoulders, and smiled into her face. It was a sweet smile, emptied of bitterness. It told Dione all that she could not say, not with the Roman standing in the gallery, alert for any treachery. Aloud she only said, "Go on, love him. He's desperate to have you back. I can feel that. I'm like Danae, all open to the stars."

"Then you know—" Dione began.

Cleopatra's head bowed, rose, in calm beyond grief. "You were right. See, I admit it."

Antyllus was dead—dead as soon as Octavian entered the palace. Caesarion was dead—killed as he fled. Timoleon—Timoleon—

Dione wailed, but not aloud, never aloud; only in her heart. She found herself clinging to the queen, to her friend whose son had died, for whom her son, her beloved, her reckless beautiful child, was dead. Cleopatra's grip was strong, her eyes dry, her voice quiet as she said, "Yes. I too curse the gift that the goddess has given us. To be ignorant as simple women are—to believe, for however little a while, that they had escaped—"

Dione stiffened and drew back. Cleopatra let her go. They stood face to face, eye to eye. They were not queen and servant then, nor even cousin and cousin. They were women who had lost children, mothers who had sent sons to their deaths. That was an old bond, as old almost as the bond of mother and child.

"Oh, how I hate war," said Dione with sudden passion.

"It's ended now," Cleopatra said. "We've wrought peace, for all our efforts to do the opposite."

"Octavian's peace," Dione said. "Rome's peace. A desert, and a nation of slaves."

"I think not," said Cleopatra. She embraced Dione quickly, kissed her on each cheek and then again on the brow. "Go, cousin. Find your beloved. Live, for his sake if not for mine."

FORTY-SEVEN

Cleopatra stood still while Dione climbed the stair with her maid behind her. They moved alike, very straight, very proud, like caryatids who bear the weight of the sky on their heads. They knew what she meant to do; approved it, she rather thought.

They paused while Dione spoke to the Roman freedman at the window. He ducked his head and let them by, even had the courtesy to help each over the sill and onto the ladder.

As he turned back, Cleopatra beckoned to her servants. Mardian brought the painted screen that had belonged first to some forgotten pharaoh. Gods marched on it through a forest of papyrus: ibis-headed Thoth, baboon-headed Ptah, falcon-headed Horus, Sekhmet like a lioness with a woman's body, Hathor the heifer, and leading them with a subtle jackal-smile, Anubis the guide and protector. As old as the image was, as faded as it had grown with the years, still the jackal-god's eyes were bright. They seemed to meet Cleopatra's, smiling as her maids took off her gown.

Over the top of the screen Cleopatra could see the freedman's back turned, sense the fierce heat of his embarrassment. Naked men were nothing in Greece and in Rome, but a naked woman was shocking.

She whispered a word. Nothing changed in the way he stood, except that he stood utterly still. Still and oblivious, set out of time until she should call him back again.

Slowly then, with the serenity of ritual, the queen's women arrayed her as if for a great festival. They bathed her in water from the barrel that had been brought to sustain her, and anointed her body with unguents. Charmion's fingers trembled as she settled the robes into place and brought out the golden ornaments one by one, but her face was quiet, expressionless. Iras, combing and plaiting Cleopatra's hair, weaving it with pearls and gold, betrayed no sign of either grief or fear.

The gods were close. Cleopatra heard them whispering. She greeted them with a lowering of the eyelids, a slight inclination of the head: no more, for she would disturb Iras' meticulous hand with brush and paint for lips, cheeks, eyes. A queen was a work of great art; it took time, and it took care, to make her perfect. If she were truly and wholly queen, she set aside her mere humanity and became all royal, all goddess.

For this she had been born. To this she had been advancing all the days of her life. The inevitability of it, the clear certainty, was almost joyful. Tragedy, perhaps; her lord was dead, her kingdom lost. But there was no sorrow in her now. She was a priestess in the rite, doing as she could not help but do.

That was not, goddess willing, what Octavian wanted of her. He would have a triumph in Rome. He would not be Roman if he forbore. He would parade his armies, his new-won gold, his captives. And before them all, chained to his chariot with golden chains, he would lead Cleopatra, Rome's great enemy, fallen to be a spectacle for the Roman mob.

"No," she said aloud. Her maid stared. Her eunuch looked simply sad. She smiled to comfort them. "No, I will not be led in Octavian's triumph."

They bowed. "No, lady," Iras said. "You would never suffer that."

Such faithful echoes; so devoted, so perfect in their selflessness. The woman that she had been might have found that faintly repellent. The queen found it fitting. She must have attendants. There were none as exemplary as these.

At last her robing was done, her hair arranged in elaborate plaits and curls, her jewels glittering at ears and neck, wrists and fingers. Her face was painted to perfection, the mask of a queen, beautiful and remote. In the mirror that Charmion held for her, it kept somewhat of its character: there was no disguising the great arched nose of the Ptolemies. But then she was a Ptolemy, incontestably, of lineage bred as close as that of any blood horse.

Charmion put the mirror away. Cleopatra reclined on the couch with its gilded frame, its silken cushions. Up in the gallery, Epaphroditus stood like an image in stone.

Iras brought out the jar that had been concealed so carefully among the rest, the jars of wine and oil, perfumes, paints, even bread and olives and fruit. It bore no other mark than one of the seals of Egypt, the cobra with lifted head. Iris carried it with care, wary of it but unflinching. Her courage had always been high.

She set the jar in Cleopatra's lap. Cleopatra curved her hands around its sides. It was cool, smooth. A pattern of papyrus crowns marched round it, simple to starkness, black on red. Red Land, Black

Land. Desert and rich floodlands of the Nile, the wastes and the wealth of Egypt.

She was dallying. Epaphroditus would stand till the stars came down, but Octavian would not. He was quite excessively clever—if he guessed what Cleopatra intended, he would do his best to stop it.

She lifted the lid of the jar. It seemed empty, nothing within but darkness and a memory of wine. For a moment she feared that she had been betrayed, even if by kindness.

Then within the jar something stirred. A hiss; a sliding of scales. A narrow head appeared over the rim, swaying slightly, questing with its forked tongue.

"Ah," sighed Cleopatra. "Such a beauty you are. Come, sweetling. Come and kiss me."

The asp had no ears to hear, but it saw the movement of her hand. It darted. Instinct cried at her to recoil. She held steady. The pain was small beside the pain of defeat and the fear of walking alive in Octavian's triumph. The gods were merciful: the asp had bitten full in the long vein of the wrist, bitten and clung, filling this unsatisfactory prey with its poison.

At last, emptied, it writhed free, slithered over her arm and down to the floor, away into the shadows of the tomb. Cleopatra lay back. She felt nothing yet but the white-hot stabbing pain of fangs in flesh.

Iras lifted the jar from Cleopatra's lap, reached in as casually as if it had been full of olives and not serpents. She gasped, nearly dropped the jar. Charmion caught it. Iras sank down, her face twisted in pain. Her hand was a mass of small doubled wounds.

"Selfish," said Charmion. "You left none for the rest of us." She upended the jar, none too gently. A knot of snakes tumbled out, writhing, breaking free and flashing into hiding. But one paused, impeded by Charmion's foot. In a fit of temper as fierce as her own, it bit, and bit deep.

She smiled. "There. Now I can keep you company."

"But there's nothing for me," said Mardian.

"Of course there is," Cleopatra said. "The window. Go while you can. Octavian will be here soon."

She thought that he would resist. But there was no poison for him, and the window was open, and it offered life, if only life full of grief. She did not tell him where to go. He would return to the palace, perhaps, or seek out Dione. Dione would welcome him.

It was his to choose. Slow chill crept through her body. She had been warned that the pain could be great, but this was almost pleasant. It was like falling asleep in cool water, except for the burning cold where the asp had bitten her.

She could just see Iras lying at her feet, head pillowed on arm, smiling drowsily. Pain had never troubled Iras.

Charmion, last to be bitten, was strongest still. She knelt by the couch. Her face, always so beautiful, shone like the face of a goddess. Cleopatra reached for it, but her hands would not obey her. Splendid, so splendid; and oh, so cold. "Goddess," she whispered. "Mother Isis . . . protect . . ."

Voices. A battering as of rams. Shouting, running feet—the swiftness of desperation.

Too late. Cleopatra laughed as her souls divided, spread wings. Too late for poor Octavian, who wanted a queen in his triumph. He would have to find another. Cleopatra had defied him. Cleopatra was queen, always, even unto death.

Roman voice, roar of outrage: "Charmion! Damn you, Charmion! Was this the right thing to do?"

"Very right," said Charmion, as from the far ends of the world, "and fitting, for a queen born of so many noble kings."

FORTY-EIGHT

Dione felt the queen die. It had taken its time in coming: she had come all the way to the temple, and even into the precinct, before she stumbled and fell.

Grief struck first after the shock of knowledge. Then a white, mad joy. Cleopatra had conquered. She had cheated Octavian of his pleasure. He had Egypt, he had its wealth and its power and its grainfields that could feed the world. But he would never have Cleopatra.

The world was a cold small place without her. Even the goddess' temple was full of Romans. They were stripping its treasury, though they had not, it seemed, seen fit to rape its priestesses.

Dione wanted to retreat to a deep and windowless chamber and lose herself in her sorrow. But there was no time. Octavian, thwarted, could turn vindictive; might turn on Mother Isis, since Cleopatra had, after all, been Isis on earth.

She dragged herself to her feet. Isis must not be profaned. Even Octavian's Romans would learn that.

Purpose. That was what this was, this urge to get up and be doing when she should have been looking for a quick way to die. Egypt was lost. Roma Dea had overwhelmed it.

Ah, and had she? Dione paused to meet the gaze of the goddess in the shrine. Mother Isis smiled her eternal smile. Dione felt no emptiness behind her, no shadow of defeat. Her living image was gone. Her substance was as strong as ever.

Even Roma Dea was a part of her. She was all that was, earth and sea, sun and sky. She comforted the least of her children, there in her sanctuary overrun with Roman feet: strong arms, warm breast, strength to face what must be faced.

Dione raised her voice. "You! Centurion! Come here."

The man came, perhaps amused to be summoned by so small a scrap of an Egyptian woman. Let him smile if he would. She had a matter to settle with him. "Centurion, it's all very well that your men have been ordered to take every coin and scrap of gold to fill Octavian's coffers. But they will please leave us enough to keep our priestesses fed, and they will by all means pick up after themselves."

The centurion blinked. He was a classic of his kind, weathered, grizzled, and solid, a practical no-nonsense Roman to the marrow of his bones. But he had had a mother, surely, and he knew that particular tone. "Ma'am," he said in a voice roughened by bellowing on a hundred battlefields. "Ma'am, we'll see to it. Sorry, ma'am."

"Be more than sorry," Dione said tartly. "Help us clean up the shambles you've made. Look at this! Dirt tracked everywhere. This is a temple, not a barn."

"Yes, ma'am," said the centurion, by now thoroughly cowed. And in a roar that rattled the rafters: "Flaccus! Bubo! Viridianus! In here, mop-up detail, quickstep!"

Half an hour's looting and trampling took the rest of the day and half the night to repair. The legionaries, having done most of the damage, did their best to make up for it. Their centurion, whose name was Flaminius, was amenable to reason once he had had it shown to him, and he knew the power of a woman's will. He had a wife at home in Volaterrae, he told Dione, and half a dozen daughters, and a pair of sons just about old enough to go into the legions. He liked Egyptian beer, and he did not object too strongly to Egyptian cooking, though it might have been better, he opined, for a little more garlic.

When he had gone and taken his company with him, leaving the temple markedly poorer but not bankrupt, and brightly clean, she let Hebe persuade her to sit down in the room that she had been craving when first she came there. It seemed small now, closed in, with the lamps lit and a meal spread on the table by the bed.

She was hungry, she discovered. She ate a loaf of flat bread and a pair of honeyed figs. In a moment she must go and be sure that her daughter was asleep and safe. She had been doing that at intervals: craving the sight of Mariamne's face, the sound of her breathing, the reassurance that she at least still lived.

She set down the third fig that she had meant to eat, and the cup of watered wine. "Timoleon," she said. Quite calmly. No quaver. No tears. "O my Timoleon."

There was a flicker in the corner, a sound like wings, or like stifled laughter. She started to her feet.

It was only a cat—the old goddess-cat that had come to her in Tarsus. Blind now, but hale enough otherwise, it approached her as she sank back into her chair, and climbed stiffly into her lap. She stroked the fur that was still, after all these years, as soft as finest silk, and rubbed the blunt chin, feeling as much as hearing the rumble of the purr.

Feet sounded in the passage beyond the door. A priestess coming up from the temple, pausing. Dione suppressed a sigh. She did not need any more to do, not tonight, except to finish eating and then to sleep.

But duty knew no mercy. The door opened slowly, as if the woman outside knew how little welcome she would receive.

Woman, no. Man, and Roman. Even to the toga, its purple stripe black in the lamplight, but never as black as his eyes under the strong brows.

There was a glint of silver in his hair. That had not been there before. Ah, she thought: we all grow old.

Lucius Servilius the Augur shut the door behind him, carefully, and stood in front of it. He did not trouble with a greeting. "I saw our daughter. She's a young woman now, almost."

"Ten more years," Dione conceded, "or twelve, and yes, she will be."

"She's as beautiful as her mother."

Dione let that die unnoticed.

Lucius frowned. Time was when he would have blushed and stammered, but he had grown out of that. "I . . . also saw the queen. Octavian is beside himself."

"I hope so," Dione said. Giving him nothing. Making him work to talk to her.

He was not as easy to master as most men were. He sat on the bed, since she had the only chair, and poured wine into the second cup that had been left there by the goddess herself for all Dione knew. "Ah," he said, sipping. "Caecuban. I thought you'd acquired a taste for raw Macedonian by the time you left Actium."

Dione opened her mouth, and shut it again. Of all the brazen nerve . . .

"I was afraid," he said after a pause, "that I might find you also—as she was. You are just stubborn enough to have gone ahead with it."

"I'm sorry to disappoint you," Dione said. "There's the matter of a daughter just out of infancy."

"And a pair of sons?"

Her eyes very suddenly were full of tears. She was furious at them. "One son," she snapped. "Just one."

He went white. He had not known. How could he not have known?

She sprang on him, sending the wine flying, hammering him with fists, shrieking she knew not what.

Astonishment and the shock of grief laid him open to her, but he was a soldier, too, honed and tempered with it. He caught her flailing wrists and wrestled her down, and shook her until she stopped screaming. "Dione," he said, conjuring her with her name. "Dione, beloved. I didn't know. *I didn't know.*"

She almost spat in his face. "How couldn't you? You're Octavian's man. Octavian had them hunted down, Caesarion and Timoleon. He had them killed."

Lucius shook his head. "No. No, that was the boy's tutor, the messenger said—"

"That was Timoleon!" Dione would start screaming again if she did not stop now. She gulped in breath, and fought to still her trembling. "It—was supposed to be—Rhodon. But he looks too odd. So it was Timoleon. They were supposed to—to be princes—in—"

Tears. Tears were better than shrieks. Lucius' shoulder was broad, she had always liked that, and solid: he was all whipcord and bone.

He was weeping, too, hard and silent. "I . . . almost killed Caesar when I heard that Caesarion was dead. If I had known—that Timoleon—" He had to stop, to find his voice again where it had fled. "Roma Dea rules me, and rightly so. But if I had known that Timoleon was dead, I would have strangled Caesar with my own hands."

"No, you wouldn't," said Dione. "He's Roma Dea's toy. Who do you think hunted them down so quickly? She wanted blood—Caesar's blood. She got it. My son was merely an appendage."

"How you must hate us," said Lucius Servilius.

She leaned back in his arms, but did not try to break away. "No," she said. "Or maybe a little. But not enough to sour my soul."

"And yet you loathe me."

"No," she said again. "Oh, no."

He did not believe her. She would not have, either, a moment before.

"I do love you," she said. "I never stopped. But you loved Rome more than you loved me."

"I wasn't given much choice," he said with sudden asperity. "I was captured at Actium. By the time I came to, I was in Caesar's hospital tent, and being told that I could either adhere to Caesar and live, or defy him and die."

"You didn't swear to Octavian, did you? You swore to Rome."

His silence was answer enough.

She nodded as if he had said it. "Now Rome rules Egypt. We've lost. Are you glad that you were right?"

"I am most deeply sorry that Cleopatra and Antony are dead," said Lucius Servilius. "As for Egypt . . ." He paused. Swallowed. "I've asked to be given a position in Alexandria. Not the governorship, that's too much trouble, and in any case I haven't been a consul and I never did get around to running for praetor, so can't hold rank that high. But they do need people to settle things. Especially people who know the city. Who know what it needs, and what it wants."

"Which aren't always the same thing." Dione liked to look at him, even when it hurt. "You'll find a Roman wife, I suppose, to keep Roma Dea happy."

He looked so insulted that she almost laughed. "Do you really think she's that petty? All she wanted was her due. She has it. And I," he said, "have a wife already."

"Not in Roman law."

"Roman law can be changed."

"I won't have any more children. Mariamne took all of that that I had to give."

"She is enough."

Stubborn, she thought, half angry, half wanting to laugh. Roman. Oh, she hated Romans. She loved them. She had to contend with them for the rest of her life, unless she took Cleopatra's way—and that, alas, was closed. She wanted to live.

Even in such a world as this. Even with Cleopatra dead.

"Egypt will still be alive," she said, "when Rome's empire is long fallen into dust."

He nodded. "Yes, I see it, too. I cherish it. As I cherish the empire that hasn't fallen yet, and won't, I think, for a while. Certainly not till I'm too dead to care."

Dione's laughter escaped for all that she could do. She never had been able to stay somber where this man was—grim humorless Roman though he might be. "I'll fight Rome. I'll do everything I can to keep Egypt, and Alexandria, alive."

"Certainly you will," said Lucius Servilius. "You wouldn't be yourself if you didn't."

"I wish," said Dione after a brief, charged silence, "that you would quarrel like an ordinary man."

"Why should I want to be ordinary?" he wanted to know.

Why? she thought. Why indeed?

"Bloody Roman," she said.

"Muleheaded Egyptian," he agreed.

They grinned at one another. It was very late, and they were profoundly silly. And alive: alive and laughing, though the world had ended.

Endings, as old Egypt knew, were seeds: seeds that sprouted and grew and blossomed, and wrought the world anew.

AUTHOR'S NOTE

The story of Antony and Cleopatra is one of history's great love stories, and one of its great examples of mythmaking on a grand scale. A novelist who wants to find the reality behind the face of, say, Elizabeth Taylor in that glorious bomb of a film, has a thin line to walk between historical accuracy and readers' expectations. The reality is there, however, and fairly easy to find. Suetonius' Lives of the Caesars has much to say of the woman who was Julius Caesar's lover and Caesar Octavian's enemy; likewise Plutarch's Lives of Julius Caesar, Marc Antony, and Caesar Octavian (who, after Actium, gave himself the title of Caesar Augustus). Of the many modern biographies of Cleopatra, I am particularly indebted to Michael Grant's *Cleopatra*. Lucy Hughes-Hallett's *Cleopatra: Histories, Dreams and Distortions* provides a useful and convenient summary of the various conceptions, both ancient and modern, of Egypt's most famous queen.

Cleopatra was not a great beauty—that much is clear from contemporary accounts. The coin portraits are singularly unflattering; they show her with a hooked nose and a ferocious lantern jaw. She was, however, both brilliant and charming, and her voice is said to have been remarkably beautiful. She was about twenty-eight when Antony summoned her to Tarsus.

Antony at that time was just shy of forty, and married to the formidable Fulvia, by whom he had two sons, Marcus Antonius called Antyllus (who was murdered by Octavian's men in the taking of Alexandria), and Iullus Antonius. His elder daughter by Octavia became the grandmother of the Emperor Nero; his younger daughter by her was the mother of the Emperor Claudius and the grandmother of the Emperor Caligula. It could be said, in fact, that although Antony himself never succeeded in ruling the Roman world, his descendants did so in grand style.

Cleopatra was not, as far as we can tell, either wanton or promiscuous. We know of only two lovers: Julius Caesar and Marc Antony. Herod of Judea (Herod the Great of biblical fame) may have had a dalliance with her; but that may simply be propaganda, and an attempt to explain why her friendship with him became a bitter and lasting enmity. In general Cleopatra seems to have been monogamous. She certainly bore Antony three children, and Ptolemy Caesar (Caesarion, born in 47 B.C.) was probably Julius Caesar's son. Caesar, at least, never repudiated him; his failure to leave his estate to the boy in his will is a factor of Roman law, not of Caesar's paternity. Caesarion was the son of a foreign woman. He could not inherit the property of a Roman.

Caesar's legal heir, his nephew and adopted son, born Gaius Octavius, assumed the name of Gaius Julius Caesar after Caesar's assassination. After Actium he took the title of Augustus, and named the month Sextilis, which happens to have been his birth month, after himself. He became the first of the Roman emperors, the first man to hold sole and undisputed power over Rome and its empire.

The battle of Actium on September 1, 31 B.C., has gone down in history (which after all is written by the victors) as a major turning point of the ancient world. In fact it was only one of many battles for supremacy in the Roman world, and not the last which Octavian fought with Antony. After the battle, Octavian built a city where his camp had been, and called it Nikopolis. For a useful overview of the battle and its consequences, see John M. Carter, *The Battle of Actium*.

Much of this novel is taken direct from the sources. Dione and her family, and Lucius Servilius the Augur, are fictional. The rest of the dramatis personae, however, are drawn as much from life as possible. The dance of Plancus, painted blue, is recorded in Velleius Paterculus. The last words of Cleopatra's maid Charmion are translated as she spoke them, according to Plutarch's Life of Antony. And Caesarion was indeed killed while attempting to escape in disguise, along with his tutor, Rhodon. His siblings did better: Selene married her Mauretanian prince, and her brothers seem to have remained with her in Mauretania; no more is known of them than that they escaped with her.

The references to magic and magical practices are fictionalized, often extensively; for an overview and sourcebook of magic as it was actually practiced, see George Luck, *Arcana Mundi: Magic and the Occult in the Greek and Roman Worlds*. I did not, however, invent Cleopatra's claim to be the incarnation of Isis (whose Greek cognate was Aphrodite), nor Antony's concomitant claim to be that of Dionysus (whose Egyptian cognate was Osiris). That much of their story, including the Great Marriage and the Triumph of Dionysus, is history.

It should be noted also that Cleopatra was renowned as an alchemist and a practitioner of learned magic. She is supposed to have been the author of a treatise on alchemy; that is much in keeping with the rest of her reputation. She was a talented administrator, a canny financier, and lover of learning and philosophy. Plutarch records that she spoke eleven languages, including Hebrew and Egyptian.

She was remarkable by any standard. Her Roman enemies, among them the poet Horace (in his *Odes* I.xxxvii), called her *fatale monstrum*, a prodigy of fate, unnatural, preposterous—and spoke with awe of her choice of death over the humiliation of a Roman Triumph. They never understood her, they hated all she stood for, but they admired her, and made her a legend even before she was dead.